SPOCK WEDS SAAVIK

Commander Saavik and Ambassador Spock, son of Sarek, were married on the second day of the month of Sharveen at sacred wedding grounds belonging to the family of the groom. T'Pau of Vulcan, former leader of the planet, presided over the ceremony.

The bride, Commander Saavik, is a Starfleet officer in good standing, late of the original *Starship Enterprise,* but most recently assigned as first officer aboard the *U.S.S. Armstrong.*

The groom, Ambassador Spock, is also formerly of the first *Starship Enterprise,* but is currently an ambassador-at-large representing Federation interests throughout the galaxy.

The couple met while the bride was a student at Starfleet Academy and the groom was assigned there as an instructor.

Ambassador Sarek of Vulcan, father of the groom, was in attendance. Amanda, mother of the groom, is deceased, as are the parents of the bride.

The bride wore embroidered silver robes that have been in the groom's family for over a thousand years.

Among the guests were Dr. Leonard McCoy, an admiral in Starfleet, Lieutenant Jean-Luc Picard of the *U.S.S. Stargazer,* Captain Truman Howes of the *U.S.S. Armstrong,* and many members of the *Armstrong* crew.

STAR TREK®
Vulcan's Heart

JOSEPHA SHERMAN & SUSAN SHWARTZ

POCKET BOOKS

New York   London   Toronto   Sydney   Singapore

POCKET BOOKS, a division of Simon & Schuster Inc.
1230 Avenue of the Americas, New York, NY 10020

Copyright © 1999 by Paramount Pictures. All Rights Reserved.

Originally published in hardcover in 1999 by Pocket Books

STAR TREK is a Registered Trademark of Paramount Pictures.

This book is published by Pocket Books, a division of Simon & Schuster Inc., under exclusive license from Paramount Pictures.

ISBN: 0-671-01545-1

First Pocket Books paperback printing May 2000

10 9 8 7 6 5 4 3 2 1

Printed in the U.S.A.

For Inge Heyer, Space Telescope Institute,
for helping us bend the laws of space-time physics

For Francis X. Doyle, USMA, 1984,
with thanks for drinks and plot conferences

ONE

VULCAN, SAREK'S ESTATE, DAY 2, FIRST WEEK OF SHARVEEN, YEAR 2329

Lieutenant Jean-Luc Picard of Starfleet, twenty-four Earth years old and, for all his Starfleet experience, feeling painfully aware of his youth amid this distinguished gathering, tugged surreptitiously at the hem of his dress uniform's tunic, trying to get the cursed thing to lie properly—and trying at the same time not to sweat. Tri-ox injections might help a human deal with Vulcan's thinner atmosphere, but the climate was still unbelievably warm, even now when it was barely dawn. It was rather flattering that his captain should have picked him to be part of this ceremonial team, but—

"Already hotter than good old Terran Hell, isn't it?" a voice with an unmistakable Southern United States accent drawled.

Picard turned sharply, and found himself staring into a weatherworn, aged face—with two of the shrewdest, least-aged eyes he'd seen. "Sir?" Picard began, then hastily upgraded that as the man's trim maroon uniform and metallic ornaments registered (despite the floppy, decidedly nonregulation sunhat): "Admiral!"

1

God, there was only one Starfleet admiral who would be this old, and this old-fashionedly Southern: "Admiral—Doctor—Admiral McCoy!"

"Doctor, please. Sounds more natural."

But this was *the* McCoy, Leonard McCoy, the one who'd shipped with Captain James T. Kirk aboard the original *Enterprise,* yes, and with Mr. Spock, Ambassador Spock, too—Picard had to fight himself not to grab the admiral's hand, reminding himself sternly, *You are not a raw cadet, you are a Starfleet lieutenant.* Of course the admiral would be here; he was one of Spock's oldest Starfleet friends. But this—this was like meeting part of living history!

"At ease, son," the famous McCoy said wryly. "This damn climate's no place for military formality."

"But, sir, I—I know—"

"You're *not* going to tell me you read about me in school, are you?"

At Picard's guilty start, McCoy snorted. "Isn't that charming. Lieutenant Whoever . . ."

"Picard, sir. Jean-Luc Picard, serving with Captain Anton Manning."

"A pleasure, Lieutenant Jean-Luc Picard. But I haven't survived a century just to become someone's folk hero!"

The world-weary grin was infectious. Picard hazarded a smile in return, then abruptly remembered where he was, and why he was here, and went back to attention.

"Nice turnout," McCoy murmured in his ear. "But then, Spock's earned it."

Picard glanced subtly about. He couldn't put names to most of the civilians, although there was no mistaking the strong features of Dr. Mbiti, the Kenyan-born Ambassador to Vulcan, in his flowing red, green, and black robes. There were no less than twenty Starfleet officers, eighteen human men and women, one lithe gray-furred felinoid Ikatr, and one startlingly blue Bolian. All of them, including his solid, middle-aged captain, looked crisp, clean, and uncomfortable in their dress uniforms, a row of muted reds and blues. The Vulcan dignitaries, a mixed lot of scientists and diplomats, men and women, were still assembling, elegant, lean figures, utterly tranquil and absolutely silent in their flowing white or brown or blue robes. Picard straightened as he recognized one of them, too, a slender woman in a long bronze robe, from the newsvids: T'Sera, who had led the second archaeological expedition to M-113. He'd love the chance to hear her lecture . . . but not in this climate.

"Not a mussed hair on any of them," McCoy continued. "But then, they're bred for this climate. A little thing like desert heat isn't going to bother them."

"This is Ambassador Sarek's land, isn't it?"

"Sure is. Been in the family for millennia."

The plateau on which they stood would have looked like a Breton stone circle—if Brittany had suddenly spouted fumaroles and its grassy fields had turned to reddish rock. Picard stifled a cough as the breeze brought him a whiff of sulfur, and watched the dark blue shadows rapidly retreat from the deeper red of the desert plains far below.

"Sir? Isn't that peak Mount Seleya?"

"That it is. The only mountain in the area with snow on it. Watch, now. You'll see something spectacular."

Above the distant Mount Seleya and the other jagged peaks, the thin air was already starting to shimmer. Then with dramatic suddenness, the rising sun, 40 Eridani A, flared off the snow capping Mount Seleya, turning the mountain's peak to blazing copper—and catching Picard right in the eye.

Wonderful. If the ceremony didn't start soon, the sun was going to be burning his scalp right through his already sadly thinning hair.

"God, what I'd give for some shade," someone muttered and Picard silently agreed. To take his mind off his discomfort, he tried to picture himself sitting in a chair in relatively cool shade, maybe even with a tall glass of iced tea, the real thing, Earl Grey all the way from Earth.

The fantasy wasn't working. Feeling a trickle of sweat tickling its way down his back, Picard fought not to fidget. "Uh . . . sir?"

"Go ahead, son. Ask away. Takes both our minds off the weather."

"About the betrothal . . . I understood that it was normal Vulcan practice for formal betrothals to take place between seven-year-old children."

"That's right. And such a betrothal's every bit as important to Vulcans as the actual wedding years later. But yes, today it's two adults getting betrothed, not two kids."

Specifically, Picard's mind filled in, Ambassador Spock, formerly of Starfleet, and Starfleet Commander Saavik, first officer of the *U.S.S. Armstrong*.

"Two people who've been colleagues and friends for decades now," McCoy mused aloud. "And why they're doing this at this stage of their lives . . ." He shrugged, a little too casually. "There are exceptions to every rule."

And there's more to the story than you're going to tell me, isn't there? "Two people who've been colleagues and friends for decades."

His mind wanted very much to make something romantic out of that. But Picard rather suspected that this late betrothal was more a matter of convenience, or maybe politics. You never knew motives for sure, if Starfleet scuttlebutt was correct, when someone as, well, cunning as the father of the groom, Ambassador Sarek, was involved.

He suddenly realized that a high-ranking officer had moved to McCoy's side—no, not just high-ranking. This was Captain Truman Howes of the *Armstrong*, Commander Saavik's ship, his fair skin and pale eyes startlingly out of place in a desert climate.

"Worried about your first officer?" McCoy asked mildly.

"Hardly! Commander Saavik can take care of herself. Best first officer any captain ever had," he added, with a glance at

Picard. "It's worth coming down into this . . . this blast furnace of a world to see this. He'd better be good to her," Howes added to McCoy in an undertone, "or, ambassador or not, he'll hear from my crew. And me."

"Just don't expect Spock to keep her safe," McCoy drawled. "It's her job to go in harm's way, and Spock who taught her that job, remember? If you ask me," he continued, "though, mind you, nobody has, I'd say this is just what the doctor ordered. Since Spock left the Fleet, they've both been too damned alone."

A rustle of the dawn wind brought with it the high-pitched chime of tiny bells.

"Ha," McCoy exclaimed. "Here we go."

The Starfleet officers straightened to attention. So did the Vulcans, though no one could have called their subtle, elegant tensing a military posture.

Two heavyset Vulcans wearing black skullcaps topped with starched frills carried out a large jadeite gong, which a third man struck. Its deep-voiced boom echoed out onto the Forge.

"Right," Picard heard McCoy mutter. "They never did get around to replacing the old one."

That didn't mean anything to Picard. The hot wind from the desert was swirling up here, nearly stifling him. If he blacked out . . . Silently, Picard breathed the ancient pilot's prayer: *Oh God, don't let me screw up.* The last thing he wanted to do was embarrass Starfleet, or offend his Vulcan hosts. After all, he hoped to be a captain someday. Stories about the fabulous Captain James T. Kirk notwithstanding, it was rare for *any* human to be invited to a Vulcan ceremony.

The gong boomed out again, to be answered by trembling showers of bells. As 40 Eridani A blazed in the Vulcan sky, the long shadows cast by the menhirs defining the meeting place converged. The humans hushed; the Vulcans were already silent.

"Here we go," McCoy repeated softly.

A figure in the dark blue-gray robes of a Vulcan ambassador stepped from behind one of the reddish, polished stones. Could this be Spock? No, this Vulcan was too old for that . . . tall and graying of hair, but surrounded by an air of matter-of-fact dignity—

Ambassador Sarek! Picard realized in awe. So that was what "august" looked like.

"Looks like one of the better Roman emperors, doesn't he?" the irrepressible McCoy murmured, almost making Picard choke. "Ah, and there you are, my green-blooded friend."

This had to be Ambassador Spock, just as impressive as his father, his rugged face composed, his tall, lean figure straight-backed in his somber ambassador's robes. Light caught and pooled in the gems of his insignia.

The bells chimed again, rising to a shrill, painful crescendo.

"There! Will you just look at her," Captain Howes whispered.

Commander Saavik glided forward from between two pillars across the central clearing, her dark hair spilling down her back, her strong, elegantly planed face unreadable. As the morning sunlight struck her, her long, traditional silver robes, the edges whispering against the sand, shimmered like water.

Picard drew in a sharp breath. He had not expected this otherworldly serenity. "She looks like something out of the Hollow Hills." Damn! He hadn't meant to say something so whimsical. Please God that no one had overheard! But of course McCoy had, judging from his sly sideways grin, so Picard tried desperately to cover with, "Do you think Vulcans have tales like that?"

"Course they do, son. Just look at the ears."

Just in time, Picard managed to suppress what would have been a disastrous laugh.

Saavik stopped beside Spock, studying the audience as sharply as though looking for threats to security—or just not approving of being so conspicuous. Her glance flicked to the two tall figures standing by the menhirs. Each guard held what looked to Picard like an unholy combination of machete and bludgeon.

"Lirpa," McCoy explained in a whisper. "They're taking no chances."

Out of nowhere, Picard remembered that Commander Saavik was half-Romulan. Had she had something to say about the security arrangements?

Spock murmured a few words to her, and she looked up at him, something that could almost have been a smile flicking at the corners of her mouth for the barest of instants.

Lucky man! Picard found himself thinking. Even if Spock was a Vulcan, not a man.

For a third time, the gong throbbed out over Vulcan's Forge. Breaking into the fading echoes came the high-pitched chime of even more bells. Two of the biggest Vulcans Picard had ever seen stalked into the amphitheater. They, too, carried *lirpa.* Following them were attendants bearing a sedan chair, gleaming with black lacquer delicately engraved in an intricate red geometric design. The chair's occupant was female and very old, so fragile that she seemed carved from translucent alabaster, yet sitting proudly erect, refusing to sway with the motions of her bearers or lean back against the chair.

"Kroykah!" Her voice was strong.

"My God," McCoy said, "it's T'Pau."

Picard drew a startled breath. T'Pau of Vulcan had been one of the most important political forces on the planet for at least two centuries!

"I thought she'd died fifty years ago." McCoy shook his head. "Maybe she won't know me after all these years."

T'Pau turned her head slowly, an empress surveying her domain. Her gaze swept over McCoy, and for the briefest instance, she raised an ironic brow.

McCoy snorted. "Fat chance. I should have guessed."

T'Pau's bearers carefully deposited her chair before the central dais, where empty chains swayed slightly in the hot wind.

"That's where the old gong used to hang." McCoy's voice was suddenly full of tension.

Spock dropped to one knee before T'Pau, who leaned forward to touch the ambassador's temple. Picard saw Spock's face go blank, as though he'd instantly entered trance.

T'Pau beckoned to Saavik. She, too, sank down in a reverence as graceful as a dance, and she, too, sank into trance at the old woman's touch.

The Vulcan guests went utterly motionless; Picard could almost feel the force of their concentration.

Facing each other, Spock and Saavik stretched their hands out to touch each other's temples. The gesture was not an embrace; Picard did not know what to call it. As T'Pau adjusted their fingers as if they were, in truth, only seven years old, Sarek moved forward, face impassive but eyes keen, to oversee the ritual.

At T'Pau's nod, the betrothed pair began to speak.

"My mind to your mind," Spock said softly.

"My thoughts to your thoughts," Saavik replied.

"Parted from me and never parted . . ."

"Never and always touching and touched."

At those words, T'Pau extended her ancient hands to cover Spock's and Saavik's fingers, as if sealing their vows.

The Frenchman in Picard caught his breath . . . but if Saavik's eyes closed or Spock's face gentled, the moment passed so quickly that Picard could have imagined it.

"Now thee are one," T'Pau intoned. "At the appointed time, thee shall be drawn together."

Sarek nodded in approval, the faintest dip of his head, and stepped back.

At a quick gesture from T'Pau, Spock and Saavik removed their hands from each other's faces as matter-of-factly as if they had merely checked each other for fever.

Spock rose and held out his hand, two fingers extended for the public contact permitted bonded pairs. Saavik brushed his fingers formally with her own and allowed herself to be raised to her feet. For a moment, each studied the other.

Something feels different, does it? Picard wondered.

Then, each raised a quizzical eyebrow, clearly concluding: *Not that different.*

Spock nodded to his father, while Saavik bowed slightly. The venerable ambassador put out a hand as if to welcome her, but did not *quite* touch her.

And that was very much that.

What did you expect? Picard asked himself.

It wasn't, he decided after a moment's consideration, that they were passionless—at least he hoped not—just so well controlled that there was no gesture of caring, of tenderness that a human might detect. Even in a couple who had known and valued each other for decades.

"Show's over," McCoy muttered. "C'mon, Lieutenant, let's get the rest of the formalities over with."

What happened next was more familiar. The Starfleet officers formed into a long line—predictably in order of rank, which put Picard near the end. One by one, they paid their respects. Simple enough if you knew the drill. March up to the dignitaries, brace oneself, formally bow one's head, say a few words—in Vulcan if possible—and move on before the next person in line collapsed.

Up ahead, he heard Saavik tell her captain, "I am relieved to see that you survived this ordeal." She was almost smiling. "We will have you out of the sun soon."

Finally, it was Picard's turn to bow with the gallantry that was as much his heritage as the vineyards of Labarre, France. He raised his hand in the split-fingered Vulcan salute he had been practicing for days and recited the Vulcan words of polite good-will he had memorized.

"Welcome to Vulcan," Spock said.

"Your presence honors us," Saavik added. Her voice was clear, but held husky resonances that sent the tiniest shiver up Picard's spine.

Greatly daring, he decided to try one more sentence in High Vulcan, this time to Ambassador Sarek: "We come to serve."

"Your service honors us," the ambassador replied.

I said it right!

Move along! The sun was growing fierce, and, what was worse, Picard felt his captain's eyes burning holes in him from a position by the gateway. Oh, but how he would have loved to speak longer with the legendary ambassador! Perhaps Sarek would consent to answer a question or two; the ambassador had spent a good deal of time teaching at the Vulcan Science Academy and as a special lecturer on Earth.

Captain Manning's glare grew hotter. Picard moved along.

After what felt like several geological eras, the reception line ended in a straggle of ensigns. The ambassadors' aides guided human and Vulcan guests into a blessedly cool underground reception hall. There, Saavik poured water for the guests in token of her new responsibilities to come, while a cluster of senior officers and diplomats surrounded Spock.

Captain Howes approached Saavik, his fair-skinned face redder than his relatively brief exposure to Eridani 40 A would warrant. "Ah, Saavik, may I ask you a question?"

She raised an eyebrow at her superior officer's courteous, if tentative, request. "As you wish, sir."

"Will you require more time here on Vulcan? You and the ambassador . . . *Armstrong* would be honored to pick you up on our next circuit."

Saavik glanced aside and downward, then at her betrothed. "Thank you, Captain Howes. But I see no logic in postponing my return to the ship. Our joint research projects are in good order, are they not?" she asked her betrothed, who nodded gravely.

"Then there is no need for me to remain here, Captain. Ambassador Spock's duties will soon be taking him offworld. I shall be ready to beam up when *Armstrong* leaves orbit."

"Oh for Pete's sake, you two!" McCoy's exasperation seemed harsh after the softness of Saavik's voice. He looked from one to the other of the betrothed pair, shaking his head in disgust.

"Honestly, Spock! I wonder sometimes if either of you learned a damn thing from . . ."

Picard would have delayed his next promotion by six months . . . no, make that two . . . to hear what it was McCoy wondered if Spock had learned—and from whom.

Maybe it's the difference between Vulcan and human customs. But they don't exactly seem reluctant to be parted.

Or perhaps he read them wrongly. Even now, as they stood with their backs to one another, a tenuous awareness seemed to join them. Like, Picard thought with a moment of sudden sharp, unashamed romance, two stars orbiting each other, maybe not touching, but never truly parted at all.

YEAR 2342

FROM: Spock, son of Sarek, on Vulcan civilian
transport Selnar, en route to Earth
TO: Solvar, Department Head, Vulcan Science
Academy, Department of Extra-Vulcan Research,
ShiKahr

I need not, at this late date, itemize the incidents surrounding the Sundering. However, after careful initial research, I must state that I believe there is no logic in further isolating those who are, after all, our genetic kin. I therefore request that a research team be assembled to study the Romulan culture, with the short-term goal of augmented information, the medium-term goal of initiating contact with the Romulan people, and, should such discussions prove productive, the long-term goal of introducing a proposal for Reunification of the two branches of our species.

Live long and prosper.

FROM: *Solvar, Department Head, Vulcan Science Academy, Department of Extra-Vulcan Research, ShiKahr*

TO: *Spock, son of Sarek, Vulcan Embassy, San Francisco, Earth*

We have considered your request. It does not, however, strike us as logical to initiate a project of this scope at this time, especially in view of the extreme emotionality and tendency toward violence of the Romulans, and the likely Federation response to any such study.

Peace and long life.

YEAR 2343

FROM: *Spock, son of Sarek, Vulcan Embassy, Andor*

TO: *Solvar, Department Head, Vulcan Science Academy, Department of Extra-Vulcan Research, ShiKahr*

Revisiting my request of 2342 that a research team be assembled with the long-term goal of evaluating the potential benefits and philosophical challenges of Reunification with the Sundered, I wish to observe that a study of Romulan linguistics (refer to attached files) does, indeed, point to a closer link between the Sundered and those of Vulcan than the Department of Xenolinguistics initially believed. In substantiation of this hypothesis, I refer you to the work of such linguists as T'Karra and Verrin, who have proven, as is evident in their monograph (also attached), that spoken Romulan is definitely related to the form of Old High Vulcan spoken a thousand years ago.

I also need not remind you that a thousand years, even two thousand years, is not long enough, under natural standards, for any major genetic changes to have occurred in the Vulcanoid somatype, even allowing for Romulus' slightly cooler, slightly more temperate climate.

Surely this link that clearly remains between Vulcan and the Romulans merits further study.

Live long and prosper.

FROM: Solvar, Department Head, Vulcan Science Academy, Department of Extra-Vulcan Research, ShiKahr
TO: Spock, son of Sarek, Vulcan Embassy, Andor

While the study of linguistics is a perfectly logical pursuit, as is the study of genetic variation, we do not believe that the cause of Vulcan would be served at this time by a research project such as you propose. We further do not believe that the cause of logic is served by an ambassador who would attempt a project, in addition to his current ambassadorial duties, that would require him to venture out of his field of academic specialization and collaborate with the Starfleet of the United Federation of Planets to an extent that we consider would interfere with the objectivity commensurate with the role of a Vulcan ambassador. In the light of continued opposition to your project, which seems ill-judged at this—or indeed at any other—time, it is the considered opinion of this department that your persistence in this course is illogical in the extreme.

Peace and long life.

TWO

FEDERATION WORLD ORIKI, DAY THREE, MONTH OF DARNAR, YEAR 2344

"Ambassador Spock! At last!"

As Spock stepped out of the small spaceport's one terminal into Oriki's warm, dry air, seeing vistas of open green plains on three sides, a small human woman came scurrying forward, clutching a sheaf of papers with one hand, running a hasty hand through her mop of brown hair with the other. "I'm Irene Sanford, from the Federation base here on Oriki. *So* glad to see you here, so glad indeed!"

Did she mean to shake his hand? Or even embrace him? Spock took the smallest of steps back, dipping his head to her politely. As though suddenly remembering that one didn't casually touch Vulcans, Sanford straightened, visibly forcing herself back to decorum. "I'm to be your aide while you're on Oriki. You . . . do understand the situation here?"

"I do," Spock assured her, absolutely without expression.

Oriki was a bright, hot little Federation world, a mix of high-tech cities and savannas, the great sweeps of grassy plains such

14

as those surrounding the spaceport, over which vast herds of woolly *thranakis* still roamed, occasionally herded or hunted by the Orikis themselves, or harried by the small, sleek-furred, nervous predators known as *chikilis*.

"Of course, of course." Reddening, Sanford continued gamely, "There's a perfectly, uh, logical reason for negotiating with them."

"I have studied the situation," Spock assured her, and she reddened even more. He continued, "The Orikis weave a cloth from *thranaki* wool that is both remarkably strong and lightweight. More, a fortuitous accident at a Federation assembly has proven that, when treated with," Spock bit back the scientific terminology and contented himself with, "a basic Vulcan chemical compound, the fabric becomes virtually impervious to flame as well. Useful to Oriki and also to Vulcan, once a trade agreement is sealed. Ms. Sanford, if I may settle into my quarters on the base before meeting with the Oriki representatives . . . ?"

"Oh, of course, of course! It's just a short ride to Kikitik: that's the capital city."

"Yes, Ms. Sanford. I know."

This assignment had not come at the most convenient of times, but one could hardly say to the Vulcan authorities, "I regret, but I have other plans in mind." Particularly when the Vulcan authorities would not approve of such plans.

Kikitik was a true city, with narrow streets in a well-laid-out grid. The brown, smooth-walled houses were not more than two stories, but quite modern: Spock caught sight of a computer in the window of what was clearly a small office building.

There was not a sign of the Orikis themselves, though this was hardly surprising: the Orikis were notoriously wary. Naturally, there was more to this mission than one small treaty; should Spock succeed in convincing them to sign, this would mark the first time that the Oriki people had actually reached out to another Federation world.

15

As I would reach out to another world . . .
But even such thoughts must wait.

The people of Oriki, Spock mused several days later, were—
if it was not too fanciful a thought to compare peaceful
humanoids to quadruped predators—very much like those
chikilis out on the plains. They also, to carry the metaphor a
trifle further, illogical as it already was, were somewhat like
Irene Sanford herself. They, too, were small, no taller than
his shoulder, and most decidedly nervous. But there the re-
semblance ended: the Oriki were covered with sleek brown
fur.

"Amazing," Sanford said yet again as they headed to the city
square. "Absolutely amazing, sir. I mean, when we all tried to
talk to the Orikis, we got nowhere. They tend to, well, collapse
into chittering little discussion groups whenever we raise an
issue. And they, they quiver visibly whenever one of them makes
a point!"

"I am aware of that, Ms. Sanford."

"But here they are, meeting with you!"

"Yes, Ms. Sanford."

They had arrived at the huge ceremonial tent that had been set
up. Brightly striped with garish red and green, it was an incongruous item there in the modern city square on this sunny, comfortably warm day.

Do not, Spock reminded himself, *let the pleasant weather lull
you.*

As Irene Sanford tactfully stepped aside, Spock bowed formally to Rakikarit, an older Oriki, fur brindled with age, standing in the tent's entrance. Rakikarit's title translated as "pack
elder," one of several such in this gregariously egalitarian culture.

"We are glad this day, yes glad," the Oriki chirped.

"We did ask for you, only you, Ambassador Spock," a second
Oriki cut in: Alnikalam, Spock recognized from the pattern of her

red and green ribbons, a pack mother. "Yes, yes, only you to negotiate the treaty."

"I am honored," Spock said somberly, and the Oriki all chittered approval, standing aside to let him enter. There was nothing inside the tent but Orikis, perhaps twenty or thirty, to whom Rakikarit and Alnikalam promptly added themselves, although it was difficult to judge numbers in that sudden tight huddle. Waiting with Vulcan patience, Spock suspected that they found a half-human a bit less . . . intimidating than a full-blooded Vulcan.

And what, I wonder, would they think of Saavik?

Saavik. One corner of Spock's mouth quirked up ever so slightly. How bizarre to suddenly find himself considering her, here and now, as though he were barely grown, rather than an adult. He and she were, of course, still very much betrothed. But so far, their work had tended to keep them apart for more than the briefest of meetings.

Still, those meetings had all been quite . . . agreeable.

And speculations about such matters were illogical.

A chitter. A cough. The Orikis came out of their huddle in a swirl of brightly colored *thranaki*-wool robes: red, green, blue.

"Ambassador." Rakikarit padded up to him.

"Ambassador Spock," Alnikalam expanded.

"This provision, here . . ."

"We are interested."

"Yes, interested. But, first," Alnikalam asked, "will you join us?"

The entire chorus of Orikis chimed in, "Drink ritual? Food ritual?"

Spock graciously dipped his head to all of them, hearing their pleased chitters, and followed the elders to where yet more Oriki were setting out pitchers and platters on a quickly erected trestle table.

Their ceremonial drink proved to be a local tea, pleasantly

sweet and harmless for Vulcan metabolisms. But the ritual food was *thranaki* meat. Spock, instantly aware that all the Orikis were watching him, their bright black stares unblinking, realized, *They know that Vulcans eat no meat.*

This, then, was a test of his honor. Which would the Orikis find more honorable: a refusal, and possible insult to them, or an acceptance and definite insult to his own people?

Irene Sanford was almost instantly at his elbow, all but trembling at the potential disaster she saw unfolding. "Ambassador . . . ?"

Spock held up a hand, forestalling her.

"Customs," he told the watching Oriki gently, "are important to all sentient beings. Indeed, customs can be said to be one of the unifying facts that define a people."

Chitterings. Silence.

"We are in agreement," Spock said. "Excellent. Then you will understand that I honor your customs even more when I show respect for my people's own."

More chitterings, this time in clear approval. The offending platter of meat was removed.

"Now," one Oriki said, "we talk."

"Ambassador Spock!" Irene Sanford scurried to his side. "May I say, sir, that that was wonderful? I mean, I know that you're an ambassador, a professional, but, well . . ."

"Yes, Ms. Sanford. They did sign the agreement. Now, kindly excuse me."

All those happy chitterings had been painful to keen Vulcan hearing, and courtesy or no, Spock knew that he could not have endured the pitch of the human's happy chirpings as well. Still, as he returned to the two clean, featureless rooms that were his quarters in Oriki's Federation base, it was with a feeling of satisfaction. The mission had, indeed, gone smoothly, so much so that its simplicity, even with all those chitterings, had been almost soothing.

Spock quickly checked the rooms' security systems, then sat at the spartan desk and accessed the computer, whispering a password that opened his personal files.

Ah, yes. Saavik had sent him her critique of his last treatise: satisfactory.

Less so, however, was the latest rebuff from the Vulcan Science Academy, informing him that his request to conduct a study of Unification had once again been denied.

You're a stubborn man, Mr. Spock. His human friends had told him that more than once. Was he, indeed, merely being humanly stubborn? Surely persistence on the side of mounting evidence was, instead, merely logical.

Ah, but here was a second message from Saavik. Spock hesitated, then scrolled past the message. He knew only too well what her reaction to his interest in the "sundered cousins" would be. At the very least, she would remind him that the Romulans had never withdrawn capital charges of treason against him, a fact of which he was quite well aware.

Spock's mouth tightened the slightest bit. He had already taken a wary, secret first step regarding Romulus. Ever since Khitomer, he had been in communication with the Romulan senator Pardek, who claimed to share a desire for at least talks between the two peoples.

Lately, though, Pardek had fallen silent. Romulan senators, Spock knew, led risky lives at the best of times.

If Pardek's populist leanings have become too blatant, Spock thought with just the smallest touch of uneasiness, *he may already have paid the price.*

But Pardek was not Spock's only informant. When he had defeated the Vulcan madman, Sered, in 2296, on the planet Obsidian, one very young Romulan centurion, Ruanek, had proved himself truly honorable. Spock and he had stayed in secret and rather friendly communication ever since then.

Infrequent communication. Ruanek's life under the rule of his patron—Avrak, sister-son and heir to Pardek—was perilous enough, what with the intricacies of Romulan politics. The illegalities of contacting a Romulan aside, Spock had no wish to further imperil him.

Ruanek is too . . . impetuous. Honest as a being can be, and quite intelligent, but yes, "impetuous" is certainly the word.

Perhaps a good word to apply to many Romulans.

Outside the weathered walls of the estate, Ki Baratan, capital of the Romulan Star Empire, was slowly settling down for the night under the usual curfew, the streets already empty of all but watchful patrols.

Enforced peace, the woman thought. But here in the estate, in this secure room, with its simple desk and chair and not much else, there was no peace. She paced restlessly, silken robes of stark black and white swirling about her legs, and dark reddish-brown hair brushing about a face that had seen too much to ever have been called anything as soft as lovely.

She was Charvanek, Commander of the Romulan Star Empire—she who had once, so briefly, so disastrously, encountered a then-Starfleet Vulcan officer named Spock. She had trusted him—

Bah, no, you fell for him like a green girl—even gave him your secret name!

But of course, he had been more sensible than she. Of course he had been there just to steal that cursed cloaking device. Charvanek stopped short at the memory, hand reflexively reaching for the disruptor that wasn't at her side, not here in the relative safety of her mansion.

At that thought, Charvanek cast a quick, automatic glance at the screens that monitored activity on her estate. Yes. All was still secure.

Her gaze fell on a blank patch of wall beside the screens, a rectangular outline lighter than the surrounding blue. A tapestry had hung there until fairly recently, an elegant work depicting Azeraik triumphing in death over his enemies. There were other blank patches throughout the mansion, though she had not sold, and would not sell, the ancestral weapons still enshrined in the main hall. Art objects, after all, were just that and could be sold. Honor could not.

Nor, Charvanek thought with sudden warmth, could *Honor Blade*. The old ship might be a little battered, worn with time and hard use—but it was hers, a good, strong, old-style Romulan warbird.

She was still a member of the Empire's fleet; but Erebus would be choked with ice floes before the praetor offered her a ship again.

No matter. *Honor Blade* had survived and still would serve. As had and would she.

And if she had narrowly escaped execution back then, when she'd been commanding that Klingon-made monstrosity and had made that . . . error of judgment, only fools bemoaned the past. And if it had taken long, perilous years for her to bury disgrace and fight her way back to power, literally as well as figuratively, that was as it was, too. Thinking of grizzled old Takvi, who had been her engineer in the old days and whom she'd managed to save from charges of treason—the treason of staying loyal to her—Charvanek smiled thinly. At least she had the satisfaction of knowing that she'd protected her people.

Some of her people. She never had learned what had become of her second-in-command, Tal. But then, in the Empire these days, people . . . disappeared.

Charvanek's thin smile tightened even more. Of course, the real reason for her own survival and restoration of rank—as well as the reason she'd been allowed to keep *Honor Blade*—had been not all her cleverness, but her kin lines.

Fortunate indeed, even now, that I am of the emperor's blood.

For what that was worth nowadays. Shiarkiek might still be emperor, but everyone knew that the weary old man was only Praetor Dralath's puppet. After Tomed, "glory" had been a word reserved for the Praetor, while "honor" . . .

The word tasted sour on her lips.

Shiarkiek is the very heart of honor. He deserves better than this.

Romulus *deserves better!*

Charvanek resumed her pacing. Resent the past though she might, not being some rigidly controlled Vulcan, she no longer hated Spock, not after so many years. He'd done only what he must do, in all honor, for his sworn allies. Had the situations been reversed, she would have done the same.

At the thought, Charvanek gave a sharp, humorless little laugh. Ironic that there were no allies on Romulus or within its empire these days, none whom she might trust—

Yet I have this honorable not-quite enemy.

One used what tools one had. Charvanek, decided, stopped before her desk. A whispered code, one she changed daily, unlocked the terminal.

Another private code, equally short-lived, set a certain program running, searching. Absently brushing her hair back from her elegantly pointed ears, Charvanek hunted through Romulan outgoing transmissions as warily as ever a hunter stalked game, careful not to reveal a trace of her presence. . . .

Ah, yes. That one. They would not think to trace a most routine communication on tariffs; they would not even realize that another, coded, message was riding it.

Charvanek's lips tightened once more in that thin, ironic smile. Once, she had given Spock her most secret name. She doubted that he, with his Vulcan memory, had forgotten it. And it would be by that name, that pledge known to their sundered peoples, that she would approach him now.

If he betrays me again, I am dead.

The thought hardly bothered her, not after all these years of hard-won survival. What was life, after all, without risk? And what was worth gaining without cost? Especially since in this case, the prize was the very honor of the Empire.

* * *

"Ambassador? Ambassador Spock?"

Spock, alone in his quarters on Oriki, straightened in his chair. No mistaking the cheerful chirp of Irene Sanford. "Yes, Ms. Sanford?"

"Sir, there's a message from Commissioner Hanover. Shall I put it through now?"

That would be Federation Trade Commissioner Robert Hanover. "Indeed."

Spock switched on the viewscreen, and watched Hanover's round face form. "Well done, Ambassador Spock. Though I probably don't have to tell you that. I'll just add that no immediate business seems pending. So go ahead, Ambassador. Take some time off."

Had it been the old Starfleet days and McCoy or Kirk (ah, Jim . . .) who'd said that, Spock would have deliberately retorted, "Take some time off *what?* And how can one remove an abstract concept at all?" Instead, he merely said, "Acknowledged. Spock out."

Oriki's savannas were intriguing, the simple sweep of grassy plain soothing to eye and mind, ideal for meditation. They were also, he thought, remembering chirping and chittering, quiet. The Orikis had already offered to arrange a brief excursion before he returned to Vulcan—

A sharp beeping from the console on the desk warned him of an incoming message. Curious, Spock accessed it.

And froze.

The message was encrypted—and what would open it was the number S179-276 SP, his old Starfleet number, still almost as familiar to him as his name. And . . . it was signed by a name he had reason to remember.

He had been watching her career from afar on and off ever since she had been returned to the Empire in an exchange, although it had, of course, not been easy to get accurate data. As always, it was agreeable to see that she still did hold rank—indeed, that she still lived! And he truly appreciated how tenaciously the woman had clung to power—yes, and without once losing her morality.

She, Spock thought, *is a sad rarity on Romulus these days: totally honorable and totally sworn to the good of her people.*

But she would hardly have risked her hard-won life and rank just to send greetings. Spock rapidly set about decoding her message.

"Fascinating," he murmured after a bit.

A more accurate word might have been "astonishing."

"I would not trouble you," her message began—meaning, of course, *I would not involve an outsider,* "but there is no other choice. Honor on a certain world"—logically, she must mean Romulus—"has been betrayed. The great cannot be trusted, nor the pyramid support its peak." That meant, Spock translated, corruption in the government—all the way up to the praetor.

Indeed. For she added, her wording carefully not quite condemning her, "Many are disgusted with Praetor Dralath," namely herself, "and at the twisting of everything Romulans hold honorable. And something dangerous is brewing, although one knows not what. A certain bloodline is hardly, after all, in the praetor's confidence."

No. Someone of the emperor's own line would hardly be a favorite with Praetor Dralath.

But her message held one more shock. It ended, *"You must look to the security of the many."*

Ah yes, a doubly alarming code, indeed! "The security of the many" could only mean Romulus *and* the Federation—and that Federation security might be at risk. And that stressed *"You"* could mean only one thing:

She could not risk sending any more data. She wanted him to come to Romulus.

Spock leaned forward, one eyebrow arched. She had sent the message with her private name, her secret name, Liviana. (Liviana, whispered to him once, years ago . . .) A name, he thought, that not even the praetor would know, a name to prove the sender was, indeed, who she claimed to be.

But to ask this of him. Spock sat back, considering, fingers steepled. Given: Commander Liviana Charvanek was honorable. But even the most honorable could be . . . coerced.

After a moment, Spock leaned forward again, fingers flying across the console's keyboard, sending a careful query to Ruanek. The message would, as always, travel a devious route from world to world, system by system, in a random pattern that could not easily be traced.

Then, calmly, he went back to his work, finishing off the details that seemed to follow every assignment.

As humans would say: Good timing! He had clearly posted his message almost exactly when Ruanek had been about to send one of his own. Within only a few of Oriki's swift hours, the Romulan's coded message arrived. And it, too, warned that "something dangerous and underhanded is definitely being planned by the Leader."

Meaning, of course, Praetor Dralath.

Unfortunately, Ruanek, a relatively lowly subcommander born into a House Minor and in service to a discredited senator's heir, knew no more about the praetor's plans than did Charvanek. Being Ruanek—that was to say, impetuous as ever—he hinted that he did know something about what happened to Pardek: "Those who sup with golden spoons need look to the envious."

That rather flowery statement could only mean what Spock already suspected: Pardek had somehow managed to run afoul of the praetor.

But how? There is an enormous difference between being disgraced in some social affair and being arrested for high treason.

But Ruanek, not being without all common sense, had ended by adding that he could not risk revealing more in a message.

No, indeed.

Spock sat back again, mulling over the facts. To act would imply going behind the Federation's figurative back—not, he thought in deliberate understatement, a desirable thing. But not to act . . .

Spock got to his feet.

"Ms. Sanford."

She appeared almost instantly in the doorway. "Ambassador?"

"I will be going out onto the savanna. Alone, Ms. Sanford," he added hastily, seeing her about to speak, "to meditate."

Alone a short while later, dressed in a plain, hooded robe, he wandered the grasslands, lost in thought. When Spock tired of walking, he sat amid the vast sweep of the plains, surrounded by nothing but the sea of grass, with no other sound than the soft whisper of wind stirring the grass, calming his mind until he could slip into meditation.

Time passed, meaningless. . . .

All at once, Spock stirred. Suddenly, he became aware again of the discomforts of the body. A chill had begun to rise from the savanna, cooling with the dusk. He scrambled to his feet, went through a tranquil series of stretching exercises, then paused, looking about at twilight. The green plains were tinted a garish red by the setting sun.

Red as human blood?

Illogical. And human *blood has nothing to do with this matter.*

Ruanek's message had confirmed his own hypothesis. Commander Charvanek stood to lose even more than Ruanek did. She would not have risked all she had regained by communicating with the one who had betrayed her unless she saw a genuine danger to her people—and to the Federation as well.

The Romulans had withdrawn after Tomed, true enough. But the Neutral Zone was an easy thing to cross, especially in a cloaked ship, as he had seen. And if the Romulan-Federation balance of power was precarious at best, Federation-Klingon affairs had deteriorated after Khitomer, while Romulan-Klingon affairs were, purely and simply, tinder needing only the proper spark to kindle an interplanetary Klingon blood feud.

The result might well be war on three fronts, with at least one culture devolving into savagery.

Spock let out his breath in a silent sigh. Pardek might well be imprisoned or, by now, dead. With no Federation diplomatic relations with Romulus after Tomed, and only the scantiest of data from Intelligence, he had no recourse. He must go to Romulus, quite outside the law—and alone.

He could even find some ironic satisfaction in knowing that he no longer needed to appeal to the Vulcan Science Academy.

THREE

ROMULUS, YEAR 2344

Spock stepped from the relative peace of the shuttle into the noisy, dingy chaos of the Imperial Customs Building of the Romulan Star Empire at Ki Baratan, a vast gray-walled rotunda badly in need of cleaning and something more invigorating than that dull, flickering greenish light. All around him were hordes of other new arrivals, busy, snarling Romulan travelers in no mood for courtesy, their sallow skin turned a ghastly green by the dim light, each intent on pushing his or her way through first. The rotunda echoed and re-echoed with a confused racket of hurried footsteps, hard-heeled boots clicking against hard floors, and luggage being dragged. And it stank with a mixture of starship fuel, tired Romulans, and too little attention paid to cleaning. Spock straightened, putting on an air of haughty indifference that he trusted should look sufficiently "noble Romulan," and at least some of the crowd stood warily aside to let him pass.

He had not found it at all difficult to book passage from Oriki to Sharnak, a trading world closer to the Neutral Zone—particularly since Sharnak swarmed with merchants of many species who did not look at anything too closely except credit itself. From such a world, messages could be sent either throughout the Federation or across the Neutral Zone into the Empire, with no one the wiser save for the message's recipient. And from Sharnak, Spock had sent a coded message to Charvanek, telling her in veiled words of his intention, then found yet another trading vessel, this one heading here, to Romulus.

Fascinating, he thought, catching a glimpse of himself in the distorted mirror of a badly scratched and dented metal column. Too elaborate a disguise would have been suspect, so he had settled for a slight thickening of his eyebrows, a slightly more pronounced edge to his brow ridges—yes, he did look quite convincing, as a Romulan from a colony world, at least, particularly dressed as he was in the severely tailored brown tunic and trousers of a scholar-aristocrat. Romulan skin did tend to be more sallow than that of most Vulcans, indicative, no doubt, of their planet's greater cloud cover, but every race save the fatally inbred contained enough diversity for slight variations of skin tone not to be an issue.

Cold-faced guards in ill-fitting gray and silver uniforms, disruptor rifles slung over their shoulders, gestured at Spock and the other new arrivals: Follow that line on the floor. A Romulan noble would never have taken such casual rudeness, so Spock turned and gave them a raised eyebrow and the slightest of sneers, making them draw back ever so slightly. Point made.

He followed the worn white line, aware of being watched by yet more bored, grim guards. Ah yes, and those were surely the electronic eyes of security monitors staring down from the ceiling and columns, half-hidden among all the imposing flock of Romulan birds-of-prey images, their blue and blood-green wings outstretched as though caught in the midst of striking down the Empire's enemies, talons forever clenched about the twin homeworlds. Here and there along the walls of the rotunda hung posters portraying a presumably glamorized Praetor Dralath, looking young and stalwart, if grim as some protective father figure, welcoming "all honest and honorable visitors." Garish red lettering on most flat surfaces repeated the same dour warnings against smuggling, spying, and other acts against the State. No one else amid all the bustle seemed to be paying the posters or warnings any heed, so Spock ignored them as well.

The white line he and the other new arrivals were following led eventually through a doorway into a smaller, just as crowded, and equally dingy gray hall, decorated with yet more images of that bird-of-prey. Nothing, Spock mused, to encourage a tourist or make a newcomer feel at home save for still another of the posters of Praetor Dralath.

"Name?" a stern voice insisted.

Spock tightened his mouth slightly, hardened his expression a touch, and raised his chin. The brusque Romulan guard, his hand resting on the butt of his disruptor, who had just demanded that Spock identify himself looked him up and down, registered "aristocrat," and added a clearly begrudged "sir."

"Symakhos, First Academician of Bardat," Spock snapped, as though offended at being stopped. He presented his carefully forged papers as if making a vast concession.

The guard scanned them quickly, frowning. Illogical to worry: The odds were 875,656.3 to 1 against the papers being recognized as forgeries. And if his charade should fail, Spock thought with the barest touch of humor, he would not have long to regret it.

But the guard quickly handed back the papers. In a tone that was almost deferential he said, "No need to go back to the main Customs Building, sir," and pointed out a Customs desk in an office set apart from the chaos.

Rank, as the human adage states, hath its privileges.

At the Customs desk, Spock turned over his papers to the young, unsmiling, cold-eyed Romulan woman seated there.

"Name?" The woman sounded bored.

Ah yes, bureaucracy is one constant to be found across the universe. "Symakhos," he repeated.

"Species?"

"Romulan," Spock replied, raising an eyebrow as if to ask: Was that not obvious?

"Birth world?" Her tone became infinitesimally more polite.

"Tarus."

"Occupation?'"

Spock straightened as arrogantly as he had with the guard. "First Academician of Bardat."

The Customs Officer raised an eyebrow. "Purpose of visit?"

"Research."

"Address while on the homeworld?"

He gave it. Fascinating. The woman stiffened slightly, then almost bowed.

"I have no more questions, Noble Born," she said. "If you will step this way?"

He faced a genetic scanner with just a touch less confidence. Lights cycled on a screen he could not quite see and there was the faintest hum of machinery. Then a metallic voice intoned, *"Genetic match confirmed."*

It would be interesting to see the Vulcan Science Academy's reaction to this! We truly are still the same race genetically.

"Please move on," the woman said. Now she sounded only bored: Spock was no longer her problem. "Belongings reclaimed in the baggage area. Life to the Empire."

"Indeed."

Spock returned her salute, his hand pressed against his chest in a scholar's vague imitation of the Romulan military salute, then stalked in his best Romulan aristocratic fashion from the Customs area to the sign indicating TRANSPORT TO KI BARATAN in faded blue letters. There, he boarded a rough-riding, unpleasantly crowded, but mercifully swift magtrain, heading for the main terminal in the capital city.

Spock leaned back against the seat he had appropriated, posture and facial expression carefully projecting the casual arrogance of a provincial aristocrat in not-quite-familiar territory. As a provincial citizen, he would most likely be excused the occasional slip of accent or lack of knowledge of current events.

It was, however, a touch . . . disconcerting to see so many almost-familiar faces and know that they were not Vulcan but Romulan. Saavik would *not* approve. In fact, she would doubtless say—

But it was illogical to once again be thinking of her in unsuitable surroundings—illogical and dangerously distracting.

Totally illogical, too, were the sudden flashes of—could it actually be anger?—he was beginning to feel whenever he was jostled by the crowd.

There is, he told himself sternly as the magtrain came to an abrupt halt, *such a thing as acting a role too well.*

"Ki Baratan," a harsh mechanical voice warned. "Obey all laws. Glory to the Empire. All off."

The Ki Baratan terminal was constructed of reddish stone. Daylight filtered in from a series of windows set high in the walls. Over each window roosted an image of the bird-of-prey, while one vast portrait of Praetor Dralath glowered down at new arrivals as though challenging them to stay. Here, as in the Customs Building, grim-faced, bored guards prowled, disruptor rifles on their shoulders.

Spock stalked on to the staging area where he was to be picked up—assuming that all continued according to plan. He would not wait. If no one was there for him, it meant either that Charvanek had not received his last message—or that she had run afoul of Dralath.

Either way, Spock told himself, he would not yield to the illogic of worry. If he was not met, he had merely to retrace his steps, a scholar whose appointment in Ki Baratan had been unexpectedly canceled, and take the first ship off Romulus.

In other words, as the humans said, what would be, would be.

With that less-than-inspiring thought, Spock stepped from the terminal and out onto Romulan soil.

FOUR

U.S.S. ARMSTRONG, STARDATE 21012.1

Commander Saavik, first officer of the *U.S.S. Armstrong*, sat straight-backed and correct in the command chair, apparently in perfect harmony with herself and the universe around her.

And all the while, she was quite well aware of the rest of the bridge crew—two humans, a young Andorian, and two feathered I'xati—subtly watching her. Such dependable Vulcan self-control was what they expected—no, what they wanted—from her.

Anything, she thought with the faintest touch of wry humor, *that keeps them at the same time suitably alert and calm is excellent.* Her keen hearing had already overheard a few whispered complaints about "boring missions" and "routine patrols." *As I am forever telling the so earnest, so green, and so illogically glory-hungry ensigns to whom I am trying to teach ethics, no patrol is ever routine.*

The door onto the bridge slid open as her watch ended, precisely on time: Captain Howes was courteous of Vulcan sensibilities.

"Captain on the bridge." Rising from the command chair, Saavik pivoted to greet Captain Howes and added formally, "The bridge is yours, sir." There was more than a little relief in her voice. She had been offered a captaincy more than once, but like Spock before her, was more interested in science than command.

"I relieve you, ma'am."

He raised an eyebrow along with that statement, as he always did at her insistence on such formality after so many years. But he knew as well as she, Saavik thought, that aboard a starship, a closed community in a hostile environment, attention to proper order meant survival.

Seated, Captain Howes studied the pad that Yeoman Ethari, the Andorian, handed him, and asked Saavik without looking up, "Everything shipshape, Commander?"

"Aye, sir. Now." She added tranquilly, "I have already canceled the order for sonic toothbrushes."

Howes glanced sharply up at that, a split second's blankness on his face. Saavik could almost see him quickly processing data: Toothbrushes? Archaic means of deck cleaning as punishment! A Vulcan making a joke?

The captain grinned. "Ah, you've been reading Patrick O'Brian novels again, haven't you, Commander?"

Yes, in fact, she had been reading those ancient sea novels. But not by the faintest expression did Saavik give away her inner amusement. "The classics, sir. And the decks truly are clean. Now."

She swept a subtle glance around the bridge, knowing that *Armstrong*'s crew usually enjoyed watching their captain's not-quite-banter with their first officer.

Howes' grin widened. "Well, as long as you're happy . . ."

Saavik obligingly retorted, "Happiness, sir, is an emotion and, as such, not relevant to my state of mind. Good day, Captain."

As the turbolift doors whispered shut behind her, she could hear chuckles on the bridge. Satisfactory. Humor in many species lessened tension, not to mention boredom.

The turbolift jolted on the way out from the bridge. Eyebrow raised, Saavik notified Engineering—which, to her bemusement, seemed to have already heard about the toothbrushes.

Her class was waiting: three humans, one stocky Tellarite, and two more of the I'xati, twins from one hatching.

Today . . . she realized with an inner frown that she would have preferred to cancel the class. Today, illogical though it might be, she suddenly had no patience for mistakes.

Nonsense.

"Have you considered the problem posed at our last session?" Saavik asked the class without preamble. "Yes? Then let me hear your solutions."

The problem had been based on the quite real, and tragic, Tomed Incident of 2311, in which an encounter between the Federation and the Romulan Empire had accelerated through misunderstanding and hot tempers on both sides into the death of thousands and the latest withdrawal of the Romulans behind their Neutral Zone. (An unexpected flash of memory: A child running from her in terror at the sight of her "Romulan" features; her own loathing at being forced to become the hunter, as once, when she'd been that poor child's age, she had been hunted. . . .)

It is counterproductive to dwell on what I saw.

Ensign Pierce, a fair-haired young man from Weapons Systems, so newly out from Starfleet Academy that his voice had barely stopped cracking, glanced around at the others, then said hesitantly, "I would end hostilities by a quick preemptive strike."

Saavik raised a brow. "You would fire against those who had not attacked you?"

"Uh, well, if it was for the greater good."

"And you would know this in advance? Congratulations, Ensign. Your precognitive skills astound me."

"But . . . uh . . . I mean, suppose you do know that they're going to attack you? And maybe kill hundreds of innocent people? Shouldn't you then, well . . ." His voice faltered under Saavik's steady, emotionless stare. "Why not simply use something so powerful they can't strike back?" he asked desperately. "Maybe, I don't know, protomatter?"

As a weapon? An unwanted flash of memory from decades ago: *the Genesis Planet.* And a sudden blaze of purely Romulan fury roused in her, shouting at her to crush this young idiot with a few scathing words.

But Saavik forced down the illogical fury and merely . . . waited. Ah yes, they weren't all fools. The I'xati both had raised their feathery crests in shock, and Ensign Musashi, an intense young human woman from Life Sciences, actually hissed at Pierce, "Protomatter's unstable!"

"Ensign Musashi is quite correct," Saavik said, carefully without the slightest trace of emotion. "Protomatter degrades. This is no doubt useful if you hurl sufficient quantities into a star because you wish to produce a supernova."

Ensign Pierce by now was an intriguing shade of red, but he couldn't quite puzzle out the way to withdraw with grace. "But . . . I mean . . . that would end the war—"

"By destroying an entire race and its culture. Indeed it would. And possibly, assuming other worlds within the new supernova's reach, you would also destroy at least one entire planetary system." Her voice wanted very much to shake with anger; she held it steady. "Quite efficient. But I must observe that I consider that to be a disquieting ambition for a weapons officer."

She paused to allow Ensign Pierce time to wish he had never been born. But he looked back at her bravely, horror in his eyes.

"I'm sorry, Commander. I, uh, guess I wasn't thinking."

"But now you *have* begun to think," Saavik conceded. "We have made at least a tiny advance today."

She listened to the other solutions: Musashi and the two I'xati were enthusiastic about sitting down and discussing matters—commendable, but not exactly practical in the Tomed affair—while Gurcha, the Tellarite, insisted that the leaders on both sides should be *forced* to meet head-to-head. Or hoof-to-hoof.

At least, Saavik reminded herself sternly, they were *beginning* to reason. And if they were wildly illogical, they were still very young.

That didn't precisely relieve the urge to pick them up by their collective napes and shake some sense into them.

Sorry, Spock. You and I know I will never, ever, quite have the self-control of one born and raised on Vulcan!

He had still agreed to their betrothal. Giving the ensigns their assignments in reading and viewing historical data—and adding a remedial study of Earth history, twentieth century—she dismissed them.

"Grow some brains!" she overheard Musashi whisper to Pierce as they hurried off. "Kill off a whole world—right, and say that to a Vulcan! Are you crazy?"

Just young.

Heading off to the ship's gym, Saavik raced through a tougher workout than usual, letting off in exercise the frustration she would never have shown to the youngsters—or, indeed, to anyone else.

Except, maybe to Spock. He has seen me at my most . . . ah . . . Romulan.

Ah, Spock. Why do I keep thinking of you? One thing I am not is a romantic human!

Chief Medical Officer Rhys, dark and stocky like many from New Caledonia, paused in his rather desultory weights routine to watch Saavik's workout.

"All this energy couldn't possibly be a case of stress reduction, could it, Commander?" Rhys asked slyly.

"Vulcans do not have stress to reduce," she replied as serenely as breathlessness would allow. *No falsehood, considering that I am not wholly Vulcan.*

She allowed her glance to linger at his midsection, which showed a good ten kilos of superfluous weight, and Rhys laughed ruefully. "Or anything else," he admitted. "Unless, of course, your observation is a case of the old Earth maxim: 'Physician, heal thyself.' "

Laughter reduced stress among humans. Therefore, Saavik thought, by the time that she left the gym, the humans there probably had acceptably low stress levels.

She, however, was still most bewilderingly . . . restless.

FIVE

KI BARATAN, ROMULUS, DAY 3, FIRST WEEK OF
TASMEEN, 2344

Spock paused just outside the terminal's main doorway in Ki
Baratan, trying to get his bearings. The crowds of arriving passengers parted about him, glaring at the aristocrat who had
stopped so abruptly yet not quite daring to touch or snarl at him.
He was aware of them, but only dimly in this moment's sudden
revelation: Not only was this the first time that he had ever stood
on the streets of a Romulan city, it was almost certainly the first
time that *anyone* from the Federation had done so. *At least,* he
thought, anyone who was not a prisoner facing execution.

But he could hardly stand here in the middle of all these irate
pedestrians. Spock moved to one side with the casual arrogance
of someone entitled to expect his driver to appear immediately.
Clearly no one in the busy crowds was seeing him as anything
but a Romulan noble, not even those stern, rifle-wielding guards
who stalked past the entrances and exits, patrolling.

So. You have a moment before they become suspicious.
Observe.

39

The air was cooler than that of Vulcan, though not unpleasantly so, the atmosphere more moist and a little thicker (approximately 0.065 percent so, his mind automatically analyzed) than the Vulcan norm, the difference in gravity so slight as to be almost undetectable. That the air here, just outside the terminal, was still tainted with oil, fuel, and other spaceport odors was unpleasant but to be expected.

The streets were, of course, paved, the buildings, again as was to be expected from those near a spaceport terminal, strictly utilitarian, plain walls, reddish stone or some dark composite material: warehouses, no doubt. Each building carried, predictably, the by-now-overly familiar bird-of-prey emblem, faded by exposure to the elements.

The people hereabouts were strictly utilitarian, too, men and women in drab brown or gray, those who clearly earned their living loading and unloading cargo, dealing with imports or exports. The only traces of color came from the food stands set up here and there, adding whiffs of slightly stale grease and not-quite-fresh meat to the odors. Spock flinched inwardly at this blatant reminder that Vulcan's sundered cousins were eaters of meat.

And over everything loomed yet another portrait of an almost smiling, paternal Praetor Dralath, shielded by the outspread wings of a gigantic bird-of-prey. Green-lettered signs proclaimed GLORY TO THE ROMULAN STAR EMPIRE or LONG LIFE AND PROSPERITY TO THE ROMULAN PEOPLE.

Could that be a corruption of "Live long and prosper"? I wonder . . . yes, and that cornice design could almost *be one from Vulcan's past—*

Just then, to Spock's quickly controlled alarm, a familiar figure nearly collided with him: Avrak, Pardek's sister-son and heir, dark hair slicked severely back from his sharp, handsome face, his silver and red uniform precisely fitted, ornamented sash at just the right angle. He was clearly en route back to Romulus, presumably from one of his colony world estates. Closely following him was his entourage of aides and guards and servants in clothing of dull grays and browns, all of them with the same grim, harried expression. No wonder. Despite his handsome arrogance, Avrak looked as irritable and worried as a noble whose head of house was in trouble dared without showing weakness.

Spock hastily lowered his head, moving aside, minor nobility acknowledging House Major, and Avrak passed without more than an absent wave of a hand.

If Avrak is still at liberty, then clearly whatever affected Pardek was of a personal nature.

It could not, logically, be a matter concerning reunification. That would have created more of a stir, and any praetor worthy of the title would have seized on that as an example of treasonous activity worth a sea of propaganda.

Someone was calling his assumed name. Fighting an illogical surge of relief, Spock turned to see a dark, wiry young man in a somber silver and blue uniform half-standing in a sleek black groundcar, searching the crowd.

Ah, then Charvanek did *receive my latest message.*

And that not-quite-military uniform could only be Charvanek's livery for civilian retainers. Spock moved without unseemly haste to the groundcar, dipping a polite head to the youngster, who was barely more than a boy, and who returned the gesture with off-hand courtesy. "First Academician Symakhos?"

"Indeed."

The youngster's quick, sharp glance had just committed him to memory. *Too professional a glance for a mere driver. And why has he given me no name? Obviously, Charvanek means for him to observe me.*

It was hardly surprising, given the distrust and uneasiness he had already noted. Logical, in fact.

Spock climbed into the groundcar. Seen at such close range, it was still imposing, but plainly well-used, scratched and dented under the slick black enamel, albeit in superb repair. "Belt yourself in," the young Romulan told him curtly. "I may need to make some abrupt stops before we're clear of traffic."

Their groundcar slowly made its way up from the terminal through streets increasingly crowded with gleaming private groundcars, blocky, ugly commercial carriers, and dead black military vehicles with birds-of-prey engraved on their sides. Pedestrians crossed where and when they could, dodging the vehicles, swearing at the drivers or at each other, occasionally even flashing knives. Spock told himself, *Accept.* These people were as they were, and it was illogical to flinch.

As his own driver skillfully wove their way along, slowly extricating them from the congestion and noise, Spock allowed himself a stranger's prerogative of glancing about. Ki Baratan was clean and elegant in its own grim way, very sleekly modern, with wide streets and smooth-walled buildings of glass and metal or sweeps of reddish stone—igneous?—that was presumably common enough to be economical. A good many of the walls bore the gaudy LONG LIFE AND PROSPERITY propaganda slogans. And here and there, Spock spotted security cameras and viewscreens.

Interesting. The praetor would seem not to be exactly trustful of his people.

The groundcar lurched as the young Romulan swerved about a crowd of pedestrians. Muttered curses followed in the car's wake, and Spock raised a brow: Profanity often did have its roots in antiquity, and those oaths had sounded intriguingly close to ancient Vulcan phrases.

Phrases, he thought with the barest hint of irony, *that no Vulcan today would ever repeat.*

He glanced up. The rooftops were decorated almost ornately with intricate stonework, figures that . . .

He blinked. *Yes, indeed yes,* Spock thought with a little shock of recognition, *those are definitely T'Karik and Sesenek from the old tales—yes, and that is, without a doubt, the image of a* sehlat!

More shocks followed as the groundcar slowed still further. The ordinary Romulans were plainly dressed, men and women both, in what appeared to be homemade clothing dyed dull gray or blue with only a few accents of color: a bright bit of yellow embroidery at a collar or red trimming at a sleeve. But the *styles* of the clothing . . . yes. Spock had seen similar designs in old volumes of Vulcan costume.

And the language, even the body language, the lift of a brow, twist of a hand—all the details continued to be jarringly not quite right yet just as jarringly familiar.

If it were not illogical, I could find myself looking for acquaintances.

"Look out!" the young driver shouted, swerving wildly to avoid a little boy who'd darted in front of the groundcar. The child's mother snatched her son back, shaking him, hissing, "Behave or the Eater of Souls will get you!"

Spock twisted about to stare after her, then sank down into his seat again.

"Are you all right?" the driver demanded.

"I was," Spock told him truthfully, "merely startled."

The driver snorted, muttering something under his breath about ". . . without the sense of a *drabbik.*"

But Spock hardly noted. The Eater of Souls. One of Vulcan's oldest archetypes: a demonic being said in the ancient tales to materialize during sandstorms to devour Vulcan souls down to the very *katra*. Not surprising that he had reacted so strongly, since archetypes were "hardwired" into every sentient being's psyche—and equally not surprising that Romulan archetypes should remain Vulcan if . . .

"The date," Spock said suddenly. "What is the date?"

"Why, Day Three, First Week of Tasmeen, of course."

Tasmeen! The Romulans had even kept the Vulcan calendar!

And in that moment, Spock knew, with a certainty above all those logical reasoned appeals he had made to the Vulcan Science Academy. Despite the changes wrought by a thousand years, these were still his people, these were still the sundered cousins who must not be lost from the Vulcan family.

But his trained ambassadorial senses were beginning to note

disturbing traces of unrest that had nothing to do with the basic Romulan hot temper. For all the crowds and hostility, people were not quite meeting each other's gazes. And the streets were just too clean, too empty of idlers. Whenever the groundcar stopped in traffic, Spock, now that he was listening for it, overheard flashes of resentment, muttered warily, at the balance of trade compared with the Way It Was, resentment at the quality of Romulan ships compared with the old warbirds, resentment at too much taxation, too many tariffs.

Almost, Spock mused, *as though Praetor Dralath were channeling resources. For what? A defense buildup? A war? And is Charvanek correct? Is there danger to the Federation?*

"There," the driver pointed with his chin. "The commander's estate."

The high outer wall was an unornamented sweep of that common red stone, somewhat chipped and worn with age. At the gate, whose intricate scrollwork did not quite disguise its sturdiness, Spock's driver reached out of the groundcar to type in a code on a recessed keyboard, then muttered a second code. A moment passed, another . . . then the gate swung slowly open, metal creaking and complaining. Poor maintenance? Or part of a deliberate warning system? Vulcan had once had such guarding walls, such deliberately noisy gates and creaking floors. . . .

The garden within the circle of the walls, smoothly twisted spires of dark lava half-hidden by vegetation, was . . . just a little too unkempt, not quite neglected. The mansion was . . . just a little too shabby, again not quite neglected. But what had once been a colorful façade in sharp, primary reds and blues was faded here and there or even chipped, and Spock noted an ornamental column no longer standing quite true. Clear evidence of what must have been a difficult—and expensive—struggle back to power. Illogical to feel guilt.

Or was it, perhaps, regret?

The not-quite-shabbiness continued within the house: too many empty spaces that might once have held art, too many shut-up rooms. Too few servants, as well, though that could indicate caution on Charvanek's part.

A door creaked open, and a stolid Romulan in the somber silver and blue livery stood aside. He looked, Spock thought, like a veteran, retired now to his commanding officer's private service, and he stared at Spock—hard. Spock met his glance blandly and entered. The door creaked shut behind him.

Charvanek stood before him.

For all his years of self-control, a stab almost of pain shot through Spock at the sight of her. Of Vulcan stock as Romulans were, Charvanek had barely been touched by the years. But the long struggle for survival had burned away all weakness, all softness, leaving her as fierce as the Romulan bird-of-prey, fierce and compelling, and like that bird-of-prey, beautiful.

Control. Spock nearly snapped that warning at himself.

Charvanek said only, "Spock."

Spock and Charvanek sat across a small, inlaid table of honey-dark wood in a small room ornamented with faded murals of Romulan wilderness. Sat as though, height of illogic, they were merely two old acquaintances meeting once more, sipping two ritual cups of *khavas,* the Romulan answer, it would seem, to Earth's coffee.

Illogical, as well, Spock realized with a jolt, to need to concentrate on what Charvanek was saying, and not simply remember the past.

You are not a human. You must not be a fool.

Spock had been under Federation orders back then, but with Vulcan honesty, he had to admit that their meeting had hardly been the hard, logical stuff of regulations.

The past is just that: past.

Charvanek must surely have been thinking the same, because she broke off, studying him, face unreadable save for the faintest of wry smiles. "We are, for good or ill, no longer who or what we were."

"And only fools wish for it to be otherwise. Charvanek—"

"We are alone. Liviana."

"Liviana, then." His voice, to his astonishment, had almost stumbled on the name (the secret name whispered to him once, so long ago . . .). "What of Praetor Dralath?"

"Ah. Indeed. Dralath." Without doing more than drawing back ever so slightly, she suddenly became not the woman but the commander. "Our brave leader is becoming increasingly unpopular with the people."

So he'd noticed on the journey here. "And the military?"

"Unfortunately, he still has a firm grip on the military." Charvanek shrugged slightly. "It was they who let him arrest several senators under trumped-up charges: Karpan, Teranas, Pardek, Gorath. And not one citizen spoke out in their behalf. Or rather, dared speak out."

Her voice was almost indifferent, as though she wasted no pity on anyone clumsy enough to be snared. Spock caught Pardek's name among the others, and kept his face studiously blank. At least, he thought, Pardek and the reunification project with him were still alive.

"Then the military is the true power here?"

"You misunderstand! Dralath is strong enough to keep them his: they haven't forgotten how last year, he gutted a general who tried to attack him. Convenient, of course," she drawled, "that the attack should happen during a planetwide broadcast."

With careful irony, Spock said, "That seems an unlikely way to win public support."

She gave a short, fierce little humorless laugh. "True enough. Most recently, Dralath has become increasing warlike. Though, I might add, not altogether convincingly."

Spock raised an eyebrow. "A cover?"

After the slightest pause, she nodded. "It's almost as though he were planning some act of 'military glory' to counter that growing unpopularity. There is nothing," Charvanek added cynically, "like some easy victories far from home to make a leader look good."

"Before I can act or make any logical recommendations, I must have evidence."

"Other than my word?" It was a warning purr.

"I do not doubt your word. But I still must see the praetor in action. And I must, to be quite blunt, have a chance to consider any potential replacement. I am assuming that there *is* such a replacement under consideration?"

"Clever, Spock."

"Merely logical. You would not have taken the risk of contacting me if you merely wished a sympathetic ear."

That forced a wry smile from her. "Indeed not. So, then: Narviat is his name, a logical—yes," dryly, "Romulans are capable of logic—a logical and clever aristocrat who is liked by the people."

And by you, Liviana? Do I read that behind your words? What are you plotting, my no-longer-enemy? "Not a comfortable situation for him."

"No, indeed! Narviat has been walking a knife's blade as far as Dralath is concerned. Particularly since Narviat is distant kin to the emperor—"

"As are you."

She raised a brow. "You've been checking on me."

"Indeed."

He volunteered nothing more, and Charvanek, after a moment, continued, "What would you? I . . . might be able to take you with me to the next session of the Senate. Academic advisors are common there. You must understand that this will involve a great deal of danger for you, for us both. The risk—"

"Risk," Spock snapped before he could stop himself. "Of course there is risk! This has all been a calculated risk!"

Charvanek blinked. "Well done!" she said after a moment. "You truly *are* acting like a Romulan! Quick temper and all—I never would have dreamed a Vulcan had such passion in him."

Spock stared at her, stunned.

It . . . hadn't been an act.

But Charvanek must not know it! Spock quickly forced his face back into its usual impassivity, hunting a logical explanation for his lapse—yes. Clearly Romulan thoughts, Romulan emotions, could overwhelm a Vulcan's self-control if they caught him off-guard. Understood.

To cover the awkward moment of silence, Spock said, "One acts the role one must."

Something dark flicked in Charvanek's eyes. "Ah yes," she said with absolutely no expression, "I had forgotten just how fine an actor you can be. So, now: At least you will need only the most minimal of disguises to pass as my distant, scholarly cousin. My very *distinguished* scholarly cousin, that is, one whose talents appeared so early that the sacrifice of a military career and a soldier's honor was seen as the only . . . logical . . . choice. And we have this advantage: No one will expect to find Ambassador Spock of Vulcan—or Captain Spock of Starfleet—in Ki Baratan. If we tell them that you are a civilian scholar, they will see only a civilian scholar."

"Indeed." It was an irony of war that hiding in plain sight should be easier on perilous Romulus than on friendly Earth.

Of course, a stray thought reminded Spock, whenever he had needed to pass unnoticed among humans, matters had been complicated by the presence of James Kirk, for whom "inconspicuous" had been impossible. What Jim would say of this mission . . .

At least I endanger no one but myself.

Correction: He also jeopardized this exceedingly unlikely ally—she who right now was studying him as she would a weapon.

"Yes," Charvanek said shortly, and called over her shoulder, "M'ret."

A dark wiry Romulan, the boy who'd been Spock's driver, shot into the room, nearly banging the door back against the wall in his haste. He grabbed the edge just in time to keep it from slamming, then turned with a youngster's desperate pride to Charvanek, saluting. "Commander."

"My aide," Charvanek told Spock, and for a bare instant, an almost maternal amusement glinted in her eyes. "M'ret, this is my distant cousin, Symakhos, First Academician of Bardat. I believe you've already met."

M'ret offered Spock a sharp, correct bow with more poise than Spock had expected. Spock acknowledged it with a solemn dip of his head. Charvanek continued, "The academician will be attending the next session of the Senate with me. His baggage was misplaced on his civilian transport, but he must be properly garbed as befits one of his scholarly rank."

Did M'ret believe that fiction? The youngster gave not the slightest clue in face or posture. He merely saluted Charvanek again and said, "As my commander wishes."

SIX

U.S.S. ARMSTRONG, DEEP SPACE, STARDATE 21018.5

Saavik woke with a start, rolling out of bed, clawing her hair out of her eyes with one hand, snatching for her phaser with the other, calling, "Lights!" She saw—

Nothing alarming. The familiar bronze-red panels of her quarters on board *Armstrong,* the tiny curl of incense from the little bronze firepot in one corner, the weapons collected over her years in Starfleet hanging undisturbed on one wall. But something was still screaming—

Not screaming. Beeping. Saavik let out her breath in a hiss. The beeping was merely her computer signaling an incoming message.

Disgraceful lapse of control, she scolded herself, though a wry corner of her mind acknowledged that even a Vulcan could be caught off-guard. Getting to her feet, Saavik stretched and breathed in deeply, pulling her composure about her along with a dark red robe. Running a hand through her disheveled hair, willing her still-racing heartbeat back down to normal, she sat at her meticulously clean desk. "Screen on."

Instantly, the insistent beeping stopped. But Saavik stiffened in new alarm, her eyes widening. Not the standard innocuous "message incoming" signal: The screen had darkened to Starfleet blue, flashing a "high-security" warning. Unusual that the message should have bypassed Mr. Watanabe on the bridge. . . .

Not unusual, Saavik corrected herself, *ominous.*

Control. That was the way of it. She was a Starfleet officer, not some ensign right out of the Academy. And more important even than that, she was a daughter of Vulcan, by blood and by choice.

But very few Starfleet personnel possessed both the technical skill and the authority to override a starship's ordinary communications protocols and bypass the bridge. Indeed, right now she could think of only one.

"Computer," Saavik ordered, more sharply than she would have preferred. "Security procedure. Classified communications access."

"Identify for retinal scan," the computer's emotionless voice replied.

"Commander Saavik of Vulcan, first officer *U.S.S. Armstrong,* Security Class One."

A beam of light flashed, recording the patterns in her eyes. The screen blinked, colors shifting, as the computer ran its testing program.

"Security clearance Class One: granted."

"Message on," she ordered.

Starfleet's insignia, overlaid with the emblem for Starfleet Ops, appeared on the blue screen for a moment, then faded, to be replaced by the still-lovely mahogany face, the corona of now-silvery hair, and the presence, simultaneously attractive and formidable, that was Captain Uhura.

Captain, no more than that—and by choice. Despite her age and accomplishments, Uhura, as head of Starfleet's elite security agency, kept what humans called "a low profile," or at least as low as was possible.

"Captain Uhura." Saavik came to rigid attention.

"At ease, Saavik. Please." Uhura's voice was still as melodious as it had been when Saavik had served as a trainee on board the *Enterprise*. "I have some alarming news, I'm afraid."

Logic, Saavik told herself. *Captain Uhura would have no reason to contact me directly, rather than going through Captain Howes, unless it concerned—Spock.*

Discipline insisted that she not question a superior. Discipline, this once, could wait. "It is about Spock, isn't it?"

Uhura didn't so much as flinch. "It is."

Not illness. There would be no need for a high-security message. And not . . . death. I would surely have sensed that.

Saavik drew in a sharp breath. "He has left his appointed post with the trade mission on Oriki."

"Now, how did you know that?" Uhura's voice was casual, but her eyes were suddenly absolutely cold.

Warily, Saavik replied, "I . . . deduced it from the fact that you called me directly. I cannot, however, hypothesize where he has gone."

Uhura studied her for a long moment without speaking, face almost as unreadable as that of a Vulcan, then said bluntly, "He's gone to Romulus."

"Romulus . . ."

Captain Uhura was waiting. *I will not disgrace myself,* Saavik snapped at herself. She forced her face back to a mask of utter calm. "I assume that you wish me to extricate him."

Uhura drew a deep breath. "Other folks might think you really did have a computer planted in your skull. Yes, and that you couldn't care less what happened to Spock. But that cool façade doesn't fool me."

No, I would guess not. But do you know the force of emotion behind it? I dare not show the slightest trace of that, or I will never control it again.

She waited. After a moment, Uhura continued, "Has Spock ever discussed his views on reunification with you?"

Saavik raised an eyebrow. "Certainly. It is a subject on which we disagree. I will not insult my future consort's logic. But . . . Spock is an idealist. His ambition is to join what Surak's choices sundered. And Surak," she added, not quite as steadily as she would have liked, "died violently."

Uhura nodded. "Precisely. So, Saavik, once again, we've got to help him. Just like old times. I'm assuming that your next step, were I to end the communication here, would be to plan your own trip to Romulus."

"That would be a highly illegal procedure."

"And you would still do it."

"Yes."

"Now, that's fortunate, because there just happens to be a Barolian freighter docked at Starbase 6, one light-day from here. We've arranged for you to take possession of it. It will get you to the homeworld, and back to the Federation as well."

She clearly wasn't going to specify details. But Saavik had never known Uhura to fail to follow through on a mission before.

"And my identity, and reason for being on the Romulan homeworld?"

"We've arranged cover for you," Uhura said. "Here's your briefing."

Lights flickered on Saavik's computer. It hummed briefly, and she raised an eyebrow: Any data taking so long to transmit must represent a satisfactorily thorough briefing.

"Intelligence has learned," Uhura told her, "that Praetor Dralath has a condition known as T'Shevat's syndrome. It involves green blood cell deterioration, increasingly debilitating pain, and a considerably shortened life span."

"Interesting . . ." Saavik said thoughtfully.

"Quite. There's a VSA paper on the subject: Healers on Vulcan are using RNA splicing and ribosome transfusions to force the syndrome into remission."

53

Saavik raised an eyebrow. Once again, Uhura's range of interests impressed her. "Am I to assume that the Romulans do not have these techniques?"

"Precisely."

"And that the Praetor has granted special privileges to those who might have his cure?"

"Exactly."

"Then I am to pass as a medic and purvey these techniques on the homeworld until I can find Spock and . . ." *bring him home, bring him home safely!* "And ascertain his mission, then help him to withdraw. Is that correct?"

"That, and keep your eyes and ears open. There's something big brewing on the homeworld, I'm not sure what. And I can't think of a better woman to find out, can you?" Uhura all but purred.

Gratitude might be an emotion, but Saavik felt it heat the back of her eyes, her cheeks. "Indeed, Captain. I quite agree." Something in her voice made Saavik add, "I assume you wish plausible deniability?"

Uhura grinned at her. It took a good thirty years off her age. "You got it. We know nothing about your mission, we don't know where you're going, we don't even know that there *is* a mission."

"Understood."

"But I don't like sending you in there cold. I think I may be able to scrounge you some backup."

"I do not wish you to risk . . ."

"Hey, risk is my business." Uhura smiled. "It's like old times, working with you, Saavik. In the thirty-three years since Tomed, information about the Empire's been at a premium. Keep your eyes open, and we'll be glad of anything you can bring us—but if you are apprehended, we'll never have heard of you. And if you run afoul of other Federation offices, or Vulcan officials, for that matter—we never even had this conversation.

"In short: Foul up, and you are either dishonored or dead. Still want the assignment?"

"I presume that is a rhetorical question."

"My God, Saavik, do you know how much you sound like him?" Uhura leaned forward in her office chair half the quadrant away. "Bring him home, Saavik. Please."

I will not stand watch, Spock, while you sacrifice yourself again. I will not be left holding a burial robe as the one thing I have left of you.

"If it is even remotely possible." Saavik paused, because in another moment, her voice would have most unforgivably shaken. "And I do promise this," she added in the Romulan language. "Neither Spock nor I will be the cause of another war between the Romulan Empire and the Federation."

Uhura blinked. "Lord. You sound so Romulan it's almost alarming."

"I merely meant to show the adequacy of my cover."

"Adequacy!" Uhura snorted in a manner unsuitable for a senior Starfleet officer. "I'm going to sign off now. I don't have to tell you to erase all traces of this communication."

She paused, looking intensely into the screen as if attempting to fathom Saavik's thoughts. "All my hopes, Saavik. I still intend to dance at your wedding."

Uhura ended transmission before Saavik had a chance to salute.

Saavik swung around—and caught sight of herself in her cabin's small mirror. She had flushed olive, and her eyes flashed: She really did look as fiercely Romulan as she had sounded.

Embarrassment was illogical.

So, for that matter, were other emotions. Saavik sat motionless, willing herself to take slow, regular breaths . . . think of nothing but breathing . . . slow . . . calming breaths . . . calming . . . calm . . .

Saavik saved her data, then delicately deleted the records of her conversation with Uhura from the *Armstrong*'s main system. Ship's time indicated that Captain Howes would have come off-watch and would logically be found in his quarters. Very well.

"Commander Saavik to Captain Howes."

The captain responded almost instantly. "What's wrong, Commander?" Surprise flickered across his face at the sight of her, so fierce and disheveled, and with the surprise was a hint of quickly suppressed appreciation. "Commander . . . Saavik, are you well?"

"My level of health is satisfactory." That meant, she thought, precisely nothing. "But I wish to request immediate and extended personal leave." She looked down, as though suddenly unable to bear his gaze. "If you consent, I can leave the ship at Starbase 6, one light-day hence at warp factor three."

Glancing slyly up, Saavik saw the captain's eyebrows rise and his fair skin redden. He had, after all, attended her betrothal; he must certainly be wondering if . . . "You . . . ah . . . do not wish to request that we divert to Vulcan?"

"No, sir. Unnecessary. Is personal leave granted, sir?"

"Certainly, Commander! God knows, you've got leave coming." She watched him suppress his questions with almost Vulcan control. On him, the effort looked painful. "I'll get someone to take over your watch."

"Unnecessary, sir," Saavik repeated more gently. She allowed herself to lower her gaze again, as if in relief.

"Saavik, you've been pushing yourself, even for a Vulcan. Consider that an order."

"Aye, aye, sir," Saavik said. "And thank you."

She cut the connection. It might be considered shameful to mislead her captain like that.

But shame was a human emotion.

SEVEN

"It's shot-rolling time," Jean-Luc Picard muttered to himself. During the Napoleonic wars, a disgruntled ship's crew would roll cannonballs belowdecks to indicate dissatisfaction. At least, in the British navy: he was certain no one on board his ancestor's ship ever would have done a thing like that.

Stargazer should have been overhauled and returned to its mission as a deep-space explorer three weeks ago. Granted, his crew was comfortable, if bored, taking turns on too-short shore leaves planetside on Mars since no one was sure how long they'd be here. By this point, though, Picard and his chief engineering officer were both ready to mutiny.

What was the point of being the youngest captain in Starfleet, with a neat, nimble ship, if he couldn't get her out of spacedock?

"I'll snake-charm them," promised Phigus Simenon, his engineering officer. He was a Gnalish, therefore of reptilian ancestry, and he would probably try.

Leaving the engineer to fight the good fight, which, from what he heard behind him, was rapidly escalating into a holy war, Picard stormed off down the corridors. Had his ancestor who had nailed his colors to the mast at Trafalgar felt so frustrated and defeated? Even if Picard lacked the resources available in a Napoleonic dockyard—bullying, bribery, and the lash, ah, the Good Old Days—he had no intentions of losing the battle with Refit.

"Jean-Luc!" a familiar voice called from a side corridor where full-spectrum lights and artificial winds stirred a carefully balanced small garden. "Come on over here. There's someone I want you to meet!"

Captain Walker Keel might be an old friend, but he was also senior to Picard. His "come on over here" could have been interpreted as a direct order—if the sight of the tall young woman who stood beside Walker wasn't enough to draw him. Entranced, Picard stood for an instant enjoying the sight of full-spectrum light turning the woman's long red hair to blazing copper. But it was more than mere beauty: the woman with Walker, that lucky, lucky man who would no doubt introduce him, possessed such a delectable poise and graciousness—

He could hardly stand here staring at her from across the corridor. "Walker!" There, that sounded almost convincingly hearty. "Good to see you." As the two men shook hand vigorously, Picard added, "What's *Horatio* doing in port?"

"Refit." It came out as a snarl, and Picard hastily stifled a laugh.

"At least I'm not the only one. *Stargazer*'s in refit too. They say they've got other ships ahead of it in the queue, *Horatio* being one of them, I daresay. Rank hath its privileges."

"Ah, well, I want to talk with you about that, Jean-Luc," Keel said. "In my office. I—"

Smiling at Picard—a charming sight, he thought—the woman coughed once, meaningfully.

"I did promise you an introduction, didn't I?" Keel asked ruefully. "Then I start fuming about my ship again. . . ."

"Come between a captain and his ship?" The woman laughed. "I know better than to even try."

"Still, I swear, my manners went out an airlock somewhere. Beverly, permit me to present my dear, not-so-old friend, Jean-Luc Picard of the *Stargazer*. Jean-Luc, this is Beverly Howard, who is in medical school on Earth."

Picard bowed stiffly from the waist in full, old-fashioned courtesy. "Jack Crusher's fianceé? *Enchanté, Mademoiselle.*"

She laughed delightedly. Despite her engagement to his best friend, Picard instantly tried to think of a way to make her laugh again. Her mouth was generous, and the artificial sunlight turned her eyes to a rich, tawny gold.

"The pleasure is all mine, Captain," she said. "I have heard much about you."

"And I've heard a lot about you from Jack."

Jack was a lucky man. Beverly had beauty, brains, charm, and poise.

"I'm planning to be a Starfleet physician," she added. "Perhaps we'll all be assigned to the same ship."

"Starfleet doesn't hand out that sort of luck," Walker cut in. "Beverly, I hate to sound rude, but I really need to talk with Jean-Luc."

She smiled at Picard, happily certain of his regard. "Captain—"

"Jean-Luc, please."

"Jean-Luc, then. I . . . don't suppose Jack is off duty?"

Picard wryly returned the smile. "Feel free to tell him to meet you. In fact, tell him this is captain's orders."

Picard's communicator suddenly beeped.

"Captain!" Phigus Simenon's voice held an unusual note of excitement. "They've moved us to the head of the queue!"

Picard frowned inwardly. Luck that good didn't just happen, save at a high price.

"Jean-Luc?" Walker gestured. "This way. I may not be able to pry my ship out of spacedock, but they gave me a suite of offices fit for an admiral."

Keel hadn't exaggerated about that suite. Settling Picard in the surprisingly luxurious hospitality area, its chairs upholstered in Starfleet blue, Keel poured tea for them both, Earl Grey served in fine Admiralty china.

He's waiting for the stress to build up. One of us will have to ask the first question. And, Picard decided, *it is not going to be me.*

"Right about now," said Walker Keel, "I imagine you're getting ready to count your blessings."

"Blessings wearing the name Walker Keel?"

"Exactly. I ordered the shipwrights to give you priority." Keel grinned at him.

"I know you, Walk. You hate delays in port as much as I do. Maybe more. You wouldn't stand down in my favor unless you needed something. So, with all due respect, what is it?"

"Jean-Luc, I need your help," Keel began, forthrightly enough. "Starfleet needs it. I could have shouted for joy when I saw you come in. We need a small ship, a fast runner, captained by a discreet officer, and you're the best I know."

I'm also your friend, Jean-Luc thought. "Trading on my sense of obligation?" he asked wryly.

"I'm counting on your sense of duty," Keel retorted. "When you see this, you'll know why." Turning on his computer terminal, he said over his shoulder, "The admiral got a call from a . . . certain lady in Starfleet. In a certain branch of Starfleet that doesn't need to be named."

"Ah. No doubt, the . . . certain lady's wish is our command. Or, rather, my command. Which is . . . ?"

"We need someone to back up a Starfleet officer who's gone undercover."

"On the surface, I've had worse assignments."

Walker grimaced. "Don't fool yourself, Jean-Luc. If this operative's caught, it could compromise topflight Starfleet officers and officials from here to Vulcan. And, quite probably, start a war with the Romulans."

"The Romulans!" Picard echoed in surprise. "You can practically hear them seething from across the Neutral Zone, but—"

"Just because the Romulans happen to be quiet just now doesn't mean that they're not out for someone's blood. Ours or the Klingons. Or possibly both . . . two birds-of-prey, as it were, with one disruptor. We've got a couple colonies exposed . . . Four Corners and Melville, over here on the border near the Klingon Empire . . .

"But never mind that." Keel tapped his screen. "Look at this." An image materialized: a tall figure striding through a crowded spaceport, a traveling cloak flowing about it. "Magnify," Keel said.

The image enlarged. The figure moved with an efficient grace that teased at Picard's memory. Then it turned and the hood of the cloak fell back. Picard started. He recognized that face. He simply didn't believe he was seeing it again.

"Three days ago," he heard Keel continue, "Commander Saavik of Vulcan, apparently under instruction from our lady friend, took possession of a Barolian freighter bound for the Empire's homeworlds." Keel stopped short, eyeing Picard. "You know her?"

Picard was studying the cool Vulcan features. A certain smoldering quality around the eyes turned the routine Starfleet ID into a challenge. Glancing up at Keel, he said, "I was at her betrothal to Ambassador Spock about fifteen years back."

"Memorable, I take it?"

Picard smiled faintly. "The sort of thing you remember when you're a young officer. Particularly since, in my case, it entailed making my bows to both Spock of Vulcan *and* his father."

"Ah yes, Sarek," Keel said thoughtfully. "Apparently, it was Sarek who made this match for his son. With, one assumes, the full agreement of both parties, since they were hardly children at the time."

"Has anyone said anything to Ambassador Spock about this?"

"Unfortunately, the ambassador has dropped out of sight. He does that from time to time. He'd make a fine spy," Keel added with a wry twist of a smile.

"And Commander Saavik's captain?"

"Captain Howes? Describes her as an 'outstanding officer,' but he's not in on this. All Howes knows is that Commander Saavik took leave for, shall we say, personal Vulcan reasons. Needless to say, he wasn't about to question her."

"And Commander Saavik?" Picard asked. "What's her cover?"

"The lady I mentioned didn't share that data."

"What is it you want of me, Walk?"

"Simply put, I want you to provide backup. Help her if she needs it, get her out of there if and when it becomes necessary. And keep your head down and your nose clean."

"Understood."

It was going to be hard on Jack, parted unexpectedly from his Beverly. At least, unlike Spock, he wouldn't return from leave or whatever to be confronted by the news that his betrothed was missing—or dead.

Picard beamed back up to the *Stargazer* without delay, and strode onto the reconfigured bridge to find that the ship's refitting had been completed in record time.

"Surprise, surprise," he murmured wryly.

He was very well aware of what Walker had not said: Succeed, and he would be officially ignored. Fail, and he'd be damned lucky if he and his crew were the only ones to die.

But then, you didn't join Starfleet for a pleasure cruise.

Taking his seat, Picard broadcast, "This is the captain. All leaves are hereby canceled. All personnel are to return to ship immediately. I repeat, all personnel are to return immediately."

He hadn't long to wait. In just under a shipboard hour, his yeoman announced, "All crew present and accounted for, sir."

So be it. Here we go.

"Set in a course for the Romulan Neutral Zone," Picard ordered. Over the involuntary gasps of the bridge crew, he added firmly, "Make it so."

EIGHT

KI BARATAN, ROMULUS, DAY 3, SECOND WEEK OF TASMEEN, YEAR 2344

Praetor Dralath glanced up from where he sat at his work desk, looking about his private study there in the Central Court. The room was large and pleasantly opulent, smooth stone walls of green-veined ruatinite gleaming, a perfect background for the war insignia and honors—some of them, he thought wryly, even earned—and the ritual weapons, none of which, for security's sake, actually were charged or bore a usable edge any longer; everyone remembered how Praetor Aratenik, not too many years back, had been dispatched by an ambitious underling who'd snatched a weapon from that fool of a praetor's collection.

Ambitious, yes . . .

Dralath had no intention of following in Aratenik's path.

The room was also brightly, almost blindingly, lit. Succession to the praetor's rank often did occur with the aid of a convenient assassination, and Dralath was not about to risk letting anyone hide in shadow. In addition, cleverly placed mirrors let him scan the entire room without seeming to look up from his work.

His life's work. Such as his life had become.

I am beset by traitors, within and without!

Dralath glanced down again at the datasheet in his hand. Another riot, quickly crushed, in the Rachan Marketplace. Someone handing out flyers on Erehani Way, flyers full of treason—well, that someone had unfortunately died in the middle of capture. The guards, of course, had already been punished; they should have known that the praetor wanted a *live* traitor. Such creatures were so much more useful! Once a would-be rebel had told all he knew, he could be put to so humiliating a death that he could never make a proper martyr.

So be it. One did not groan over slain prey. But . . . Dralath glanced at the next datasheet, detailing a crop failure in the Rarathik District, and the next, which described an abortive attempt at rebellion by the district's farmers, then brought his hand down on the desk with an angry slap.

Do they think me a god, to control the rain? That technology we do not possess, curse them for idiots!

But a second glance at the sheets showed that the unrest was as much due to claims of inferior seed, blighted seed, provided by the government, as it was to the vagaries of weather.

Damnation.

"Serik!"

The clerk, a thin young *rharit* of a man, nervously poked his head into the room. "Praetor . . . ?"

"Who is in charge of seed distribution for the Rarathik District?"

"A moment, please. . . ."

As the clerk scrolled frantically through the data on his handheld console, Dralath barely fought down a sneer. Bah, Serik's lips even quivered like those of a *rharit*! Next thing, he'd be down on all fours and twitching his nose.

"Uh . . . I have it, Praetor. Senator Tharnek."

"Indeed." Dralath waved him away. "Back to whatever it was you were doing, Serik. Yes, close the door after you."

Tharnek. A pity. The senator did give him such agreeable and of course quite voluntary . . . donations. But if Tharnek was working a bit of secret, illicit business on his own, there could be no choice. Dralath quickly keyed in his private code on his console's board, then sent Tharnek a personal message, advising the senator to meet with an unfortunately fatal accident. That done, Dralath, smiling thinly, accessed another code and scanned down the list of the soon-to-be-late senator's holdings. How honorable of Tharnek, he thought, keying in a new set of commands, to assuage his shame by transferring all his wealth to his praetor.

Wealth that was very much needed just now.

A sharp beep warned of incoming data. Dralath scanned the new message, then let out his breath in an angry hiss. A brawl between two spaceport workers had quickly escalated into a near-riot. And though the local guards had swiftly restored peace with only two deaths, still, the gist of the shouts, at least according to the spy's report, had been not directed at the fighters but at *him*. And yes, yes, look at this: In the confusion, someone had actually managed to tear down one of his posters and deface another! The sheer arrogance of it left him breathless.

As did the warning behind the act. So much unrest! Or rather, so much new unrest. One could do only so much with guards, spies, and secret police. The last thing he wanted, Dralath mused, was an outward use of any more force than was needed for the putting down of a spaceport brawl: start attacking one's own people in earnest, and one had best commit suicide there and then to spare the inevitable mob the trouble.

Yes, but if one could not win the people's love by ordinary means or ordinary force, there was yet another way. Dralath pursed his lips, considering. He had already begun his plans for this: an off-planet, outside-the-Empire war. A small war. An *easy* war. A quick victory with low casualties, one to dazzle the people and turn him into a popular hero. Much more credible, then, when he blamed all the troubles, the economic shortfalls, and even the occasional crop failure, not on the poor, long-suffering

praetor, the Fearless Defender of Romulan Honor laboring endlessly on the people's behalf, but on the selfish, grasping senators.

Indeed. Give the commoners something seemingly glorious,
Dralath thought, something larger than their little lives, and their
eyes were blinded to fact.

I need them blinded for as long as possible. Another advantage
to that nice, glorious little war: a chance for aging patricians to be
rid of recalcitrant and overeager heirs. It never hurt to woo more
allies.

Even with all these mirrors. Dralath grimaced, and saw the gri-
mace reflected a dozen times over. The problem with so many
security mirrors meant that one had to see oneself, yes, and
denuded of any fancies.

Suddenly pushing back his chair, Dralath stood, daring the
mirrors to do their worst, the metallic fabric of his uniform glinting with medals and clan sigils. Of medium height and slightly
stocky build, he still held himself with the upright carriage of the
active warrior he had once been. No problems there.

But the ruthless mirrors showed him flesh beginning to sag at
jaw and chin, showed him the paunch that insisted on remaining
no matter how fiercely he exercised, showed him the first lines on
forehead and cheek—those first warnings that his time was short,
shorter than others of his kind.

"No!"

But the mirrors revealed everything. Everything except the
traitors in his blood, the tiny killers that ate away at his life and
his glory.

So far, he'd held the damnable sneak of a disease at bay for
longer than any of a series of now late, not particularly lamented
physicians could have anticipated. The sickness in the blood gave
him an aristocratic pallor, more than anyone would attribute to a
man whose origins were really anything but Noble Born.
Analgesics too subtle to register on bioscanners brought him
release from increasingly nagging pain. Cautious doses of stimu-

lants restored brief moments of nearly youthful energy. He could take the few good years he had remaining to make a name for himself that would outlast him—

"And be nothing more than a cursed footnote? I will not have that! I will not surrender!"

No? What of the emperor? Look at him! Once Shiarkiek had been a figure of true splendor, tall and lean, proud as a god. Now he had shrunken to nothing more than a tired old man who dressed like some backcountry noble and who wanted nothing but to retire to his country estates to tend his pet fish.

Ancient as the emperor was—past two hundred—he would still outlive Dralath unless someone pushed the ancient fool into the Halls of Erebus. There had been times, many of them, that Dralath had been tempted.

Not yet, Majesty. Not while you may still be of use to me. Not while I am still in control. And I am in control.

A shudder shook him. Dralath frowned at his image and straightened. Foolish to let fear enter his thoughts. Perilous to show weakness, even here. Perilous—

And perhaps unnecessary? Yes . . . his spies had brought him word of a recent arrival in Ki Baratan, some colonial female, Evaste, a medic or mystic healer or whatever she was, who had made claims of possessing gene-splicing techniques that might extend life . . . and might just possibly provide treatment for his own condition. A cure . . .

At first he'd thought her nothing but yet another fraud, someone to be casually eliminated. Pest control. But one of those spies had been Kharik, one of Avrak's House Minor underlings: unreliable, granted, since Kharik, all hot temper and bluster, lacked most of the cunning of his patron—and just might be occasionally reporting to said patron. Still, Kharik was not without his uses. And he had said that the medic was a beauty. Even allowing for the lout's usual exaggeration, Dralath had decided that meant Evaste was probably at least passable. Worth a brief interview.

Dralath glared unflinchingly at his reflection. Evaste had been more than passable, but that was less important for the moment than what she'd said . . . So sure, so logical . . .

Maybe this time, he thought. *Maybe this time there is no fraud. To live in full possession of mind and body . . .*

Bah! He sounded like a fool. This Evaste might or might not live up to her promises, but at least she was quite . . . beautiful. Dralath smiled ever so slightly.

A knock sounded at the door. "What?" he snapped.

Serik poked his nervous head inside once more. "I—I would not disturb you, Praetor . . ."

"Then don't!"

"Uh, but . . . but the emperor . . . he seeks admittance, Praetor. What should he be told?"

Dralath smiled inwardly. It said a great deal about his status, civil unrest or no, that the emperor came to *him!*

"Let him wait—no." Why make so trite and obvious a gesture of contempt? "Usher him in. Bring the usual amenities, drink, food. Then leave us alone."

Serik bowed, straightened, bowed again, left. In another moment, he entered again, holding open the door and announcing nervously, "His Imperial Majesty, Emperor Shiarkiek, Master of the Romulan Star Empire, Lord of—"

"Yes, yes," a weary, cultivated voice murmured. "I am certain our noble praetor knows all my titles. Now, do stand aside, there's a good youngster."

With no more fanfare than that, Shiarkiek entered. Once, Dralath thought, he had been an impressive figure, lean and wiry as a hunting *kharakh,* his hair that odd shade that sometimes appeared in the Romulan royal line, a light reddish-brown. But now that hair was liberally streaked with gray, and the elegant leanness had fined down almost to gauntness. His robes, some dull metallic-gray fabric trimmed with faded reds and blues that gave only the vaguest nod to military splendor, seemed almost too big for the thin body.

There it was: all the transitory nature of glory. Shiarkiek was, Dralath mused, now no more than a tired old man, so frail he would surely break at a harsh word.

I will never sink to this. No matter the pain. Never.

The praetor got to his feet, just a touch too slowly for true deference, saluted, just a touch too casually for true respect. "Emperor Shiarkiek." It was almost a purr. "How kind of you to visit my offices. Please, be seated. Serik! The food and drink I requested. Bring it. Swiftly!"

Serik, wide-eyed, sped away, closing the door behind him.

"Your courtesy," Shiarkiek commented, so smoothly that Dralath could not quite have called the retort sarcastic, "is well known. As Senator Tharnek has reason to know."

Dralath just barely mastered a start. So, now! Time for some secret . . . inquiries. Someone on his staff was clearly in Shiarkiek's employ.

Foolish to waste time in false puzzlement or denial. "The emperor is amazingly well informed."

"The emperor," Shiarkiek countered, "*is* still the emperor."

"As he is. For now. Oh, no threat was implied, Your Majesty! Of course not! I merely meant . . ." With a melodramatic sigh, Dralath said, "It is a shame, a true shame, to see the mighty brought low by the one enemy none can overturn."

"By age, you mean." Irony flashed in the ancient eyes for an instant. Then Shiarkiek was once more a weary, passive figure. "So it is, even for you, Dralath."

"I am not—"

"Yet old? No longer young, at any rate. And death may come to anyone, old or young. As Senator Tharnek has so recently learned, with that so-tragic fatal accident he must even now be experiencing."

"Senator Tharnek," Dralath said flatly, "was betraying his own people, supplying the farmers in the Rarathik District with inferior seed. He was a traitor, Your Majesty, not someone on whom pity should be wasted. He had committed a crime both against his own and against all the Romulan people—as I am sure you agree."

"A crime has certainly been perpetrated," Shiarkiek agreed blandly.

"Clever, Your Majesty. Quite. May I remind Your Majesty that cleverness is a double-edged sword? Too much cleverness can, alas, sometimes prove quite dangerous to the . . ."

"Puppet?"

"Why, Emperor Shiarkiek! What would make you say such a terrible thing?"

"Honesty?" the emperor asked with a raised brow. "Dralath, we both know exactly how matters stand. 'He who rules the military rules the Empire.' And I did not come here to argue what is and what must be. I am not yet ready for *my* fatal accident."

Serik, with perfectly terrible timing, chose that very moment to knock on the door. "Your Majesty? Praetor? I—I have the refreshments you requested."

At Dralath's impatient wave, Serik brought in the tray, placed it on the praetor's desk, and scuttled out again. Dralath stared after him for a thoughtful moment. *Had* that been terrible timing? Or deliberate? Was little Serik in the emperor's pay? Sometimes meek little *rhariks* did go mad. In which case one snapped their necks with one's heel.

Shiarkiek glanced wryly at Dralath, as though understanding exactly what the praetor had been thinking. "I am *not* to meet with a fatal accident just yet, am I?"

"The Powers prevent! It would be . . . awkward."

"For both of us, yes."

But while Shiarkiek took the glass Dralath filled, he did not drink, only, after a moment, returned it to the tray. "Dralath, this is not a social call. I . . . would not seek to criticize you or the way in which you handle the tedious job of government. But . . ."

Suddenly the spark of life animating the emperor seemed to vanish. Sagging, he murmured, "Where is glory these days, Dralath? Where is honor? Once to be a ruler was to serve the people, the Empire, once to be a Romulan was a matter of pride, of knowing that one's word was good, one's way was pure, one's heart and soul were sharp and clean as the edge of a blade. Now . . ."

"Now," Dralath said, letting just a touch of impatience show in his voice, "we are as the times have made us. No more, no less, than we need be."

"A sad thought. Hear me out, Dralath, I pray you. Once, there would not have been a need for these 'accidents.' Once, the accused would have been honorably charged, honorably offered the choice of death by ritual or by combat. Once, there would have been none of this sly secrecy. There would have been no need." Shiarkiek paused, blinking weary eyes. "Is that it? *Was* there such a need? Why has there been such a sudden gathering of funds? Yes, yes, even an outdated old man such as your emperor is aware of it. A war, Dralath? Is that what you wish? A dishonorable war? A war for your own glory? Can you, even you, have sunk to mere *profit?*"

"Enough," Dralath snapped. "This conversation is pointless." A heartbeat. "Your Majesty."

"Is it? Dralath, think! Without our honor, what are we? Not Romulans, not beings of pride and grace—without our honor, we are *nothing!*"

"I hear and heed," Dralath recited by rote. "Now, if you will kindly—"

"It will happen to you, Dralath. Each day, the flesh grows a little less firm, the will a little less sure. Someday some younger soul will sit in that chair and tell you that you, too, are . . . obsolete."

Damn him, can he know of my disease? How can he know?

"I have," the praetor said, biting off the words, "work to do. Even if you, O Emperor of the Ancient Days, do not. Go away, old man. Go home and tend your fish!"

But Emperor Shiarkiek was already moving slowly away. The door shut silently behind him, and Dralath was left alone.

Alone with the ruthless, merciless mirrors. And the truth.

"The healer," he murmured. "Evaste. Evaste, and her miraculous medicines . . . they had best be as miraculous as she claims." If they were: excellent. If not . . . Dralath shrugged. People did tend to . . . disappear.

Raising his voice, he snapped, "Serik!"

The door opened just enough to let Serik poke a nervous head into the room. "Praetor?"

"The provincial healer, Evaste by name. You do know of her? Excellent. She is to be granted an audience. At the Hall of State. Yes, I said at the Hall of State!" A minor noble, she should know how to behave. If not . . . others' embarrassment was always amusing, too. "Oh, and Serik . . ."

"Praetor?"

"It is not a request."

As the emperor left the room, his bent-backed shuffle took him slowly down a less-used corridor, unnoted by guards or underlings.

Servants, he thought, *and ministers, spies, courtiers—bah, that much I don't miss, all the lives surrounding me, never letting me be.*

Shiarkiek headed on down the empty corridor till he had reached that one brief stretch of hall that was unmarred by monitors or electronic spies. And slowly his back straightened, slowly the shuffle became a determined walk. *Still old, yes,* he thought dryly, *but not quite obsolete, not yet. Oh, and Dralath, my fish, my pretty little pet fish, are garahk. They have fangs.*

A man fell in beside him at his signal, a figure as tall as Shiarkiek, almost as lean, the hood of his cloak pulled back just enough to reveal keen dark eyes in a clean-featured, handsome face that gave away almost nothing of its emotions. *No longer precisely young, our Narviat,* the emperor thought, *but quite the elegant figure. I would expect no less from a kinsman. However distant.* That brought another face briefly to mind: Commander

Charvanek, of the royal line as well, though just as far removed. *Fortunate for you both. Were either of you closer in the direct line of succession, were either of you named my heir, I fear Dralath would be racking his brains to come up with yet more "fatal accidents."*

"Well?" Shiarkiek asked. "Did you see and hear?"

"Everything. You play a dangerous game, my emperor."

Shiarkiek raised a wry brow. "He will not kill me. At least not before I've named an heir. That One—" Even in these secure surroundings, it was wiser not to name names. "That One doesn't want the throne himself, not when it's so much handier and safer for him to use an emperor as . . . figurehead. He hardly wants the civil war and chaos that would follow my sudden demise."

Narviat's fingers flew in a ritual gesture. " 'May you live a hundred years yet.' "

Shiarkiek shot him a cynical glance. "Wait till you are my age, then see if you make that same wish. But as I say, That One hardly wishes civil war."

"Yet he does want a war. For," Narviat added coolly, "his own glory."

"We are in agreement, then. He must be stopped. But . . . how?"

Narviat frowned slightly. "How, indeed?"

And for an instant that handsome, well-schooled face did show a trace of the thoughts behind it. For an instant, Shiarkiek read, quite clearly, *And how am I to take the praetor's place?*

NINE

There were yet more guards within the maze of the Government Center, stalking about the red or gray buildings with disruptor rifles at the ready.

Of course, Spock thought. *With the senators and the praetor all about to assemble in one site, it must be the proverbial nightmare for Romulan Security.*

The Hall of State, predictably, was also built like a fortress. Of smoothly polished red stone, it had few windows save for a row of narrow slits near the domed roof. There were no indentations in the walls at all, nothing to provide handholds for any would-be assassin.

Paranoia? Or brutal honesty?

"Have I been here before?" Spock murmured to Charvanek, following her up the Hall's wide, shallow stairs. "Am I expected to display a provincial's awe?"

Charvanek, coldly elegant in a stark black uniform, her short crimson cape fastened by a golden badge in the shape of the imperial eagle, flashed him the hint of a sardonic smile. "You have never been here before. But you need not be awed, my cousin. After all, were you not just recently accorded audience with His Imperial Majesty, who presented you with that bauble?"

The tunic and breeches she had decreed proper for one of his scholarly rank were of a slate gray so dark as to be nearly black, half-hidden under a heavy, equally somber gray tabard. About his neck was Charvanek's "bauble," what Charvanek had assured him was a perfect copy of the golden medallion awarded to eminent civilian researchers.

She caught him glancing at the Hall's immense metal doors, and explained, "Those were cast from the hulls of the ships that brought us here. Each panel is engraved with a different scene from our journey. A pity," Charvanek added with sharp irony, "that you have no time to appreciate them as they deserve."

"Hold!"

Two young Romulans in dull silver uniforms and bright scarlet capes, heads shielded by crested helms, barred their way with disruptor rifles. Their challenge was merely a ritual, surely, since they must have recognized Charvanek at once—but Spock saw the indifferent coldness in their eyes. They would think nothing of firing at anyone's wrong move. In another time and place lacking the military discipline, Spock thought, these two boys would be casual killers.

What is Romulus breeding?

"Uhlans of the Romulan Guard," Charvanek said, nodding with a commander's crispness at the guards as she and Spock passed, granting the boy on the left the barest hint of a chill smile.

"Young Neral," she explained to Spock, "is right out of the Academy. Yet he has already made friends with every faction of the court—a most desirable talent."

The boy stiffened to attention. At his crisp order, the doors swung wide. Charvanek strode forward down a wide hallway without another word, and Spock followed. The faintest of whirrs and a quick flash told him that they had just been scanned, definitely in a search for concealed weapons, for retinal identification, and probably down to their genetic level as well to be sure they weren't impostors. Security in the Romulan Star Empire, Spock thought, was thorough.

"Your records are already in the databanks," Charvanek said casually before he could ask.

Well, perhaps not *that* thorough.

Their footsteps rang against the polished red and gray stone. More guards passed them on patrol, rifles in hand, glances wary; each guard in turn granted Charvanek a somewhat grudging salute.

Back in favor, then, but not entirely. Or, more correctly, not totally in favor with Praetor Dralath.

A whiff of incense caught his attention. Small, intricately worked bronze firepots that could well have been of Vulcan design were set in niches along the smooth red walls. But no Vulcan firepot ever had been bolted to the floor, or had a protective grille welded over it.

"It would seem that the senators do not wish to risk a literal firefight."

Charvanek raised a wry brow. "It did happen. Once."

Rather incongruously, low tables placed at regular intervals held shallow bronze bowls of flowers with huge, fragile petals, red and purple set among leaves the color of fresh-shed blood.

"The emperor," Charvanek commented without expression, "is very fond of flowers. He is also, by the way, quite an esteemed marine biologist. Better for him," she added, so softly that even Spock's Vulcan ears almost missed her words, "had he been allowed to be that. Only that."

At least the flowers softened the hall's austerity. How cool such stonework would have been during a Vulcan summer, Spock thought, like a deep well in the shade. Here, it was merely . . . chilly.

Two more of the cold-eyed young uhlans met them at the end

of the hallway, also with their disruptor rifles at ready. The settings, Spock observed, were on Kill.

"No dramatics," Charvanek snapped at them. "You know me. And I vouch for my cousin, Academician Symakhos of Bardat. Now—*stand aside!*"

It was a commander's stern voice—and it was instantly obeyed.

"Come, cousin," Charvanek said. "Here is the Council Chamber. We're early," she added, glancing about.

A few Romulan men and women in dress uniforms glinting with metallic thread and harness had already gathered. They stood stiffly near the council table, not quite at attention, all but radiating their wary discomfort. The curt snatches of conversation Spock caught sounded less like true gossip than military dispatches:

". . . another lady for our praetor."

"She is a medic."

"A faith healer."

"A fraud."

"He wishes her as 'guest-friend.' That is enough."

They act like so many predators forced into the same lair, Spock thought, then scolded himself for that emotional metaphor. Whatever latent mental talents these people might possess, their ancestors had left Vulcan long before the arts of the mind had been perfected: their unschooled emotions were perilous—even for themselves. No wonder they hated this type of proximity.

Study your surroundings. Concentrate.

The council table was a large stone rectangle of so dark a green that it was nearly black, polished to a fine gloss that would show no stains. On it sat small, individual terminals—bolted to the table.

Nothing that can be moved—or is that, perhaps, thrown? Nothing that can be used as a weapon.

Then Spock froze as a new group of Romulan senators entered, boot heels clicking against the smooth floor. No Pardek, of course; Pardek was still in prison. But there, unmistakable as he had been at the terminal, was Avrak. An ambitious man, Avrak: no doubt he regarded Pardek's imprisonment as his opportunity, assuming he survived it.

If Avrak recognizes me . . . Illogical. He has not seen me since the Obsidian affair.

With Avrak were two others Spock remembered, the cousins Kharik and—Ruanek! Ruanek, with whom Spock had been corresponding secretly since the events on Obsidian.

Avrak might not recognize me. Ruanek, though . . . impetuous as he is, can I trust him not to accidentally betray me?

Hiding in plain sight never seemed so utterly illogical.

And yet . . . Charvanek, it would seem, had been quite right: Romulans, like humans, saw only what they expected to see, and neither Avrak nor the cousins paid Spock the slightest notice. After a few moments, he dared study them.

When he had last seen Ruanek and Kharik, they had been barely more than boys, part of the Vulcan fanatic Sered's strike force on Obsidian. Now, Kharik wore a centurion's insignia, but still smoldered with the same illogical anger as before; not surprising that he had not risen above that rank. Spock was gratified to see, however, that Ruanek appeared less . . . unfinished than he had on Obsidian.

Only a subcommander, though? I should have thought a man with your intelligence would have risen further—or is that the problem? Your intelligence, and your impetuous honesty?

And . . . could the fact that the now-grown Ruanek's features looked more Vulcan than Romulan have helped restrict his career? Humans had once based prejudices on nothing more than racial appearance. Were Romulans so illogically sensitive about the past?

Ruanek and Kharik had always been rivals. Judging from their surreptitious glares at each other, the feud had grown worse over the years. Amazing, given Romulan tempers, that they were both still alive.

Perhaps it amuses Avrak to keep them that way.

"Well, cousin?" Charvanek asked. "Nothing like this on Bardat!"

"Indeed not," Spock agreed with utter honesty.

Classic Romulan architecture, it would seem, included high, arched ceilings. Wind rushed in from those narrow windows up near the roof: Vulcan design again, intended to catch the faintest cooling breeze off the desert. Not logical in this cooler climate, particularly not now, when chilly drafts were swooping down, carrying the mineral-sharp tang of the Apnex Sea. A shiver ran through Spock before he could suppress it, and he warned himself, *A Romulan would not feel this as cold.*

Breaking the vast sweep of the stone walls were blue, red, and blood-green mosaic scenes of military glories. There were also more than a few war trophies—welded into the stone so that no one could snatch one free. An array of Klingon arms and banners crowded one entire wall. Spock turned from them and found himself staring with a shock almost of horror at a jagged segment of a Federation starship's hull, set in the place of honor, directly behind the high-backed chairs of emperor and praetor, the emperor's one step higher. Traces of the ship's identification number still showed, and Spock instantly memorized it. He would confirm that number with Starfleet when he returned.

An immense brazier wrought in the form of a giant Romulan eagle stood at the far end of the Council Chamber, welded to the floor and covered with protective mesh. As each new senator entered, he or she approached the brazier, scooped up incense in a gold cup from the bowls on the nearby offering table, and cast it into the embers, adding to the growing miasma of too-sweet incense.

"Come," Charvanek said suddenly. "Time for the offerings."

A tall, dark-haired, immensely strong-looking man in the gray and red uniform of a commanding general was also striding toward the offerings. Charvanek raised her chin but did not alter course in the slightest. She reached her destination an instant after the man and met his eyes unflinchingly. He set down the cup, stood back, and bowed . . . grudgingly.

"Noble Born," he managed to say.

She dipped her head ever so slightly, then turned away. Scooping up her offering, Charvanek bowed deeply, then cast the spices into the brazier and watched as they sparkled into bright flame. Only when the last grain was consumed did she turn back to the man whose turn she had preempted. "General."

The general flushed angry green, rendering his face even more intimidating. He clicked his heels, bowed sharply from the waist, and stalked off, leaving the shrine unhonored.

"Volskiar," Charvanek spat the name as she guided Spock back to the council table. "A brute, a fool, and an agent of the praetor, with an upstart, downworld title. He," she added fiercely, "argued I should be executed when I returned from Federation space."

Spock raised an eyebrow. "To be blunt, he cannot have been the only one."

"Indeed not. But he was the only one who did not care that I overheard him."

"My dear cousin!" a sudden male voice exclaimed.

Charvanek turned with a warrior's speed. But in the next second, her tenseness melted, and her smile was, Spock thought, almost genuine. "Ah, Narviat."

The man who strode toward her was as tall and lean as Spock, his strong, narrow face handsome in a deliberate, polished way. His sleek black hair, its length indicating membership in the Imperial family, was pulled back in an elegant knot. He wore the dress uniform of an admiral of the fleet, black boots, fitted black trousers, and a severely tailored tunic of metallic silver cloth crossed with a crimson sash and glittering with awards—but he was too politically elegant to be convincing. Spock suspected that it had been years since he had seen active duty.

"Narviat," Charvanek repeated, holding out a hand. Spock raised an eyebrow slightly as the man brushed her fingertips lingeringly with his own. Were these two pledged? Acknowledged lovers, perhaps?

No, logically *not* acknowledged. They were both, after all, related to the emperor, and Dralath would surely view any union between them as a threat to his power.

Narviat's glance turned toward Spock, a searching personal and political appraisal performed at light-speed.

"My cousin," Charvanek said, "may I present Symakhos, First Academician of Bardat, and a family connection on my mother's grandmother's side? Symakhos, Admiral Narviat."

"An honor, Admiral," Spock said. Picking his way carefully, he added, "The admiral's service record compels admiration even on the frontier."

"Long retired now," Narviat confessed. "I count myself fortunate to have served at all before retiring into public life. You, too, have steered a hard course," he added with only the briefest of hesitations. "A mere veteran can only imagine the discipline it takes to turn from the path of arms to research. The Empire needs its scientists."

Decidedly, a political type.

"Your acknowledgment honors me," Spock began.

A blare of noise interrupted him: a harsh fanfare from a hidden speaker, making everyone in the chamber wince. Narviat's face hardened ever so slightly. "Our praetor approaches. To business."

All around Spock, the others straightened to stern attention. Not a trace of their thoughts could be read from the suddenly stony faces, but Spock nearly swayed under the sudden blaze of raw emotion: Hate? Envy? Ambition?

It is their emotion. Not your own. There is no emotion. There is calm. Logic. Only logic. Only calm.

"And there is our noble praetor," Charvanek murmured for Spock's ear alone.

Starfleet and civilian intelligence had made Praetor Dralath's disillusioned features almost as well known to Spock as his own. But it was not the praetor who captured his attention, or the faces, almost equally familiar to Federation Intelligence, of officers and ministers of state. Who was that tall, lean figure sagging at Dralath's side? Spock heard Charvanek's sharp hiss of indrawn breath and knew: This could only be Emperor Shiarkiek.

And the man was deathly ill.

Or . . . was that, perhaps, heavily drugged? As everyone saluted him, a full military salute with an added lowering of their heads, Shiarkiek glanced at them all, his eyes not really tracking. He made an abortive gesture that might have been an answering wave, sank with an audible thump into his seat, and vanished into a world of his own. Dralath stood a moment longer, eyeing the senators with casual arrogance, then sat. With a loud scraping of chairs, so did everyone else.

"Terminals on!" Dralath ordered, and each screen blazed into life. "Senators," he began, allowing them only an instant, "do you see these reports before you?" He gave them a few moments for frantic scanning, then added, "Have you read these examples of mismanagement on so many levels? A dockyard riot in Argat. A fuel spill near Tartak. Seed shortages. Crop failures. Even the as yet unsolved sabotage of Senator Branak's groundcar!" His voice snapped out, sharp as a whip's crack "Are you not *ashamed,* each of you, to confess such ineptitude?"

A few angry murmurs started up at that, a few angry glances flicked at Dralath, then away.

"Or can it be," Dralath shouted, "can it truly be that some of you are feeling more than mere shame? Come, look up at me, all of you! How many of you can meet my gaze without flinching? You, Senator Erket? You, Admiral Narviat?"

A mistake, that. Narviat could, Spock saw, and did return Dralath's stare, his handsome face absolutely cold.

Dralath glanced away, out over all the others. "No, Senators, not all of you *can* meet my gaze. And we all know why! Not all have been true to the Romulan people!"

More murmurings, and some uneasy glances, senator at senator: Who was going out of favor?

"I will be blunt, Senators!" Dralath shouted. "Some among you are nothing less than *true enemies of the state!* Some of you are *out-and-out traitors!*"

"No!"

"That cannot be!"

"My loyalty is unquestioned!"

Romulans leaped to their feet, their chairs crashing over backward in the haste to outshout everyone else. Denials and accusations echoed off the high dome of the roof. Hands flew to Honor Blades.

But in all the chaos, Spock, forcing inner calm on himself with every bit of his will, looked only at Dralath. And Dralath . . . was leaning back in his chair, watching the panic like one enjoying a mild entertainment, on his lips the faintest of thin, cold smiles.

He knows exactly what he does.

Sure enough, at the precise moment when blood would have been shed, Dralath leaned forward, both hands on the table, and shouted, *"Silence!"*

It was a voice trained to override riots. Senators froze, blades in hand. Into the sudden startled quiet, Dralath continued, scorn in his voice, "Look at you! What, have you all turned to squabbling *children?* Or have you, perhaps, decided to show me your imitation of the Federation? Or is that of the Klingons?"

A few uneasy laughs swept about the table.

"Sit down, Senators. Sheathe your blades and *sit down!*"

Warily, the Romulans found their seats again, like so many predators who would spring up again at one misplaced—or carefully placed—word.

"Look at the documents," Dralath continued. "Read them carefully. See the report from Tralath Province. And Harkan County. Grain shortages, faulty starship engineering—I need not tell you that there have been shortages, delays in shipments, accidents, Senators, more accidents than are credible. Warning signs,

Senators. Dangerous signs. Now, some among you have been blaming me."

Shouts of denial rang out, from the faithful—or the most politically wary. Dralath, smiling that cold little smile, held out his hands for silence.

"Your denials do not make the danger any less. Senators, think. Only fools would try explaining away all these problems as mere mischance, unrelated mishaps. No! There can be only one explanation, one hard, cruel fact tying together all these *shortages*"—his finger stabbed at the screen—"all these *failures*"—stab—"all these so falsely named *accidents!*"

Dralath froze dramatically over the terminal, hands on either side of it, glaring around the room. "There can be only one explanation, Senators, and I shall be blunt about it: Some among you are in the pay of enemies of our Empire!"

Over the cries of outrage and fury, Dralath shouted, "Yes! I shout with you! I am your praetor, and I am angrier than you can ever be. There is treason among us! *And it must be torn from Romulus' heart!*"

One unfortunate senator, a burly young man, made the mistake of continuing his outcry a second after everyone else had fallen silent: ". . . treason torn from the very top!"

He froze, staring at Dralath.

"Senator Erket," the praetor said very softly. "I wondered. Are you not kinsman to the so recently deceased Senator Tharnek?"

"I am," grudgingly. "But I am loyal—"

"Are you? Are you indeed?" Dralath got slowly to his feet. "What about the reports from your own district, Senator?"

"Everything was filed properly! And no one can blame me for—"

"For what, Erket?"

"I was assured that the grain was good! I—"

"Checked it yourself? Imported grain from offworld that so coincidentally was tainted. Was that all it was, Erket? Tainted grain from a Romulan colony? There were irregularities in the ship manifests, were there not?"

He is manipulating you, Spock thought, *surely as a* le'matya *stalks its prey. And he, too, enjoys the hunt. Can't you see that?*

He risked a glance at Charvanek: cold eyes, rigid posture, a survivor not about to draw attention to herself. Narviat: the same.

"They were minor points!" Erket protested.

"Were they? Could the grain have met with deliberate tampering? From enemies, perhaps? Maybe even *Klingons?"*

Erket shot to his feet, whipping out his Honor Blade in a quick blaze of metal, so shocked and outraged he could only choke out, "You dare!"

Dralath's guards came to instant alert, but the praetor waved them back with a casual hand.

"What's this?" Dralath purred to Erket. "Would you challenge me?"

The chamber had fallen utterly still. Erket, eyes wild, began, "I never meant—"

"Are you afraid, Erket? A coward, perhaps?"

With an anguished roar, Erket charged. Dralath, teeth bared in a savage smile, waited, poised, his own blade glinting in his steady hand—then twisted aside. Before Erket could recover, Dralath had caught him from behind, pinning the younger man against him. And the edge of Dralath's blade was against Erket's throat.

"Drop the knife, Erket. Now."

Gasping, wild-eyed, the younger man obeyed.

For an agonizing moment, nothing happened. There was no sound save the panting of the two men.

And then, shockingly, Dralath laughed. "Did you think me in earnest, Erket? Did you really think that I would kill you over mere accusations?"

Just as Erket, wild with hope, began to laugh with him, Dralath added, "I would."

With one quick, efficient movement, he cut Erket's throat.

TEN

KI BARATAN, ROMULUS, DAY 5, SECOND WEEK OF TASMEEN, 2344

Spock leaped to his feet with everyone else in the room, staring in sheer disbelief.

With one quick, efficient movement, Dralath had cut Erket's throat. In the next moment, the praetor sprang fastidiously back from the thrashing victim so that none of the green blood stained him. As Erket, struggling uselessly for air, slid to the floor and finally moved no more, Dralath stood motionless over his prey, face utterly calm.

"Thus to all traitors," he said.

As though he'd given a signal, the room erupted into noise, claims of loyalty, shouts of patriotism.

I have just seen murder. The thoughts came slowly to Spock's stunned mind. *I have just watched a man be killed, and I—I did nothing.*

He was going to die, Spock realized with the same stunned detachment, he was going to attack Dralath and be torn apart by the Romulans—

No! I will not yield to emotion. I will . . . use it.

"I—I am ill," Spock murmured to Charvanek in the broken voice of a scholar who has never seen violence. "I must . . . quickly . . ."

Her sharp glance told him she understood this must be a ploy. A swift gesture said, *Go! That way.*

As Spock staggered across the room, hand over mouth in imitation of a spacesick yeoman he had once seen, not a few harsh laughs followed him.

I care not what they think of the academician too weak to watch their praetor kill.

But his mind was working logically again. And logic insisted that he must, as the humans said, risk all on a fall of the dice.

This will be my only chance to approach Ruanek.

On Obsidian, the younger Ruanek had become entranced, courtesy of the then-hostage Dr. Leonard McCoy, by the subject of Terran horses, "those swift, exotic war-beasts." The Romulan's fascination had continued over the years; Spock had once, bemused by this oddity, even managed to send Ruanek an image of a racing horse, and received almost wistful thanks.

Now, Spock deliberately stumbled against him and, before Ruanek could react with a Romulan warrior's automatic anger, whispered in his ear, in Federation Standard, *"Horses."*

Ruanek's quick glance was nothing short of wild. His thoughts were clear enough: No one but Spock could possibly know of his fascination with those exotic Terran beasts! But with amazing self-control, he turned his startled yelp into a convincing snarl. "What do you think—"

"No insult," Spock gasped out, like a man at the edge of collapse. "Academician Symakhos . . . Bardat . . . please, need help . . . have to find the—the facilities. Can you . . ."

Kharik, predictably, snickered, muttering something about "baby-sitting" and "fitting role." Avrak merely gave an impatient, over-the-shoulder wave of dismissal: Yes, go on, what happens here is too important.

Once they were safely out of the Council Chamber and down one of the hallways, momentarily out of sight of the guards, Ruanek whispered, "I don't suppose you really do need—"

"Merely a moment to sit and catch my breath," Spock said, which was true enough. "An academician rarely sees such sights." He sank to a bench as though badly shaken—which also was not too far from the truth—and Ruanek perched nervously beside him, waiting as tensely as a hunter not sure if the prey will turn on him.

"Guards will certainly be patrolling," Spock murmured. "I am a very boring pedant, and you will be doing your best to get away from me."

"Understood."

As the first of the expected guards passed them, frowning warily, Spock said in a dry, scholarly voice, "I am recovering. You do understand—the shock? But let us not waste this moment. I am doing some research on the pastimes of the military." He whipped out the small recording tablet that Charvanek had insisted was part of an academician's outfit. "I would consider it an honor, Subcommander, if you would spare me a few seconds more."

The guards glanced at each other, shrugged, and moved on.

"It's been a long time," Ruanek burst out. "Damn, no, that sounds stupid. Of course it's been a long time! It's just that—Light and Darkness, I never expected to see you *here!*"

"And so," Spock said calmly, pretending to write, "you are often a part of these gatherings." Very softly, he added, "The need was great, or I would not have come. My life is in your keeping, Ruanek. Can I, on your honor, trust you?"

"Of course!" That was said from the heart. "First, though," Ruanek continued, "first we must have the rules set straight in front of us. I have not forgotten Obsidian, or what happened there. I have not forgotten that you saved my life and honor. But . . ." He shook his head. "All bets are canceled here and now unless you can swear to me on *your* honor, yes, and that of your Federation, that you mean no harm to the emperor."

Spock raised a brow, startled at Ruanek's vehemence. "To the emperor? Not to . . . others?"

A shudder shook the Romulan. "I am not a traitor," he murmured. "But I hold faith first to my emperor and my people above all else. Let that be understood."

"It is, and no dishonor to you or them. And I do swear as well that I mean no harm to Emperor Shiarkiek. I pledge this as well," Spock added softly, "as least as much as it is logical for one to speak for many: The Federation has no quarrel with your emperor or, indeed, with the common people."

Ruanek stared straight into Spock's eyes, as though hunting for even the slightest hint of falsehood. "I have heard that Vulcans never lie," he said at last. "And . . . I cannot believe treachery would ever come from you. Not after the honor I saw displayed on Obsidian."

The next patrol was passing them.

"Yes," Ruanek said in the voice of someone utterly bored, "that is, honestly, truly, how we entertain ourselves at court. Do you *finally* have that all down, Academician? Good. Now I must return to my patron!"

"A moment, more, please. This detail, here . . ."

The guards moved on, one of them with an audible snicker, and Ruanek's face hardened. "There is no dishonor in what we say," Spock murmured. "Ruanek, *was* that slain senator a traitor?"

Ruanek snorted. "Corrupt, maybe. But he was far too stupid for anything more. As Dralath knew. That was a lesson to the rest of us: Behave or die." He muttered something sharp and ugly under his voice. "There is glory in war, but not in slaughter."

"Then the praetor is, indeed, planning war?"

"War," bitterly. "War for profit. For . . . prestige. *His* prestige. And no, I do not know his planned target. Yet." Ruanek paused, pursing his lips, plainly fighting a fierce inner battle. "I will tell you this," he said in a rush, "and will deny having said it: Many of us, those raised on tales of honor, of how it was and still should be—many of us do *not* want lives, any lives, to be thrown away just for the praetor's glory."

His voice was rising perilously. At Spock's warning raise of an eyebrow, the Romulan hastily fell silent. As the next patrol passed them, Spock asked, as though making a casual note, "And how is that spelled? *T-r-a-y-t-i-k?*"

"*T-r-a-y-a-t-i-k,*" Ruanek corrected absently, "a dice-throwing game." His voice sank to a murmur. "We are, some of us, trying our best to change our world. But it is slow work, so slow that I—I sometimes despair of our ever succeeding. And yet—but you would not understand something so illogical as 'hope.'"

I understand, Spock thought, *that you are your own best argument for the need for reform. That the Empire should blindly waste so promising a one as you is the height of illogic.* But he could not tell Ruanek that.

"Hope," he murmured, "may not be truly logical, but it is never useless." In the academician's precise voice he added, "Thank you, Subcommander. You have been very helpful. I will, with your patron's permission, gladly send you a copy of my finished paper."

Ruanek got brusquely to his feet. "Papers are for scholars. You may stay here, Academician. I must return to my patron."

They reentered the Council Chamber together. The body, Spock saw with the faintest shiver of distaste, had already been removed, and every trace of blood had been wiped from the smooth table and floor. Dralath was back in his high-backed chair, calm and unrumpled, revealing not the slightest sign that he'd just killed someone. And the uproar in the chamber had died down to murmurs.

Spock heard Kharik snicker as Ruanek took his place, and saw Ruanek's angry flush. But the subcommander clearly was too used to his cousin's barbs to react. A ripple of harsh amusement at the scholar's weakness followed Spock back to Charvanek's side; he ignored it utterly.

"Have I missed anything?" he asked Charvanek in a totally innocent tone.

She ignored him, staring at Dralath, who was clearly in the middle of a spate of rhetoric, saying, ". . . regrettable. But there shall be worse, Senators. Prepare yourselves, prepare your people. There shall be no more sly attacks on Romulan men, women, and children. There shall be no more poisoned grain or faulty equipment, all those incidents meant to wear us down, make us quarrel among ourselves—when we now know the truth! The enemy is not here, not on Romulus—the enemy is out there! And if we must fight to guard our own, then fight we shall!"

And, "Fight!" the Romulans echoed, pounding the table with their fights. "Fight!"

"If there must be war," Dralath trumpeted over the din, "then *let there be war!*"

"Let there be war!"

But then the fierce shouts turned to horrified gasps. Emperor Shiarkiek, ignored all this while, slowly and without drama, toppled forward to lie sprawled across the table. Spock, on his feet with the others, caught a glimpse of Dralath's face, torn between triumph and fury that Shiarkiek should spoil his moment.

Then Dralath shouted, *"Evaste!* Here! Hurry!"

Spock saw a straight, slim, figure rush forward, dark hair caught in a multitude of beaded braids, a flash of flowing robes, russet, bronze, and deep red, startlingly vivid among the somberly dressed Romulans. She bent over the stricken emperor, murmuring to him, then treated him with what Spock presumed was a medkit. The woman straightened, signaling to the guards to carefully help the emperor to his feet. She followed them out, braids swirling about her face. Whoever this Evaste was, Spock thought, she must either be a fool or a skilled player of a very deadly game.

As if sensing his scrutiny, the woman glanced sharply at the crowd, her dark eyes searching the sea of faces. Spock saw a fierce, sharply planed face framed by dark, barbaric braids. A face as familiar to him as his own.

Saavik!

Dralath, his moment utterly gone, was doing his best to recover, proclaiming, "Tomorrow, the Lady Evaste of House Minor Anat-Vorian will be presenting a medical paper at the Ministry of Science, one that I assure you will prove of immense interest to us all. You will all wish to attend."

It was not a request.

Yes, Spock repeated silently. *Ah, yes. I will, indeed. But only to learn how my betrothed has come to be here in this nest of vipers.*

ELEVEN

KI BARATAN, ROMULUS, DAY 6, SECOND WEEK OF TASMEEN, 2344

Kharik had begun grumbling complaints almost from the moment of Praetor Dralath's proclamation yesterday. "Ministry of Science . . . boring, incomprehensible yammer . . . no place for a soldier." He had not stopped for most of that day and well into the night—save for those moments when he'd gotten in yet another gibe at Ruanek for "wiping the scholar's chin—or anything else."

Thank whatever Powers there be, Ruanek thought, with a final tug of his tunic into rigid order before his less-than-perfect mirror on this new day, *that my rank entitles me to private quarters.* Cramped the room might be, barely more than the space allotted a soldier's bunk and locker in the barracks, and hardly truly private, but it was, at least, his! *Were I still sharing with Kharik and the others, I would have murdered him long ago.*

A cynical corner of his mind whispered that then he'd merely be following in Dralath's footsteps.

I am not, Ruanek told himself dourly, *Dralath.*

He glanced about the room once more. Allowed so little space, Ruanek had been forced into scrupulous neatness even beyond a soldier's necessity. That wasn't such a bad thing, since it also meant that whichever of Avrak's agents came nosing about in here had less chance of hiding any more of those tiny surveillance eyes. Ruanek gave his reflection a wry grin. He had a few gambits planned just in case Avrak felt like testing the quickness of his wits again.

He'd gotten pretty efficient at hiding things, as well. So far, no one had found his contraband tapes: science data, linguistics— forbidden subjects, downright perilous for a true Romulan warrior, who must never be distracted from his role by anything as unimportant as learning anything more than the art of war.

Ruanek let out his breath in a silent sigh. Unlike Kharik, he did not expect to be bored by today's presentation. And there was something wonderfully ironic about being *ordered* to attend a science lecture.

On their way to the Ministry of Science as part of Avrak's entourage, Kharik, predictably, began his angry mutterings all over again, but softly, so that their patron wouldn't be disturbed. "What are we doing going to the Ministry of Science?"

Ruanek glanced sharply sideways. "Obeying orders. And who knows? You might actually learn something."

"Such as what? Better ways to guard? To kill? I'm not a scholar's nursemaid, cousin."

Ruanek raised an eyebrow at Kharik and quite deliberately glanced down at his insignia. *Remember your rank, Kharik. Your lower rank.* "The academician turned out to be quite . . . interesting," Ruanek countered, deliberately vague. "Quite interesting, indeed."

That, he thought, had to be the most ridiculous of understatements. He had very nearly shouted out "Spock!" back there in the Council Chamber, confronted with the last being in all the universe he'd expected to see. There could have been no secret Federation invasion. Ruanek knew he was hardly in the front line of information, but even the best of Romulan Security could never have kept *that* quiet! Spock really was only one Vulcan, alone on this world. The raw courage of it, the sheer, Romulan-war-tale *arrogance* of walking alone into a nest of enemies . . .

What does he hope to achieve? Hope, as he'd said to Spock, wasn't logical, and yet . . .

But there'd been too many disappointments down through the years. *I wonder,* Ruanek thought bitterly. Can *Vulcans go insane?*

Sered, his mind prompted, unbidden.

Yes, he answered his own question, *unfortunately, they can.*

Dressed again as Academician Symakhos, Spock followed Charvanek into the main seminar room of the Ministry of Science, looking down the sloping tiers of seats to the podium far below. His mind touched on memories of similar rooms on Vulcan and Earth. All lecture halls on Vulcanoid or humanoid worlds did seem to follow the same basic lines of an amphitheater—and all seemed to have the same hard, unpadded seats, presumably to prevent attendees from dozing off.

Yes, consider such matters as these. Do not think of Saavik—

Definitely not. His human side had most certainly been overwhelmed at the sight of her. It would not be disagreeable to discuss with her that most human and bewildering concept of "love" when they were both safely away from Romulus—safely alone—but he was, first and foremost, of Vulcan.

Are you?

Yes!

Spock resolutely turned his attention back to the consideration of the Ministry: a featureless, utterly functional gray building. When compared to the garish splendor of that elaborate Hall of State, this blandness said a great deal about the way Romulans viewed science.

As an afterthought. Or rather, as a boring but necessary source for weapons.

All around Spock and Charvanek as they took their assigned

seats, the room was filling with gray-robed scientists and a growing crowd of Romulan nobles, incongruous in their glinting metallic uniforms—the senators, Spock thought, from yesterday's council, here at Dralath's "request."

Guards were, of course, also filing into the room, lining the walls. They all bore the standard disruptor rifles, they all wore the same dull silver uniforms, and they all had the same cold, blank expressions. They, at least, need not even pretend any interest in the lecture to come. Spock's sideways glance noted a few familiar faces among the attendees: Avrak, clearly intending to snatch any advantage he could from the meeting; Kharik, already utterly bored; and Ruanek, looking alert as a warrior . . . no, Spock corrected himself with some surprise, as the scientists.

Again: Fascinating.

Bad enough, Ruanek thought, that Kharik should be here at all. Worse that he should have been the one to bring the mysterious Evaste to both the praetor and Avrak's attention. Avrak had been quick to claim the credit, which was a patron's right; but he owed Kharik now, and Kharik would let neither his lord nor his cousin forget it.

"When I attended the Lady Evaste's briefing," Avrak commented seemingly casually to Ruanek, "Kharik came with me as security, but I don't suppose he paid attention to anything but the lady's . . . eyes."

Catching Kharik's frown, Ruanek thought, *Oh, clever, my patron. You forever keep Kharik and me at each other's throats, never giving us quite the room to strike at each other—or at you.*

Rather than risk saying something that was certain to be destructive, Ruanek merely smiled. Tightly.

And for an instant, he allowed himself to escape into *the* daydream: an empty, lovely sweep of desert such as he imagined might be on Vulcan, a peaceful place where nothing terrible had ever happened, nothing terrible ever would. . . .

Akhh, nonsense! He was a Romulan subcommander, not a—a weakling of a poet!

A fanfare blared from hidden speakers. The praetor's personal guard entered, grimly elegant in silver and red uniforms, fanning out along the stairs. Senators and scientists alike rose to welcome Praetor Dralath, who entered glittering with awards and smiling like a well-fed predator.

"Honored Senators, honored scientists." His sweep of a hand took in the entire room. "Welcome. I have brought you here to listen to a most remarkable presentation. One that may, in fact, change the entire course of all our lives. Lady Evaste, if you would . . . ?"

As she reached the podium, red-crimson-russet robes swirling about her, a guard warily protecting her back, Ruanek settled back into his seat. Inexplicably, his heart had suddenly started racing.

". . . granted, our control group was small," Saavik continued, "and the study has been going on for only fifteen years."

And it feels as though this presentation has, too. But then, she had never expected to actually give it. *I seem to have fascinated Dralath utterly. It is illogical to complain of being overly successful.*

Still, she had not enchanted him so thoroughly that he would share his plans with her. Yet. And . . . then there was Spock. Spock, unmistakable even in those drab Romulan robes, Spock staring at her, his face impassive as always, but his eyes . . .

Saavik quickly looked away before her voice could betray her by shaking.

Spock, what are you doing to me? I am no green ensign with, ah, what is the phrase, my "first crush." And we have known each other for so long without . . .

"But each of the controls had begun to deteriorate before tests started," she continued with fierce determination. "I will transmit hard data once I am granted computer access." Saavik paused for dramatic effect. "My research institute even managed to . . . acquire Vulcan test results. As you may know, their Science Academy's work on genetic splicing and ribosome transfusion is some years in advance of our own."

"Yes," came grudging mutters.

"So. Preliminary trials there showed detection rates fifty percent more effective than conventional methods and a thirty-five percent remission rate after first crisis of the following diseases, for which, as we know, my colleagues, there is as yet no cure." She read down the list, listening to the growing murmurs of disbelief from the audience, and quickly concluded, "And there have been no adverse reactions, and no allergic reactions, to the medications."

"So far!" a scientist shouted, ignoring Dralath's frown.

"So far," Saavik agreed. "I applaud your caution. Now, let me show you some diagrams, scholars and Senators."

And here I believed the mission was merely to get in, get Spock, get out. Had Captain Uhura already known that Dralath was planning war? Unlikely; she would then have sent in operatives more professionally trained in espionage. *It is illogical to think that Spock might have been, as the humans say, set up.*

Romulans were not logical. As the presentation continued, Saavik was forced to stop now and again as an occasional debate—no, call it honestly, a fight—broke out among members of the audience. Not from the senators, though: they seemed to have perfected the skill of sleeping with their eyes open and their backs straight. Saavik met Spock's eyes once again, and instantly regretted it.

Oh. The sudden thought struck her so strongly that her calm voice faltered. *It could be . . . no . . . I couldn't have lost track of the days so thoroughly.* But the relativity paradoxes of space travel wreaked havoc on the body's calendar, sometimes by as much as years. It could logically be that . . .

No. Concentrate! Your life—and Spock's—depend on it.

"Now, scholars and Senators, if you will watch this . . ."

Saavik rotated the helical projections on the display platform, then projected a simulation as modified by her prototype drugs. There in the audience, Spock frowned judiciously, silently analyzing.

Others in the audience were not so restrained.

"What about genetic variation?" a man called out. And a woman's voice added, "Have you ruled out chance mutations?"

"One can, by the very nature of 'chance,' " Saavik retorted, "hardly predict what may or may not happen." She spread her hands, smiling. "I make no claim to soothsaying abilities."

That earned her a ripple of amusement, mostly, she noted, from the males.

"And climatic influences!" a scientist shouted. "What about those? Does the model take into account *those* potential variations?"

"Yes, climate!" another yelled. "Vulcan is a scorched wasteland! How can we compare it to—"

"Can we reverse—"

"The altered genes! Will they breed true in successive generations?"

Romulans, Saavik mused, turned even scientific disputes into blood sport.

Ruanek sat in silent, utter horror. He'd just been an idiot, a damned suicidal idiot. He had lost himself so thoroughly in the presentation, struggling his way along to understanding, that he had actually shouted out that cursed question about genetic variation.

Why not just turn your disruptor on yourself while you're at it? You're too stupid to merit the Final Honor.

But there was worse to this than Avrak's questioning frown, worse than his happening to know a scientific concept that should be beyond a good, honorable soldier's interest or understanding.

Worse was that he *did* understand. There could be only one

reason why Dralath should be so interested in advanced medical techniques. And Evaste's techniques might work. They might add twenty, forty, even a hundred years to Dralath's life, letting him outlast his emperor, outlive any hope of rebellion. . . .

No. It must not happen. Ruanek glanced warily about, but of course none of . . . the others were here. This problem was his to solve.

". . . and there, scholars and Senators, you have it. Preliminary, yes, but as my colleagues and I see it, most promising."

Dralath, to Saavik's relief, was getting to his feet. Her ordeal— at least this part of it—was now officially over. Senators quickly stood at attention, while the scientists, less formal in their excitement, collected their notes and scrambled to their feet to congratulate the praetor's latest favorite, making the guards glower and close ranks.

"There is no need," Saavik said in Evaste's most charming voice. "These are my fellow scientists!"

She stood acknowledging their thanks, smiling past them at the praetor. But . . . Spock had joined the line of well-wishers. And as he neared her, Saavik *knew* with utter certainty.

The Fires of Pon farr *are upon me, but only the first stages, not the blood madness. Does Spock feel the burning yet? Not fully; he's older than me . . . and he studied on Gol. His control is logically stronger. But I—I mustn't let us touch; that will surely kindle the bond. . . .*

"A stimulating presentation, lady," Spock was saying, revealing absolutely nothing in face or body language, and something deep within Saavik was pleading with herself, *No, please, not now. . . .* "Thank you." *Oh no, don't come any closer, I can't . . .* But she had to pass on a vital bit of data. "He wants to dine alone with me tonight," Saavik whispered.

"Refuse!" Spock hissed.

She felt an alarmingly illogical flash of triumph: He was protective. Or jealous. In another moment, the flames would leap up—*No, no, emotion on his part means that he's starting to feel it, too!* Frantically, Saavik whispered, "How else can I find out what he hides?"

"You should not be alone with him."

"On the contrary, it is you who should not have come to Romulus alone. Then perhaps neither of us would be here."

But Spock had a point. Should her nighttime interrogation of the praetor go sour, Spock's presence would be highly valuable. Saavik hastily clasped her hands to keep from reaching out to Spock. Instead she whispered to him the location of her suite in the praetor's compound.

And then, not daring to wait a moment more, she murmured an excuse and hurried off. Ah, a terrace, with fresh, mercifully cool air! Saavik stood in the doorway, breathing deeply, willing *calm . . . you are calm. . . .* She'd been through the Fires before, of course; she knew her own body, knew that it wasn't too late to keep this—this appalling case of bad timing under control a while longer.

That was, if these Romulans only left her alone long enough to collect herself!

"Get away!" Saavik snapped at the guards who were crowding in behind her. *No. Wrong. Evaste wouldn't sound so commanding.* She forced herself to smile at Dralath, standing behind them, to look somewhat abashed at her outburst. "It's nothing; I'm always like this after a presentation. I just need a few moments by myself."

At the praetor's wary nod, the guards withdrew. "Praetor Dralath," a male voice murmured.

Dralath turned with deliberate lack of haste. "Senator Avrak. What do you want?"

"May I present two of my sworn guards, Subcommander Ruanek and Centurion Kharik? They will guard the entranceway to give the lady the privacy she seeks. None shall pass them."

"Of course not," Dralath agreed. "Not if you wish to remain what you are."

"And in the meantime, Praetor Dralath, might we not talk together?"

"So be it," the praetor snapped. "You're safe here, Evaste," he added over his shoulder as he and the senator strolled away. "Just don't stay away too long."

Saavik made herself return his smile. She let out her breath in a slow sigh of relief, and headed out onto the terrace to lean on the smooth coolness of the stone balustrade. She would have steepled her fingers as she had been taught, but someone might see: that was too Vulcan. Silently, she recited, *I am Saavik, daughter of Vulcan. I am in control of my being . . . I am in control of my mind . . . heart . . . soul . . . I am . . .*

Among the enemies who begot me. In a place I never thought to see. . . .

Saavik's first sight on Romulus had been a Customs officer there in the noisy, crowded Ki Baratan terminal. He was a grizzled old man with the bearing of a soldier. He had also had one sleeve neatly fastened above the elbow and a patch covering his left eye. *Don't they heal even their own?*

"Evaste of Anat-Vorian?"

"Yes, sir." Saavik kept her voice soft and level. *I did not expect this; after so many years, I did not expect to still be harboring a latent hatred for . . . my half-kin.*

"You've the accent of the frontier all right," the officer said. "Been a long time since I've heard it. Served with a man from the Outmarches, oh . . . you would barely have been in school. Vorian. Do you have an elder brother?"

"I . . . had."

His muscles ticced around the eye patch. Saavik heard herself ask, "Centurion, are you in pain?"

He gave her a startled glance, then shrugged. "You get used to it."

"But why . . ."

She had meant to ask, *Why weren't you healed?* Misunderstanding, the old centurion muttered, "You can't be wondering how I got these, can you? Not if you knew enough to call me by my old title. *Akhh,* my ship took a direct hit. The shields went down, and my console exploded. Lucky to have a face, they told me."

"Lucky to be alive!"

"You think so? Like this? Not enough money to buy me a new face and arm, they said. Nothing to be done about it, but my uncle went to his commander. Fates speak his name gently where his spirit wanders; he never came back from the Barrier. He got me this job. Otherwise, I'd have taken refuge in the Final Honor, aye, and my wife and children with me."

There had been the slightest hesitation on those last words, the slightest unexpected warmth. With a shock, Saavik realized, *He would not have abandoned his children, his wife.* How illogical that she had never thought that a Romulan might actually be a loving husband and father!

The old centurion snorted. "You just listen and it all pours out, does it? You'd have made a good priest, lady. Bah, enough of that. Why are you here now?"

"At the praetor's call."

Music blared from the immense viewscreen. The centurion grimaced. "Not again." Outside the tiny office, people sighed and looked up at the screen.

An image of the Imperial bird-of-prey, with the crown that looked like golden talons, filled the viewscreen. The screen flashed, and an impressive figure in a military uniform bright with awards replaced the Eagle.

Dralath, Saavik thought, *that is certainly Praetor Dralath.*

"My beloved fellow citizens," his voice rang out. "I, your praetor, come before you to caution you that the emperor requires a sacrifice of us all:

"After much thought, and with the Senate advising us, we have reached a decision concerning recent trade talks with the Klingons. We are breaking them off and canceling the remainder of our contract for their birds-of-prey. We have demanded a return of our earnest money. Although demanding a return from thieves seems an exercise in futility, I would not, as praetor of our great empire, allow it to be said that we have gone back on our debts.

"Furthermore, our scientific and engineering advisors speak well of our new prototype warbirds."

An image of a ship, the eagle on its underbelly freshly painted, formed on the screen, and Saavik straightened in alarm. This ship was perhaps twenty percent bigger than the old warbirds, with more graceful lines than the *K'tinga*-class Klingon vessels that the Empire had used in recent decades.

"Why indeed, you may ask, my friends, should we send our treasure to the barbarian Klingons when we possess such ship-building capabilities ourselves? Furthermore, with unemployment up and inflation at an all-time high, constructing these ships, the prototypes of a fleet of much larger vessels that we hope, one day, to build, will employ many loyal Romulans."

Glyphs replaced the warbird: addresses at which men and women seeking work might apply.

"You are offered the chance to serve the Empire, once, through your sacrifice, expressed in taxes."

Was that a sigh Saavik heard in the Customs Building?

"Twice, through your own military service, which I cannot commend in high enough terms."

"A third time, in your work and your continued loyalty. We bring you now . . ."

Old officers, some known even to Saavik thanks to intelligence briefings, appeared on screen, criticizing the quality of Klingon vessels and praising the spaceworthiness of the new ships.

The praetor reassumed control of the screen. "We are naming these ships *Amarcan*-class warbirds, after Commander Amarcan, late of the Imperial War College, who disappeared into the Barrier. What you are about to see is the Consecration, performed by the Noble Born commander out of reverence to her teacher's spirit, of the ship that she will command."

Odd that he doesn't mention the commander's name. Almost as though he's . . . reluctant to do her that honor. Or . . . wary.

A woman no longer young, but still marvelously fit and supple, approached a small crucible. She kept her eyes fixed upon the shimmering metal, and her lips moved in what Saavik recognized with a start as the most ancient memorial incantations— originally of Vulcan. The woman drew a blade that glittered with the subtle, watery sheen of the most treasured ancient Vulcan weapons and cut a lock of her own hair. She threw the hair into the molten metal, in token of personal mourning, then slashed her palm and let the blood flow.

The Noble Born's ceremonial chant was replaced by martial music as the screen went blank, only to have the image replaced by a view of the Valley of Chula as the moons rose. A chorus of children's voices rose, celebrating the valley's flowers.

Does the Federation know—no, of course they don't—I must get word out—

The former centurion cleared his throat, startling her out of her stunned thoughts.

Then Dralath's guards had arrived, to take her to him—and it was then Saavik realized that there must be much more to her mission than simply locating and extricating Spock.

I am Saavik, daughter of Vulcan. I am Saavik, Commander, Starfleet. I will withstand the Fires in my blood for as long as it is logically possible. Regardless of the Fires, I will complete my mission.

I will do what I have sworn to do.

Somehow.

TWELVE

KI BARATAN, ROMULUS, DAY 6, SECOND WEEK OF TASMEEN, 2344

Ruanek let out his breath in a long, shuddering sigh. Why had Avrak loaned him to protect Dralath's latest favorite? Oh yes, granted, the senator would have seen an ideal chance to better his standing with Dralath.

But . . . assigning me, here, now, to . . . guard the lady . . .

The Fates seemed to be pushing him this way, no matter what he wished. And their humor was as twisted as ever.

But—one's honor, even one's life, was a small, small thing when balanced against the future of a people.

Whatever must be done, Ruanek told himself resolutely. To Kharik, he said quickly, "The lady has been out there alone a little too long. I doubt there's a problem, but I'm just going to check, be sure that all's well. You stay here to guard the doorway."

He hurried out before Kharik, blindsided for once, could summon an argument.

Evaste stood leaning on the smooth black stone balustrade.

The balustrade of the terrace that hung out so nicely over the ground so far below . . .

Fates, oh Fates, I have killed before, but never murdered . . . certainly never a civilian. She is blameless. . . .

Is she?

"Lady? I do not mean to disturb you. I merely wished to see if you were well."

Oh, you hypocrite! You murderous hypocrite!

The lady glanced coolly at him, showing not the slightest sign of alarm, and he . . . *akhh,* how could she not hear the pounding of his heart? He froze as she returned to leaning on the balustrade, her profile wonderfully clear against the sky, the beads in her many braids glittering in the light of the one risen moon, her wild, bright robes like the petals of some exotic flower. . . .

If he didn't act now, he never would. "Lady Evaste . . ."

She turned back to him with the smallest sound of impatience. "Yes? Subcommander . . . Ruanek, is it?"

"Yes. Lady, the . . . the drugs you've brought and the ribosome transfusions." He nearly stumbled over the technical terms.

"What of them? You seem far too healthy to need their aid." That charm again, directed now against him, disarming him.

"Then . . . they . . . do work." *Say no, oh say no, say that you're a fraud, that you're a liar, anything to let me spare you!*

But she, unheeding, asked, "Do you think I'd risk my life on a sham?"

"Lady Evaste, do you—you can't know—you can't give them to the praetor."

"Strange words from a subcommander! Is this treason, Ruanek?"

"No! I only . . . please, you come from a frontier world, a distant colony, you can't know what life is like here. . . ."

But anything else he said really would be treason, so Ruanek contented himself only with, "Just believe this, lady. For your sake, for all our sakes, get back on the ship that brought you, go home with your drugs and don't ever, ever return."

She didn't need this, Saavik thought, she truly didn't need this, particularly not now when she had just barely managed to will herself back under control. But this wasn't merely a political matter. Subcommander Ruanek was showing far too much anxiety about Evaste's mission, and his stance was far too alert for someone simply on guard duty.

Just what I didn't need: a rebel.

And what would Evaste of Anat-Vorian, provincial medic from a backwater world, do? Scream? Run? Not know how to fight like a Starfleet officer, that was certain. For that matter, would a scream bring help, or only wagers on her likelihood of survival? She was hardly about to let Ruanek kill her—but she could hardly "break cover," either!

Stall, Saavik told herself. *Don't let him get a hand near that dagger. Don't let him get between you and the doorway, either.*

Too late for the latter. He'd already maneuvered himself between her and escape; he hadn't risen to the rank of subcommander by chance.

Not surprising that the warnings of *Pon farr* had utterly subsided; violent emotion could have that effect. And there was nothing like suddenly confronting a would-be assassin to stir up violent emotions, even in a half-Vulcan.

"It's very charming of you to worry about my safety," Saavik began warily, watching him for any telltale tightening of muscles, the warnings that he was about to move, "and I do appreciate your concern, but I assure you—ah, look!" The relief in her voice wasn't feigned. "Here comes your colleague." Unless he was in league with Ruanek . . . ? No. Not with that look of utter hatred for the subcommander. "Why, Centurion Kharik," Saavik said with Evaste's lightness, "did you think my honor was in peril?"

"From *him?*" Kharik snapped. "From that *boy?*"

"I am," Ruanek reminded him curtly, "your senior."

"An accident of birth."

"No accident surrounded my birth. *Or* my engendering!"

"Are you insulting my—"

"I am insulting *you*, Kharik, only you!"

No male posturing here: genuine hatred blazed behind the insults on both sides, just barely kept in check.

Your problem, soldiers, Saavik thought, *not mine.*

They weren't paying the slightest attention to her. Not sure if she was angry at being suddenly forgotten or wildly amused, Saavik hurried back into the Ministry of Science. There, the dangers were merely those of being revealed for what she was, of being killed or captured—and right now, something so plain and uncomplicated was almost welcome!

Ruanek knew what was happening; he knew that he was taking out all his anger and despair over Evaste—and what he'd almost done, *would* have done—on his cousin. He also knew that this was a damnably stupid time and place to be doing it.

But all at once he simply didn't care. After all the long years of subtle taunts, of hatred kept fiercely in check, it felt so savagely wonderful to spit out bitter words, enemy to enemy, to know that at last there would be no one to say, "Enough!"

"Keep your voice down, fool!" he snapped at Kharik. "We don't want the others rushing here to stop us."

"You fear them seeing us!" Kharik snarled. But at least he didn't shout it. "You slimy coward!"

"I am no coward, Kharik! You and I both know that well! My honor is strong, Kharik—while yours is the weak, stained falseness—"

"I call doubt upon your courage!"

"I call doubt upon your honor!" Ruanek retorted. Blazing with the years of suppressed rage, he snapped out the ritual words: "Hear me, heed me: I call Declaration of Challenge upon you!"

"I accept!" It was a roar. "I accept!"

"But I," a sudden cold voice cut in, "do not."

The cousins whirled as one. *Spock!* Ruanek thought. *Yes, and—Commander Charvanek!*

Vulcan and Romulan . . . together? Allies? These two?

Yes, and both of them looking cold as Death itself. "This," Spock snapped in a voice sharp as the edge of a blade, "is *not* the place for a Combat of Honor."

Ruanek, shaking with the sudden release from tension, bowed in reluctant submission to Spock—and to the equally cold-eyed Commander Charvanek. And after a moment, so did Kharik.

"It seems the scholar you tended intervenes to save your life. Another time," he snarled at Ruanek, straightening. "Another place."

"So shall it be," Ruanek snapped.

With a second curt bow at Spock and Charvanek, Kharik stormed off.

Ruanek, still shaking, struggled to get himself back under control and not present such an undignified image to a Romulan commander of the emperor's House. How could anyone expect a man to go in one instant from a death challenge to—nothing—and not react? Still, they had been quite right to stop the duel before it began: Now that his head was clearing of rage, Ruanek had to agree that the Ministry of Science was certainly no place for a duel.

"The woman, Evaste," he began in an awkward attempt to explain, then stopped at Charvanek's frown.

"The woman," she said, "over whom you were fighting."

"Commander, pardon, but it wasn't quite like—"

"Silence! Do you know how close you came to causing a public scandal?"

No, he hadn't. Caught up in the heat of the pending battle, he hadn't realized a thing other than blood lust. But if he'd happened to embarrass his patron, embarrass Avrak—oh yes, Avrak, who was probably already furious with him for that blurted remark about genetic variants.

Suddenly overwhelmed by constraints of patron, rank, lineage, and a system that seemed designed to keep him trapped, Ruanek erupted, "But the woman! The Lady Evaste is a threat—"

"The Lady Evaste," Spock cut in, his words clearly as much for Charvanek as Ruanek, "is an *ally*."

There was a moment of startled silence. Then the commander, eyebrow raised ever so slightly, murmured, "What a fascinating . . . complication."

Too much was happening too quickly—with too little hard data behind it. Ruanek snarled at Spock, "Someone pledged to tell me the truth. Someone should begin to do so *now,* or I may make another mistake."

Was that, could that possibly be, the quick flash of answering anger in Spock's eyes? Oh no, that was impossible—

No more impossible than everything else happening this day.

Charvanek's hand closed on his arm before he could react, the firm, strong hand of a commander used to calming warriors in battle. "Peace."

One did not argue with a commander's order. Ruanek bowed his head, letting himself submit for the moment, and Charvanek nodded in satisfaction and released him. "Subcommander, I agree: It is wrong to keep an ally in ignorance. We shall tell you as much truth . . . as you can stomach."

Complications, Charvanek thought. *When has my career—my life—been free from them?*

She led her unlikely allies, Spock and Ruanek, careful that no one followed, to a quiet, unornamented little room. "This is one of the Ministry storage chambers. Rarely used," she added, brushing dust off a sleeve.

"Safe, I assume?" Spock commented.

"It should be," she assured him with the faintest wry upward quirk of her mouth. "I debugged it myself, just as I've debugged a great many rooms in recent years. Now you, warrior, are Subcommander Ruanek, in service to Avrak, Senator Pardek's own sister-son. You do, I assume, know who we both are?"

He nodded, still young enough, for all his military experience, to be flushing slightly that a commander—or was it awe over her Imperial lineage?—should know him. How he and Spock should know each other, Charvanek mused, was another matter—but she had learned long ago not to be surprised by anything Spock might accomplish. Still, she was certainly impressed that he'd already managed to find one of the best of the younger generation!

So, now. "Subcommander, are you loyal?"

She'd snapped that out too quickly for him to think about his answer. "To our people and the emperor, yes, I so swear it!"

"I see." She had noted that careful omission. Intriguing . . . Spock was right, then, about him. Very delicately, Charvanek suggested, "There are those who are not happy with things as they are," and saw by the slightest of flinches that he was one of those. "A clever man might manage to hold to honor by . . . ever so slightly altering the way he sees the world. By . . . ever so subtly shifting sides. By serving . . . my cousin. Both my cousins."

"The emperor," Ruanek said with an archaic little gesture of reverence. "And . . . your pardon if I guess wrongly, Commander, but do you not refer to Admiral Narviat?"

Charvanek glanced at Spock, saying with a glance, *He is clever!* "And . . . ?"

"And I—I am trusting you, both of you, with my life, Commander."

"Understood. And what," she added dryly, indicating Spock, "do you think we do?"

She saw him register the fact that just being seen with a Vulcan—and one already under a death sentence—would condemn them both. "Ah. Yes. Well." Ruanek hesitated a moment longer, then admitted in a wild rush, "I am with a—a certain group, Commander, a secret group, those who seek to replace the praetor."

"Ah, a secret group," she murmured, more to Spock than to him. "With, no doubt, a charmingly dramatic name: Fighters for the Way, perhaps, or—no, Subcommander, I am not mocking you." *Quite. It is just that you are still, underneath all that harsh warrior façade, so . . . young.*

"You must understand," he stammered earnestly, "w-we are not seeking the overthrow of everything! I can ask no better than to live and die for the emperor."

"Then," Charvanek said, "we are on the same side. Most . . . convenient."

Spock straightened. "But our friend clearly has another question. What?"

"Who is *she?* Evaste, I mean. Who is she?"

Charvanek turned to study Spock. "A most excellent question. Who *is* this Evaste?"

"Her true name is Saavik." The briefest of pauses, then: "My wife."

Only by stern self-control did Charvanek keep from echoing that—at a shout. Contenting herself with raising an eyebrow, she murmured, "A complication, indeed."

Very much of a complication. Studying Spock, she knew, ah, she knew just how much of his old attraction toward her still lingered—but she also had seen quite plainly just a short while ago that he was even more strongly drawn to the woman he'd just named as his wife.

The woman who, if Romulan Intelligence was correct, was an officer in Starfleet. A half-Romulan Starfleet officer . . . yes, of course. There could only be one such Saavik.

Bah. The Empire was foolish to abandon her. Just another sign of how far we have slid.

Ruanek glanced from her to Spock. "Your pardon," he said with just a touch of anxiety in his voice, "but while the world may yet change about us, right now the truth of the matter is that I cannot stay away from my duties too long. Kharik will already have alerted our patron to my absence and I—"

"Need a good excuse. Understandable." Charvanek pulled a tiny silver box from her belt, carefully opening it, seeing from Ruanek's start that he recognized the tablets inside.

"*Turath*, Commander? Do you . . . mean to poison me?"

Charvanek was busy breaking off the smallest corner of one pungent tablet with a precisely placed thumbnail. "Not with a . . . dosage this . . . ah! . . . small. All you will get from this, at worst, is a dense sleep—and from the look of you, Subcommander, a little enforced rest won't hurt you. Yes, and anyone finding you will get a telltale whiff of *turath* and know that you weren't shamming."

She saw what might almost have been ironic humor glint in Spock's eyes. But, Vulcan that he was, he wasn't about to help her fabricate a lie. *So be it.*

"You have been poisoned in the line of duty, Subcommander," Charvanek said, as Ruanek, grimacing at the taste, swallowed. "You were heroically trying to protect the lady from would-be assassins. She fled back into the Ministry of Science, but you attempted to follow the assassins. Unfortunately, before you could summon help, the poison overwhelmed you. Fortunate for you, the assassins were in a hurry, and the dosage wasn't . . . ah, yes, *turath* works swiftly."

Together, she and Spock lowered the unconscious Ruanek to the floor, then stood for a second watching him tensely.

"Breathing," Charvanek said after a moment.

Was that actually a sigh of relief from Spock? "He will not betray us."

Charvanek gave Spock a wry glance at that. "You sound as though one could carve that in stone."

"One could, if one wished. It is, nevertheless, the truth."

"Ah well," Charvanek said, almost lightly, as they left. A wary glance this way, that: Safe. "If you are mistaken, there is at least this comfort: Neither of us will be worrying about it, or about anything else, for long!"

THIRTEEN

Outside, Romulus' twilight was slowly deepening into true night, and one moon had already begun its climb into the sky. Within Charvanek's estate, artificial lighting was automatically switching itself on, the pools of sudden illumination startling the insects and small, chirping *hataki*. It would have been agreeable, a corner of Spock's mind noted, to be no more than a visitor, free to wander out there in the evening. With . . . Saavik.

Impossible.

". . . and so," Spock concluded to Charvanek in the secure room in her mansion, "Saavik and I agree that I must be present when she meets with Dralath."

Charvanek stared at him in utter astonishment. "Are you *insane?*" she exploded at last.

"I do not believe so."

"Do you realize—Spock, if you are taken, I cannot protect you."

"Then, obviously, I must not be taken. Charvanek, we must know anything that Dralath says."

116

"And which 'we' is that?" she demanded. "Be *logical,* curse it! Your objectivity is compromised—how could it not be compromised under the circumstances? Spock, I would not have expected this of you!"

On Vulcan, that would have been grave insult, but a reluctant little smile flickered across Charvanek's face as she finished. Romulans valued loyalty, Spock recalled—and Romulans certainly appreciated a dangerous gamble.

He waited.

And with a sharp sigh, it was Charvanek who yielded. "It may prove well for me after all. I have only rarely been able to place spies in Dralath's house—unfortunately short-lived spies. Perhaps Evaste—Saavik, rather—will prove more effective. Didn't you train her?"

"Yes."

"Well, then! All you Starfleet officers are half spy."

"Charvanek—"

"I know. The past is the past. In this case, however," she added, almost gently, "Starfleet connections or not: Fortune attend you."

Not just fortune, but a wholly illogical jealousy and fear attended Spock as he slipped through the shadows toward the praetor's compound, the night darkening around him. Nor was it logical that he blamed himself for his mate's decision, yet so he did. He had permitted his mate to expose herself to danger.

"Permitted"? Spock questioned himself. *She is not my property! Or . . . my mate . . . yet.*

Faint lights showed a guard station up ahead. Spock crept forward till he was close enough to see and hear the two Romulans inside, then went utterly still. He might be long retired from Starfleet, but he could still kill, logically and efficiently.

Kill? You are Vulcan, not Romulan. Do not let their emotions affect you.

But if his mate—if Saavik were in danger—

You will do what is logically necessary. No more than that.

A guard chuckled. "I'll wager a five he breaks down her defenses, or anything else tonight." He held out his hand so that green light could shine upon the crystals he rattled enticingly: high stakes at a guard's pay.

A second guard snickered. "What makes you think he hasn't already?"

"Maybe he'll keep this one. Especially if she has the drugs she says."

"Not likely he'll share with the likes of us."

"The drugs or the woman?"

Both guards laughed. Spock, hands clenched, reminded himself that he was a man of peace, and crept closer.

"Don't be so gloomy. We've come in for our share before. But this one—if he discards her, she's the type who would choose the Final Honor. They raise them strict on the frontier."

"Side bet on that? How about two? It doesn't seem quite honorable to raise the stakes any higher."

"Done."

Crystals spilled from the guards' hands onto a table.

"Did you hear anything?" one asked his comrade, then toppled as Spock's hand squeezed the nerve plexus between neck and shoulder. His companion leapt forward, reaching for his sidearm, then fell as Spock applied the nerve pinch to him, too, with perhaps more force than was absolutely necessary.

Would the guards report this assault? The odds were logically low, perhaps 78,836 . . . no, that was not right, 93,465.66666 . . . no matter, no matter.

With a great effort, Spock forced his mind back onto the proper path of Vulcan logic. No, the guards would *not* report this. Admitting that they had been incapacitated by an unknown foe or foes who had then gained access to the praetor's compound would be as good as cutting their own throats.

Slipping past the unconscious Romulans, Spock warily hunted for electronic sensors . . . yes, and yes again. A quick study showed that they operated on relatively uncomplex mathematical codes. Easy to bypass. The softest of hums, barely audible even to Vulcan hearing, warned him of yet another trap—yes. Light beams, possibly from an old-fashioned but still potentially deadly laser. A handful of dust lightly tossed at them made the invisible beams temporarily visible, long enough for Spock to safely duck under and step over them, and enter the gardens surrounding the praetor's mansion.

Spock paused, listening, looking . . .

No. He was alone in the middle of lush greenery that rustled in the soft breeze. Ahead, Spock saw fountains plashing in the moonlight. A stream, its banks too regular to be natural, ran swiftly down from the fountains beneath the night sky, the water where it passed through shadow turned as dark as his mate's hair. . . .

That is illogical.

All this greenery. He could not help but find it . . . extravagant, a waste of precious water—then, bemused to realize just how much of a desert dweller he still was at heart, reminded himself that this more temperate world was hardly Vulcan.

And what of the Romulans? Is the desert still in their hearts after so many years? Or has so much water made them all as drunk on their appetites as the praetor?

Lights glowed on the terrace he sought, marked by an arcade of slender uprights carved from translucent white stone. Spock took cover behind a tall block of lava, whorled and hollowed by time and some craftsman's skill into something as aesthetically pleasing as it just now was tactically useful.

No sign of danger. He risked stealing closer, catching the scent of wine and the pungency of burning fat. His nostrils flared with disgust.

"You do not eat enough!" came Dralath's too-hearty voice, followed by a sizzle as if he had just set a skewer of meat into a pot of bubbling oil. "Here. Come, to please me."

Spock knew that Saavik had grown up eating meat—that, and anything else a half-starved child could find. And even now, what would sicken a Vulcan would not distress her in the slightest.

"I have already eaten, my lord—oh, very well, I can refuse you nothing."

Her voice was soft with an implied surrender. And without warning, a sudden hot fire blazed up within Spock. How dare she sit out there with the praetor, lingering over a late-night supper, eating meat, of all barbarities, and murmuring so provocatively? A fierce, jealous little voice whispered in his mind that she had never used that tone on *him*.

All at once there was no logic to the world. All at once he ached to vault onto that terrace, to kill this other male! Hunter-instinct narrowed his sight, and his blood roared in his temples—

No! I must not—must not . . .

He had not felt this disoriented, this outraged since . . .

. . . since his last attack of *Pon farr.*

The realization stunned him back to sanity. Illogical to deny fact. Not even Vulcans had been able to compensate for what warp speeds did to their systems. Not even a mathematician as accomplished as Spock could accurately calculate how much "real" time had elapsed since he had last entered the Fires—particularly with the added complication of his human genes. And the chaos of Romulan emotions all around him had completely disguised the first warning symptoms.

Relativity has turned deadly on me.

Drawing a deep, sobbing breath, Spock sought the inner stillness, but found only leaping fire.

No! I am not a mindless beast! I . . . will . . . be . . . logical!

He leaned his brow against the coolness of the standing stone. In what felt like a totally different space-time continuum, Spock had taken all but the last vows of *Kolinahr.* He should have—he must have—sufficient discipline to keep the blood madness at bay, at least until his work was done.

Yes, but if he sank into meditation, he would be left defenseless before any patrolling guards—

And if I do not, the Fires claim me and I attack Dralath—

Overhead, the second moon had joined the first, casting silver and faintly green light over the garden, double shadows forming and mingling like spectral guards. Spock gripped the standing stone with desperate force, barely aware of the roughness of the rock. Sink into *Pon farr,* and he threw his life away. Worse, he would be throwing Saavik's life away.

There was no choice. Fingers steepled, Spock turned his mind and will inward, seeking the center, seeking control . . . down through levels of flame . . . down to the center . . . cool, logic at the center . . .

The outer world was not important.

The outer world did not concern him.

The outer world did not exist.

"You found my gift, I see," Dralath purred.

"There was no need for it, my lord." Saavik touched the silver pendant at her neck. "But I do thank you." *And I will melt this collar down as soon as I may.* "I only regret you did not wake me."

"Ah no. You are very lovely when you sleep."

She had been calming the Fires through deepest meditation when Dralath had entered her room. He had seen her defenseless, open to his view—

Only Spock has that right! Only he!

Control, Saavik commanded herself, repeating her personal mantra: *Logic is the cornerstone, logic, not emotion. I . . . cling . . . to . . . logic.*

Her hands were shaking. Let Dralath think it was because of him.

"I hope to further remedy any omissions tonight," Dralath was continuing. "Come, lady, what would you have of me?"

A pause. Then Saavik said, as though having just thought of it, "A story, perhaps. A true story. Tell me of the Empire and—and how you will restore it."

Dralath chuckled. "What a charming picture you make. Can I believe it?"

"My lord, can you doubt? All my life, I have longed to be precisely where I am now."

"With me?"

With Spock! "With a man able to shape the destinies of worlds! You are such a one, are you not?"

Dralath chuckled again, and poured some more of the blood-green, faintly sweet wine into their glasses. "My dear, have you ever met any Klingons? No? Just as well. A lovely thing like you should not be exposed to such creatures."

"But, my lord, are they not our shipwrights?"

"That," Dralath said shortly, "is about to end."

She nearly spilled her wine. "How fascinating! The day I landed on Romulus," Saavik all but babbled, "I heard you speak against the Klingons. How could I have known that I would actually listen to you telling me these things? And so, do you reclaim our economy from the Klingons?"

"Evaste, my clever Evaste, I am minded to teach the Klingons a lesson."

"Indeed?" Saavik asked. "Oh, but your glass is empty! Let me serve you."

Dralath covered his glass with a hand. "Not far from the Boundary between the Empire and those Klingons, even closer to those interfering fools that call themselves a Federation, there is a Klingon base called Narendra III. It menaces our trade routes."

"Why, I've heard of it! Is that not the only civilian outpost in the entire Klingon Empire?"

"No Klingon is truly a civilian," Dralath said flatly. "Even the children are savages. They build nothing, are worth nothing, live for nothing but violence. If we attack, quickly and with no warning, we can destroy this base and eliminate a security risk to the Empire."

Saavik put down her glass with such force that the fragile crystal nearly cracked. The annihilation of a base, a dishonorable surprise attack on civilians—the children slain or abandoned . . . as she had once been abandoned, left to struggle on as best she could on a world laid waste . . .

"Evaste?"

Steady. He must not suspect. "I—I was merely overwhelmed by the astounding daring of your plan! To destroy all of Narendra III in one bold strike . . ."

He nodded, pleased. "And there is more to it than the elimination of one potential threat. Think of the game of *khariat,* my dear, wherein the removal of one piece can cause a cascade of others, till nothing is left of what was a carefully balanced pattern but chaos."

"The Federation . . ." It was the barest gasp from Saavik.

"From an easy victory at Narendra III to a quick strike at Melville Colony. They call that a colony world, but it is, *of course,* a secret Federation military base. And from there . . ."

There was, Saavik thought, more blood lust in Dralath's smile than desire.

Spock came back from the inner world of cool tranquillity to the reality of the Romulan night with such a sudden jolt that he nearly cried aloud. What—

Guards! Some primal instinct had warned him of danger. He dove into shadow, willing his racing heart to calm, too stunned by the sudden transition to think clearly. The Fires were banked, but as the two guards stalked by, Spock could feel the embers stirring, urging him, *Strike. Kill.*

No, he told himself. These men were merely doing their job. And yes, he was in control . . . he was in control . . .

But then Spock heard Dralath boast to Saavik about Narendra III, about the massacre he had already set in motion. And that it would be followed by a stealth attack on a Federation colony as well—

We have just run out of time!

Spock clenched his teeth to keep from what would have been

a totally illogical, utterly suicidal shout of rage. Did that—creature not see? Narendra III's destruction might indeed be the spark to turn the Klingons not only against the Romulan Empire but against the Federation—and none would prosper, all would lose.

And Dralath called it a game. A triumph. The potential for sundering the intricate web of civilization that was the Federation—a game! Here was the treachery Charvanek had suspected, only exponentially worse. And Saavik had been right: It had taken her own cleverness and courage to expose it.

Dralath was boasting freely now, figuratively marking Saavik for death with every word.

Why should he not boast? His fleet is away, and he no longer needs to be discreet in her presence.

"I have prepared no less a fleet than seven of our new-model warbirds," he told her.

Only seven ships in the newly configured fleet? Spock wondered. *Fascinating. It would seem that seven of the new craft are all the Empire can afford.*

But seven ships were more than enough to take out a civilian outpost.

Excellent, Saavik told herself. *You've found precisely the information you were apparently sent here to find. Your objective now is simply to escape with Spock.*

Oh, easy.

She forced a laugh, looking up into Dralath's eyes, hoping he could not read her expression clearly. "I could almost wish you had not told me this."

He chuckled. "Why not?"

"My lord, I may be from an outlying world, but did you truly think me naïve? After this night, what need would you have of me?"

"Have you looked into a mirror lately, lady?"

"You flatter me, my lord. One disposes of liabilities."

"I would never—" Dralath protested. He reached out as if to pull her back against him.

"Do you not think, my lord," Saavik purred, evading him, "we must . . . bargain a bit? I would not wish to sell my . . . secrets for too little."

"No fear," Dralath retorted. "I always pay for what I want."

She pretended not to understand him, watching his smile broaden. But of course she understood only too well what a dangerous game this was. Let Dralath cease to be amused—or let arousal overpower his humor—and she was in deadly trouble. She—and Spock.

Spock is out there, listening.

Saavik shivered. Instantly, Dralath moved between her and the wind. The warmth of his body eased her trembling . . . he wasn't all that unpleasant to the eye, not really . . . something to be said about the attraction of power and—

Saavik stiffened with horror. In a moment, she was going to find him attractive, and he was anything but that! She could see finality in Dralath's eyes: Why not, he was plainly thinking, enjoy her before he killed her? In celebration of his triumph.

Killing him would be my quickest escape, but my odds of getting offworld would drop . . . I do not have time for these repulsive games!

She must, above all, remain calm. If Spock was out there, he was fighting the Fires himself by now. Any fear or rage of hers might well plunge him into the all-out combat rage of *Plak-tow,* and that would be fatal for them both.

It should not be this way, a wistful little thought whispered. If only she could run to Spock, disappear with him into the shadows . . .

No retreat for you, she told herself.

But then, there never had been.

Praetor Dralath held out his hand, two fingers extended. She made herself touch his outstretched hand, but could not quite manage not to flinch.

"Are you still shy, my pretty Evaste?" he asked. "Don't be afraid of me," he coaxed. "No lady has ever complained of me."

More likely, none of them survived.

Saavik made herself laugh softly, as though aware of nothing but the way Dralath's fingers caressed her palm. She looked down to hide the fury building in her mind. Or . . . was it just fury? Rage, jealousy, desire . . . She heard herself cry out in sheer, maddened frustration.

"Ah, Evaste," Dralath crooned, "do you know how exciting you are now? Did no one ever tell you? What you feel is a condition some women of our race fall prey to. Atavistic, yes, but it need not prove unpleasant. Come, let me show you."

Now Dralath was stroking the fingers and palm of Saavik's other hand. He bent forward, pressing his cheek against her hair, pulling her into his arms, and she wasn't sure how to get free, or even if she—

No! Oh, no! Why hadn't she considered this before? Dralath was of approximately the correct age—what if he had been there on the planet of her birth? She moaned in genuine loathing as Dralath pulled her closer, but desire still burned within her, not for him, never for him—

Spock!

No, no, she could not endanger him as well. But—

Let them fight, some ancient shadows in her brain whispered. *How else will you know to choose the stronger?*

No! It is only Spock I wish!

"Stay here with me," Dralath murmured against her shoulder, nuzzling her neck. "Stay. You shall have everything you want, and I shall protect you. You truly are in no danger, my dear— because it is already too late for any betrayal. The orders have already gone out, and the fleet is away. Three hours after it crosses the accursed Barrier, it will hunt Klingons. And kill them."

She could not suppress her gasp of horror, nor her involuntary glance up at the night sky as if she could expect to see Romulan ships, streaking off to do murder. To start a war.

"Ah, my Evaste, you do understand!"

I do, Saavik thought. *I understand that you mean to bring madness down upon us all.*

She must end this, here, now, before she could no longer think. Dralath's hand moved over her shoulder, easing the clinging silk back from it. Saavik shut her eyes as if in surrender. Gently, she slid a hand up his arm, caressingly brought it onto his shoulder—

Then closed strong fingers on the praetor's neck in the most enthusiastic nerve pinch of her life!

FOURTEEN

KI BARATAN, ROMULUS, DAY 6, SECOND WEEK OF TASMEEN, 2344

Spock edged out from around the tall, pitted stone just in time to see the praetor press Saavik down beneath him onto the cushions.

No-o-o!

Snapping Dralath's neck would be too quick. Spock would strangle him, yes, see his face darken, his eyes pop, feel his futile struggle for air—yes! His vision narrowed to his quarry.

Just then, Saavik freed one arm, slid it up Dralath's arm in a travesty of passion—and administered a meticulous nerve pinch. Spock held back a shout of triumph. *Atavism,* he rebuked himself. *Pure atavism—but how satisfying.*

Saavik was muttering a disgusted oath and pushing the praetor away. His limp body toppled from the cushions onto the tiles.

As Spock vaulted onto the terrace, Saavik rose to face him. And he—he stood frozen, staring at her, unable to speak. She wore a filmy gown the deep green of heart's blood, the vivid shade that once, long ago on Vulcan, had meant passion. Now, Vulcan women rarely wore it. And about her neck glinted a silver pendant. One of the praetor's gifts? No matter, no matter . . .

So beautiful. So very beautiful. His.

Her hair was still mostly coiled in a low, loose knot. If he reached out, twined his fingers in it and tugged, it would slip free over her shoulders. To touch her now . . .

"You left yourself no margin for error," he forced out in an almost rational tone.

She brushed back the stray tendrils of her hair with a weary hand. "You might have trusted me. You did once."

"I do." He could say no more, aching to shield her from all harm, hold her in his arms—*take her now; she will welcome you*—

Here? Now? Illogical, utterly illogical. Control . . . for her life as well as yours, control. "Saavik . . . you must leave immediately."

Saavik nodded. Matter-of-factly, she picked up the praetor's feet; Spock grasped his shoulders. No guards were about: Dralath had banished them all from the immediate vicinity. Spock and Saavik carried him inside her suite and deposited him, by unspoken agreement, on a low couch rather than Evaste's bed, then stood looking down at him, each, Spock knew, fighting an inner battle.

"We must give the praetor some false memories to cover your departure," Spock said at last. "I regret having to violate even his mental integrity but . . ."

He had forced a mind-meld before, on a woman; in his present emotional state, the memory of Valeris shamed him.

Saavik, misunderstanding his reluctance, raised an eyebrow. "This is war," she told him sharply. "Your skills are stronger than mine, but if you do not wish to perform the mind-meld, I will. A woman's touch—my touch—might be more effective."

She reached out her hand toward Dralath's temple, but Spock quickly blocked her. "Not alone, Saavik." He too made contact. Their fingers brushed, clung briefly, then separated.

"You ask, you do not order," she whispered. "So I will consent to what you ask. Anything you ask."

She had to know what she was saying. And its effects on one in the grip of the Fires.

Resolutely, he forced his attention back to the task ahead. This mind-meld would not be easy, not with an enemy, a rival. Not with fire racing in his blood. And most certainly not with Saavik's thoughts touching his.

Entering Dralath's mind was like struggling through a wasteland—a savage wilderness that could well have been found in Vulcan's most barren regions. The praetor might not be a telepath, but his subconscious fought them, mind to mind. The outcome was never in doubt, but Spock and Saavik both were breathing hard by the time they finished.

Spock withdrew from the meld, feeling an illogical need to wash his hands. When the praetor woke, he would have nothing but vague, groggy memories of too much wine and passion spent.

"I suppose his women flee after he's possessed them," Saavik whispered. "Assuming they survive."

She wiped her hands against her robe, in the process molding it to the curves of her body. At Spock's intake of breath, she looked up. The fire in her blood had burned away the weariness and humiliations of the role she had played. Now, she was clearly struggling not to hurl herself into his arms.

Without thinking, Spock put out his hand to touch her temple, the light touch Vulcan teachers and adepts used to invoke a mind-meld. He had soothed her that way when she was a child who flashed into panic or blind fury if she was restrained.

The touch was electrifying, a blaze of pleasure, desire, and triumph that she responded so completely. For an instant, Spock's fingers brushed her lips to still their trembling, and then he was reaching for her, heedless of anything but the need to make her his, to ease the fever in his blood, the madness in his mind and spirit then and there. And she—

She stepped back, forcing discipline upon herself with an effort that made them both ache. He dropped his arms, his breathing harsh as if he had been fighting all day.

"What a treasure you are, Saavik. I ask forgiveness." Somehow, he managed to keep his voice level. "I assume you had some plan to escape this place."

"Yes. Spock—"

"Then you must implement it now, while there is still a chance for reinforcements to come in time to Narendra III. Set your course for Narendra III and send a subspace message to Starbase 9. Then, head for Vulcan."

"But you—" Saavik's eyes blazed with longing. "You will not leave, too? Spock, come with me!"

The idea of traveling back, alone with her, to Federation space . . . the wondrous, tempting idea . . .

"I . . . cannot." The words seemed to tear themselves from him. "Saavik, you are strong and competent, but you are only one. Should you fail and your message not arrive—yes, that might well happen, we both know it. I must do what I can here." *The emperor,* he thought, *weak though he may be, still holds the people's loyalty. If I can reach Shiarkiek, he might be convinced to recall the fleet.*

If recall is even possible—

And, though Spock didn't say it, he must also find a way to unseat Dralath. Even should Saavik deliver her message, even if Narendra III and the Melville colony could be defended, there must be no more such plans.

Saavik glanced back at where Dralath lay. "We could simply— eliminate him, here and now." It was a temptation.

"That will not recall the fleet. Dralath controls the military with an iron hand," Spock said flatly. "No matter how precarious his balance of power may be, it is still a balance. If the Romulan generals are released from his yoke, each will seek his own glory in combat. They might run riot from Narendra III toward as many Federation colonies as they can strike."

Saavik shuddered. " 'And the war-beasts are let loose from their chains.' But you, too, are only one. What can you—"

"What I must." Spock interrupted. For a moment, the sheer

enormity—the sheer arrogance, perhaps—of what he meant to do overwhelmed him. "I have unfinished work here and allies that I cannot abandon. You understand." *Please. Understand.* "I shall follow you home . . . if I can."

Saavik went white to the lips. "So this is *Kobayashi Maru,*" she murmured. "Endgame. Admiral Kirk called it a test of character."

"Jim also said that you could take the test again if you were displeased with its results. Believe me, Saavik, you have no need."

Saavik bowed her head.

And Spock . . . remembered how he had once, long ago, left the *Enterprise*'s bridge and entered a contaminated engine room, knowing he would not survive. *How do you like my solution?* he had asked Jim. If he failed now . . .

If he failed, if he never returned to her, Saavik would face a slow, painful death as her systems shut down and madness erupted from the fire in her blood, while the best Spock could hope for was the violent mercy of a Romulan disruptor.

But the needs of the many on Narendra III and beyond—the needs of perhaps thousands of innocent civilians—outweighed the needs of the one. Or even of the two.

"Spock!" Saavik's voice was husky. "Parted from me . . ."

"Never parted," he completed in the whisper that was all the voice he could find. "Never. Now, go."

While I can still bear to release you!

The effort ached all through Spock's body, but he turned away into the night. He dared not know how she escaped. If Charvanek were defeated, Romulan interrogation techniques might not break him, but then again, they might tear data from his mind. Then they would kill him, possibly as painfully as *Pon farr.*

Even so, if Saavik's warning alerted the worlds, they would not have failed.

For Saavik to disappear, Evaste of Anat-Vorian had to die. As the sound of Spock's long strides faded away into the gardens,

Saavik ran for the too-lavish bedchamber of the suite she had never wanted to occupy. She threw the silver pendant across the room, then stripped off the loathsome, clinging silk that was the color of an Orion slave. It tore with a moist sound she found highly satisfactory, imagining she was rending the praetor's flesh. Tossing the ruined gown on the floor, she struggled into a ship-suit, then into drab Romulan traveling clothes until, finally, she felt decently covered.

Spock wanted her as much as she wanted him. She could not have mistaken the longing in his gaze. Or the fire in the brief touch that was all he dared give and all she dared accept.

"Come back to me, Spock." It was the faintest whisper. "Come back to me."

Saavik shivered. So cold—or was she burning up? She had to get offworld before the fever robbed her of wit and strength. She turned to the equipment that "Evaste" had brought to Romulus with such high hopes and wiped its files as if, disillusioned, the trader-medic had destroyed her small stock-in-trade.

One last task remained. A quick search of the praetor's tunic turned up a pouch of high-denomination crystals, a finely wrought knife, and a disruptor. She left the crystals where they were, but took the weapons. And for a moment, for all her need for haste, Saavik hesitated.

I could kill him, here, now. I could kill him as he lies helpless.

She hefted the disruptor, thinking that she would rather snap his neck.

Of course, Saavik told herself, she would never do anything so dishonorable. Or foolish.

So be it. You get to live, Dralath. And I trust I don't regret it.

A rejected gift, a torn gown, missing weapons—the disruptor for protection against recapture and the knife for honor—and files erased. With luck, the Romulans would ask no further questions. Suspecting that she would need speed as well as luck, Saavik raced across the garden. No problem with security devices: Dralath in his confidence had told her where and what they were.

At the nearest checkpoint, two guards lay unconscious, a pile of crystals on a nearby table. They had probably been gambling when Spock passed this way. *Well done!* she congratulated him without seeking to touch his mind. No use in drawing out their farewell. Grabbing a cloak from an open locker—if these fools had been under her command, she would have put them on report—Saavik wrapped it around herself to provide a safely military appearance until she could discard the cloak, the praetor's weapons, and anything else that was of Romulus.

What else? Did she need money? Saavik had no false scruples about appropriating the guards' money, or even that of the praetor if it were necessary.

Saavik bared her teeth at the night and turned her back on the praetor's mansion. Hailing ground transportation, she rode down into the city, then changed, rode, and changed again, stopping about half a kilometer from the Customs Hall. Discarding the warrior's cloak, she burned it to ash with the disruptor, then threw the weapon down before the Guard could come. Another clue.

Saavik produced her identification disk and held her breath through emigration processing, then strode as rapidly as she dared to her ship.

As Saavik activated the ship's hatch, she heard long, measured steps. A flash of illogical joy erupted: What if Spock had followed her? Whirling, she reached out to touch him through their bond—

—then saw, instead, the one-eyed centurion whom she had met on landing.

"Lady Evaste!" he gasped.

A shout from him now could summon reinforcements. Her ID would not stand up to any serious investigation.

If I kill, I will go mad. And I do not wish to kill, not him.

"Oh no . . ." he muttered and drew closer, holding out his one hand.

Saavik shrank back, blood fever overwhelming logic, telling her: Male. Outsider. Unacceptable. If he came any nearer, she would attack. She drew the praetor's knife, and sanity returned, making her hold it not as a trained warrior but as Evaste might, uncertain of her grip. The fine blade shimmered in the dim light of the port's night watch.

The centurion took a wary step back. "Lady . . ."

She shook her head, warning him off. "I have to get offworld. Let me go. Please let me go." She kept enough of her wits to let her voice shake with seeming terror and shock.

"You poor thing," he said, and lowered his hand as if he realized why she might dread being touched. Saavik caught a glimpse of herself reflected in the battered side of her tiny ship. Her hair was wild, her eyes were wild, and her lips still trembled from the aftermath of her parting from Spock. A spasm of desire shot through her at the thought of him, and she shuddered as the blood fire rose. Her eyes were flame. Her blood was flame. If this outsider touched her, she would turn to ash.

"Let me see your identification," the centurion ordered, standing back. "Set it on the deck."

How very strange: She glared at him, yet he was not consumed by the fires she felt darting from her eyes. . . .

No. Think. Be logical.

As logical as she could be just now. Still holding the praetor's blade, Saavik set out first the disk, then the transponder, telling him, "I was legally cleared for takeoff."

"Scans showed you carried a weapon. I said I'd deal with it. Give me the knife, lady." A touch more gently, he added, "Set it down, if you will not hand it to me."

She set down the blade, and he, moving very slowly, picked it up. Pity made his remaining eye too bright. "An Honor Blade and a fine one," he murmured, searching the knife for owner's marks.

Then he stiffened in sudden stunned realization. "Evaste, did you take this from . . ."

Saavik made herself look down as if ashamed.

In the next moment, she forced herself not to raise both eyebrows in appreciation: Some of the words the old man was using were not only obscure but viciously inventive. "Why did I even let you through Customs?" he groaned. "One-Eye, they call me. Blind! Blind and foolish. Night and day, I wish I had not listened to those young men, so sure, so damnably sure of themselves. Those aristocratic oafs. And now look . . ."

She could see from the pain in his face how deeply he regretted that he had not acted on his first impulse and sent back offworld a lady who had played for stakes too high for her. "Please," she whispered. "Just let me go."

The centurion put her ID disk down. "I can get you offworld and through the Boundary without trouble, but only on conditions."

"What else?" she asked, then broke off because her voice had nearly betrayed her. "What must I do now?"

"Promise me three things. And swear by the Eagle."

Damn! "Name them." She let her voice quaver as Evaste's might have.

"You will not retreat into the Final Honor. You may not believe me now," he added, very gently, "but people do survive what you've been through, yes, and go on to build themselves decent lives." She could practically sense his thoughts, male and misguided but well-meant: *Women live through these things. If she can only get through the first few nights, she will survive.* "So," he continued, "you will promise me you will give yourself a chance."

"What else?" she asked.

"You will go straight home."

The irony was enough to almost make her weep. This time the quaver in her voice was quite real. "And the third condition?"

"That you plan no vengeance on the Empire. You *will* swear that on the Eagle." He pointed to the representation of the great blue and green bird-of-prey on the wall over their heads.

It was not vengeance, Saavik thought, to stop dishonor. Here was a Romulan centurion who had a wife, children he loved, and he was risking their future to help a woman he had seen only once. She suspected that he would claim the Final Honor himself rather than support a sneak attack on other people's children.

Honor still did remain in the Empire. Just because she had never seen it as a child did not mean it did not exist even here. She hated knowing this, but like any hard lesson, it was worth the learning.

"By the Eagle," she whispered. If Spock respected it, if his friend Commander Charvanek reverenced it—and if this veteran, battered as he was, could still swear by it—it was worth a promise.

The centurion removed her ID from his reader, then set it down again. As she bent to snatch it up, he saluted her.

"Safe return, lady. May the fates be kinder than they have been." His scarred face twisted in what she realized was a smile. "I know it seems impossible just now. But you'll turn out just fine."

She could imagine him twenty, thirty years ago, assuring his ship's "eaglets," some of them younger than she had been on her trainee cruise, that they'd do well, they'd survive, they'd turn out just fine if they worked hard and trusted him.

Had they? Would she? "Your name," she cried suddenly, "what is your name? Give me some term of honor by which to remember you."

"I am Hasmonak," said the former centurion. "Life to the Emperor."

He saluted her, stiff-backed and proud, the remnant of the warrior he'd been. Her vision suddenly blurring, Saavik activated the tiny ship's hatch, and thrust herself into its security. Seat and schematics were blessedly familiar, and clearance came promptly.

Moments later, Saavik was in space.

Leaving Spock in the snare that was the Romulan Empire.

Leaving Spock, and in him all that was her life.

FIFTEEN

KI BARATAN, ROMULUS, DAYS 6 AND 7, SECOND WEEK OF TASMEEN, 2344

It was very late when Spock made his way back to Charvanek's estate. The last of Romulus' moons had set, and the air was still and cool enough to make him shiver. How could the first settlers have endured so sharp a change in climate? Or had they just been so thankful after the long journey to find twin worlds with breathable atmosphere and tolerable gravity that all else had not mattered?

At least the chill was cooling his blood, calming his thoughts—

Thoughts of Saavik, so beautiful, so wondrously beautiful—

So lost to him.

As, Spock reminded himself fiercely, he would be lost if he did not concentrate on the here-and-now. At least it was a touch simpler *to* concentrate now, without her presence so tantalizingly close. . . .

No. He would not think of her. Of them. Of anything but completing what he had come to Romulus to do!

Charvanek had given him the proper codes by which to gain entry through the outer gates. Within, the gardens were a mass of black, though Spock did not doubt that they were also a mass of sensors. Just because Charvanek didn't wish a blaze of thief-deterring light didn't mean she would take risks. Let him make one wrong step, and there would be a blaring of alarms—at least.

But Spock stole silently along without mishap. He had, he realized, become rather adept at slipping through shadows, and thought with the faintest touch of irony that Jim Kirk would have been amused.

So now, here was the mansion. Spock keyed in the proper code, then slipped inside, wincing at the creaking of door and floor. Charvanek—

—was awake, sitting there wrapped in a silky blue robe, watching him. For a moment, the Fires flared up within him, unbidden and unwelcome—then faded again at the sight of the disruptor pistol in her hand.

"I could hear you," she said, voice and face utterly without expression. The quick, ridiculous thought flashed through his mind, *So much for a career as a thief.* "I assume," Charvanek added, "that your goal is political, not personal."

But then she paused, considering, and her gaze softened ever so slightly. *"Akhh,"* she said softly. "Is that the way of it?"

Putting the pistol aside, Charvanek got smoothly to her feet. "Your blood burns," she murmured. "We are not so long sundered from the Mother World that I do not know it. You . . . may not survive to see your home."

Spock barely shrugged.

Charvanek frowned at his acceptance. "And if you go mad?"

"Then I must not let myself go mad."

"Ah, Spock . . ." She drew closer, the folds of her silken robe whispering softly together. "We are allies. And, I hope, friends." It was said with infinite gentleness. *With pity,* Spock thought. She wore some subtle, barely sweet scent, she was warm and alive and asking, "May a friend . . ."

139

Spock held up a hand, stopping her before she could say something from which there would be no drawing back. "Long ago, another friend touched me in just that wise." His voice was harsh with strain. "Saavik. I have just sent her off. She, too, does not expect to survive." How could she, kept apart from her bondmate and knowing she had only a scant chance of reaching Vulcan? "I cannot dishonor her sacrifice by surviving it."

"Ahh . . ." It was the softest of pitying sighs.

Spock looked at her, not daring to move, remembering how he had once desired her, knowing how he still desired her and would, he thought, even without the urging of the Fires. "Regret," he said, almost gently, and meant it for them both, "is useless."

"And you," Charvanek agreed almost brusquely, "are wiser than I." She reached out and briefly caught his arm in a warrior's strong, passionless greeting. "Wait."

She disappeared into another room, from which she reappeared in a remarkably short time, dressed now in full uniform. "Report, Spock. What have you learned?"

It was the Romulan commander who spoke, the crisp tones allowing for nothing as weak as passion. *Thank you,* Spock thought. *Thank you for the return to sanity.*

Swiftly, leaving out all but the essential data, he told her, "The praetor has already dispatched his fleet to attack the civilian Klingon colony at Narendra III."

"There?" Charvanek erupted. "There are almost no warriors in that outpost, nothing but women, children, helpless elders— Dralath cannot possibly be unaware of that. Even for him, such an attack would be obscene!"

"Nevertheless, that is his plan. And he further plans to use Narendra III, once he has secured it . . ." He hesitated, wondering if he should tell her what, as a loyal Romulan, she would surely not regret—no. She was his ally. And honorable. "As," Spock continued, "a staging point for an assault on the Federation's

Melville Colony. From there, he can strike deeper into the heart of the Federation itself."

He stopped, watching her. Charvanek's smile was sharp and thin, utterly without humor. "What, did you think I would rejoice?" she asked. "Yes, the Federation is no friend of Romulus—but only a fool welcomes a sudden return to chaos! And does Dralath believe that chaos would stop dead at the edge of the Empire, most courteously leaving us all untouched? Or that once he breaches your Neutral Zone, the Federation will not return the favor?"

"It would appear so."

"Damn him. He dishonors us all." It was said with cold rage. Biting off each word, Charvanek continued, "I will, no doubt, be called to some form of briefing, all lies and wasted time, tomorrow—no, curse it," she added, glancing out the window, "not tomorrow, today."

"We have two point five hours before dawn," Spock began. "Time enough—"

"For me to get to my ship!" Charvanek sprang to her feet, pacing fiercely. "The fleet has a sizable head start, but they will be running cloaked . . . draining speed. If *Honor Blade* goes uncloaked . . . engines at full . . ."

"There are seven warbirds," Spock reminded her.

" 'The greater the odds, the greater the honor,' " she flung over her shoulder as she all but attacked a computer console, keying in figures with Vulcan speed. "Yes! It can be done—*Honor Blade* will head off the fleet. Turn it if we can. If not . . ."

We fight. The unspoken words seemed to echo.

Another few keystrokes, and Charvanek turned to Spock, eyes fierce. "I have just put my crew on alert. I will—"

"You will first, I trust, get me to the Imperial Palace. While you intercept the fleet, I must meet with the emperor."

"Ha, yes!"

She sprang to her feet, belting on her disruptor pistol. "Emperor Shiarkiek is far from the feeble-wit our praetor thinks him. If Fortune—or blind luck—is with us, my kinsman will countermand Dralath's orders, or send the recall order after me. Let it be so!"

They sped to the Imperial Palace in a small, silent, two-passenger vehicle.

Ahead, a great building loomed out of the night: the palace, without a doubt, featureless in the dim light.

Charvanek pulled over into shadow and stopped the engine. "We dare drive no closer, or risk detection."

Spock came sharply alert. "We are being followed."

They waited tensely.

"Subcommander Ruanek!" Charvanek exclaimed. "What are you doing here?"

"Commander Charvanek!" Ruanek erupted. "I was on my way to you. Saavik is missing!"

"No," Spock began, but Ruanek continued, unheeding:

"I've been hunting her in every possible place, thinking who'd be interested in her and her gene splicing, the praetor, the emperor, but she's gone! Kharik must have stolen her away and—"

"Heed me. Saavik has not been 'stolen away' like some prize. She has escaped on her own, under no one's will but her own."

"But she—you—I don't know what you're doing here, but—" He threw up a hand in surrender. "I'm already absent from duty without my patron's permission, and Kharik is probably already reporting that fact. But what can I do to help?"

"Follow us," Charvanek snapped. "Guard our backs. We've made more than sufficient noise as it is. I'm amazed that a whole patrol hasn't already come to—oh, hells!" Spock, Charvanek, and Ruanek ducked into cover behind a fold of the wall—

Just in time.

"Guards," Ruanek whispered. "Praetor's guards."

They were an arrogant lot in their stark, glittering, metallic uniforms, secure in their employer's power. Their leader, a brash-faced youngish centurion, held up a hand to stop his men.

"If I am seen, they'll hold me for questioning," Charvanek

whispered. "I'll arrange a diversion before I beam up to my ship. They will be so busy investigating that your escape will go unnoted." She nodded to Spock, her eyes warmly eloquent, then saluted Ruanek with a quick, "Life to the Empire!" and ran back toward the groundcar. Spock could feel Ruanek tense as the patrol's centurion surveyed the ground. Let the officer pull out a scanner, and they'd either have to make a run for it or try their chances against the praetor's forces.

Then, with a curt gesture, the centurion motioned his squad onward. Spock closed his eyes in what he had to admit was relief. The place at his side where Charvanek had stood felt unguarded.

Now he had only Ruanek to aid him. Would that be enough?

Such speculation was illogical. Quickly revising his plans, Spock turned to Ruanek as, years ago, he would have turned to one of his own crew.

"I remember," he began, "that you like to gamble."

"Sometimes," Ruanek said warily. "What . . . did you have in mind?"

Just then, he reminded Spock of one of the subcommander's beloved horses—one that might, wild-eyed with alarm, bolt at any moment.

"What the commander ordered," Spock told him calmly. "A meeting with your Underground. And," he added with deliberate drama, "with your candidate—for praetor."

The next moment, the ground rocked as Charvanek's ground car exploded—her promised diversion.

They ran.

SIXTEEN

UNDER KI BARATAN, DAY 7, SECOND WEEK OF TASMEEN, 2344

"This way," Ruanek urged.

Spock glanced about in growing . . . was it illogical for him to feel uneasiness? Surely not. Granted, Ruanek had so far proven himself quite trustworthy—but if Spock himself could wear a false face, so could the subcommander. And Romulans thought nothing of lying.

Nonsense. Illogical, indeed. Ruanek would never play him false.

And yet . . . they had escaped the palace grounds, which swarmed now with security, investigating the "incident" Charvanek had staged. They had long since left the better part of Ki Baratan, and now made their way through a narrow, convoluted maze of streets, some of them little wider than alleys. No, some of them actually *were* alleys, lined with blank stone walls—the chipped and weathered backs of buildings—and smelling objectionably of what Spock thought was a disconcertingly poor Romulan sanitation system.

Not that the streets themselves were much more agreeable. The buildings were crowded together, one right after another, plain red or gray stone façades with few attempts at differentiation or ornamentation save for the predictable posters—mostly weatherworn or deliberately defaced—of Praetor Dralath. Judging from the condition of those posters, Spock thought, Dralath's guards rarely bothered patrolling here.

No greenery here, either, not the slightest hint of a garden. Nothing but stone walls and stone pavements, and the faint scent of boiled vegetables, the diet of poverty, that seemed the same in every poor section of every world.

The hour was still too early for many people to be about: a few dull-eyed workers off to the spaceport docks, or one of the ubiquitous old ladies with brooms who each seemed determined to sweep her patch of pavement into submission.

Bah, you let yourself grow fanciful.

Better that, he retorted to himself, *than alarmed.*

For this would, indeed, be such a perfect place for a trap. So many false turns, so many strange alleys—was Ruanek trying to lose him? Spock had no illusions as to what would happen to a Vulcan alone here.

But, he thought, feeling the blood fire stirring, *if it comes to that, I will not be the only one to die.*

"This way," Ruanek said suddenly.

Spock moved to block his way. "Is this a trick, Ruanek? Are you planning to betray me?"

The Romulan's surprise seemed genuine. "No! I would never be so dishonorable! I owe you my *life!*"

He stepped around Spock and went through the ritual—*the cliché,* Spock thought—of rapping a particular pattern on a barred door.

The door opened. Ruanek exchanged quick words with an unseen someone inside, then turned to Spock. "Follow me. And—you *can* trust me."

"I must," Spock murmured dryly.

He followed Ruanek down a long, narrow stairway smelling of rock and damp earth and lit only sporadically by daylight filtering in through cracks in the rock overhead, and was very much aware of being watched with every step. But no one interfered, no one even spoke as they reached the bottom, a floor of natural rock. Ruanek led him on through a new maze, this one a network of tunnels that might, Spock thought, have mostly been ancient lava tubes deliberately linked over the years. Possibly the original settlers, still figuratively looking over their shoulders, had felt the need for such a hiding place.

Others were using it as such now. A wary, very mixed group of Romulans was gathering in a large cavern reachable by no fewer than four tunnels and two stairways—one of only four steps leading down from a narrow, sloping tunnel, the other a true stair leading down from an unseen upper level.

Like the communal lair of Vulcan keerik, *or a Terran rabbit warren. No danger of being trapped in any one spot.*

No chance of easy defense, either, of course.

A mixed group of Romulans, indeed, judging from their clothing and the way they carried themselves: the robes of a scholar, the uniform of a centurion . . . nobles, techs, and intellectuals, young and old, men and women. Not all that many for a true revolution, but that they should come together at all said something very powerful about the genuine discontent at least in Ki Baratan.

As the capital goes, so goes the culture, or so the Federation has often learned.

Out of the crowd, a blunt voice called to him, "Who are you?"

Before Spock could answer, Ruanek cut in, "This is the Academician Symakhos of Bardat."

"Like the Pit he is!" the voice shot back. A stocky man in scholar's robes pushed his way to the front. *"I'm* from Bardat— and damned if I ever saw any Symakhos there!"

"True," Spock said, raising his voice just firmly enough to be heard clearly over the murmurs, skilled as he was in the vocal tricks of the ambassador's trade. "I am, indeed, not Symakhos. That fiction was necessary for a time. For I am not," he continued levelly, "a Romulan. I am, in fact, a Vulcan."

If the murmurs had been fierce before, they were almost a true uproar now. Spock held up a commanding arm and said, not quite shouting, into the chaos, "Now, is this *logical?*"

That startled most of them into momentary silence, and Spock continued, a father scolding noisy children *(And thank you, Father, for the memory)*, "Where are we? Well? Where?"

The quicker ones got his point instantly. "Under the city," they muttered. "Under Ki Baratan."

"Precisely. If you continue to make such a noise, we shall have the city down about our ears."

"But you," a woman in a centurion's uniform protested, "you tricked us. How do we know you aren't also a traitor to your own people?"

Ruanek hotly cut in, "I *know* this man. I . . . cannot name him," he added with a wary glance at Spock, "but he is honest! My life and honor, and the honor of my family, answer for him."

"Exactly," someone snapped.

It was Narviat, descending the longer stairway with calculated drama. "Tell me, Symakhos-who-is-not, does *she* know of this matter? Or have you tricked her as well?"

He meant Charvanek, of course. Spock, who suspected that Narviat would soon, if indeed he had not already, puzzle out his true identity, said flatly, "I have done, and will continue to do, nothing to harm her life or honor. And as for anything else, you may recall a matter of some years back, along the Neutral Zone. Then, it was this young man alone who upheld Romulan honor when others sought to exploit a criminal madman in destroying a world. His honor speaks for itself."

A flicker of comprehension crossed the handsome, well-schooled face: Narviat had clearly heard—and not approved—of Romulus' role in the Obsidian affair.

"As," he murmured, "does your own honor."

Ah, he does realize who I am. No danger there. Being the politician he is, Narviat will say nothing that might in any way implicate himself.

The others were hardly so calm. Arguments were breaking out again, and a flash of Fire-born anger erupted within Spock. "So does the honor," he continued, aware of how his eyes must be blazing with the blood fever, "of your praetor, of Dralath who attempted to debauch and destroy a woman—and who, to impress her, revealed his plans. He has sent out your empire's fleet not against some worthy foe, not some great and terrible peril to the Romulan people—but children. Unarmed women. Crippled elders. Unarmed civilians!"

Over the renewed storm of murmurings, Spock asked, "How many of you know of Narendra III? How many know of that unarmed colony—"

"Klingons," a man began tentatively, and Spock whirled to him, finger stabbing at him, making him shrink back in surprise.

"Klingons," Spock agreed. "But unarmed *women*, unarmed *children*—open war can be honorable, but where is honor here? Open war can be honorable—but such a cowardly attack, such a sneak attack, can not!"

He had struck home with all of them with that—

All but one. Spock met the gaze of the still-skeptical Narviat, and fought down a new surge of rage. That his word should be doubted, and by a—

By a politician, he told himself, *and one who has every right to be skeptical.*

But there was no time for subtlety. "I have heard a great deal about establishing my trustworthiness," Spock said to them all, but looked directly at Narviat. "It seems reasonable that you establish yours as well."

Narviat quirked an eyebrow at him. "Brave words from the only Vulcan on Romulus. Or are you going to say that we are *all* Romulans? Or, as in the old tales of the Sundering, Vulcans?"

"Words are easy," Spock retorted. "We can trade barbs until the praetor's ships attack, or we can act now."

I must know what you are. I must know if you are better than Dralath.

"Wait, wait," Ruanek broke in. "You both wish proof of each other? We all know that Vulcans have amazing mental disciplines, such as the—the 'mind-meld.'" He stumbled over the unfamiliar term. "Use it now, so that you both may know the worth of the other."

Ruanek, Spock thought, had some very elevated ideas of what Vulcans could and could not do! Narviat, studying him, said with just the faintest undertone of wry amusement, "The subcommander has a spirit of fire. But I have heard from no less a personage than our emperor that Vulcans do, indeed, have a way of knowing if a man lies—although it is also said that Vulcans cannot lie."

"Much is said," Spock told him flatly.

"Yet Vulcans do have such a discipline—that, I believe. Nothing magical about it; this is merely one of the skills we have forgotten. And are you skilled in this 'mind-meld'? Yes? Then let us take the test, here and now."

It would, Spock thought, be the most dangerous mind-meld he had ever attempted, what with the Fires in his blood barely quelled by meditation, and his judgment might well be impaired. But he could hardly refuse.

"We must be in physical contact," he told Narviat, moving to his side, the others edging back out of his path. "It should not be unduly uncomfortable, but whatever occurs, the link must not be broken by others."

Narviat nodded. Spock put his hands, fingers spread, on Narviat's temples, feeling the man hold resolutely still, then began:

"My mind to your mind . . ."

And . . .

His own mind fought him, the blood fever tearing at his will, trying to attack the other consciousness, the other male—

No. Control. Partition off emotion. Partition off mere animal instincts. Narviat must know nothing of that. See only Narviat, feel only Narviat . . .

But the Fires raged, there below the surface, distorting his sight, his will, his mind, and it was too soon since he had forced the mind-meld on the praetor, too soon since he and Saavik had been linked—

Suddenly Spock had to break off, staggering back, struggling not to pant, fighting for self-control.

"That," Narviat said after a shaken moment, "was . . . interesting."

"Decidedly."

All he had gained, Spock thought, all he had read for certain, was—nothing specific. Yes, Narviat was ambitious and, in his own honorable way, ruthless—no surprise there, not from a member of the Imperial family who'd survived so far. He was also far less venal and warmongering—more sensible, was it?—than Dralath.

And that, Spock thought, *will have to do.*

Particularly since, judging from Narviat's expression, he had picked up a fair amount of emotional backlash that had left him . . . quite bewildered.

"I trust," Spock said laconically, "that doubts have been erased?"

A quick nod from Narviat. "If we move," he told them all, "we must move swiftly. For your sake," he added to Spock, "as well as our own." Glancing around the group, catching each man's or woman's gaze with his own, Narviat added, "What we are about to do could mean our deaths. For we do not seek merely to recall the fleet; what we are about to do is nothing less than plot the overthrow of the current government. You cannot be surprised by this; this next step was inevitable. But there can be no turning back, no retreat save death." A well-timed pause. "Are you all agreed?"

Nods. Murmurs.

"Then: To Dralath's defeat!"

"To Dralath's defeat!"

The shout from them all was warily muffled, but it still, Spock thought, sounded alarmingly loud. But Narviat was already pointing out possibilities with the air of a man who has thought them over many a time and worked most of them out.

"We cannot risk anything as chancy as straight assassination. Dralath is never seen in public without a guard, and there is almost certainly some form of body armor under that pretty uniform."

"Armor," a man shouted, "can be pierced."

"It can, yes," Narviat agreed. "But what if you miss? Wound Dralath or miss him altogether, and you have ended any chance of getting close enough to him again. Hit the wrong target, and Dralath has a lovely chance to turn the victim into a martyr—'He died for his praetor.' "

That started some uneasy murmurings. Narviat held up a hand. "Wait, there is worse. Miss and *be captured*—I don't have to spell out what happens to the rest of us then."

"And assassinations," Spock added, watching Narviat closely, "tend not to lead to an orderly transfer of power."

"How nicely you put that! No, they do not." For an instant, what could only be genuine concern for the people flashed in Narviat's eyes. "I would not wish civil war on Romulus. Not again. But," he added briskly, "there are other methods."

Spock straightened. "Someone," he said very softly, "is watching. Keep talking."

As Narviat began a bright pattern of words, Spock edged subtly away into shadow, as though weariness from the mind-meld had suddenly caught up with him, as though hunting a place to rest . . . hunting . . . Across the cavern, he could see Ruanek doing the same thing, edging up the taller stairway for a better view . . .

A shout. A flurry of motion and—

"Kharik!" Ruanek erupted. "Watch out—he's trying—no, you don't!"

Kharik, snarling, was trying to make a break for it, clearly meaning to flee back to Avrak with the tasty news that Ruanek was a traitor. But Ruanek, leaping off the stairway, blocked his escape. Kharik whipped out a disruptor pistol, but before he could fire, Spock caught his arm, tearing the weapon from his grip.

The two cousins stood staring at each other, years of mutual hatred in their eyes.

No, Spock thought, *not here, not now.*

The others seemed to expect a fight, closing in around the cousins. "No," Spock began. "This is not—"

"Honor," Ruanek snapped. "I call challenge on Kharik, he of no worth."

"And I," Kharik snarled, "accept challenge from Ruanek, he who is *nothing!*"

"To the death," they said as one, clearly reciting a ritual chant. "We challenge and accept this combat to the death."

"But this is the height of illogic!" Spock protested. *Never mind that duels are, in themselves, illogical; these people won't accept that fact.* "This is a terrible time for a duel."

Time? There is no time!

"Honor," the Romulans told him in a rush. "This is a matter of honor!"

"But we are right below the city! Anyone might overhear!"

They shrugged that off. And even Narviat, whom Spock had expected to be more logical, said, "It must be. A Vulcan cannot understand our ways."

I cannot understand what is nothing short of human illogic! No, no, humans would never be so insane!

But he had no choice but to yield to the situation as the Romulans backed up, clearing enough space for a combat ring. Ruanek, his eyes shadowed, came to military attention before Spock.

"I ask honor of you. I ask that you be my second."

It was clearly meant as a great compliment. "If it must be," Spock said reluctantly. "Yes."

Not surprisingly, no one wanted to second Kharik. After a few moments of awkwardness, Narviat sighed, muttered something about "Honor must. I will do it."

Madness. They are all quite insane.

As, then, were his own ancestors. He was, Spock realized with the smallest of chills, seeing a virtual window into Vulcan's bloody past. "If you must fight, fight. But above all, be *quiet!* I remind you again, these tunnels are perilously close to the surface, and any sound of fighting will alert the city guards."

"Agreed," Ruanek snapped. "My enemy, what weapons shall we use for the kill?"

It was a ritual request, since all Kharik had left to him was his blade. "Knives," he said, as though it really had been a choice.

"So be it."

The combatants circled, each with knife in right hand, their blades glinting, their eyes glinting, each watching for an opening, waiting—

A lunge, a blur of action almost too quick for the eye to follow—

And they'd drawn back again. A streak of stark green blood marked Ruanek's upper arm—not, Spock noted with uncontrolled relief, his knife arm—and green blood trickled down Kharik's cheek. Nothing serious, not yet, but small, cumulative wounds could yet take their toll. . . .

Another lunge, quick thrust, quick parry, forearm blocking forearm—

Separate again. No damage done this time. Circling, circling . . . not a sound to the fight save the hiss of the duelists' breath—

Lunge! Ruanek feinted to the left, took Kharik with him, risked crippling as he blocked Kharik's knife with his left arm, hissing as the blade tore a jagged rip through flesh. Continuing the motion, he twisted, knife hand forcing forward in a short, brutal underhand stroke, up under the ribs with such force that the breath left Kharik's lungs in an audible groan—

Ruanek leaped back, panting, blood dripping from the blade—

blood surging as well from Kharik, stabbed in the chest but still living. A collective hiss rose from the crowd, another from Spock, the metallic reek of blood filling his nostrils, the savagery of the Romulans filling his mind, the blood, the blood fever, rising, blazing—

Kharik lurched forward, knife reaching for his cousin. Ruanek dodged sideways, blade level—

And Kharik's own movement impaled his throat on the point. He choked, blood spouting, then convulsed so strongly he pulled free, staggering, the knife falling from his hand. One last surge at Ruanek—

Then he fell, twitching, writhing—and at last lay still. A few of the crowd, the scholars used only to verbal violence, turned away, retching. The rest stood silent as Ruanek warily checked the body for any last sign of life.

There was none. He straightened, gasping out, "It is done," his face torn between ecstasy and a strange . . . emptiness.

Of course, Spock thought, the Fires blazing. *For all the hatred, they had been part of each other's existences. Ruanek has just cut a piece of his life away.*

For a time, he could not frame another thought, could only force his will inward, inward, seeking the coolness, the tranquillity . . .

Control. Logic. Logic is the cornerstone, not violence, not blood—logic.

Logic and civilization. As Ruanek stood over the bloody corpse, struggling for breath and self-control, Spock gradually dared surface back to the world around him. The struggle for self-control had taken little real time; no one seemed to have noticed how he had suddenly gone blank.

He said dryly, "I trust that Romulan honor has been satisfied. Now, may we go on to the matter at hand? Overthrowing a government is no small task."

Narviat's laugh was clearly forced. "Indeed. First . . ." Ruanek was hesitating over the body. "What?" Narviat asked.

"The ritual . . . I *am* his kinsman. Was."

Spock and Narviat exchanged wry glances. "Honor," the latter murmured, just for Spock's ears, "can be a genuine . . . nuisance sometimes."

Narviat moved to the corpse's side, set the outflung limbs more or less straight, said what sounded to Spock like a singularly perfunctory prayer, then added, all but snapping his fingers in impatience, "Crystals."

Ruanek fumbled in his small money pouch, came up with two crystals, which Narviat snatched and placed on the corpse's eyes.

"May his journey to the next world be a swift one. Now, you and you," pointing to two of the burlier men, "see if you can't find some nice, tranquil final resting place for the less than dear departed, someplace his patron's guards won't locate too quickly."

Ah yes, Spock thought, *the consummate politician, indeed. A careful mix of concern and utter pragmatism.*

But, like it or not, that was what often made the best politicians.

And, just possibly, it was the mix that would create the Romulan Empire's next praetor.

SEVENTEEN

NEUTRAL ZONE AND FEDERATION SPACE, STARDATE
UNKNOWN, YEAR 2344

"Personal log, Stardate . . ." But she couldn't seem to remember the exact date. "I am Saavik of Vulcan, Commander, *U.S.S. Armstrong*. This is my report of an unauthorized mission into the Romulan Empire for which I assume entire personal and independent responsibility."

Saavik paused. To the best of her knowledge, she had not been expelled from Starfleet. Yet.

"Course heading . . ." She read in the coordinates, adding, "Departure from the spaceport at Ki Baratan, bound through the Neutral Zone to the Klingon civilian base Narendra III."

Saavik checked her instruments. In ordinary times, she would have found the opportunity to fly the lively, unpredictable little craft highly agreeable. One thruster was decidedly out of alignment, and the ship had needed nursing along after liftoff.

It still did. If she concentrated, she should be able to properly adjust the matter/antimatter feed rate, gain more efficiency out of the ship's computers.

If she concentrated . . .

A sudden insistent *beep beep beep* brought her sharply alert, realizing that it was the navigation computer's emergency signal warning her against a change of headings. What—she had been staring into the blinking lights of her instrument panels as if meditating on nothing at all!

Hastily, Saavik checked the navigational settings. The port at Ki Baratan had set her course; diverging from it while in the Neutral Zone could result in her ship's being boarded or destroyed.

Open the log, Saavik. Document the homeworlds' planetary defenses.

What was wrong with this wretched ship's autocontrols? Had the Barolians cheated her? She had a mission worth dying for, but damned if she was going to die because of defective instrumentation!

For at least the fifth time, Saavik ran diagnostics. Normal, normal . . . the lights were blinking steadily . . .

Once again, the navcomp's shrilled distress signals jolted her awake.

On course to Vulcan. Again.

Saavik rubbed a hand over her face. Couldn't blame the shipboard computers. It was all too clear what was happening.

Sometimes, meditation could overcome the effects of *Pon farr.* For her, meditation seemed only to set *her* on autopilot.

If only Spock had agreed to escape with me, we could have put this damnable hulk on autopilot for Vulcan, and right now be . . .

No. Definitely no. Dreaming of Spock, especially dreams like those, would make her go mad even faster.

So be it. She was bonded to a member of one of the most ancient and honorable families on Vulcan. She had an obligation to at least try to set the record straight.

Talk, Saavik. Talk.

She heard her voice grow fast and shrill as she gabbled another log entry. If Captain Uhura's people ever wanted to break into the

157

praetor's mansion, they would know everything she did about his security. About Dralath. Court gossip that Starfleet anthropologists would prize; rumors about the Underground; details on every person in the court—including the emperor—with whom she had come in contact. Like that one-eyed centurion and the implications for Counterintelligence of his lack of medical treatment.

Could she fly free yet? Not quite.

No. Wake up. There is one thing more you must do. Damn you, you're still Starfleet! Wake up!

A timed-release message, Saavik decided.

"Saavik of Vulcan, Commander in the Starfleet of the United Federation of Planets, to all ships. Seven Romulan warbirds approach Narendra III with hostile intent. At maximum warp, assume attack in . . ." She struggled to calculate the time, and abandoned any attempt at precision. "In approximately three hours after the Romulan fleet exits the Neutral Zone." She would have to trust that the Federation—or the Klingons—had ships on patrol. "A second stealth attack is projected on Melville Colony. Warning. Warning. Warning."

She added every distress code she could remember in at least ten languages, then set it to broadcast at a later, programmed interval—whether or not she was conscious—and turned back to her personal log. Captain Uhura had warned her that she was on her own. Was there any way to explain what really did look like espionage, defection, treachery, an act of war, or any number of acts that could not only get one court-martialed, but executed?

Why not take ship for Talos IV, while you're at it? Get that automatic death sentence.

Was the ship's climate control malfunctioning again? She had set it for Vulcan normal, but she was so cold . . . no, she was burning, burning . . . oddly difficult to distinguish between the two . . . Saavik shut her eyes, reaching for body sense, knowing she was too far gone to enter a restful trance.

There went the cursed alarm again! She slammed her fist down on the arm of her chair, denting it.

The pain she could no longer deny alerted her. The problem wasn't the navigational computer. Each time she slept or, to be more accurate, when she blanked out, her survival instincts, honed so fiercely in childhood and sharpened still more by *Pon farr,* determined to get her home. To Vulcan.

If I had any doubts about which half of my genome was dominant . . . I suppose I truly am Vulcan after all.

She turned the cabin temperature up again. After a time, she ceased shivering. . . . It would be easy to just slip away, to acknowledge that she wasn't going to survive. . . .

She had spent her life fighting that knowledge.

Her will was on already on file. It would be logical to prepare her last messages while she was still almost sane.

"To Captain Howes, *U.S.S. Armstrong.*" Her captain had always been both professional and kind to her. If she had not outraged him past forgiveness, he would be experiencing what humans called hurt. "Forgive me," she said at last.

Now, Sarek. She closed the high, confining collar of her shipsuit and touched her hair, a futile attempt at tidiness. Spock had wanted to pull it down about her shoulders.

"To Sarek, Ambassador of Vulcan, from Saavik, Commander in Starfleet and, as he was once generous enough to call her, his daughter-in-law."

Saavik flinched from the awareness that, after her next statement, Sarek would call her a traitor.

"Sir, I give you my word by my faith and the faith of the person who means most to me in all the worlds that I have committed no treason. You have given me great honor, my father. Knowing you has enriched my life. Live long and prosper, Sarek. See that there is no war."

She attached her personal log, her navigational records, and then, impulsively, medical and navigational telemetry. Sarek of Vulcan would require complete data.

Whom else did that leave? Spock? No, she could not bear to say farewell to him!

She was too weary to sit upright. And Spock was not there to raise an eyebrow at her. Saavik slipped down in her chair until her face pressed against the metal of the equipment console. It was cool, smooth . . .

Saavik came awake with a start. Too quiet in here . . . One good scream would break the silence . . . *and leave me irrevocably mad.* Instead, she checked her course.

Finally! She was far enough from the Empire to race for Narendra III. She red-lined the engines. If they blew, at least she would have delivered her message and she would be out of torment. . . .

No. Think of Spock. How his face had lit when he first saw her on Romulus! Love had been warm in his eyes, whether he would ever admit the word or not. Memories to take into the dark.

Husband, have I done well? May we rest now?

She knew she was hallucinating when he answered her.

Soon, my wife. Just one more duty to perform.

She programmed a broadband distress call. Perhaps a Starfleet ship on patrol along the Neutral Zone would hear the ancient human cry of sheer disaster, *Mayday! Mayday!,* coming from a Barolian ship and investigate.

The fires she had kept at bay so long could no longer be resisted. Her last thought was wonder. She had survived *Pon farr* before with no difficulty at all. But she had never been bonded mind to mind before.

Or . . . in love . . .

EIGHTEEN

Rachel Garrett, captain of the *U.S.S. Enterprise,* ran a hand through chestnut hair cut short for convenience and almost allowed herself to lean back in her command chair and stretch out long legs. Then, she straightened again. Whether or not all was quiet, she was still what Starfleet slang persisted in calling a "straight arrow," and straight arrows did not, repeat not, relax on the bridge of any ship they commanded.

At least, this was not one of the "interesting times" that seemed to occupy the various *Enterprises*—from blue-water Navy to her own ship, the *Ambassador*-class NCC-1701-C.

She glanced around her bridge, then allowed herself to look out at the stars. They had drawn her ever since, as a girl, she had stayed out all night gazing up into the vast Indiana sky and promised herself she would one day be one of the people who—what were those lines from the old poem? "Slipped the surly bonds of Earth . . . and touched the face of God."

She allowed herself the smallest touch of pride. So many of the pioneers in space had been Midwesterners. From Ohio, John

Glenn, the first man from the old United States to fly an orbital mission; Neil Armstrong, the first human to walk upon the moon; Judith Resnick, of *Challenger*, for whom an entire wing of the Early Aerospace Museum at Wright-Patterson was named; and, perhaps the greatest legend of all, James T. Kirk of Iowa, captain of the first *Starship Enterprise*.

It had been their duty to serve. And their passion, as it was hers. Which didn't mean that even a captain of the *Enterprise* couldn't appreciate an interval of peace now and then.

"Captain," Lieutenant Commander Varani said suddenly, glancing up from his communications console, narrow gray-skinned face earnest, "sensors are registering a distress signal from a small craft—registration indicates a Barolian ship. Heading 65X 35Y mark 42." He paused, glancing at the human beside him, Helmsman Richard Castillo, for help. Lieutenant Castillo added, "It's signaling Mayday. In Federation Standard."

"Mayday?" Garrett echoed in astonishment. An ancient human distress call coming from a Barolian ship? "Life signs?"

Lights blossomed on the science officer's duty station.

"One occupant . . ." Commander Tholav, Andorian and soft-spoken as always, said slowly. "The basic life-form appears to be Vulcanoid, Captain, but with major anomalies."

"Yellow alert," Garrett ordered. "Patch the display through to medical."

She brought up the display from Tholav's station—life signs on scan measured against a Vulcan-norm baseline—and grimaced at the divergences. If this pilot was indeed a Vulcan, he or she was desperately ill.

Nothing's ever simple, is it?

Garrett was not about to risk taking some exotic disease—or worse, some Romulan who somehow knew "Mayday"—onto her ship, but she also had no intention of abandoning someone in genuine need of aid!

"Tractor beam on," she ordered. "We'll beam whoever it is on board and take the ship in tow. I'm not having any Trojan horses on board my ship. Or Trojan freighters. Security team to transporter room now. Sidearms. Send a medical team in decontamination gear. I'll join you there." She keyed open the bridge arms locker and chose a phaser. "Mr. Varani, get to work scanning that ship. Mr. Castillo, help him." Castillo was the best helm officer she'd ever had, but he also had a damn good tactical secondary specialization. "Commander Tholav, you have the bridge."

Three "Aye, aye's" sounded almost simultaneously.

Three men from Security awaited Garrett in the transporter room, flanking the transporter chief and Dr. Frances Stewart, the junior medical officer on board, a compact blond woman from Earth's West Virginia. Stewart's field was psychiatry—which, as she put it wryly, was why she was called in every time an alien came on board.

"Energize," the captain commanded.

Security braced. The transporter lights flickered. A column of shimmers formed on the pad, solidified into something that turned and screamed in fear, rage, and the despair of a cornered animal. It—no, she—dropped into a fighting crouch and tossed wild hair back from her face, baring her teeth in defiance, then screamed and leapt straight at the security team, long fingers curving into talons, strong arms reaching for the nearest man.

"No! Outsiders . . . *Alien!*"

Garrett fired, phaser on stun, but the woman's frenzy carried her on. "Dammit!" the captain snapped, and fired again. To her relief, this time the woman fell, still clawing toward the guards for a frantic moment before she finally lay still.

Dr. Stewart threw herself down beside the stranger, cradling the limp form in her arms. "Intraship beaming!" she shouted at the intercom. "Get us to sickbay *now*! Decontamination team to the transporter room."

Doctor and alien disappeared in a fast shimmer.

So much for my nice, peaceful cruise! Garrett thought, and signaled her bridge. "Varani, Castillo? How's the scan of the Barolian ship progressing?"

"The drive signature looks clean." That was Castillo's voice.

"And I am trying to access computer via the comm link that brought us the Mayday." That was Varani. "Doesn't look like a trap," he concluded.

"You think it's clean?"

"Captain, your pardon, but I am Ochati, not Vulcan to calculate the odds in my head. I would need further data."

"I want that ship *searched,* understand? Mr. Castillo, select your away team and assemble in the transporter room at ten hundred hours. By the time you finish, I want you to know it so well that you can even report what shipyard welded her deck-plates."

"Aye, ma'am."

"Signal if you need me. I'll be in sick bay. And Richard . . ." Garrett paused and saw the people around her grin. *Only my mother ever calls me "Richard,"* Castillo always said.

"Yes, Captain?"

This time even Garrett had to suppress a grin at the good-little-boy voice. Yes, Captain: Yes, Mother. *Mister, just you wait till you get back to this ship.* "No unnecessary risks."

"Aye, aye, Captain."

Chief Medical Officer Aristide, his thin, dark-skinned form elegant as always, was waiting for Garrett in his office. "We've got our . . . guest stabilized," he began. "Or as stable as she's going to get. Your phaser almost killed her, Captain."

Garrett ignored that. "Where is she? And, for that matter, *what* is she?"

"Where she is: We've got her in isolation. What, is another matter."

To Garrett's surprise, the doctor made no attempt to accompany her into the isolation area. She studied the medical staff hovering around the figure on the biobed: all women. Garrett caught Dr. Stewart's glance and raised an eyebrow. Stewart hurried to her.

"Captain, you remember, in the transporter room, the stranger attacked Security when she probably could have taken out either LoPresti or me, or gone straight for your throat? When we brought her round from your phaser—"

Damn, does everyone in sick bay have to blame me for protecting my crew?

"—we found out real fast that our guest here seems either to panic or go berserk in the presence of men. She took one look at Commander Aristide, screamed again, and tried to take him apart. We set up this isolation unit because, frankly, I don't think she's got the strength for another attack. Whatever is wrong," Dr. Stewart continued, "it's nothing contagious. Nothing to affect humans, at any rate."

"Amen to that. Any idea of who she is or what *is* wrong with her?"

"We're running standard ID scans. Unfortunately, her condition's deteriorating. Can't restrain her either," Dr. Stewart added, "for fear of another episode. You . . . ah . . . may want to stay back on the off chance she comes round and recognizes you from the transporter room."

"I'll take the risk." Garrett moved as quietly as she could to the biobed and looked down at the *Enterprise*-C's involuntary passenger. Vulcanoid, all right. The elegant pointed ears, the arched eyebrows, the dark, thick hair, and the skin with its green tint underlying the pallor of critical illness were all Vulcan. Unconscious, the woman's face was inhumanly serene. That, too, was Vulcan.

One of the techs, a young Bolian woman, blue skin darkening with sudden surprise, said, "Captain, we're confirming ID on her. This woman is Starfleet."

Damnation! This was getting more complicated by the moment. Starfleet personnel in a Barolian ship coming off a heading that could be traced back into the Neutral Zone?

"Her name?" Garrett asked sharply.

"I am Saavik." It was barely a whisper from the Vulcan woman.

Rousing herself with what was plainly a great effort, she opened fierce dark eyes and fixed them on Captain Garrett's face.

"I am Saavik," she repeated. "I sent a warning. Narendra. Narendra III . . . and Melville Colony . . ."

Saavik! Garrett had heard good reports of Commander Saavik, who was first officer of the *Armstrong*. The woman's long career had attracted some fairly interesting rumors. . . .

"Oh my *God*," the captain muttered under her breath as she put together some pieces of the puzzle. She pressed the Vulcan's hand, feeling it hot with fever. "We haven't heard any distress signals." Was Commander Saavik hallucinating?

"Subspace . . ." Saavik sighed. "I sent that message!" Her eyes opened again, a touch more sane, her gaze scanning her surroundings. "What ship?"

"This is the *U.S.S. Enterprise*. I am its captain, Rachel Garrett."

"Enterprise," Saavik repeated. Her gaze seemed to focus, even to brighten. Her lips parted as if she had much more to say—but then her head lolled sideways.

Stewart was instantly at Saavik's side. "Pulse is shot to hell, so fast I can barely count it. She's the one who's bonded to Ambassador Spock, isn't she? In that case . . ."

"My thought precisely, Doctor."

Even now, comparatively little was known about Vulcan biology, but ever since the days when Ambassador Spock had been Science Officer Spock of the first *Starship Enterprise, Pon farr* had been an open secret.

Then Saavik, poor woman, must have been overwhelmed while on some Federation mission. "No wonder she relaxed when I told her she was on board *Enterprise*," Garrett breathed. "She served on the first one. With James T. Kirk."

"She looks too young for that!"

"She *is* young, relatively speaking. For a Vulcan." Garrett turned back to Saavik. "We'll get you to Vulcan. Is that what you want? Is Ambassador Spock there?"

Maybe mentioning his name broke some rule of Vulcan etiquette, but at least it got Saavik's attention. She forced herself halfway up with a frantic "No!" and grabbed Captain Garrett's hand. Even now, Garrett thought, trying not to wince, that Vulcan strength could break every bone in it.

She needs the physical contact. That's right: Vulcans are touch telepaths.

"I crossed the Neutral Zone," Saavik whispered. "From court . . . at Ki Baratan . . . Romulus . . . Narendra III . . ."

Garrett listened to her story in growing horror. Oh God, no, let it be only a sick woman's hallucinations! As Saavik, exhausted, sagged back against the bed, the captain shouted across the room at the wall communicator, "Mr. Varani! Any record of transmissions? Any sign of warbirds?"

"No warbird sightings, Captain. We are beginning to receive a message, however. Timed at regular intervals. Directed at Starbase 9 and the Klingon Empire. First one should be reaching Starbase 9 . . . right about now."

"I want you to raise Captain Walker Keel. I want a reply in the next fifteen minutes. Encrypt it."

"Spock . . ." It was a heartbroken murmur from Saavik.

"While you are attempting the impossible, Mr. Varani, I want you to contact Vulcan too. Ambassador Spock, if at all possible—" If Ambassador Spock's bondmate was this ill, Garrett doubted he would be fit or willing to be seen. Still, he'd have to have some sort of confidential aide.

And Vulcan was a damn sight closer than Starbase 9.

Communications signaled from the bridge.

"Yes?" Garrett called at the wall unit.

"Piping Lieutenant Castillo through to you, ma'am."

"Castillo, any information yet?" she asked.

"Captain, I'm pulling our guest's reports out of her ship's computers. She's also left a personal log and a couple of letters. To Captain Truman Howes of the *Armstrong*. And to Sarek of Vulcan. Marked private, but I think . . ."

"Send 'em through to sickbay," Garrett ordered. "Dr. Aristide's office."

In that relative privacy, she quickly accessed the information from the Barolian ship—then sat back, a cold weight settling in the pit of her stomach.

My crew . . . oh God, my crew.

"Get back over here, Mr. Castillo," she ordered. "We may need to move in a hurry."

To Rachel Garrett's astonishment, the Vulcan who awaited her onscreen in her cabin was not some aide or even Ambassador Spock, however much the worse for wear. It was his father, the legendary and formidable Sarek, senior ambassador of Vulcan.

"Captain Garrett of the *U.S.S. Enterprise*." To her astonishment, his eyes held a hint of warmth even though they seemed to be looking at something very far off. "It has been approximately fifty-three point six of your years since I have been contacted by a captain of the *Enterprise*. How may I serve you, Captain?"

God, Garrett thought, this was one charming Vulcan! Granted, he had plenty of practice. He and his son probably knew humans better than any other Vulcans alive. "I am looking for Ambassador Spock. Do you know where he is? Can you deliver a message to him?" That ought to leave Sarek enough of an "out" so he would not have to speak directly of *Pon farr*.

"My assumption," Sarek said, "is that Spock remains on Oriki."

Garrett stared at the Vulcan, the beginning of a truly horrible surmise forming in her mind.

"What is it, Captain?"

Sarek's glance was far too perceptive. "Not two hours ago," she began cautiously, "we rescued a very ill woman, who has been identified as Commander Saavik of Vulcan. She left a message for you."

Sarek went absolutely motionless, the warmth in his eyes disappearing. "Transmit immediately," he snapped, the calculated urbanity of his voice gone.

As he absorbed the message without waiting for it to be decoded into ordinary Vulcan script, Garrett saw what she never expected to see: a Vulcan desolate and terrified. Now, Sarek looked every day of his age, which had to be somewhere close to two hundred.

"Captain, are there any other data? I would examine them."

No point in explaining that Commander Saavik's reports should be classified; Sarek had helped preserve the Federation's direst secrets long before Captain Garrett's birth. She transmitted Saavik's navigational records, her medical files, her personal log. Sarek's proud carriage sagged more with each report.

"Thank you for contacting me," he said at last. "I am much in your debt, as is the Federation. But I have an additional request to make of you. Bring my daughter home. Please."

For what? So she can be debriefed? So she can be cured? If Spock isn't there, they'll both die. Maybe, Garrett realized, *he just doesn't want Saavik to die among strangers.* She felt her vision blurring and told herself fiercely, *Stop that!*

Rumor had it that the Vulcan watching her had not wept even at the death of his human wife. Rumor was often wrong.

"I promise," she said.

To her amazement, Sarek smiled bleakly. "The promise of the captain of the *Enterprise?* I require no better assurance." And broke contact.

Garrett headed back toward sickbay. An aide hovered over Saavik, attempting to make her drink water through a straw; an IV went into one arm, where a greenish bruise was forming. Recognizing Garrett's footsteps, Saavik tried to rise, then sank back down onto the biobed.

"I just spoke to Ambassador Sarek," Garrett told her. "We're taking you home."

"No!" Saavik interrupted. "We must go to Narendra III."

"We'll get it all done," Dr. Stewart said, her voice almost a croon of reassurance. "Trust the captain."

Saavik sighed. *"Enterprise."*

Her eyes shut.

"Doctor!"

"Don't worry. That's natural sleep. If we're really lucky, she'll go into healing trance. If not, well . . . I've studied some of the Disciplines. Most shrinks do, sooner or later. I know a little Vulcan, too. I've been talking to her in it. It seems to anchor her."

"Can you get the whole story out of her?" Garrett asked.

"I've tried. I think she's hiding something."

"Like why she crossed the Neutral Zone in the first place?"

Dr. Stewart nodded. Garrett stared down at her hands, aware that she had clenched them into fists. Deliberately, she forced herself to uncurl her fingers. "Keep trying, Doctor. Report to me anything you hear."

"Yes, Captain."

Returning to her own quarters, Garrett checked for messages. No word yet.

So. She sat for a moment, fingers steepled, resting her chin on them. Sarek had thought Spock still on Oriki. Easy enough to follow up on that.

But, as Garrett was coming to suspect, he might be on Romulus itself. If Spock were on Romulus, it stood to reason that Saavik might have followed him, to provide backup.

She accessed navigation and tapped in a theoretical course. Yes. If *Enterprise* diverted to Narendra III at warp nine, the Klingon base was some nine hours away.

Saavik's message had warned that the fleet would initiate attack three hours after emerging from the Neutral Zone.

Alone. Against a fleet of brand-new warbirds with unknown

capabilities that a half-Romulan Starfleet officer with Command training regarded as formidable.

You know, if you divert without orders, people will think you're as crazy as Saavik.

Let them.

She leaned forward to signal the bridge.

"Divert course to Narendra III," she ordered. "Maximum warp. Tell the engineers to give me everything she's got. Yellow alert."

"With all due respect, Captain . . ." began Tholav's soft voice.

"Do it!" She heard orders relayed, took a breath, and asked, Any word from Captain Keel yet?"

"Ma'am, I have Captain Walker Keel on screen now."

She heard the relief in Varani's voice. *Attaboy,* she thought, but did not say, and leaned forward, both elbows on the table, to greet the image on the screen. No point playing poker with this one; the term "poker face" could have been invented to describe him. And she'd known him long enough to be blunt.

"Walk, I'll put my cards on the table. I've just diverted course to the Klingon base at Narendra III on the word of a possibly deranged Vulcan woman. She's telling me I'm going to face seven Romulan warbirds solo. Tell me she's wrong."

She had to give Keel credit. Not even an eyelid twitched. "I think, Captain," he said, all traces of humor gone, "that you had better explain."

Garrett keyed open a channel to Communications. "Transmit Commander Saavik's tape."

"Transmitting now."

"There isn't a whole lot of time," Garrett said, quickly filling Keel in on the rescue of Commander Saavik. "Now that I'm about to put my head in the warbird's beak . . . You'd better level with me, Walker."

Keel stared at the coffee cup in his hand as if it were an alien object. He drank, then clearly came to a decision that tasted worse than the coffee, and set the cup down.

"I'll let Admiral Lynn fill you in." Walker's face faded out and for a moment Garrett was staring at a blank screen.

As the admiral appeared onscreen, Garrett rose.

"As you were, Captain." Acknowledging her salute, he added, "Finish your meal."

She sat down, remaining at attention as she had every dinner of her first year at Starfleet Academy. If Admiral Lynn wasn't close to retirement age, he had probably intimidated Records into shaving a few years off his date of birth. Despite his years in space, he was as weathered as a downworlder, with white hair and a white mustache that gave him the look of a predator: a deceptively mild predator who would smile before he struck.

Without any soft words, he began, "Staff indicates that if you divert now you'll reach Narendra in five hours."

That was the admiral she'd heard about: Never mind the covert ops. What was the old saying? "Damn the torpedoes. Full speed ahead."

"I diverted one point five hours ago, sir. ETA now at four point three hours." By the time *Enterprise* arrived, Narendra III would already be under attack. If Saavik wasn't crazy. "Admiral, what's the time horizon until you can send reinforcements?"

Meeting her eyes, the admiral gave the bad news to her straight. "The protection of Melville Colony must be top priority if we're to have any hope of avoiding all-out war. Under the circumstances, Captain, you're on your own. I don't need to tell you to govern yourself accordingly."

"I understand, sir."

"I thought you would." Lynn's face was very bleak. "As for Saavik, Sarek of Vulcan has contacted me. Commander Saavik must be returned to Vulcan for debriefing. She has vital information about the Romulans.

"Godspeed, Captain," Admiral Lynn continued. "If my physician wouldn't knock me down, sit on me, and certify me unfit for command, *and* if I had a ship I could commandeer in time, I'd come and back you up myself."

"We'd appreciate that, Admiral." Garrett sighed. "I'll send Commander Saavik back to Vulcan."

"I'll get you reinforcements as soon as I can, Captain," Admiral Lynn said bluntly. "So hold out. You don't need old-style Fourth of July speeches about how important this situation is. But, *Enterprise* . . . " He grinned without humor, looking remarkably like an enraged predator. "Do your best."

"Aye, sir. If you'll excuse me now, I must go inform my crew."

By rights, she should have let Admiral Lynn break communications. She paused, but the admiral had risen and was saluting her.

"Godspeed," Admiral Lynn said again.

He knew better, she thought, than to wish her good luck.

Discussion in Garrett's ready room had been brief. Course had been set; nothing more remained to do but wait. And fine-tune the weapons systems. Lieutenant Castillo left, his eyes bright with interest. Normally, doctrine discouraged some tactics. But when a ship was as badly outnumbered as *Enterprise,* he was damned well going to try them.

Garrett accompanied Chief Medical Officer Aristide to sickbay. She knew he was watching her. Evaluating her fitness. Damn.

Saavik would no doubt perceive distress. Garrett attempted to calm herself. By the time her breathing had steadied, she had managed her grief, her fear to the point where she could hide them. Was this how Vulcans did it?

Already, Saavik looked paler, thinner than she had the last time Garrett had seen her. But she roused the instant she heard footsteps, and her eyes were very bright.

"Is the word given?" she whispered.

"The word is given, Commander. *Enterprise* is bound for Narendra III. Maximum warp. As for you, we're going to get you home, where your own people can take care of you. We'll have you on board a shuttle to Vulcan within the hour."

"Begging the captain's pardon," said Frances Stewart. "Just who do you think you can send on board that shuttle? We're going into what may be a war zone, and you're stripping the ship of essential personnel?"

"You'd kill me if I said 'nonessential passengers,' Frances," Garrett told her. "I want you to volunteer to escort the commander to Vulcan."

The psychiatrist's gaze flashed to her chief. Aristide spread out his hands: *What do you want?*

"I'm sending two security guards and a pilot," Garrett continued. "A ship with a complement of seven hundred can spare four."

At least they would have a chance to go on living.

"But why me?"

"You like this woman, don't you? She trusts you? That makes you, pardon the expression, the logical choice."

"Captain, I took an oath . . ."

"You took several oaths, only one of which was to obey all lawful orders of your superior officers. Now, will you volunteer or do I make it a direct order?"

"Aye, aye, ma'am. Request permission to escort Commander Saavik to Vulcan."

"That's better. I don't like it either, Frances, but . . ." Garrett shrugged. "We can always hope we'll all be luckier than we deserve.

"By the way, just in case, I want to tell you, I respect the way you've cared for your patient. I'll note that in your file before . . . before . . .

"Dismissed."

Garrett walked beside Saavik's gurney on the way to the shuttlebay. In general, one did not touch Vulcans, but in a brief interval of consciousness, Saavik had grasped Garrett's hand and pulled at it, drawing her down so she could whisper hoarsely, *"He* is still out there."

Saavik would not have revealed that information if she expected *Enterprise* to survive.

Garrett squeezed her hand. "I thought so. There's a ship out there, too. It'll bring him home."

Saavik sighed. " 'The needs of the many outweigh the needs of the few. Or the one.' "

Do they?

The Vulcan seemed to read her hesitation. "*Kobayashi Maru,* Captain. Thee understands."

Garrett patted the other woman's hand.

"Take care of her, Frances. And of yourself."

Stewart drew herself up and saluted formally. The shuttle's doors sealed. Garrett left the deck.

"Depressurize," she ordered.

Godspeed, Rachel Garrett wished the departing shuttle as it dwindled among the stars.

She returned to the bridge, going the long way round to take a last look at her ship—and to let her crew see her.

NINETEEN

SPACE, THE NEUTRAL ZONE AND BEYOND, YEAR 2344

As the *Honor Blade* sped out and away from Romulus, Charvanek, seated in her ship's command chair, allowed herself a quick glance about the bridge. *Akhh*, yes, as cramped and awkwardly designed as it always had been—what idiot could have placed the controls for the left thruster away from the other set? The lighting had a greenish cast that made everyone look newly deceased, and the once-elegant red and silver bulkhead had faded to an un-Romulan . . . pink, ghastly in the green-tinged light. It was, without a doubt . . . timeworn (Charvanek's hand searched for and found the frayed patch on her command chair's left armrest). And they never had been able to get rid of that mysterious hint of burnt wiring.

Still, the bird-of-prey guarded *Honor Blade*'s bridge, and her engines were as fine and as finely tuned as Takvi could make them.

Her ship, restored with her own treasure. Not some unblooded new design or some Klingon trash, but a solid Romulan vessel as well known and reliable as its crew.

"Orbital defenses successfully jammed, Commander. Leaving homeworld orbit."

"Once out of weapons range, cut transmission," she ordered. She, who went to defend the Empire, would not leave her home-world defenseless.

No one on board had questioned this. They were hers, from grizzled old First Engineer Takvi, with her since the old days and loyal as they came, to lean, wild-eyed Subcommander Durnak, to her eager young aide, M'ret, who'd followed her here gladly. She had chosen only those whose utter loyalty lay not to the praetor, not even just to her, but to the emperor and Romulan honor.

Subcommander Durnak, pilot, sat all but welded to his con-trols, murmuring steadily under his breath. Nothing wrong, Charvanek knew; he merely begrudged even the slightest dust particle striking *his* ship. She had seen less reverent faces in shrines. Beside him, Centurion Ekenda, Navigation, a grim-faced middle-aged woman, awaited orders.

"Navigation. Lay in the following course."

Unblinking, Ekenda absorbed its audacity: cut across the Neutral Zone, uncloaked for greater speed, and, if the Fates were with them, outrace the fleet to Narendra III. Durnak glanced at the new heading, raised an eyebrow, but complied without a word.

"Five seconds to warp speed," Ekenda called off. "Three . . . two . . . one . . . warp speed!"

As the universe blurred and blazed about them, Charvanek leaned forward slightly.

We're coming, Volskiar, my old foe, we will overtake you and your arrogantly named Victorious, *and that so dishonorably launched fleet.*

And if some Federation ship spots us before then? Do I . . . inform upon Romulan ships to my enemy?

In this case, I do.

I must.

Her hand stole, just for an instant, to the amulet about her neck: a childish charm for good luck such as even nobility some-times wore. But this one held a tiny, undetectable, and exceedingly powerful recording chip. The events of this mission would not go unnoted.

How long has it been since we last went into battle? How long since the old days, when Subcommander Tal was at my right hand and issues were simple: good or evil.

Bah, no, they had never been *that* simple.

And I was never that naïve.

Spock, her mind told her, unbidden, First Officer Spock of the *Starship Enterprise.*

Ah well, Charvanek thought wryly, *maybe I was that naïve. Once.*

"Subcommander Selta," she snapped. "Open a channel to all within *Honor Blade.*"

His hands flew over the console. "Ready, Commander."

Charvanek took a steadying breath. They had this precious time alone while in warp drive, and she would not waste it. "My shipmates, you are no doubt aware of the new fleet and of the praetor's plans to restore our ancient glories. What you may not know is how he plans to do so."

As meticulously as if she laid out a battle plan in a council of war, Charvanek explained the situation: what, exactly, Narendra III was, the hazards and the political situation, and the cost to the Empire.

The bridge crew's discipline held, but the softest of snarls came over the ship's speakers from First Engineer Takvi:

"Dishonorable."

"You need not fear to say the word more loudly. Yes! It *is* dishonorable! If we submit to be used, and used on this raid, this one-sided massacre, it will be the blackest stain ever to mar the Empire's name."

She got to her feet, stalking about the bridge, catching the eye of this man, that woman. "Those of you who have served with me in the old days know my history. You others surely have heard the tale, in one form or another, of how I was kidnapped by the Federation." This was hardly the time to burden them with too many facts; the official version would serve. "You know how, in the years that followed, I waged a long, fierce battle to regain rank, honor—to, in blunt honesty, save my own life. Some of you were with me."

Charvanek paused, hands on hips, listening with a concealed wild delight to the murmurs of agreement, even of approval. *They are mine.*

"You have heard. You know. You know me. So you can believe this: I would not risk my life, my honor, after that long, long struggle were it not that I believe the cause is just. I have killed in battle. We all have. But I have never yet murdered an unarmed foe. And I have never yet, and never will, slay children. And no, it matters not what race, what species:

"I will not slay the helpless.

"I will not so stain my honor."

She paused, waiting. "Nor will I." That was Durnak's mutter.

"Nor I." Centurion Ekenda.

"Nor I," came in from First Engineer Takvi.

And now the voices were joining in quickly, "Nor I! Nor I!"

She held up a hand for silence. "Easy words. But do you know what lies behind them?"

She waited. They were all too well trained to ask the questions she saw burning in their eyes. M'ret, Charvanek decided, and whirled to him, commanding, "Ask!"

He was still young enough to actually flush. "Who—this is not the emperor's command, this can't be!"

"It is not. Think. All of you. Would Emperor Shiarkiek ever, *ever* do anything that would harm Romulan honor?"

"The praetor," someone muttered, as she had expected.

Charvanek pounced. "The praetor, indeed! It is he, it is false Praetor Dralath who would turn our Honor Blades into butchers' knives." *Softly, softly, you rant like Volskiar.* "We all know the unrest at home, we all know that Dralath is . . . less than popular, we all know the economy is less secure than it should be. A quick, easy war is so nicely dramatic, such lovely glory—for *him!* There is no honor in this mission, no brave defense of our race, no advancement or glory—nothing but shame in the name of the praetor's greed!

"Understand this now and utterly: I spend no lives without just cause. I will do my best to sway the fleet. I do not want violence against our own. But if talk fails . . ." Charvanek paused just long enough to make her point. Then, quickly, concisely, she told her crew what they must do. They must already have guessed. Still, shock, even horror, flashed from face to face.

But no one stirred. No one said a word.

"Will you do this?" Charvanek asked.

The blood was rushing in her ears. Returning to her command chair, gripping the armrests so fiercely she knew she must be denting them, she heard their answer:

"Yes!"

Oh, my brave ones! But some of you have families, aged parents. I must leave you one last escape.

"*Any* action that we take will be construed as treason. If any of you have any qualms about following my orders *to the letter,* you may take a rescue pod and leave the moment we return to sublight speed. No shame, no questions. Just leave."

She waited, heart racing.

No one so much as moved.

So be it. Deliberately rousing them anew, Charvanek cried, "I ask you now: Do you serve the emperor?"

"Yes!"

"Yes!"

"Forever!"

They were glad of the chance to shout. Charvanek sprang from her chair once more and prowled among them. "And the Empire! Do you serve the Empire?"

"Of course!"

"We do!"

She stopped, staring at them all. "And what of honor? Do you serve the name of Honor?"

"Yes!"

"Yes!"

And a chant started up there and then: "Emperor, Honor, Charvanek, Empire, Honor, Charvanek!"

"And what will you do?" she asked.

"Whatever we must!" M'ret cried.

"Whatever we can," Durnak growled.

The shouting broke out again. "We will defend the honor of our race!" "We will do whatever we must!"

She must ask this. "And if you must . . . die?"

M'ret snapped back without a moment's hesitation, "Then we die with glory!"

It was a boy's fervor. But—no one argued. No one so much as winced. For a moment, Charvanek could not speak, nearly choked with a rush of emotion so strong she had to fight to show nothing. *Nothing but pride in this my crew.*

Whom she just might be leading to their deaths.

Then Navigator Ekenda said, absolutely without tone,

"Coming out of warp speed in twenty seconds . . . nine-teen . . ."

"So be it," Charvanek said softly, and returned to the command chair. Then she added in sharp command, "Subcommander Durnak! At my order: As soon as we drop out of warp, full ahead on sublight engines. Understood?"

A quick nod.

". . . ten . . . nine . . ."

". . . five . . . four . . . three . . . two . . . one. Sublight."

Charvanek had a quick glimpse of this new section of space, sighted the glow that marked the Narendra III colony. No sign yet of the fleet—*hei-ya-hai,* they had won their race! "And—now! Full ahead!"

She was, Charvanek realized, clenching her teeth, and forced herself to relax. She had studied the data. The fleet must emerge from warp drive some distance from Narendra III: too many navigational hazards in that sector for anything but sublight flight.

If the Fates were kinder than they had been, there would not be much time to wait.

* * *

Seven ships as one flashed out of warp speed, drawing the suddenly curving light of space about them like a cloak of blazing colors, too many for the eye to interpret. Charvanek allowed herself one quick flash of exultation at the glory of the sight.

But what use was glory without honor?

"I think I can tap into fleet communications without being detected, Commander," Selta said without looking up from his screens.

"Do so."

The bridge's main viewscreen blurred from a view of space and stars and the vulnerable colony ahead to Volskiar's face. He glared fiercely out at them from the viewscreen, the very essence of the Noble Warrior. "Romulans, honorable warriors of the Empire . . ."

Ah yes, the Speech to the Troops, Charvanek thought. *We are embarked upon a glorious mission,* she predicted.

Sure enough, Volskiar was continuing, "We are embarked upon a glorious mission, one to bring new honor to the Empire and increased security to our borders."

Now we bring in the melodrama, about the colonists in peril of foreign invasion. . . .

"Think, Romulans, of our colony worlds. Think of the honest, hardworking, loyal men and women who ask nothing but to serve the Empire. Now picture foreigners imperiling those Romulan men, women, yes, Romulan children. And such invaders *do* threaten, brutish creatures who know nothing of honor, nothing of glory: Klingons! Klingons who know nothing but blood lust!"

Trite, Volskiar, trite.

"You ask, how can this be? Have we not dealt peacefully with the Klingons, even purchased warships from them? Yes!" Volskiar's fist slammed down on the console. "We made that mistake! We let them sell us faulty ships—but no more! That was all part of their plan to weaken us, then overwhelm us."

Oh, well done, Charvanek thought. *You parrot Dralath's propaganda flawlessly. Why, I can almost hear his voice.*

"We cannot let our own, our brave Romulan colonists live in peril!" Volskiar roared. "We cannot let them be murdered by these *aliens!* And *we shall not!* We strike first, my loyal warriors, we go to destroy the menace to our worlds now! We go to smash the Klingon base, the military base of Narendra III—and we go now! Now!"

Akhh, listen. Some hot-blooded—or politic—warriors on the other ships were echoing that "Now!"

"We go to fight not for personal glory," Volskiar shouted. "We fight for our people, for our homeland, for Romulus! We fight for the heart and honor of the Empire! And we shall return only as victors! Is that understood? We shall return victorious!"

"Victorious!" the echoes rang from ship to ship. "We return victorious!"

Victorious over the helpless, Charvanek added darkly.

For one wistful little moment, she pictured them all, the crew of all the ships save, of course, for *Victorious,* saying, "No. We will not do this thing."

Don't they know? Don't they have the data—

But why should they? Most Romulans, including, she thought, a good percentage of the military, knew nothing of Narendra III beyond the one word: "Klingon." Why should they know more? The rest of the commanders weren't struggling to hold on to their lives and ranks; they had no need for serious Intelligence information. And even if they did know that Narendra III would be an unarmed, undefended target, they could afford to be obedient warriors, warriors untroubled—at least publicly—by questions of honor or morality.

"Commander," Selta turned toward her, his face pale. "Communication coming in for us from *Victorious.* From General Volskiar."

"Put him on, Selta," she said. "Shipwide."

Let my eaglets all hear this, too.

"Honor Blade!" Volskiar shouted. "You are in-system without orders!"

Are we? How clever of you to notice.

"Honor Blade, you will stand down. Lower shields. Take your weapons systems offline and prepare to be boarded!"

I think not.

Charvanek signaled to Durnak: On! Out of firing range, at least for now.

"All engines stop. Subcommander Selta, open fleetwide hailing frequencies. Visuals on."

"Done, Commander."

Straightening in her chair, Charvanek broadcast to Volskiar's fleet, "This is Charvanek, Commander and Noble Born, of *Honor Blade.* I need not say more; you all know me, or of me."

She would, Charvanek knew, have only a few precious moments before Volskiar began jamming her transmission. "Dishonor is being cast upon you, vital data withheld! Know this, warriors: Narendra III is no military base. They are *civilians!* Do you copy that? They are *unarmed civilians!"*

"Frequency's being jammed, Commander."

"Then find a different frequency! Keep a channel open!"

A few frantic moments, then: "Go ahead, Commander."

"Do you hear me, Romulan warriors?" Charvanek continued fervently. "This is *truth!* Our orders came not from the emperor, not from the Empire—they came straight from Praetor Dralath, and *he knew,* he knew full well that this is no mission of defense! Yet he sent us out to win nothing but shame!"

Subcommander Selta's fingers were flying over the console in a duel with *Victorious'* communications officer, struggling to keep a channel open.

"Wait, Commander, wait . . . yes! Go ahead!"

"Warriors, hear me!" Charvanek cried, voice sharp and clear as the call of a war trumpet. "If we obey, if we massacre the helpless, then the praetor has, indeed, sold our honor. We will have become only his butchers—and butchers for hire. We will never, we *can* never, cleanse ourselves or our children of the shame!"

"Signal coming in," Selta warned, "overriding ours."

Volskiar's fierce image formed on the screen—laughing.

"Now, is this not tragic?" he gibed. "She is still the Federation's pet! Have you ever heard such a foolish tale? As if we would ever be sent out on such a shameful mission as she claims—Set it to music, Charvanek! Let the street musicians sing it!"

Behind him, she could hear the others, his favorite officers, laughing, too.

"Damn you, Volskiar, this is not—"

"No use, Commander. It's not getting through."

In more ways than one.

"She is still unstable!" Volskiar was proclaiming. "A danger to us all! Ah, but worry not, warriors of the Empire: When we return in victory, she will no longer inflict her madness *or* Imperial connections on us!"

If *you return,* Charvanek told him silently.

But the other commanders were chiming in, laughing, mocking her, a hard, almost desperate edge to their jests.

They will not listen to me.

And then, the sudden harsh realization struck: *They do not want to listen. They want nothing that will spoil the sport! Akhh, my people, my people, what have we become that killing should have become no more than a game?*

Not for all. Someone must—someone *would* take a stand. Here. Now. She glanced up at the Romulan Eagle insignia, differenced as befit one of the imperial line, there on the bridge, told it silently, *Life to the Empire.*

Volskiar's image vanished from the viewscreens, replaced by a vista of space and the six other Romulan ships.

So this is what our death looks like, Charvanek thought. Then, suppressing emotions as ruthlessly as any Vulcan, she ordered in a harsh voice she barely recognized, "Attack."

No time to think save in the most basic terms. Dive directly at the nearest target, *Swift Kill* (*akhh,* ironic name), firing full, blazing blue-white flame:

"Direct hit!"

"Hard left!" Charvanek ordered, just as the *Swift Kill* erupted into a blinding red-yellow-white fireball, just as Durnak, anticipating—bless his insane heart—banked sharply left, taking them swiftly away from the shock wave.

Turn, get off a quick shot at *Sharp Sword*—near-miss, only minimal damage. Another volley, and *Sharp Sword* careened out of control, tumbling into *Battle Helm* and joining it on the fiery path to Erebus.

Three! The Fates had been kind.

But the element of surprise was gone now, and Volskiar was shouting orders at the fleet:

"Close ranks—*close ranks, damn you!*"

At Charvanek's signal, Durnak took them zooming in a daring rush between two closing ships, *Honor Blade* firing at them while they dared not lest they hit each other. Zooming out again from those close, confused quarters, escaping untouched, registering a clean miss to one target, direct hit to the other—

No, not a kill, curse it, and now the *Honor Blade*'s own flank was exposed—

"Deflectors up!" Charvanek shouted.

Too late! *Honor Blade* lurched wildly, lurched again, and Charvanek, ears ringing with explosions and cries of pain, thought, *At least we bloodied them, at least we die with glory*—

But they weren't dead. Yet. The main lighting was out, and for one heart-stopping moment, Charvanek was sure that life-support had gone with it. But then the fainter emergency lighting switched on, turning the bridge to a smoky red cave. All around her, the bridge crew were staggering to their feet, some with faces streaked with blood, muddied to greenish-brown by the lighting, some cradling arms or hands.

"Damage report," Charvanek snapped.

"Weapons down three-quarters."

"Deflectors at minimum."

"Life-support holding at seventy-eight percent."

"Engines . . ." A pause, then Takvi's growl, "Warp out. Sublight engines down."

"Casualties?" Charvanek asked sharply.

Twenty dead, forty-seven more injured.

Volskiar's crippled us. Why doesn't he finish us?

Because, of course, that wasn't Volskiar's way. Arrogant creature, he'd rather run the risk of leaving a foe alive so that there could be more glory for him. If he had the education to match his bloodlust, Charvanek mused bitterly, he would know how greatly he tempted the Fates.

Sure enough, she suddenly heard a static-filled transmission from the *Victorious,* Volskiar's voice, fairly dripping contempt, "Leave the traitor there. She isn't going anywhere."

"Am I not?" Charvanek murmured.

"We will take the ship in tow on our way back to the homeworld after our glorious victory!"

"Will you?" It was a snarl.

She watched the surviving ships of his fleet streak on toward their prey, *Honor Blade* helpless to stop them.

Helpless for the moment.

And then Charvanek began firing off orders to the crew. "Engineering! I want those engines back on-line as quickly as possible."

"Commander—"

"Yes, I know it won't be easy. Do it! I also want our weapons back in some semblance of order. Don't waste time on the deflectors. Medic! See to the wounded. Give the worst-off the Final Honor. Your hand is mine."

She paused, seeing the tension in all the bridge crew; they knew as well as she that the mercy of a quick death was something they well might not receive.

"All of you, hear me. We may not see our homes again. You knew that. We may well die reviled as traitors. But—by all the Powers That May Be, if we must die, it shall be as warriors! We shall die with *honor!"*

"With honor!" came the answering roar.

TWENTY

KI BARATAN, ROMULUS, DAY 7, SECOND WEEK OF TASMEEN, 2344

Kharik's body had been carried off without any drama at all—almost, Spock thought, as though what had been a living, albeit unpleasant, being just a short while ago had become in death no more than so much rubbish. The only sign that someone had died here were a few green streaks of drying blood on the stone floor. And on the still-shaking Ruanek.

Spock was hard-put not to tremble as well. The violence of the knife fight still echoed within him, striking ancient chords Spock most firmly refused to hear.

Control, he told himself, *control.* Reaching within himself, he sought the inner tranquillity, silently reciting the soothing mantras that almost worked.

He dared not even consider that he had failed at Kolinahr.

As calmly as though the cousins' duel to the death had never happened, Narviat said, "Come. There are plans we must discuss."

His glance took in Spock and a few men and women whom he

apparently considered more trustworthy than the others. It did not include Ruanek.

Of course not, Spock thought, blood fever blazing up within him at the realization. *The pack shuns the wounded member.*

As he would not. And he would *not* surrender to the rage! Very deliberately, Spock moved to Ruanek's side. "Let me see your injuries."

Ruanek shrugged, but spoiled the casual effect by an involuntary wince. "Mere cuts. I've endured worse."

"I am sure." That was said with utter lack of tone. "Nevertheless even the smallest of wounds may weaken one."

Ignoring Ruanek's protests, Spock stanched the blood with a wad of torn-off tunic, then bound the slashes as best he could, thinking about his handiwork, *Dr. McCoy would most certainly not approve.*

Narviat glanced at Spock, then at the subcommander. "You do realize, of course," he commented almost casually to Ruanek, "that after what has occurred, you cannot possibly return to your patron and your old life."

Ruanek nodded stiffly. "No need to tell me, sir. I . . . had no future there."

Bravely said. But he had the look about him of someone so fragile he might shatter. Shock, Spock knew, understandable after that deadly duel, and from the wounds that, while not serious, were still injuries. And Spock could not help but sense the blaze of Ruanek's emotions, strong as a psychic scream to a Vulcan: The Romulan was, under his resolute warrior's façade, desperately afraid, the foundations of his existence destroyed all too suddenly.

"Ruanek . . ." Spock began, not certain of what to say.

"I will not be a liability."

"So be it," Narviat snapped. "Come."

He led them through a maze of the tunnels to a cave furnished with a makeshift table and chairs—nothing about them to link them to anything more than, perhaps, some homeless folk. As the other members of the underground, warriors and civilians alike, entered after him in wary ones and twos, Narviat held up a cautioning hand. "Remember where we are this time, namely, practically under our noble praetor's feet."

Someone snickered. "Next time he will be under ours."

All the Romulans laughed at that, softly but, Spock thought, with a great deal of venom.

All, that was, save for a stocky man in the dark robes of a scholar—the same scholar, surely, who had accused Spock of not being Symakhos. Narviat frowned slightly.

"Therakith? Is something wrong?"

"I . . . merely think it less than wise to celebrate before the battle is begun, let alone won."

Narviat studied him a moment longer, eyes narrowed thoughtfully, then shrugged. "Wisdom. Come, let us begin our, as you put it, battle."

But Spock continued to watch the scholar, wondering. Therakith met his gaze for an instant, then frowned and looked away. Nothing there to arouse suspicion, nothing overt, at any rate. And yet . . . something about the man's demeanor failed to ring true. Were it not a breach of courtesy, he would already have a hand on Therakith's temple; peril or no, he would insist on knowing something of Therakith's thoughts—

What had courtesy to do with it? Even now, he could easily force a mind-meld—

You are a Vulcan, Spock reminded himself sharply, refusing to consider the mental invasion he'd inflicted on Dralath, *not a savage. Even now.*

"Are you with us?" Narviat asked, and Spock turned his attention to the table and the unrolled charts.

Tried to attend. Tried to focus on what seemed the same plans, the same useless, endless debates—

There is no logic to anger. . . .

The cave was cool, unpleasantly cool, and close. He had never before been bothered by the phobia humans called claustrophobia. Why now? Why was this cave so shadowy, distorted, dark, dark flame—he glanced at the smooth walls and saw himself reflected, distorted by distortions in the stone. His face was wild and pale, his eyes, his eyes were flame—

This was more than the Fires. The realization struck Spock with the force of a savage blow. What bothered him had nothing to do with some suddenly acquired phobia. The fierce surge of emotion blazing through his mind was not from him alone, but from all around him, and he shouted out:

"A trap! We have been betrayed!"

He had destroyed the element of surprise. Members of the praetor's guards rushed forward as he shouted the warning, storming in from both entrances with disruptor rifles ready and knives drawn, blocking escape, and Spock—

—*suddenly saw nothing but* enemy males, *felt nothing but flame, hot flame within him, his mind, his eyes, flame, and he*—

—fought. He fought with bare hands and ferocity, sent a warrior flying, twisted and pulled two more crashing into each other, hurled another against a wall with stunning force, moving with the quick efficiency learned in his Starfleet days. At the heart of him a cold, utterly rational core reminded him, *They cannot fire their disruptors in such close quarters, not without killing their fellows. Knives or bare hands only.* Illogical, terribly illogical, to be feeling such undeniable joy in violence, in triumph, but just now, it was most wonderfully satisfying to see enemy after enemy fall.

But I have not killed. I . . . will . . . not . . . kill.

The Romulans were under no such constraint. They fought with the sheer ferocity of those who know that death in combat is far preferable to death by slow, humiliating pain. Ruanek hesitated for a moment, and again, that small, rational fragment of Spock's mind produced the reason: This was the first time the subcommander had ever fought against his own. But then, with the air of someone cutting his last tie to reality, Ruanek hurled himself into the battle. Knives flashed, men and women fell, and the reek of blood . . . the reek of blood . . .

I am not a savage! I will not kill!

But all at once there were no more foes to fight. As Spock stood panting, Narviat's allies moved from fallen body to fallen body, hunting remaining signs of life. The wounded guards received no mercy, only the flash of knives falling with quick, deadly efficiency. Those of the Underground who were too badly wounded to stand were granted the Final Honor. Spock dared not watch, dared not see *hot blood gushing forth, filling his mind with renewed fire—*

There! One foe remained, backing away: Therakith! Spock lunged at the scholar, caught him, the Fires blazing up so fiercely he could barely see, barely think—

"Symakhos." Then, more cautiously, "Spock!"

He was Spock. He was Spock, not some mad thing, not some mindless beast, and he—

—collapsed back into himself, his mind clear enough to recognize Ruanek's voice—and to realize that he had Therakith by the throat and was nearly strangling him. Spock loosened his grip just enough for the scholar to catch a ragged breath, and Narviat, leaning over Spock's shoulder, hissed one word:

"Why?"

"Why do you think?" Despair blazed from Therakith's eyes and voice. "Dralath has my family—had them. He . . . I . . . once I . . . I betrayed you, curse me for a fool, for worse than a fool—I trusted Dralath to keep his word just once. But once he had all the data I could give him . . ." Therakith's voice broke. "He has betrayed me. He has murdered my sweet Katara, my poor little babes. . . ."

Spock, shocked back into total sanity, released him, asking as gently as he could, "How could you know that?"

"How? How? Did you see that guard, the monster who lies there? I have never killed a man before, but that one, *akhh,* that one I took great delight in killing! He is Dralath's living message:

He wears my wife's marriage bracelet on his belt! It could not be removed while Katara lived: See? I wear its mate, welded shut about my wrist. And . . . that is . . . those are . . . that is the most terrible, the most terrible . . . those are locks of baby hair, my babies' soft young hair, twisted into the belt as well. . . ."

There was stunned silence. Then Narviat said, "I must ask you this: How long have you been his spy? How much have you revealed?"

Blinking fiercely, Therakith said harshly, "Not that much, nor that long. Long enough. The tunnels . . . he knows we meet down here. But I did not betray you by name! I swear this by what is left of our homeworld's honor. That fact alone he does not have."

"For what good it does," Narviat muttered. "And no, I do not blame you." He put a hand on Therakith's shoulder, squeezed gently. "We all have our breaking points. It is no dishonor to admit exhaustion of the heart. But—this place is no longer safe." He withdrew that hand as though scorched. "Nor, alas, are you, not now that Dralath knows who and what you are."

"I am aware of that." Therakith stiffened proudly. "I shall not be a burden. A scholar I may be, not a warrior, but I have a true Romulan's honor—and no wish to live further." A knife flashed in his hand. "Triumph, Narviat. Slay Dralath for me. Send him to burn forever."

With that, with quick, academic precision, he slashed open his throat. Narviat, face naked with horror, caught his sagging body, heedless of the spouting blood, and eased the dying man to the ground. Therakith glanced at him, at Spock, saying without words, *Avenge us. . . .*

"He is dead," Spock said softly.

"I know." With the smallest of shudders, Narviat let the body go slack, then fumbled in his belt pouch till he had found two crystals and placed them on Therakith's eyes. The politician murmured a prayer that was, for once, utterly free of artifice.

Covered with Therakith's blood, Narviat got to his feet, stalking grim-faced among the others, counting heads, murmuring to his surviving allies. He paused to disentangle the pathetic strands of baby hair from the guard's belt, his hands gentle as he slipped the hair into his own belt pouch, then turned to rake everyone with his gaze.

"We cannot linger. Some guards might have escaped, and at any rate, other guards are going to be checking up on their fellows soon enough. All of you, leave! Wait for my signal. We shall meet again."

He waited until, judging from the undisturbed silence, the others had gotten safely away, then told Spock curtly, "Follow."

Without another word, Narviat began climbing the nearest stairway to the surface. He was outlined against the sky for a dramatic moment, the clean lines of his aristocratic face in sharp silhouette. But suddenly his outline was obscured by others. Spock heard a crisp voice say, "Admiral Narviat, you are under arrest."

Narviat, wonderfully self-possessed, drew back in apparent astonishment—effectively blocking the entrance to the stairway and hiding Spock and Ruanek as well. Spock motioned to Ruanek: Back! They retreated down the stairs, avoiding the dim green glow from the grimy lighting tubes set into the rock.

"On what charge?" Narviat's cool voice was the essence of patrician disdain.

"Treason, Admiral. High treason against the praetor and the Romulan state."

"How utterly ridiculous! But," Narviat added with a sigh, "I suppose you must do as you are ordered. You will, of course, permit me to send a message to my staff. And to my Imperial kinsman."

"We will," the arresting officer said flatly, "do as we must. If you will come with us, Admiral, we shall forgo restraints."

Spock felt rather than heard Ruanek's horror, and moved ever so slightly to block him from lunging up in any foolish attempt at a rescue. "We can do nothing to help," he murmured.

They stood in utter silence as Narviat was marched away. Spock, testing, found his mind remaining mercifully clear. Of course. He had already proved more than once that violent activity—and the fight with the Romulan guards certainly qualified as that—together with emotional shocks, such as Therakith's death and this sudden arrest of Narviat, temporarily banked the fires of *Pon farr*.

Logic told Spock that Narviat would not be executed immediately; the admiral was too important in rank and bloodline, and was too popular with the people. Nor, for the same reasons, would he meet with an "accident." There must be a trial, undeniable—if forged—proof of treason against the Romulan people. That bought the rebellion a little time. . . .

"Gather the others," Spock told Ruanek. "They cannot have gone far."

No, they had not. They hurried forward, eyes wild with shock and fury. "What are we—" "How can we—"

If he let this continue, they would, being Romulans, fall to bloody quarreling, or they would launch some insane attack on Dralath's guards. And Spock was hardly about to watch a revolution devolve into a massacre.

"Silence!" he commanded. "You sound like children crying for their nurse!"

That stunned the rebels into a moment's silence. Before they could snarl at him, Spock continued, "How long have you been meeting? How much time have you wasted talking without accomplishing anything?"

A centurion stiffened, eyes blazing with outrage beneath the helm he still wore. "How dare you, *outworlder!* You cannot know—"

"I know delay when I witness it. Hear me out, all of you. We can do nothing to help Narviat—not yet. But losing the security of the tunnels is no true obstacle. It is, instead, a goad to action."

"Is it, now?" the centurion challenged. "And where, O wise general, would you have us meet? In Dralath's own offices?"

"Why not?"

"Why—"

"Hear me out." His mind was still working with cold clarity; he must take advantage of the brief respite from *Pon farr.* "On Earth, on the Terran homeworld—"

"We have heard of Earth," a woman in scholar's robes cut in dryly.

"Excellent. Then you may even have heard of a rebel named Vladimir Lenin. Lenin was hunted even as you are hunted, but the enemy never found him—because he had cleverly hidden himself in the headquarters of the Secret Police. Now, if a human can do that . . ."

He heard the Romulans mutter, and thought, *I have them.* "Some of you, I know, work in the government bureaucracy." Seeing a few grudging nods, Spock continued, "Being who and what you are, do you not have access to a great many offices?"

"Yes," someone muttered, "but . . ."

"Then here is what we shall need."

At first, the Romulans stirred as he told them his plan, some of them murmuring uneasily, others giving him sharp, speculative glances. Then one gray-clad woman straightened. "Yes," she said. "Yes, we could do this. In fact . . . we can do it. And we will. For Narviat's sake, not yours."

And a sardonic smile touched the corners of the centurion's mouth. "Be glad you are a Vulcan, clever one. Were you a Romulan, we just might have to . . . have you eliminated."

Ruanek drew in his breath in an indignant hiss. But Spock met the Romulan stares without flinching. "Believe *me,* all of you, I do not doubt that for a moment. But we are wasting precious time! Go!"

And, considerably to his relief, they went. Ruanek, with a gesture to Spock that clearly meant *wait,* cautiously climbed the stairway, cloak gathered about himself to hide his bloodstained clothing. After a moment, he signaled down to Spock, *All safe.*

"Now," Ruanek muttered, as they left the alley and entered a street busy with groundcars and other transports, "we have a new problem. You can hardly return to Commander Charvanek's empty house, and you can certainly not go on to Admiral Narviat's estate." Ruanek's eyes widened as it struck him that he, too, no longer had anyplace to go. "I can't bring you to my . . . to my former quarters, either."

"Indeed," Spock said with an ambassador's soothing calm. "However, I have a better site in mind."

"And that is . . . ?"

"The Imperial Palace."

Ruanek stopped short, openmouthed with surprise. "You are— damn, you are—that is the most—you are—"

"Audacious?" Spock suggested serenely.

"Audacious, hells, yes! But how in the name of all those hells are you going to get in? Just walk right up and order the gates to open?"

"Precisely." Spock showed him the forged Imperial medallion that was part of Symakhos' disguise. The gold glinted as a narrow shaft of sunlight caught it.

Ruanek's laugh was almost a gasp. "And yet, and yet, why not?" he said wildly. "What better place to hide? Who would think of looking for us in the Imperial Palace? And here we Romulans believe we are gamblers!"

"Come," Spock said before Ruanek's burst of humor could overwhelm him into hysterics or utter collapse. "Let us see if the emperor will receive us."

TWENTY-ONE

KI BARATAN

Dralath's guards, predictably, were still patrolling outside the Imperial Palace. And, predictably, they tried to block the way. Spock merely . . . looked at them, the aristocratic scholar who had every right to be where he was, and showed them the glittering, seemingly authentic, imperial medallion. Ruanek, playing along in the role of bodyguard, snapped:

"This is the Academician Symakhos of Bardat, honored by His Imperial Majesty!"

"Academician," the guards' centurion muttered, and gave Spock what might almost have been a salute.

"Precisely," Spock said in his most pedantic tone. "Now, kindly step aside. You would not wish the emperor to learn that I had been detained."

Logically, the guards will now believe that we have an appointment.

Of course, the effect would be spoiled if the emperor refused them admittance.

He did not. The massive gates swung open with a suddenness

that clearly surprised Ruanek all over again. "But then," the Romulan murmured, "Emperor Shiarkiek *is* renowned as a scholar. New things fascinate him."

Not quite certain how that was meant, Spock entered through a gate cut through the massive walls—as thick as those of any fortress of Vulcan's warrior past—and found himself confronted by a maze of paths that wound through a network of streams and ponds too regular in shape to be natural. The water sparkled in the sunlight, and fish glinted here and there below the surface like so many living green and yellow jewels.

"Fish," Ruanek said, "are said to be the emperor's special study." He straightened. "That—there—that is the emperor himself."

Spock heard the softest gasp of awe from Ruanek as the tall, lean figure approached, long brownish-gray hair flowing unbound about his thin, refined face. Emperor Shiarkiek wore what had once been an elegant blue and gold robe, but the gold threads had faded to dull brass, and the silky blue fabric was close to threadbare, just short of downright shabby. "Comfortable," Spock suspected, was the word Shiarkiek would have chosen.

Interesting. The emperor was clearly no young man, but there seemed to be nothing of the decrepit figurehead who had collapsed during the meeting of the Central Court.

He has been playing a role, Spock realized, *fighting for survival. Like Narviat. And Charvanek. And, presumably, most of the Romulan nobility.*

"How interesting," the emperor said. "I have never given a medallion to you. Who are you?"

Ruanek, with a second gasp, fell to one knee, head bent, clenched fist over his chest.

"*Akhh*, stand," Shiarkiek told him. "You make me uncomfortable." As Ruanek straightened, awe shining in his eyes, the emperor frowned. "But you are injured!"

Ruanek clearly was too exhausted—and too overwhelmed—to

speak. Spock said for him, "Subcommander Ruanek has been in a duel of honor. And won."

But Ruanek had just won the battle over his own awe. This time his salute was less melodramatic, more properly military. "Your Majesty, if I may be more precise?"

"Please."

"I am indeed Subcommander Ruanek, sworn to Commander Avrak, sister-son to Senator Pardek. And . . . the one I slew was also sworn to Commander Avrak, Centurion Kharik."

"I see." Was that the faintest hint of wry amusement on the emperor's face? "And why, young eagle, did you feel obliged to provide me with so much detail?"

"Why—you are the emperor! It would not be honorable to hide the truth from you!"

"I see," Shiarkiek repeated. "Quite admirable." He turned to Spock. "And you are . . . ?"

Ruanek cleared his throat uneasily. "Your Majesty, may I present . . ." the smallest of awkward pauses, "the Academician Symakhos, a distant kinsman of . . . of the Noble Born Commander Charvanek and Admiral Narviat."

"And thus, kin to myself, eh?" The ancient eyes studied Spock shrewdly: the gaze of a scholar used to searching out the most obscure data. "Very distant, perhaps," Shiarkiek murmured after a moment. "*Akhh,* but the subcommander is weary from his wounds." A casual wave of a hand brought several servants running. "Summon my physician. Make this officer comfortable. Go with them, Ruanek."

Not exactly subtle, are we? You do wish to question me, Shiarkiek. But then, I wish to question you as well. Can you, I wonder, sense the Fires burning in me?

Seemingly not. They stood in silence for a time, gazing after Ruanek. Then the emperor murmured, "That is a dangerous man."

Spock raised an eyebrow. "How so, Your Majesty?"

"Why, he is *honest!* Honest, honorable, and, no doubt,

absolutely incorruptible." A hint of sardonic humor flashed in Shiarkiek's eyes. "Definitely dangerous."

"Truth often appears dangerous."

"Indeed. Walk with me, Symakhos. Or," the emperor added with a sharp sideways glance, "whoever you truly are."

So! "I fail to see—"

"Come, now. I am old, no denying that, but I am not yet feeble of memory. I can account for each and every honor I have awarded. And I would remember a fellow academician named Symakhos, were there such a one."

"Ah." Time for the greatest gamble yet. As he had told the Underground, Spock said, "I am a Vulcan."

"*Are* you?" It was almost an exclamation of delight. "How fascinating! I have often wondered what genetic and cultural differences might have grown up in the years since—ah, but we can hardly arrange a symposium, now, can we? Or even indulge in a genetic sample."

A scholar, Spock thought, bemused by the use of that familiar word "fascinating," *a true scholar.*

Which did not make him any less an emperor—or a danger. Shiarkiek paused by a small pool, deep enough for its water to be dark blue. "Where are they . . . ? Ah, there they are, my beauties. Do you see them?"

Spock, standing warily back from the edge, saw small, sleek shapes, bluish-gray, fins, dorsal spines. . . . "I do not know the species."

"They are called *kharah*. Observe how quickly they surface! They know I am here with a treat for them." The emperor removed a small covered bowl from the folds of his robes. "Patience, my pretty ones. Let me but remove the lid . . . there, now, there."

What he tossed into the pool was small, red, and squirmingly alive—until it hit the surface of the water. In an instant, two *kharah* had seized it, torn it apart, and devoured it, leaving a small swirl of greenish blood on the surface. Spock, certain the emperor was testing him, kept his face resolutely blank. No logic in revulsion; these were only animals behaving as they must.

Not unlike someone in the grasp of *Pon farr*—no! He would not think such improper thoughts! He needed his wits about him in front of this man who, for all his scholarly mannerisms, was still emperor of all the Romulans.

"Well done, my pretty ones!" Shiarkiek told the fish, tossing them a second . . . morsel, which met the same fate as the first. The emperor offered the bowl of squirming red creatures to Spock. "Would you like to feed them?"

"With all due respect, Emperor Shiarkiek—no."

It had, indeed, been a test. "Ah, you truly are a Vulcan. So consistent. So very . . . vegetarian."

"We follow our beliefs."

"As do we all. Or at least as we may delude ourselves we do." The emperor quickly emptied the contents of the bowl into the pool, then put the bowl aside. "Now," Shiarkiek began, "knowing of the Vulcan reputation for reasonable honesty—and do not quirk that eyebrow at me; we are all mortal and, therefore, fallible—knowing, as I say, of that honesty, I believe I can ask with a fair expectancy of truthfulness from you:

"Are you here as a vanguard to Federation attack?"

That was said with utter sharpness, the ancient eyes suddenly fierce as those of a warrior. Spock met the emperor's gaze directly. "No. I am not. My word on my honor and the honor of Vulcan, I am not."

"And why, then, *are* you here? I cannot believe you a common spy. You are clearly too civilized an individual for that." The emperor paused, studying Spock thoughtfully. "Or . . . can you possibly be here without official sanction?"

"Your pardon, but that is hardly a question I will answer."

"Understandable. But . . . yes, I do believe I am correct! How very daring of you! Of course, Vulcans *were* warriors once. But again, why are you here?"

So, now! "There is one," Spock began, picking his way with

care, "who imperils us both, the Empire and the Federation. I do not name him."

The emperor snorted. "You mean Dralath."

Eyebrow raised, Spock countered, "Do you know of the attack in motion against Narendra III?"

The wise, fierce eyes glanced away, blinking, blinking. And suddenly the keen scholar was gone, replaced by a weary, sad old man. "Oh yes." It was the harshest of whispers. "I know. I knew. But . . . I . . . could . . . do *nothing!*"

He turned sharply back to Spock. "I was a fool, a fool, so seduced by my scholarly research I forgot what I was. Never do that, never forget. For once you do, once you begin trusting others with what should be yours, you never, ever win it back. And that," Shiarkiek added bitterly, "includes command of the military.

"*Akhh,* well, what is, is. You are Narviat's associate, however you came to be so—and no, I do not wish to know of that, or of who else might be involved. There is a limit to blunt honesty, and I did not live so long by learning what I could not later deny having heard. I can make an extrapolation easily enough as to what you two mean to do."

"Then you *do* support him."

"Ah, you, too are a scholar, wary and testing each step of the experiment! Yes. Our Narviat is ambitious, even ruthless, though he thinks I realize it not, but he is, underneath it all, a worthy son of this House and I must respect his honor. And," the emperor added with Romulan bluntness, "there is no one else. No one who can be trusted not to destroy the Empire. No one who would not be assassinated on the day he took power. If Narviat dies, I see no way to replace Dralath. And now Narviat has been arrested—yes, I have my sources of information. But it is up to you to see that he is set free. However you mean to do that."

A casually imperious gesture brought a servant running. "Send word," Shiarkiek said. "By the usual means, the usual targets. Spread the usual rumors. There must be no stain on Narviat's honor," he added to Spock as the servant hurried off again, "so the proper whispers in the proper ears will keep him in the public favor. More than this, however, I cannot do. Yes, again, I wish you both success. But hear me out," the emperor continued, blinking fiercely, "whatever you do, I pray you, since I may not command you, do it *not* for honor, do it not for personal pride or political advantage:

"Do what you must do only for the sake of the *people*."

Utter honesty blazed from the ancient eyes, so strong an emotion that Spock, more shaken than he ever would have admitted, glanced away, saying softly, "We do. We shall."

Dralath sat at his work desk in his office, studying the computer screen, not bothering to glance at the guard standing at attention before him. "And . . . ?" the praetor snapped over his shoulder.

"And there is nothing else to report, my praetor. Yes, the Academician Symakhos did visit with the emperor, but they stayed out near the fish ponds for nearly the entire time, where there is no place for spy eyes or ears. We do not know what was said, though it seemed to simply involve," the guard added with distaste, "fish."

"And Symakhos' aide?"

"Ah. That *might* have been one Subcommander Ruanek, in service to Senator Avrak but now reported missing."

Wasn't that . . . yes. The officer who'd been poisoned defending Evaste—for all the joy Dralath had had of that whole sorry interlude. What was he doing with Charvanek's pet academic? "You say 'might,' " Dralath said sharply. "Do you not have confirmation?"

"I regret, my praetor, that none of our people could get a clear image. And Emperor Shiarkiek's physician is quite honest and honorable: We cannot reach him."

Disgustingly true. "Go on."

"Academician Symakhos and his aide left the palace long before nightfall, and took lodgings near the Imperial University of Ki Baratan. There, he filed for permission to use an office in the Bureau of Statistics and Information."

"I am aware of that." The file was on Dralath's screen right now, together with the research proposal: *A comparison of grain consumption by the military versus the civilian population on the Romulan colony worlds, dating from the establishment of those colonies.* Just the sort of pedantic rubbish scholars adored. "Permission was granted," Dralath murmured, reading on. "Of course it was granted. The study might well be genuine, even potentially useful."

He glanced up at the guard, who straightened to attention. "I wish a close watch kept on the research. See to it. Now, go. And send in Serik!"

The little aide scurried inside, blinking nervously. "My praetor?"

"The emperor is about to be ill. A most lamentable relapse of the condition that caused his recent collapse during Court. His own physician is no longer sufficient. Emperor Shiarkiek will be committed to my guardianship for medical treatment. For his own safety, of course." Dralath paused, glaring impatiently at the horrified Serik. "Well? See to it—or see to your immediate suicide!"

Ah, that made the creature scurry out!

Dralath waited till Serik had closed the door behind him, then permitted himself the smallest of smiles. Security Chief Zerliak had reported far too many innocent meetings lately, between Shiarkiek and Narviat, between Narviat and Symakhos, between Symakhos and Shiarkiek . . .

Innocent, Dralath thought sardonically.

He turned back to the console, keyed in certain security codes, then added a whispered code as well. In a few seconds, the image on the screen sharpened from text to visual: a spy eye staring into a prison cell. There was no shadow here, nothing but blazing light. The man who sat on the cell's cot, a bare shelf extruded from the wall, wore prison garb, a simple tunic and trousers, no belt, no sash, nothing with which a prisoner might attempt suicide. His hair, hanging loose about his face, looked as though he had combed it with his fingers. His eyes were deeply shadowed. The eyes of someone who has been kept from sleep for longer than he would have wished.

Still attempting to keep up appearances, Narviat? As well as your dignity?

Dralath's smile thinned. Narviat was entirely too secure in the knowledge that the praetor dared not torture him in any way that would leave physical marks. Mustn't show the people a poor, battered martyr; they must be convinced that what they saw was a hardened enemy of the State, a senior officer, an Imperial, no less, who had betrayed their trust.

Drugs? Too risky with so important a prisoner. Too many chances for an overdose, or a fatal allergic reaction.

But there were tortures other than physical. So far, Narviat was showing an infuriating ability to escape the double torments of light and noise. He managed to slide into meditation like some cursed Vulcan—presumably a survival trick he'd learned during his military service.

Dralath flipped open a secure channel. "Add variable-frequency subsonics," he ordered. "But carefully! If he is reduced to lunacy, you will join him!"

Narviat, though, Dralath suspected, was too strong—and too stubborn—to go mad.

Still, meditation could take the place of sleep for only so long. Eventually, Narviat would break, and surrender the details of his treasonous plot.

And then, of course, during the forthcoming victory celebrations over Narendra III, he would die a traitor's death—humiliating, protracted, and agonizing.

TWENTY-TWO

NARENDRA SYSTEM, STARDATE 21096.4

As the *Enterprise* sped toward the Narendra system, Captain
Garrett held a final situation-analysis meeting in the small,
sparsely furnished briefing room. Senior staff sat tensely around
the oval table studded with computer consoles and holographic
projectors. *We will pretend that we have a chance,* Garrett
thought.

The chronometers all told her the same cold fact: Three hours
had come and gone, and they were still a ship's hour from
Narendra III.

Varani's soft voice came over in-ship communications. *"I have
attempted to raise the stations along the Neutral Zone. By the
time they reply by subspace transmission, Captain . . ."*

The battle will be over one way or another. No help there.

"Still no word from Narendra III?" *The colonists couldn't
already all be dead. Could they?*

"My regrets, Captain," Science Officer Tholav said. "The
system now contains a sizable uncharted anomaly that is putting
out bursts of chroniton radiation. It's enough to make communi-

cation difficult and to mask traces of cloaked ships. Commander Varani and I were unable to separate out emissions from the aftermath of the storm."

So I am going on the word of a sick woman—and my own instincts, Garrett thought. *Well, I've always trusted my instincts, and when the woman is Commander Saavik . . . No use delaying this.*

"We can no longer second-guess ourselves," she said. "We are committed to this fight and, as the admiral said, we cannot expect reinforcement for . . . some time. So we'd better review what kind of assets we have."

She nodded to Tholav. "Narendra III is, indeed, unarmed," he reported in his soft voice.

"—or at least hasn't got anything I'd call a serious fighting ship." The Andorian's fingers tapped a few keys on his console, bringing up a display of Narendra III's ships, crew complements, and projected firepower. "As you see: some scouts, a few shuttles, the occasional personnel carrier. Nothing fit to take on a warbird."

Garrett frowned at the projection. Helm was going to have to avoid that anomaly; chronitons could play hell with a warp drive. "If we do, somehow, make it in-system before the Romulan fleet," Garrett continued, "the system's asteroid belt looks like a promising hideout. What's the assay on the biggest rocks?"

Commander Tholav brought up a new projection. "Metallic content is sufficient for us to power down and pass undetected— unless, of course, the Romulans are on the lookout for us."

Hiding out in an asteroid belt, with only life-support and scanners active, was a calculated risk in case they had to come up to combat readiness fast. "If the Romulans arrive at the party late," Garrett said, "we might conceal ourselves there to await reinforcements, then set up a kind of cordon to warn off those warbirds. I'd seed the perimeter with mines, only that would be a sure giveaway of our presence. I want your best estimates on how quickly we can get engines, shields, and weapons systems back on-line. Then, figure out how to cut that time in half."

Mutters of "aye, aye" reassured no one.

"Already working on it," said Lieutenant Kepler, the tactical officer. A human from the Alpha Centauri systems, she had red hair and a hair-trigger temper—until the fighting started.

"At least," Castillo said, clearly trying to look on whatever bright side there might be, "the warbirds can't shoot while cloaked."

"We cannot count on that," Tholav warned with his customary fatalism, antennae drooping slightly.

"Yes," Garrett cut in before the Andorian could add any more discouraging comments, "but at the very least, the cloaking device is a tremendous power drain." *Grant us that much hope, Tholav.* She rubbed her eyes, reddened from the ferocious refresher course she'd been giving herself in Klingon and Romulan ordnance. "If it's worst-case, and these new warbirds can fire from beneath the cloak . . ."

Castillo glanced at the others, then shrugged. "As I see it, worst-case is that we get to Narendra after the Romulans have destroyed it. That gives us not only a massacre to deal with but the Klingons' reactions. They could be as likely to turn on us as the Empire. We could face war on two fronts."

"Nasty, clear-minded way he has of putting things," Aristide commented to no one in particular. "I don't see the Romulans responding to a charge of human-rights abuse."

"Human?"

Aristide shrugged. "Intelligent beings. Intelligent unarmed beings." He met the captain's gaze, his narrow, elegant dark face expressionless. Aristide, Garrett knew, was a son of a highly political family from Earth's Caribbean Alliance, specifically from an island that had in the past been tortured by one revolt after another. Garrett suspected that the only reason he'd thrown his support behind the mission to Narendra III was that the Romulans' hatred of Klingons amounted to race prejudice.

"Captain!" Lieutenant Commander Varani called from his communications station on the bridge. "Long-range scan's picking up something now that we're closer to Narendra system. Before, it was hidden by the star's energy emissions and the anomaly. I've got a fix on them. Two . . . three . . . no, four warbirds."

"There's our confirmation," Garrett said. "On my way," she told Communications. "Here we go."

"Only four?" Castillo asked as they entered the bridge. "Down from seven? That's progress!"

Two ensigns cheered.

"Shut it down!" Garrett snapped, taking her seat. "They might have left a third of their complement in reserve."

"They're decloaking," Castillo said in sudden alarm.

So, Garrett thought, they couldn't fire while cloaked. Thank heavens for small mercies, which were probably all the mercy anyone was likely to get.

"Captain." Tholav's voice was very soft, his body and antennae rigid with outrage as he stared at his data. "Bad news. Very. The Romulans have begun to fire on Narendra III." In their ancient past, Andorians had been warriors as savage . . . as Klingons. Now, Garrett's science officer stood so tense he nearly quivered with the strain, waiting for commands.

A voice from Earth's past echoed in Garrett's mind: *"This is a day that will live in infamy."*

"Warp eight," she ordered. "As soon as we're in-system, raise shields and go to red alert. Earlier, if the warbirds make any move toward us. Lieutenant Kepler, put that tactical display on screen."

The display enlarged just in time to reveal three Klingon scoutcraft exploding into white-hot fireballs. A personnel carrier still docked at the station opened fire on the Romulans, and a warbird seemed to swoop in toward it like one of the predators for which it was named, precision-firing disruptors. The Klingon ship cast off from the space station. Garrett's heart went out to whoever was captaining it, knowing that attempting to draw the warbird's fire was a suicide mission.

Disruptors engulfed the Klingon ship. It exploded into a blinding blaze of light, debris, and slag toppling slowly back onto the station, pulled in by its artificial gravity.

Utter silence fell on the *Enterprise*'s bridge as the light from the explosion faded. Garrett almost started when Varani cut in, "Captain, I'm picking up a Klingon message."

She'd never heard of a Klingon asking for aid—or even admitting needing it. "On screen."

The dagger triskele of the Klingon Empire appeared on screen, followed not by a message, but by howls of mourning.

"All ships!" rasped a harsh Klingon voice, echoed a moment later by computer translation. "To all ships in this sector! Now hear this! Our Empire's civilian outpost on Narendra III has been attacked in overpowering numbers without declaration or challenge by enemies devoid of all honor!"

Two shuttles blew up onscreen, as though underscoring his words. A small flotilla of one-man ships struggled up from the planet's gravity well. A warbird that seemed to be hovering, a predator with outstretched wings, waiting for an opportunity to swoop upon its prey, picked the Klingon ships off almost lazily, one by one, as they crossed the terminator between light and darkness.

"The Romulans have got this massacre all planned," muttered Castillo. "Dammit, it's not *fair.*"

"Fair?" Garrett asked. "You still expect the universe to be fair, mister? Even now?"

Damn, now the warbirds had veered to fire directly on the space station. Garrett didn't need Tholav's quiet voice to tell her the personnel in there were taking heavy hits.

The Klingon message broke up into static, then reformed. "Image onscreen," Garrett ordered.

A elderly Klingon propped himself up against his console. Violet-colored blood dripped from his mouth, and he held his arm awkwardly, as if it were broken, but warrior pride still blazed in his eyes. Flames surged in the background, then subsided as Klingons attacked the fires with as much rage as if they fought Romulans hand to hand.

A cool voice in Garrett's mind observed that at least the warbirds were not equipped with the plasma device that had destroyed outposts on the Neutral Zone two generations back. At least not so far as she could see.

Yet.

Thank heavens for large mercies as well as small.

Maybe they just haven't needed to deploy it yet. But there was no point second-guessing her enemy. That was the kind of thinking that woke you in a cold sweat in the night watches for years to come. Assuming you survived to get the nightmares.

"Narendra station, this is the Federation starship *Enterprise!*" Garrett called. "We're on our way!"

To her astonishment, the Klingon gave her an almost gallant salute with his uninjured arm. "Well met, *Enterprise.* Trust you to scent action. We offer you a priceless opportunity for honor. Hunt with us, *Enterprise.* Fight at our side. Go to the Black Fleet with us! Win such glory that warriors will howl to honor our memory!" The old one's grin showed broken, discolored teeth.

"Captain," Tholav said quietly, "two of the warbirds have opened fire on the planetary installation. Awaiting orders, sir."

The image suddenly flared, broke up, reassembled as the station took yet another blast. Through the static, Garrett could see the old Klingon clinging fiercely to his station, surrounded by swirling smoke. He bent double, choking, but somehow remained on his feet.

"Narendra station!" Garrett shouted, hoping to be heard.

"Yes, *Enterprise?*" His voice came through clearly enough despite the undercurrent of physical pain and sorrow. He gave her her ship's name rather than her own. Klingon honor, Garrett knew: Her ship's name *was* her own.

"We are coming, Narendra. Helm, give me everything you've

got!" Garrett cried. "Listen to me, Klingon. Listen to *Enterprise*. Hold out. Hold on."

Again, the Klingon laughed. "Before I jettison station records, have you a word for our poets to remember, *Enterprise?*"

Behind her, Garrett heard Tholav's sharp intake of breath. "Captain," he reported, "we're getting some gravimetric anomalies. Some manner of rift's opening up. It resembles a Kerr loop. . . ."

Garrett waved him to silence. The only thing she wanted to do with superstring theory right now was use it to garrote Romulans. She turned back to the dying Klingon station.

Damn! Now what? She had never been much for fancy speeches, yet here this Klingon was, asking her for the kind of words it took a Churchill of Earth or a Korask of Rigel IV to invent. She had no ringing words for Klingon bards!

Yes, but Earth history had, and, if words could comfort a gallant old warrior about to die, she would borrow them.

She matched the Klingon's fierce grin. "Tell your bards and those point-eared Romulans," she shouted, "that before we're through, the Romulan language will be spoken only in hell!"

He would not have understood the reference; he understood the message. The Klingon roared with laughter.

"Well said, *Enterprise*. Welcome to our war!"

Klingons around him took up the ritual battle cry. *"HeghlumeH QaQ jajvam!"*

She didn't need the translator to tell her that one:

It is a good day to die.

The station shuddered. The old Klingon screamed in pain and rage as a piece of debris struck him, almost toppling him. Blood gouted from a gaping wound as he clung determinedly to his post. He howled once for himself, but the cry ended in a gurgle as more blood sluiced from his mouth. The Klingon looked straight into Rachel Garrett's eyes.

"Qapla'!" The word was forced out. *Success.*

He toppled, his head striking his ruined console, in death yielding only his life.

"Station's going to blow!" Castillo warned.

"Filters up!" Garrett ordered. "Now!"

Even with filters up, the explosion was blinding. Garrett's mind filled in sound where, of course, there was none.

"What do they want?" That was young Ensign Fredericks, sitting in at communications. "Romulans usually want something!"

Dear Lord, when had the Academy started graduating them this young? His superior, Varani, was snapping "Quiet!" at him, but for once Garrett overrode one of her officers' commands.

"It's all right, Ensign. You're right. Romulans usually want something. In this case, it would appear that the praetor's out for glory. Romulans hate Klingons, so they're out for terror. Destruction. As much hatred as they can sow. And that's one battle they're going to lose!"

"Gravimetric anomalies are increasing exponentially," Tholav reported suddenly. On one screen, graphs replaced the fireball that had been a Klingon space station. "If this keeps up, we could have a wormhole. Or a chronological aberration."

"Worry about the warbirds, Commander," Garrett snapped. She heard Castillo groan. "They look like they're going in to scorch the planetary surface. Captain . . ."

"Steady there, Castillo. Steady. Bring phasers on-line. *Enterprise* to Narendra III, ground command. We have lost contact with your station's commander. What do you require? How may we assist you?"

No insignia opened the downworld installation's transmission. Instead, a montage of images flooded the ship's viewscreen: dead and dying, adults shielding children, far too many children, some clutching the sticks and rocks they had snatched in frantic, useless self-defense when the first fires had lanced down from suddenly deadly skies. The children closest to Garrett lay hugging each other as though hunting comfort even in death, and she only just bit back a cry of anguish.

They had died *surprised*.

"This is the captain," Rachel said to her crew over ship's

speakers. *"To the crew of the* Enterprise: *What you see is what we have sworn to stop, with our lives if need be. I ask you to give me your best as you always have. And—I thank you."*

Something was lacking. Admiral Lynn's old-fashioned farewell resonated in her mind. *"Godspeed,"* she added.

In that moment, she almost envied the Klingons their fierce freedom of emotions. She wasn't Klingon, but she felt like howling too for the coming destruction of her crew and her ship.

"Captain," Varani said, "one of the warbirds is headed toward us. Heading 83 mark 9."

"Load photon torpedoes. Shields on full."

"Warbird's almost within range."

"Steady," Garrett told Lieutenant Kepler. Not that the tactical officer needed the caution. "Lock on target."

"Locked on, Captain."

"All ship, secure yourselves. Prepare to engage."

The cheers pouring onto the bridge from speakers shipwide made Garrett blink furiously.

"Belay that!" she shouted. "The cooler we are, the longer we can hold out."

She nodded at her bridge crew. The best in the Fleet.

"Very well, Lieutenant Kepler," Captain Garrett said calmly, formally, "you may fire at will."

"Aye, sir," Kepler replied, almost as calmly. "Hold her steady, Castillo . . . and . . . photon torpedoes away!"

Castillo held course during the tense seconds as the torpedoes sped toward the approaching warbird—

"A hit!" Kepler exclaimed. "Torpedoes both hit!"

"Not hard enough," Garrett corrected after a moment. *Hell of a tough ship. Or else the Romulans don't care about protecting anything on their vessels but their weapons systems.*

The warbird's disruptors blazed with sudden poisonous green light.

"Evasive action, Mr. Castillo!" Garrett ordered. "Now!"

The Romulan moved with them, fired. Garrett's crew braced, then fought to retain their seats as the *Enterprise* shuddered, then rocked from side to side.

Damn those Romulans; they were fast. Fast and tough, as you'd expect of Vulcanoids. Giving no quarter—but then Romulans never did.

"Romulan ship down to one-half power." Tholav's voice never wavered from its usual soft monotone.

Garrett fought back upright. "Let's hit it again!" she snarled. "Kepler, lay down a trail of photon torpedoes"—no use saving them—"and follow up with ship's phasers at max."

She braced for the characteristic ship's lurch as torpedoes darted from the ship.

Nothing.

"Kepler?"

Garrett saw red hair fanned out over the body that slumped motionless over the tac station.

"I'm afraid Kepler's dead, sir." Lieutenant Castillo's face showed nothing and his voice didn't shake, but Garrett knew that the operative words were the first two he'd said.

Me too, mister. Garrett quickly transferred helm function to her own workstation. They'd lost the strategic moment to fire; she had better try something else. "Mr. Castillo, take over Tactical. Heading 38X 49Y mark 270, Mr. Castillo. We're going to dodge that warbird and try to protect the planetary installation. On my mark. *Now!*"

Enterprise's sudden change of attitude caught the warbird by surprise. By the time it shot after them in pursuit, *Enterprise* was that much closer to the base.

Nice work, Garrett thought. But the only problem with nice work was that it embarrassed Romulans, and an embarrassed Romulan was a vindictive enemy. So nothing much had changed; her ship had simply drawn a little closer to their allies. As sapients, the Klingons were worth dying for. As fighters, they were worth dying with.

"Fire aft phasers," she ordered. "We'll cut our way through, if we have to. Mr. Castillo, fire!"

"Fluctuations increasing, Captain." Tholav, Garrett had always thought, was the sort of science officer who, if the Four Horsemen of the Apocalypse were charging him, would comment on the conformation of Death's pale horse—and now she saw that she was right.

She spared a glance at the screen where the gravimetric fluctuations were indeed building up. As the anomaly grew, space tore, revealing churning lights in all the colors of heaven. They danced, forming patterns, then breaking up. Worse luck, the damned anomaly *moved*. Maybe she could drive a warbird into it.

"A hit," Castillo reported. "Got them—no, not enough damage—They're firing!"

Disruptor fire blazed from the pursuing warbird. No time for evasive action—*Enterprise* convulsed. The restraints on Kepler's chair snapped as debris hit it, catapulting her body across the tilting deck. Someone cried out in dread, then fell silent too quickly. Someone else was swearing horribly, monotonously, but without raising his voice. On every console red lights burned or, worse yet, showed no lights at all, indicating burnout of critical systems.

"Engaging secondary life-support," Tholav reported.

"Damage control, report!" Garrett snapped.

"Deck Five . . . shields down to forty-two percent."

"Deck Three . . . Compartment Five, isolated . . . hull breach . . ."

God help those poor bastards, vented out into space, Garrett thought. *At least it's a quick way to die.*

"Captain, this is Singh in Engineering . . ." The Indian was coughing so hard Garrett wouldn't have known if he hadn't identified himself. "Coolant leak. Twenty dead. We're getting it contained." Another racking cough, and Garrett wondered how long until the casualty count was twenty-one.

A deadly light bloomed on her board. Fluctuations in the structural integrity field. Damn!

"Singh!" Garrett shouted. "Singh! Divert auxiliary power to shields and structural integrity field."

"Aye, sir."

"We've got two of 'em coming straight at us, Captain," Castillo warned sharply.

Damnation!

The warbirds bracketed the ship, firing with a systematic, efficient viciousness.

All right, Intelligence reported that Ambassador-*class ships can outmaneuver warbirds. They'd damn well better be right.*

Garrett took *Enterprise* to Mark 270, "below" the warbirds' plane of fire so fast that warning lights lit on the internal damping system readouts. If she wasn't careful, she'd tear her ship apart before the Romulans got to it.

Mind you, if we're close enough to a warbird, an exploding nacelle will take them with us. Not quite the defense I have in mind.

One warbird began almost instantly to correct course to cut *Enterprise* off. Quick learners, these Romulans. Like fighting Vulcans who'd turned vicious. Still, Garrett thought, she had some tricks left. She bared her teeth, tasting blood. She didn't remember biting her lip.

"Mark 15Y 90 degrees!" she ordered, and the ship veered away.

Not fast enough. A Romulan disruptor raked across the starboard nacelle. *Enterprise* shuddered.

"Structural integrity field compromised," Tholav intoned. If the SIF field failed, the ship would tear itself apart before the Romulans could blow it out of space.

"Engineering!" Garrett shouted.

The ship bucked again, rocking almost out of control. Sparks cascaded from installations all over the bridge while, over the cries of the injured, the deep shuddering of what might already be a mortally injured ship, came the ominous warning from the SIF readouts.

Tholav hurled himself from his station to the security console, his hands darting over the board, bypassing Engineering to channel power directly from Command to the SIF. Disruptor fire struck again. The console erupted in lightnings. They surrounded Tholav with an unholy halo. His white hair ignited as the charge that electrocuted him flung him across the bridge. Garrett managed not to gag at the reek of the blue, burning flesh of his ruined hands.

But the SIF warning subsided. The ship held together.

Tholav, Garrett grieved. *Tholav. You could at least have waited and gone with the rest of us.*

She felt a lightness as if weight, motion, and pressure had suddenly grown uncertain. Never mind the gravimetric fluctuations from the rift; the internal gravity generator had just glitched.

"Singh!" she shouted.

"Mr. Singh's down, Captain." A young woman's voice fought to be heard over the frying sound—don't think of that—of deteriorating speakers. "We're trying to get gravity back to full strength."

"Sickbay, Captain." That was Aristide's precise voice. "Thirty-three more dead." A pause, and she heard him order, "Have three of the medtechs suit up and go in! Someone may still be alive in that corridor."

The ship jolted again.

"Dr. Aristide?" That was one of the medtechs: LoPresti? "Commander?"

Too long a pause.

"Oh. My. God. Captain, Commander Aristide's gone."

Dead, then, Garrett thought with a flash of anguish, just one more among the casualties he had fought to save.

One by one, and ten by ten, ship's communications brought Garrett news of the loss of irreplaceable people as the ship failed. Engineering decimated; Aristide gone; Tholav dead, Kepler; so many others of her seven hundred, dead, dying, burning with her ship. If she lived, she would mourn them: a reason to wish not to go on living.

"Steady as she goes," Garrett said, as much to herself as to the others, and entered the ship's final course. Buffeted, reeling, *Enterprise* somehow held that course toward Narendra III, then turned at bay.

Castillo turned from the tac station to grin at his captain in admiration, white teeth flashing in a mask of ash and sweat.

"Now we make our stand," Garrett ordered. The survivors on the bridge managed a ragged cheer. This time, she did not stop them.

"Photon torpedoes," she ordered Castillo hoarsely. "Fire at will. Come on, Lieutenant, this is your chance to test out all the wild tactics you've been talking about all these years."

The ship rocked slightly as the torpedoes sped away.

One of the warbirds went up in gouts of flame.

"Good shot! Try for two!"

The ship took another tremendous hit from one of the three surviving warbirds. Debris buffeted Garrett, and she grunted at the impact, feeling something snap deep within her. A rib, hopefully only a rib. People had survived worse.

Smoke and gas erupted from one of the maintenance tubes. It was going to get really hard to breathe in just a few seconds. "Emergency O^2 masks on!"

Assuming the oxygen masks hadn't been pinholed by all the debris.

Another hit. A console came crashing down across her legs, and she nearly screamed at the sudden white-hot blaze of pain. Drugs . . . there were painkillers stored in a compartment beneath the arm of her command chair. She had never used them, never needed them. Now, she fumbled the compartment open, groped for the spray hypo, and injected herself, fighting the black mists threatening to engulf her.

"Shields down to fifteen percent, Captain. The next disruptor . . ." Castillo shrugged finality, then slammed a hand down, firing photon torpedoes.

Varani had moved over to Science. "Captain, I'm getting a reading from that anomaly, the rift. It's moving in on us."

"Evasive," she whispered, but her gaze was on the warbirds preparing to fire what she knew would be a fatal salvo. —A flash of memory: herself as a tall, gawky young girl who had looked up at the stars from the fields of home and staked her claim to them.

And had I the choice, I'd do it all over again, Garrett assured that younger self.

"Into Thy hands," she whispered as she had not since she was a child, then straightened as best she could. "Evasive action, Mr. Castillo. Where there's life, there's hope."

"Warp engines are off-line, Captain." The young voice from Engineering sounded exhausted and infinitely regretful.

Aren't we all? "Get working, mister!" Garrett snapped.

"Captain," came another voice from Engineering, sounding just as young as the first. Damn, were children all that was left down there? "Captain, there's a power drain. Our dilithium crystals are degrading. I think it's that anomaly—if we don't retreat, it'll pull us in." The voice cracked.

The warbirds had stayed with their prey, following *Enterprise*'s every move. With a blaze of green, disruptor fire engulfed the ship.

"Shields down, Captain."

Debris raked the bridge. Garrett heard Varani scream, raising his voice for what surely was the first time in his life. And, a quick glance told her, the last.

They were trapped. With warp drive down, they could not run. With shields down, they could not stand. Could they fight?

The ship's gravity quivered again, released, then secured itself. Someone, whoever was left in Engineering, must have gotten that fix to work. But to Garrett's horror, she saw an amber light flicker to red on her board. There went life-support on the bridge. What about the rest of the ship?

"Damage control!" she tried to shout, but all that came out was a gasp. She coughed up blood. Nasty way to die, drowning in your own blood.

A warbird veered, banked, and circled back. *Fight,* she told herself. *You're not dead yet.*

"Fire!" she gasped.

Castillo must have blacked out. Garrett overrode Tactical and fired. Got him! Phaser fire raked across the warbird's hull—

But then the Romulan returned fire. And this time, her own weapons systems did not respond.

Castillo raised his head, his face a bloody mask. "Sorry, Captain."

"I'm picking up an image from the planet, Captain," said Ensign Fredericks.

"Screen . . ." Garrett coughed again. "On."

A few buildings, charred and smoking, still stood amid the ruins, a few lights still flickered within. Some survivors, then . . .

"My God, Captain, will you look at the readings from that warbird?" Castillo gasped, then collapsed across his console.

The Romulans did, indeed, have those plasma weapons. A burst of immense power erupted from the Romulan ship, blooming, expanding as it exploded out toward Narendra III, engulfing it in blue-white fire that sent tears sheeting down Garrett's face. The screen filled with flame—then went dark. All those lives, all the installations downworld . . .

. . . Nothing left.

Nothing at all.

And soon, not even us.

"Suit up!" Garrett ordered. "Man the stasis units." That might save a few. "Release the log buoy." That order hurt; she had given it last during the *Kobayashi Maru* examination. So strange that Starfleet still had its cadets fight Klingons, not Romulans.

Of her bridge crew, it seemed that no one was left to obey her. Varani lay facedown on the deck. Fredericks slumped in his chair, overcome by smoke. Garrett released the buoy herself. With her exec and Engineering officers dead, she could not destroy the ship. The Romulans' plasma bursts would take care of that. At least, she hoped they would blow up the ship, rather than try to take it in tow.

One last duty to perform. She opened a hailing frequency to the broadest possible band.

"This is Captain Garrett—" She broke off with a gasp. Oh God, she hurt. Even through the painkillers, she could feel the pain constricting her chest, the bones of her broken leg grinding together. She gagged, nearly choked, panting through clenched teeth, struggling for enough breath to finish her distress call.

A racking cough told her that Castillo had fought his way back to consciousness. He stiffened with horror as he stared at the screens. "The anomaly." It was the barest rasp. "God, it's *moving!*"

Garrett ignored him. She might have only seconds left to send out her warning.

"Captain Garrett . . . of the *Starship Enterprise*. We . . . have been attacked by Romulan warships. Require . . . immediate assistance. We have lost warp drive . . . life-support is failing . . ."

"Captain, we're being sucked into the anomaly!"

It was the last thing she heard. The anomaly loomed on the flickering viewscreen, a vast jagged tear in space. Her head spun in the foul, thinning air. The rift twisted as it opened, taking on the aspects of a wormhole. The colors within it formed patterns like snakeskin, luring her, drawing her in . . .

White light erupted, shading up to purple. Even the raving of the Romulans' disruptor fire paled by comparison.

Everything went black.

TWENTY-THREE

SPACE, NARENDRA III

Charvanek impatiently hit a communications button on the arm of her chair. "Well?"

Takvi's gruff voice, the gruffness just barely hiding bone-weariness, said from the engine room, "Done, Commander. At least as good as it's going to get, given what we have to hand."

"Meaning?"

"Meaning that we've finally got *Honor Blade*'s engines functioning well enough to get the battered lady back into the security of *her* cloak."

"And warp drive? What about that?"

"Yes, Commander. Not much of one, but we do once more have a working warp drive."

"Excellent. Dismissed. Go and rest." Charvanek glanced about the wreckage of the bridge, seeing at least some order where there'd been nothing but chaos. The crew might be sagging with exhaustion, but they'd done an amazing job. "At ease."

She courteously failed to notice how they reeled when they no longer had to brace to attention.

"Open shipwide communications. I assume we still *have* ship-wide communications? Good. Hear me, all of you. Now that the *Honor Blade* is in no immediate danger of blowing up, I am ordering the following division of labor. A third of you will stand down immediately, a third will keep stations as . . ." As they limped along? No. "As we proceed toward Narendra III. A third will continue repair, maintenance, and . . ." She stopped short, because her voice had been about to quiver. "And preparation of our dead comrades," Charvanek continued, "for the Last Review in the halls of Erebus."

She got slowly to her feet, holding herself erect by sheer force of will. "One last point: I am briefly leaving the bridge. While I am gone, you will poll the crew. Make *Honor Blade*'s shuttles and emergency supplies ready for those who choose not to . . . continue the fight. There is to be no shame attached to any who do so."

Managing not to stagger, Charvanek made it to her small, neat, so-familiar cabin, and sat for a precious few moments with head in hands. *"It is no dishonor to admit exhaustion of the heart."* Her old teacher Amarcan's *Axioms* could break your heart. If it were not already broken.

You waste precious time. Charvanek forced herself up again, snatching a few seconds to wash and tend her scrapes and burns: The ship's physician would be occupied with serious injuries. Wearily, she pulled on her dress uniform, then hacked off a handful of her long hair with her Honor Blade, a token sacrifice to her dead whose blood, even more than hers, justified her injured ship's name. Properly, she should fast until she had performed the Rites for the Dead; yet the living needed her alert.

Forgive me, she wished her dead crew, and ate the hastily prepared food her orderly had left for her. *Soon, I will see that you have your proper honor.*

Soon, her mind added unbidden, she would see them again.

Leaving the suddenly tasteless meal unfinished, Charvanek returned to the bridge, pausing just outside to straighten her back and force her face into an impassive mask.

Her officers stiffened to attention as she entered.

"Commander," her First greeted her.

"Have you polled the crew?"

Here at the end of things, she found herself particular about the company in which she died. No cowards, certainly, and none whose spirits quailed at the last.

"I have, Commander. They stay at their posts of their own free will."

"My eaglets," Charvanek said, her voice going husky despite her best intentions. "You will snatch honor from the Halls of Erebus itself."

She seated herself, drew her Honor Blade, blooded it against a thumb in ritual sacrifice, and sat, keeping station. *Honor Blade* crept toward Narendra III.

The first thing that greeted *Honor Blade* in the Narendra system was a scream in the barbarous noise that Klingons called a language.

"It is a good day to die!"

That had been an old man's voice. But he'd shouted not an appeal for help, but a challenge. A brave one, that grandfather, whoever he was. She could value courage, even in Klingons.

Echoing that challenge, tiny ships rose like sparks from Narendra III, only to be shot down by General Volskiar's four remaining warbirds, swiftly as sacrificial spices consumed by flame. Charvanek could hear the mourning howls of the remaining pilots, and thought, in a warrior's brief sympathy, *Honor to them.*

Once again, shouting over the disruptor static that bombarded the station circling Narendra III, came the old Klingon's voice.

"We have been attacked in overwhelming numbers by a dishonorable enemy . . ."

Dishonorable, indeed. And she—

"Commander, systems report power drain from the cloaking device."

"Boost power," she ordered automatically, then held up a hand. "Wait." Opening in-ship communications, Charvanek asked with deceptive softness, "Engineering, need I order you to run diagnostics?"

"I mean no disrespect, Commander." Takvi's voice was its usual gruff self. "But there's only so much my crew can do. The cloaking device takes a cursed amount of power. If we are to have energy for ship's engines and weapons systems . . ."

"Understood. Concentrate on those."

Volskiar was picking off the Klingon scouts in quick bursts of fire. The personnel carrier that had disengaged from the station died in gouts of flame. But then, shouting over the static, came a new voice. A *human* voice. "This is Captain Rachel Garrett of *U.S.S. Enterprise* . . ."

Enterprise.

A little shiver of memory shot through Charvanek, and she thought, *I should have known.* Of course this was not *that Enterprise,* the first of its line, the ship she had not quite sworn feud against—the fates only knew why—but it was still *Enterprise* in a newer, mightier guise. She watched, breath caught in her throat, as it sped to the attack, engaging Volskiar's fleet in gallant, outnumbered combat. Charvanek's crew stood at their duty stations, awaiting orders to fight.

"Engineering," she snapped. "Report."

"Commander, power consumption up 58.32 percent. Estimate critical in 9.75 unless economies are instituted."

"Decloak," Charvanek ordered. Space shimmered about them. "Weapons, Takvi, do we have weapons?"

"Powering up, Commander. But it's going to take time—"

"We don't *have* time! Selta! Open communications with the flagship." *Maybe we can at least distract them!*

"Transmission jammed."

"Break through."

The communications officer winced at the terrible squeals of static, but tried again. A savage burst of sound erupted from his headset, and he ripped it off in agony, bleeding from the ears, glancing at her in wild appeal.

"Cease," Charvanek ordered.

And all the while, the brave, doomed *Enterprise* fought on. *Salute, sister,* Charvanek wished its commander, this Captain Garrett. *May your gods grant you honor in whatever Afterworld is yours.*

A cold, clear thought twisted its unwelcome way into her mind: *The* Enterprise *is wounded, dying. When you have weapons back on-line, you could destroy it, atone for attacking your own—*

And destroy her honor and that of her crew?

It probably wouldn't work, anyhow.

Charvanek reopened a channel to Engineering. "We need weapons, dammit! Shut down all nonessential systems. Lights at minimum, and lower gravity by 0.10 percent."

That should save some power but not interfere with anyone's efficiency.

"This is Captain Garrett." *Enterprise* sounded mortally worn, mortally wounded. "To all Federation ships. We . . . have been attacked by Romulan warships and require . . . immediate assistance. We have lost warp drive . . . life-support is failing . . ."

All space suddenly seemed to blaze with a blinding blue-white light, a blaze into which the *Enterprise* vanished. Charvanek blinked her eyes, dazzled. "What in the name of all the Powers is *that*?" Her mind cried wildly, *A Federation weapon, something more terrible than any plasma burst—and we never, never knew . . .*

"An anomaly, Commander, a rift in space!"

Here? Now? The Powers truly had a perverse sense of humor! The anomaly was breathtaking, shimmering with more colors than Charvanek had ever seen, but if they were drawn into it—

"Evasive action!" she shouted.

The overworked engines groaned into life, then suddenly stopped. *Honor Blade* shuddered violently as if it were taking heavy fire.

"Damage control, report!" Charvanek snapped.

"Commander!" That was Engineer Takvi, sounding almost indignant. "Engines just shut themselves down."

"Commander," her bridge crew reported, voices overlapping in their astonishment, "ship's instruments just reversed themselves." "Instrument readings went wild!" "All of *space* just wavered!"

Now what? How do I fight space itself?

But in the next instant: "Commander, instruments are returning to normal!"

The ferocious rainbow patterns of the rift shimmered, subsided, then, abruptly, quickened again. Lightning seemed to lash out of a rip in the fabric of space itself, and—

Enterprise was visible again, and fighting more fiercely than before, almost as though the ship itself knew this was its final battle.

It was not enough. The Federation ship took hit after hit. Disruptor fire raved out, followed by a salvo of photon torpedoes. The wildfire of laser fire attempted to circle *Enterprise*'s hull, then ceased. Its shields wavered and fell.

The Empire's once-mighty enemy hung dead in space.

Charvanek drew in a shaken breath, only then realizing that she'd been hoping against all logic that the *Enterprise* could have somehow summoned its customary wizardry—and spared her the decision she knew she had to make.

And only now, with dreadful irony, came Takvi's report, "Weapons powered up."

She'd always known that the Fates were perverse. So be it. "Prepare to attack," Charvanek said quietly. "Open in-ship communications."

No time for anything more than brief words. They were all going to die, and they must all already know that. "My eaglets, my children," *my heir whom I shall never now have—no. Do not think of that.* "We are here today to conquer or die. But if we die, it is with honor. In death or in victory, we shall win immortality!"

They cheered her. Even though she was leading them to their deaths, they cheered her. Charvanek rose to salute them, then sat again and strapped herself in.

"Attack."

Honor Blade leapt forward, disruptors firing even as its engines faltered. The sheer vicious impetus of its attack took out the most badly damaged of Volskiar's surviving warbirds, which exploded in a blaze of white-hot light, debris tumbling in all directions.

Bank, dive, overloading engines groaning . . . not a word of complaint from Takvi; he knew it didn't matter now what happened to them. Full power, nothing in reserve, no worries about coming home, spend it all on—

Someone got in a glancing shot. *Honor Blade* jolted wildly, lights dimming, acrid smoke swirling onto the bridge, but her ship kept flying. No time to ask for damage reports, just keep going in the name of Romulan honor and—

Charvanek leaned forward in her chair, staring through the smoke with savage joy. *Victorious* lay dead ahead, a huge green demon aimed at them. *Now we die together, Volskiar!* "Ramming speed!" she shouted.

All power for this, no lights, barely life-support enough to keep them breathing, the groan of the engines growing to a desperate roar—

She touched her amulet. *Do you see this? Record it for our honor!*

"Coward!" Charvanek heard herself shriek as *Victorious,* at the last possible moment, banked away. "Fire!"

Energy blazed from *Honor Blade.*

"Victorious hit!" someone yelled in savage joy. "No," he corrected a second later. "A glancing blow. No real damage. And— Commander, we have no propulsion, no weapons. We can do no more."

Victorious was turning, the other ships backing off. It would be Volskiar's kill.

"Life to the emperor! We die for Romulus!" Charvanek shouted, and heard her crew's answering roar:

"We die for Romulus!"

The first onslaught took out *Honor Blade*'s shields and sent her bridge crew hurtling across the deck. Three failed to rise. The second broadside disabled its warp engines. Whooping erupted in in-ship communications, heralding a major power leak. *Honor Blade* and its crew waited for the third salvo, which would surely send it to the Last Review. This was, at least, an honorable way to die.

And waited while the distress calls from Narendra III died.

And waited while their life-support faltered. The air grew thick and the smoke thicker.

No! This shall not be! My crew deserves to die in battle, not of suffocation. Time to end the waiting.

Charvanek uncapped a switch colored blue and green and marked with the sigil of the warbird. Light shot out, verifying her retina pattern. "Initiate Final Honor sequence on my mark. Now!"

For one breathless moment, the sequence began. But then circuits exploded, fused, fell still. Charvanek bit back a cry of utter despair. She could not even release her ship!

"My children," Charvanek whispered, "I offer you my profound apology."

She held up her Honor Blade, kissed the gleaming ancient steel, and saw grief glint in her crew's eyes—*Is she going to abandon us after all the promises she made?* Charvanek saluted them all, this once as equal to equal. "Did I not give you my word I would not abandon you?"

Setting the gleaming blade gently down on the bloodstained, battered deck, she drew her sidearm and vaporized the ancient blade. It, at least, would not be stained by captivity.

Violent red shimmers erupted directly in front of her command chair: Soldiers, enemy Romulans, materializing on *her* bridge. If she fired, she would get one, maybe two—

No. They held not just pistols but disruptor rifles, and they guarded General Volskiar, who never could resist being in at the kill.

One of Volskiar's guards drew his disruptor and fired at the eagle on Charvanek's bridge, defacing its imperial differences.

Durnak broke. "You profane the Eagle!" he shouted, and vaulted over his duty station—to vanish in a crackle of disruptor fire.

Charvanek never flinched. "Do you expect me to thank you," she asked Volskiar coolly, "for giving my pilot an easy death?"

Volskiar glowered at her. "You will beg me for death, Charvanek."

"*Akhh,* you always were a braggart."

"What I am is the victor! One who shall hear you plead for life before you die."

"Indeed," Charvanek retorted. "My felicitations; you will be long-lived if you wait for that."

For a moment, she was sure he was about to strike her. But Volskiar contented himself with tearing the disruptor pistol from her, thrusting it into his belt. She heard him swear softly, and laughed. "That's right, Volskiar. No Honor Blade left for you to disgrace."

With a snarl, he ripped her insignia from her uniform. She laughed, soundlessly, and this time he did slap her. Charvanek delicately touched the tip of her tongue to the blood of her torn lip, making that a silent blood oath: *Give me the smallest chance, Volskiar, and you are dead.*

"My lord general!" a security guard cried. "We can't maintain life-support much longer. Hull integrity is compromised."

Die swiftly, my Honor Blade, *as I cannot.*

"Bring the survivors onto my ship!" Volskiar ordered.

Charvanek had time for one last glance about *Honor Blade*'s ruined, smoky deck. Then the transporter beam caught her, red as the firefalls of Gal'Gathong . . .

That I shall never see again.

TWENTY-FOUR

NEUTRAL ZONE, YEAR 2344

Charvanek glanced up from where she knelt by Takvi's side. A warbird's image glared down at her and those who remained of her crew from a bulkhead of *Victorious'* brig. She suspected that the glowing spheres representing the homeworlds were actually spy eyes.

He profanes an honorable symbol, she thought wearily, *but then, I should hardly be surprised at that.*

At her side, Takvi bit back a groan, and Charvanek winced and turned her attention back to him, struggling to keep from showing her despair at the sight of his broken form. So badly injured . . . why had he awakened? Why couldn't the Fates have given him the mercy of a swift death? And there was nothing she could do to help him . . . no medicine, no bandages more than strips torn from uniforms.

In a flash of pure fury, Charvanek feigned a lunge at the guards there beyond the forcefield, and watched them draw sidearms.

Go ahead. Fire into a forcefield and let me watch the ricochet kill you. I would relish the sight!

She had already all but begged them for medical supplies, and been mocked: no aid for traitors.

"Commander . . ." Takvi's voice was a whisper. "Commander, I beg you, do not . . . do not demean yourself."

"There is no dishonor for any of us." Reaching for his left hand (the right was wadded in a tunic so smeared by now with green that she wondered how much of the hand remained), she clasped it as firmly as she dared.

He shuddered. "A damn shame the engines didn't hold out just a little longer. We'd have had the bastard."

"Next time," she murmured and saw his face twist. Night and day, was that a smile?

"The youngster told me . . ." He fought to bring the words out. "M'ret said you destroyed your Honor Blade."

"I could not let it be taken."

"Too bad."

Agony blazed in his eyes. Charvanek bent over him so none but he could hear. "Takvi . . . I can still grant you the Final Honor. Do you consent?"

"Yes, Noble Born." Relief filled his voice.

"Guard us," she ordered over her shoulder. The men and women who clustered around Takvi's pallet, keeping death watch, turned their backs. A shadow fell across her: M'ret, blocking the guards' view with his body.

Charvanek traded her grip on Takvi's hand for one on his shoulder, then rested her other hand against his face.

"Thank you for these many years, Takvi," she whispered as intimately as if they had been lovers, not commander and officer, all that time. "I will honor you as long as memory remains. Go before me now. Tell them in Erebus of the *Honor Blade*. And when they ask whom you serve, tell them: I am herald for Charvanek. For Liviana."

As Takvi's eye widened in amazement that she confided her secret name, she snapped his neck.

The others helped her lift his body, laying him gently to

rest against the wall. Charvanek straightened the slack limbs and brushed her fingers across his eyelids to close them, wishing she could do more, then stood and saluted, fist to chest.

Who would say the Rites for her? Narviat, perhaps . . . Narviat, she thought with a touch of regret, who had always wanted so much more of her than she had given him. Now they would never be able to resolve . . . anything.

A commotion in the corridor beyond the forcefield brought her to stark alertness. The field hummed, then snapped inactive as a man wearing a commander's insignia stepped in: Volskiar's Fleet Second. The guards greeted him with chest-thumping salutes. *Ostentatious,* thought Charvanek.

Then he removed his helm, and only by the sternest will did she keep from crying out.

"Tal." For an instant his name was all she could say. "Sub-commander Tal."

He was still thin, kept lean by impatience and an anger that fed on him as much as it fueled him. The wavy hair was silvered now, but the eyes, intent on hers, had not changed in all the years since he'd stood at her right hand.

Since I betrayed him, Tal and all my crew, for Spock.

"It is Commander now, Commander. Fleet Second."

All she could think to say now was an inane, "You look well, Tal." *As though we were merely meeting at court.* "Careerism agrees with you."

"What else was I to do?" The smoldering temper she remembered was still there, just below the surface. "What do you think would be left to a subcommander whose commander had . . . disappeared? Even one who brought safely home the fleet you abandoned?"

"Tal . . ."

"I secured a position at the Academy on Bardat. As a junior adjunct lecturer. It was the best I could do, as far as I could safely get from Romulus. Then, in the last purge, my loyalties were considered suspect."

"So you were dismissed?"

"Oh, hardly. The praetor ordered me back to ship duty. Assigned me to General Volskiar. 'He's used to ground assignments; advise him,' they ordered. Mine was to obey. I never expected . . . this . . ." He hesitated, and for a moment his eyes were those of the Tal she'd known, empty of bitterness. "I have heard that you asked for aid for your crew. And I . . . bear you no hate, Commander, not any longer. I want you to believe that."

"I do."

"I would do more if I were able. But . . . this should help."

He'd palmed a small, carefully wrapped, packet. As he warily unwrapped a corner, Charvanek caught a trace of a familiar, pungent order.

Turath. Quick, painless suicide. Almost reluctantly, Charvanek shook her head. "There is not enough here for all my crew."

Tal flushed as awkwardly as young M'ret. "If I could . . ."

"No need. We are dying already. Do you remember Engineer Takvi?"

Tal glanced at the engineer, laid out with what honor prisoners could manage, and sketched a reverence. "I shall send guards for the body and perform the Rites myself." But then he paused. "Is there truly nothing else I can do?"

Angling her body to avoid the spy-eyes, Charvanek broke the chain holding her amulet. As she'd hoped, Volskiar, mocking her for her superstitions, had allowed her to keep the "childish trinket." The trinket that held the true record of Narendra III.

The trinket that might help save her people's honor.

"An offering for the dead," she told Tal, pressing the amulet into his reluctant hand. "It is all I have, and I—I would like a kinsman to have it if possible." She saw by his slightest of starts that he knew she meant Narviat. Charvanek met his eyes in the way that had always meant "pay attention" when he had served her. "Do what you will with it. Do what you must. For the Empire."

He would, of course, puzzle out the truth about the amulet's contents once he was back on Romulus. What he would do with that knowledge . . .

I can still trust him, Charvanek assured herself. And wondered if she was a liar. If so, then her last hope had just come to nothing.

No. She would not permit such self-defeating worry.

Casting a wary glance at the raptor guarding the brig, Tal gave her the briefest of hand-to-chest salutes, then put his helm back on and left. The forcefield shimmered into life behind him.

But in only a short time, it went down again as sullen guards lugged in emergency rations and rudimentary medkits. Almost apologetically, they bore Takvi's body away.

Almost before they were out of sight, a party of heavily armed guards pushed new prisoners into the brig. Charvanek's first thought was a weary, *We shall be crowded now.* Then she saw one of the prisoners fall, leaving a smear of red blood on the deck, and amended her thought to, *Maybe not. Not for long.*

Red blood, though?

Her crew stirred, someone muttering, "A disgrace, thrusting humans in among us."

Charvanek raised her hand, freezing her crew in place. "There is no shame in sharing quarters with humans from *Enterprise.* They fought well."

But a ship like *Enterprise* carried a full complement of approximately seven hundred beings. Only ten survivors . . . ? Captain Garrett was not among them. Not surprising.

Charvanek's glance fell on a tall, dark-haired young man whose eyes gleamed with almost Romulan fire. At his side stood a fair-haired woman who carried herself like a trained fighter.

Guessing, Charvanek nodded to the young man. "You command now that your captain is safe in the Final Honor?"

He dipped his head in hesitant courtesy. "I hadn't thought of it that way. But, yes. Sir."

Alien stared at alien until noise outside the brig made them all turn around.

Escorted by his guard, Volskiar strode in.

Once again, in at the kill, eh, Volskiar.

The guards in the brig snapped to rigid attention. Ignoring them, he . . . smiled at Charvanek. She forced herself to unclench her hands, to not even think of how much she would enjoy cleaning her sullied name in his blood.

"You know where you are headed," he told her. "Back to Romulus and public execution. I will see that noble blood of which you boast shed, and be honored for it."

"How boring you are, Volskiar. The humans have a saying, 'He won the battle, but not the war.' I may have lost this battle. But the war remains to be won."

Volskiar's laugh sounded almost genuine. "I give you my oath: I will hear you scream on Romulus before you die."

"And to think that *I* cautioned myself against self-indulgence!"

Volskiar turned his back on her and rounded on Fleet Second Tal, one step behind him. "Have you discovered why the human ship exploded?"

Had it? Then there would be no hull segment bearing the number NCC-1701-C in the Hall of State at Ki Baratan. A pity: So brave a ship should have been memorialized. At least, though, Volskiar had been denied the triumph.

"The matter-antimatter feed in the ship's engines degraded catastrophically," Tal said. "The ship's explosion took the prize crew with it. I beg forgiveness."

Only Charvanek, knowing him all those years, could have caught the faint edge of contempt in that.

Volskiar glanced at Tal a bit too long, then grumbled, "At least we have Federation prisoners. Have you questioned them?"

Tal came to attention before his general. "They fought almost to the last, as the general can see. That one"—he pointed at the tall young man—"assumed command. He is called Castillo."

"And that woman?"

Ah yes, the golden hair. Always predictable, our Volskiar.

"She was found at *Enterprise*'s tactical station," Tal said. "She is called Tasha Yar."

The blond woman did not even shrug. Charvanek had seen that fatalistic expression before, on prisoners who had faced death so long that they almost welcomed it.

"It would be well," Tal added hastily, reading the same signs, "if I questioned her about Federation tactics."

"Well thought, Tal, for once," the general said. "*I* indeed wish to question her. Privately."

Tal met Charvanek's eyes, saying plainly without words, *Outmaneuvered.*

But Volskiar's smile at the young woman was amazingly free of lust. Fascination, Charvanek thought, or maybe, bizarre thought, even a stirring of something far sweeter. He had always been a creature of impulses. Now, he reached out a hand to touch that golden hair—

"Let her alone!" Castillo snarled.

Dodging one of the guards, he hurled himself at the general's throat.

Oh, you young idiot.

Another guard, not bothering to draw his sidearm, slammed his fist into the young man's temple, and hurled him against a bulkhead. As the human crumpled, red blood trickled down the metal.

"Richard!" The young woman's voice and training broke as she shook off Volskiar's hand and flung herself on her knees at the young man's side. Blood poured from Castillo's mouth and ears, and his neck was twisted at an impossible, fatal angle. "Richard . . ."

"Carelessness," Volskiar snapped at the guard who had killed the human. "You are reduced two grades in rank. Now, see that the dead are removed. I wish the living still healthy on our arrival!" Approaching the human woman with what might actually have been genuine gentleness, he murmured, "Come away. Here is no place for you."

With the Romulan strength that humans could not withstand, he compelled her to her feet, then toward a waiting guard. "My orders are that she be tended. Gently. Then bring her to my quarters. See that we are not disturbed."

The woman turned, looking about the brig as if the Romulan and human prisoners were the last thing she would ever see. For a moment, her glance locked with Charvanek's. In that instant, differences of race and culture dropped away. They were only two women, in perfect understanding.

In war, *all* men were women's enemies.

For a bewildered moment, Tasha Yar had no idea where she'd awakened. Then she saw the blues and greens of a Romulan eagle glaring at her from a bulkhead, and memory returned in a rush.

The battle . . . the deaths . . . and this . . . Romulan. The "private interrogation" by General Volskiar had ended as she had suspected it would.

The body lying next to her, one arm flung possessively across her chest, was inhumanly warm. She froze beneath its weight, glancing about the cabin: large, austere, only the bed (with its silky sheets), a supply locker (elegantly black-lacquered), a desk welded to the floor, and that damned warbird welded to the wall—nothing that could be used as a weapon.

What difference does it make? a bitter little voice in her mind asked. After all, she had already struck so many hard bargains in the past few days that she was almost numb. Traded one *Enterprise* for another. Bargained away a life to which she was not entitled in a doomed timeline for a chance at a death that might mean something. This was just one more trade: the lives of her adopted crew in return for her place in the general's bed.

Remembering Romulan strength, she had half-expected to die there. But surprisingly, alarmingly, he had been almost gentle.

Of course he was gentle, damn him. Don't want to break the golden-haired prize, do we?

Well, she'd survived the predators of Turkana IV. At least here, the Romulan was the only male she had to worry about—she hoped.

Richard would have wanted his crew to live. Richard . . .

Abruptly revolted, Tasha rolled out from beneath her captor's arm and off the bed's silken sheets. One quick punch would crush whatever passed for a windpipe among Romulans.

And if I kill him, what happens to my crew?

"Excellent reaction time," the Romulan commented, opening his eyes. "Very agile. All quite satisfactory."

He stretched self-indulgently, his eyes heating as he surveyed her. Damn this Romulan bastard for lying there as if she were no threat! How long had he been awake, studying her?

She snatched up the brocaded robe he had let her wear all too briefly the night before, and belted it about herself. Tightly.

Something approaching amusement flickered in his eyes. "Modesty? Somewhat late for that, isn't it?" He paused, head cocked. "Blood-green becomes you. I chose well."

"We made a deal," Tasha reminded him. *Watch him go back on his word,* she told herself. *He might find it really funny to make me sell myself, then execute my crew after all.*

"A deal." Smiling, the Romulan repeated her words. "Remind me."

She forced herself to meet his eyes without blinking. He was taller and bulkier than many Romulans and, as she now had personal knowledge, immensely strong. His face was powerful rather than aristocratically chiseled—*not exactly unattractive, though,* a traitor corner of her mind noted before she repressed it firmly. That was the body of a fighting general, not an administrator. Trouble.

Intelligence briefings claimed that Romulans had a strong honor code. What if Romulan honor was strictly reserved for Romulans?

"You remember," she told him flatly. "You wanted me. I wanted my crew's lives."

"Ah, so that was why you didn't try to kill me!"

"Would your guards honor your word posthumously?"

Shockingly, Volskiar laughed. "Not just beauty and that golden hair, but almost Romulan wit and spirit. I honor you with the truth: My guards are sworn to me. If you had succeeded in assassinating me, they would have killed your crew. You, too, but lingeringly. Now, come here."

Remember your bargain. Time to pay up. Again.

She sat on the edge of the bed. But instead of pulling her to him, he merely caught her by the chin with delicate care, turning her to face him. His eyes were . . . what was hiding in that darkness? Not anything as uncomplicated as lust.

"I have decided," Volskiar said after a moment. "I want more from you than our bargain."

Her astonishment must surely be showing in her face. "What does that mean?"

But without a word of explanation, he released her and got to his feet, pulling on a robe as elegantly brocaded as her own, and switched on a comm set at the desk.

"Volskiar to bridge. Maintain course to the homeworld. Top warp speed, *Victorious* alone. I shall deliver my report to our praetor myself. No, I still do not wish to be disturbed. Out."

Glancing back at her over his shoulder, he added, "This victory means I can afford to be generous." But then he paused, frowning. "You tremble."

Damn him. "I'm chilly," Tasha said flatly.

"Easily remedied." Volskiar opened the supply locker and took out a bottle and a goblet—metal, Tasha thought, since you didn't keep anything breakable on a warship, but intricately engraved. Pouring out something that she recalled went down like oranges, fire, and engine-room jungle-juice, he sipped, then handed it to her.

Is he showing me there's no poison in the goblet? Why else would he want me to drink from his cup? God help me, he's not going sentimental, is he?

"This will warm you," he told her. "Drink."

She was still shaking, curse it.

"Your eyes are blue fire," Volskiar murmured. "I told you: drink." He placed the goblet in her hands, folding his around them, watching her, always watching.

Already, she knew what was and what was not a request. She sipped cautiously at the liqueur—which, curse it, *was* warming.

He nodded encouragingly and sat down beside her, not quite touching her, his higher-than-human body heat almost comforting.

Tasha sipped again. As a security officer, she found the Romulan's tactics familiar. In fact, he was damned good at playing good cop/bad cop all by himself. Did Romulans also have the equivalent of what used to be called Stockholm Syndrome back on Earth? Volskiar acted as if he was just waiting for it to kick in.

"I don't know what lies they tell of us in the Federation," he said in a voice that was just a shade short of cajoling, "but, for a woman like you, the Empire can hold many very . . . pleasant things. You shall see them at my side."

"As a prize of war?"

"As my companion. My consort." And then he spoiled that by adding, "I shall be much envied."

"A prize," she said dryly.

He touched her hair, smoothing it back. "You misunderstand. Many other rewards await me. The disgrace and death of that overprivileged traitor. This time, the old emperor won't be able to protect her, and you shall watch her punishment with me, and know how I have risen in importance."

Tasha froze. She remembered the Romulan woman, clearly an officer, who had been in the brig when she and the other survivors had been transferred, and the look of perfect understanding that had flashed between them. It had been the only clean thing that had happened all that day.

Dammit, she was shaking again.

Volskiar pulled her into his arms. "I know that humans weep. If you wish to do so, there is no shame. I know so much has happened that it has made you ill. But I wanted to claim you quickly so that all might just as quickly know you are now a woman of status. And so that we could start to reach an understanding."

Wrong order, Tasha thought sardonically. Nevertheless, there seemed to be genuine concern in his voice, in the premeditated gentleness of his hands. He could simply have used her, then ordered the deaths of her crew and her along with them. But he hadn't.

Maybe I can use that, get him off guard. . . .

"I want to keep you with me," Volskiar murmured into her hair, "bind you to me. And not as a prize, never merely that."

He must have felt her tense, because he drew back, smiling at her. "Does that surprise you?"

"I have only one question: Why?"

But with a sudden shock of insight, she knew, and knew what had been hiding in those dark, alien eyes.

My God. You're smitten, aren't you, Volskiar? God, yes, you are. Oh, what a weapon you've just given me!

"Would it be so very terrible if you responded to me?" Volskiar asked, and now that Tasha understood what lay behind the words, she had to fight not to laugh in his face. "Or started by simply not resisting me?"

She said nothing.

"I can wait for you to yield," he said. "Time is on my side, and I like a challenge."

She remained silent.

"Are you afraid I will break my word? Never. You will see, Tasha. We will have no further talk of bargains."

No, mister, she told him silently, *you'll see.*

He eased her back down against the pillows. With deliberate gentleness, he traced her throat with a finger.

"Your skin is so cool," he whispered. "Delightful."

Tasha forced herself not to resist as he caressed her. There could be no escape aboard this ship. But later . . . on Romulus . . .

Her breath caught in her throat as his hand stroked downward.

On Romulus she would have time to plan. It was difficult to think clearly right now. But love-struck as this fool was, once he thought she was gentled, acquiescent . . . and once her crew was safe . . .

It was worth the gamble. After all, she had not expected to live even this long.

TWENTY-FIVE

KI BARATAN, ROMULUS, DAY 8, SECOND WEEK OF TASMEEN, YEAR 2344

All bureaucracies, Spock thought, looked remarkably the same. There might be an elegant or imposing façade to impress outsiders—but the real business of running a government or a world or, for that matter, a Federation or Empire, went on in plain buildings such as this gray, faceless complex that loomed up before him. The morning sunlight, breaking through heavy cloud layers, made it no more appealing.

By now, those rebels who worked in the government should have the false research project—innocuous and utterly boring—well under way. The subject of grain consumption was large and intricate enough to require various aides and assistants to calculate, track, and correlate its many details. Not surprising that the Academician Symakhos should find it all . . . fascinating.

It is a project suitable for a noble scholar with good intentions and far too much free time. As those in Starfleet might say, "a perfect cover." And as Dralath investigates, he will find nothing at all suspicious.

Of course, Dralath would be investigating: There were certainly spies within the Imperial Palace, as well as spy devices just outside the walls to keep track of Shiarkiek's latest visitors, and of their utterly conventional departure yesterday from the palace.

At the same time, Dralath's interrogation clearly had not broken Narviat—not yet. Had the praetor succeeded, armed guards would be waiting to greet Spock's approach.

Instead, there was only the one bored guard at the plain metal door, clearly wishing himself anywhere even remotely more suitable to a warrior's honor. He glanced at Spock and his "aide," Ruanek (unhappy in dull gray clerical robes), with all the casual contempt of a true Romulan soldier for civilians, then shrugged and waved them in without so much as a word.

Too easy an entrance?

No. A sudden quick flash and an almost inaudible *whirr* warned Spock that once again he'd been scanned down to his genetic code. He knew a moment's uncertainty—

But no alarms erupted. The guard never stirred from his post. It would seem that the security scan for all government buildings was based on the same program and received the same data as did the Central Court: a definite weakness in an otherwise excellent system. The greatest risk was that someone in Dralath's security system might match the genetic pattern of this scholar's aide with that of Subcommander Ruanek of House Minor Strevon—but it would take that "someone" time to make the connection. After all, what Romulan warrior would want to break into a bureaucrats' stronghold? Particularly (much to Ruanek's discomfort) a warrior who was unarmed save for his Honor Blade?

Ahead, drab gray corridors radiated off a central atrium, monitored by a dour clerk at a battered desk under a grimy skylight. The clerk seemed engrossed by the pages of a scholarly journal. *Or,* Spock thought, catching a glance of a decidedly unscholarly illustration, *perhaps not.*

Ruanek, meanwhile, was grumbling under his breath over the situation, as he had from the moment they'd been snubbed by the guard outside. His pride or dignity were hurt—but any concerns about his status were illogical. And the not-quite-audible complaints were rapidly growing . . . irritating. Spock whirled on him with a sharp "Silence!"

Ruanek blinked, startled. Very warily, he whispered, "Are you all right?"

"I am," Spock snapped. "I was merely impersonating a genuine academician scolding an unruly research assistant."

"Of . . . course."

Ignoring that wary irony, Spock approached the clerk, who had been watching them as though glad for any disruption. "I am the Academician Symakhos—"

"Corridor B, Room 235."

With an abstracted wave at the proper corridor, the clerk returned to his . . . reading. And Spock . . .

. . . *felt a renewed stirring of the Fires, a fierce, irrational surge of* how *dare* he be so contemptuous—

No!

No. Rudeness such as this was unimportant; strong reaction was illogical. And he—he had known the respite from *Pon farr* would be only temporary.

There is only logic . . . logic is the cornerstone . . .

Silently reciting Discipline after Discipline, Spock stalked down Corridor B, Ruanek in his wake. He knocked on the door to Room 235 in the double-single-double pattern on which he and the rebels had decided.

Room 235 was as gray and bland as everything else, a small chamber crowded with antiquated files, old-fashioned tape storage, and somewhat more modern consoles. The rebels who had found an excuse to be in here sprang up in alarm, eyes fierce. Then, recognizing "Symakhos," they settled back again, looking once more like minor civil servants, right down to the careful blandness of their expressions. Piles of printouts and books surrounded them, and they wore gray robes to protect their clothing from the dust. Ruanek stifled a sneeze.

"Academician," a woman said warily. "You spent a restful night, I trust?"

"That," Spock said without expression, "is not precisely the word." After leaving the palace, he and Ruanek had taken a room in a lodging catering to provincial scholars, an austere place with the sour smell of genteel poverty clinging to it. There, they had been relatively safe in academic anonymity, although they had cautiously alternated standing guard. Neither had rested very well. Once, Spock had opened his eyes to see Ruanek watching him as if he were a disruptor that just might explode. "Has all been made ready?"

"The others are already here. Fewer than before, of course. You can hardly expect everyone to have the freedom granted a scholar of your social standing."

"Of course." It was only logical that the excuse of scholarly research would allow for a very finite number of "aides." "We will work with what we have. Have there been visitors?"

"Oh yes," said a thin-faced young man . . . Jarrin, Spock recalled. "Two times so far, 'attendants' have stopped by to see how we were managing."

Ridda, a sturdy woman of no certain age, snorted. "And checked our materials too thoroughly for mere 'attendants.' *He's* going to be disappointed to learn that the Academician Symakhos really is studying grain statistics!"

Spock gave her a sharp, warning glare. With meticulous pedantry that made the Romulans mutter under their breath, he paged through every bit of the gathered material, shuffling printouts and rearranging books, until he had found: "What is this? Surely some manner of security device?" Before the others could react, he added, "Tsk, carelessness. Carelessness and waste. Someone must be wondering even now where he lost it. We shall keep it safe till that someone returns for it."

Spock wrapped the tiny spy eye up with fussy care, so securely that no signal could be received by anyone watching or listening. A continued search revealed no other devices, at least none that he could find. Ruanek, leaning against a wall, grinned maliciously.

"Poor 'attendants.' How frustrated they're going to be! And—"

"We have delayed long enough," Spock cut in. "Leave those statistical charts and guard the door."

Were the others startled by his sudden curtness? Spock received several uneasy glares as two burly "clerks" identified as Darit and Gerrack moved to obey. The others lifted a massive file cabinet to one side, careful not to scrape it against the floor, to reveal a ragged opening in one wall. Clearly, it had been created by disruptor fire just a short while ago: blackened ash still flaked off the edges.

That was finished before Dralath had the chance to plant any spy devices, or we would all already be under arrest.

With a wary glance back at Spock, Ruanek crept through the opening. Spock cautiously followed him into a dark, windowless room thick with dust and the webs of the Romulan equivalent of arachnids. The computer consoles that had been set down in a hastily cleared area seemed almost jarringly modern amid the dust.

"We asked for Corridor B," Jarrin said, grinning, "because I remembered that it was slated for renovation. My excuse was that the Academician Symakhos needed *quiet* if he were to concentrate. That Room 235 should happen to adjoin this ancient storeroom was pure luck."

"Luck," Spock said, "is not logical. And while you are congratulating yourself on your cleverness, let me remind you that Dralath is not a fool. He is certain to have already puzzled out that Symakhos, Commander Charvanek, *and* Admiral Narviat are connected. Narviat clearly has not yet been forced to betray us, but his release must be our first priority."

Spock heard mutters of agreement. As the rebels had made clear to him back in the caves, their loyalty was to Narviat, not to him.

No matter. As long as we continue working toward the same goal.

Dralath sat in the main conference room, at the head of the

long oval table guarded by well-hidden sonic devices and disruptors, as his advisors droned on about crop failures in this district and grain shipments in that province. And all the while, he maintained just enough control to keep from tapping his fingers impatiently on the shining stone.

Where was Volskiar? How long could it possibly take to clean out a nest of Klingons? Surely it was time and past time for the attack on Narendra III to be over and for the fleet to be returning to the homeworlds—yet he had received no word at all. Volskiar could not possibly have been defeated, not by a puling group of Klingon children and elders!

I need that easy victory, that triumphal procession, all that heroic glitter and glory. I truly need *it. And if he does not give it to me . . .*

Narviat continued to resist all attempts to wear him down. Unless Dralath could extract a confession and the names of accomplices from him, Narviat's death would smack of personal revenge rather than a credible State execution of a traitor. . . .

The sudden discreet buzzing of his wrist comm brought the praetor starkly alert. News at last! Holding up a hand for silence, Dralath said into the comm's tiny speaker, "Well?"

The messenger knew not to waste his praetor's time with nonessentials. "General Volskiar has returned—"

"Ah!"

"—alone."

"He *what*?"

The advisors were all staring at him. Dralath brusquely waved them away, waiting impatiently as they filed meekly out. Once they were gone, he hissed into the comm's speaker, "You are certain he is alone?"

If Volskiar had somehow managed to lose his entire fleet at Narendra III, there was going to be a public execution over which the entire Empire would shudder for years!

"Yes, my Praetor. The general is receiving clearance to land even now, and has asked for audience with you."

"He will speak with me. Indeed. I will take the message in my private quarters. Out!"

Spock clenched his hands behind his back, both to hide their unseemly trembling and to keep from roughly shoving the earnest young Romulan, barely more than a boy, out of the way. Even with his hands shaking, Spock could see the job done some much more swiftly, and done *right!*

"Micromanaging again, Spock?" a corner of his mind asked in McCoy's dry drawl.

Yes. He was doing exactly that, which was quite illogical. The young Romulan's fingers were sure on the console keys; he gave every aspect of knowing what he was doing. But . . . the Fires were rising anew for all Spock's mental struggles, battling with logic, with sanity. *Pon farr* could only be denied so long.

A bit longer, he told himself. *Hold out just a bit longer. Let me only finish my mission here.*

"I have it!" the young Romulan said triumphantly, and stabbed at a volume control. There was a loud crackle of static, and he hastily turned it down, frowning slightly with concentration as he adjusted the gain. "Sorry. That's as good as it's going to get."

Spock brusquely waved him to silence. "Dralath," Ruanek murmured after a few moments of listening to the faint, not-quite-clear voices, "and . . . who is that with him . . . ? I can't quite make out . . ."

"General Volskiar," Spock cut in.

"Ha, right! You've got a good memory for voices."

The room fell quiet. Everyone there listened intently. . . .

The mirrors lining the walls of the praetor's private study reflected a Dralath almost dark olive with rage. "You lost *how many* ships?"

General Volskiar stood at full military attention, fairly radiating defiant arrogance. "Four," he repeated reluctantly, "but we did fully achieve our objective—"

"You lost *five* warbirds out of *seven?*"

Volskiar's gaze wavered. "Hear me out, my praetor. One was lost to the *Enterprise,* as I say, and no shame in that. The others were lost not to an honorable, honest enemy, but to *treason!* To the darkest, foulest *treason!*"

"I am not your troops, Volskiar. No need to orate."

"But what I have to say is too terrible for small words. My praetor, I hold as prisoner the woman who was once known as Commander Charvanek—she who set an ambush and most treacherously fired upon our fleet! She who has murdered our own!"

"Why?" Dralath exploded. "Why would she do such a thing?" Zerliak had reported that that obsolete warbird she maintained had left orbit and disappeared, and there'd been that infuriating instant when orbital defenses had crashed . . .

Oh, the Klingon-loving woman was clever, clever . . . why else had she survived the first time she'd played traitor for the damned Federation?

"My praetor, I, ah, thought interrogation might better wait till she was safely in your hands."

"Yes, of course." *Clever, Volskiar. I hate cleverness in my senior officers.* He thought of Volskiar's prosperous estates. *Any more cleverness, and you may make me richer than I already am.*

Struggling for composure, Dralath said, "I take it that no one has seen her being brought back to Ki Baratan."

"Only my crew."

"Excellent." But why would Charvanek have taken such a wild chance?

Narviat. The name shot into his mind without warning. Narviat, so quietly defiant in his prison cell. Narviat, who was such a blatant friend of the people. And who, together with Charvanek, was linked by blood to the emperor, and who made such frequent visits to the Imperial Palace . . .

"Excellent," Dralath repeated with barely concealed satisfaction. "All Romulus shall celebrate, General Volskiar. There will be a grand public festival to honor our glorious victory over the aggressor Klingons and the treacherous Federation."

"And . . . the traitor?"

"The woman shall, of course, be questioned, but discreetly. We do not wish a martyr." Like her cursed cousin, Narviat, she was far too popular with the mob. As well as being of the Imperial blood.

But she would still die, she and Narviat together, with the crowds jeering them as traitors. Ah yes, none so quick to hate as those who have their faith broken! And that would shatter the prestige not only of Charvanek and Narviat, but of their kinsman as well: Narviat, Charvanek, and Emperor Shiarkiek in one swift, efficient blow!

"Very well, General Volskiar, you shall—" Dralath broke off with a muttered oath as a warning light on his desk console began to flash. He mouthed, *Talk, keep talking,* and while the puzzled Volskiar obediently began to speak of ships' supplies, Dralath began his hunt. Someone was spying on him. . . .

Keep spying, he told that someone, fingers flying over the console's keypad, *just a little longer . . . I will have you in just a little while longer. . . .*

And if it is you, my mysterious Academician Symakhos, akhh, if it is you, I shall not need my operatives to report from Bardat. If it is you, then there shall be three traitors, not two, bound to the execution frames!

TWENTY-SIX

Narendra III, Spock thought, listening in despair. *The massacre successful . . . and Saavik, ah, Saavik . . .*

Had she gotten through with her message or . . . died en route? Illogical. The action of the doomed *Enterprise* showed that she had delivered her message—but what had happened then? Had she died on *Enterprise?* No, no, the irony of that was too strong. He would not believe it. Could not. Illogical or not, he would not believe her dead!

Wouldn't he?

But . . . something was wrong. The truth seeped gradually through Spock's shock and turmoil. Something was very wrong with what they were hearing, and it had nothing to do with the horror of Volskiar's report or the banality that he droned on about now. . . .

That was it!

"Break contact!" Spock shouted. "Now!"

When the startled young Romulan failed to act swiftly enough,

Spock shoved him out of the way, disconnected the system himself, and snapped into the stunned silence, "Overconfident amateurs!"

"What—"

"What do you—"

"How could you—"

But Ruanek held up a hand for silence, nodding in terse understanding. "He's right. Didn't you hear what Volskiar was saying? How he suddenly went from making a proper report to his commanding officer to vague rambling about ship's supplies?"

"Exactly," Spock cut in. "Dralath doesn't remain praetor by being trusting. He knew someone was spying on him and was trying to keep the contact open long enough to trace us!"

He was talking too excitedly.

Control, he warned himself, and knew the warning failed to cool his anger. Underneath the *Pon farr*-heightened anger, he felt an equal surge of anguish tearing at him. Saavik and her warning, *her life,* had gone for nothing and he—

Let me accomplish something here. Let my life, here at its end, mean something.

To his dismay, his hands were trembling, too violently for accuracy on any keyboard. Instead, while the others plotted, Spock took Ruanek aside and asked softly, fighting to keep his voice level, "How adept are you at breaking into systems, coaxing out records?"

"No one trains a warrior for that," Ruanek admitted with a trace of his old resentment. "Ah, wait, but Kerit is!" Ruanek snagged a scrawny teenaged girl by the arm and pulled her over to them. "Kerit here can work wonders, crack just about any electronic system, can't you, Kerit?"

She was thin, narrow-faced, and shabby in a deliberately unkempt way. And in her eyes burned that almost fanatic light Spock had seen in many a . . . ah, what was the old Terran term . . . yes, in the eyes of many a "hacker" in the Federation. The Underground united strange companions: how else would a subcommander know a streetwise youngster and her dubiously acquired skills?

"Excellent," Spock said to her, and pointed at a console. She sat down with a thump, wriggling her fingers to loosen up. Spock continued, "Before we may reveal Dralath as the 'enemy of the people,' which, rhetoric aside, he is, we must have evidence."

Ruanek's eyes widened in sudden comprehension. "You're planning to break into his private files!"

Kerit underscored that with a little gasp and giggle.

"As far as seems prudent," Spock said coolly, "yes. We—"

Thin-faced Jarrin burst out, "Have you gone mad? Do you, do you think it's just a matter of breaking into some merchant's records for a *joke?*"

Kerit started guiltily at that, and Ruanek raised an eyebrow at her.

"These are the records of one of the most suspicious officials on the planet!" Jarrin continued fiercely. "Why do you think none of us ever tried to break in? He has alarms on top of alarms!"

"All the more intriguing the challenge, then," Spock said to Kerit, and won a sharp, nervous little grin from her. "What other choice is there?" he added to the others. "Are we to stall and bicker as you did in the caves beneath the city, talking our lives away while Dralath claims victory? Yes, and while your Admiral Narviat and Commander Charvanek both pay what is so casually called 'the ultimate price' and any hope of change dies with them?"

No one spoke. No one moved. But then Ruanek shrugged. "You're right. And, damn Dralath to the darkest hell, there's more at stake than anything so—petty as personal safety."

"Petty!" someone exclaimed, and Ruanek glared, for a moment all warrior again, impatient at a civilian's qualms.

"Are not all Romulans gamblers at heart?" Spock cut in before an argument could erupt. "Begin, Kerit." As an ambassador, Spock had learned when to apply a touch of melodrama to logic:

"Let us cast all upon a single throw of the sticks, and see what Fortune sends us!"

The technique worked. With a happy little giggle, Kerit set to work. And no one even tried to argue.

Ruanek shifted his weight subtly from one foot to the other, and fought the urge to rub his aching arm. The emperor's physician had had a deft touch, even to sealing up the deepest of the knife wounds so well that there would be no lasting harm to nerves or muscles, but that didn't mean the injuries were healed. And the pain-numbing drugs were rapidly wearing off.

Pain is nothing. He began the Warrior's Creed without hesitation. *Are you not a warrior of the Empire? Are you not a subcommander—*

Akhh, no. He wasn't. Not any longer. The shock of that renewed realization hit Ruanek so strongly he nearly staggered. He was . . .

What? No family, no rank, no status of any sort in Romulan society—Terrifying, genuinely terrifying, to think that the only stability in his life right now, the only person he could truly trust, wasn't even a Romulan.

And that person, Ruanek thought, glancing uneasily at Spock, who was leaning over Kerit to study the screen, almost laughing with her as he did so, just might be following in the path of Sered of Vulcan so many years ago, back when Ruanek still thought he had a promising career.

Spock just might be going insane.

Very much aware of Ruanek's eyes on him, Spock spared a thought almost of pity for the Romulan. What reassurance could he possibly give Ruanek? *I am merely undergoing a natural phenomenon, one that will eventually kill me. Do not let that concern you.*

At least the blood fever wasn't high enough to force him to react to immature little Kerit. She was giggling again and muttering softly to herself in concentration.

"Uh-oh. No. False path. Heh. Spider waiting, ready to catch—not me. Turn this way . . . pathway . . . yess . . . bet you think you've got that safe. No no no, this way . . . try this code . . . Yes! Got something."

"Yes, you do," Spock agreed in genuine appreciation, studying the screen. He asked the others, "Who is—rather, who *was* Senator Tharnek?"

Ruanek straightened. "I know that name. I remember Avrak talking about him, fairly recently, too . . . Tharnek . . . Senator Tharnek—right! Until just a short while ago, he was the overseer of the Rarathik District. Until, that is, he suffered an unfortunate and quite fatal confusion about the proper dosage of a heart medication."

"Fascinating. He must have truly been loyal to the praetor."

"How so?"

"See for yourself! Either he had no heir, or the late senator cherished his praetor over all others."

He moved aside to let Ruanek see, watching the Romulan's face as Ruanek scrolled down the file.

"Uh-oh," Kerit cut in, "on to us. I'm downloading—damn! They're moving data—got it. Come on, come on, stupid slow machine . . . yes, no! Damn! All right, all right, they haven't found us yet. No spider pouncing. We wiggle in this way . . . ha! There. Safe." She twisted about to give Spock a feral grin. "What do you want now?"

"See if you can access some death records," Spock told her. "Senators, Kerit, who met with fatal accidents within the last . . . mm . . . five years."

"Oh, easy! They don't guard those! Been in there before—whoo, no! Got guards now. Wait . . . try . . . twist about like this . . . and this . . . code . . . code . . . yes, almost . . . there. That what you want?"

Spock and Ruanek studied the data together.

"Fascinating," Spock said at last. "Your Romulan senators seem to be a singularly unfortunate lot. They would appear to have suffered an astonishing number of fatal accidents, far greater than the statistical probabilities would allow."

"And," Ruanek said, "there are a lot of transfers of estates into the praetor's personal accounts."

"Indeed. Kerit, one more search, if you would. Political records, now. See if you can cross-reference how many of the deceased were known to be activists, preferably those actually on record as speaking out against the praetor."

"Right. Here we go . . . yes . . . ease out . . . don't leave a fingerprint . . . eeee! Almost got me there! Spider code, down like a knife." She paused, panting as though it had been a physical struggle. "Right. Here we go. Shouldn't be a problem; public records . . . no. No, they're not. Suspicious dreeb, puts everything under guard . . . Ethak Code, clumsy stuff, should upgrade if he really wants to keep 'em secure—there."

"Interesting . . ." Spock scanned the list of names, quickly matching the names with the list of the deceased. "To speak out against Dralath too openly does seem to increase a senator's risk of meeting with a fatal accident. And there also seems to be a remarkable coincidence: Every one of the deceased left his or her estate to the praetor. How very . . . patriotic of them."

Ruanek snorted. "That's one word for it. But, yes, all this is conclusive evidence against Dralath, showing he's corrupt, but it's not going to help Admiral Narviat. We can't leave him in Dralath's hands. Yes, and we can't give up on Commander Charvanek, either!"

The Fires surged up at the thought of Charvanek, nearly blinding Spock, nearly devouring rational thought. "No," he agreed shortly, fighting for control again. "We cannot. Proof of corruption, as you so casually belittle political murders, is clearly not enough to sway the Romulan people." As Ruanek frowned at the matter-of-fact—if true—insult, Spock continued, "What we do need is an undeniable link between Dralath and the massacre of Narendra III, irrefutable evidence that Dralath, not Charvanek or Narviat, is the traitor. Without that evidence—"

"Uh-oh." That was Kerit, fingers flying over the keyboard. "Bad. Someone's on to us. Better try . . . right. There. Got by 'em. For now. Make it quick, get your data. They're going to be sending the spiders in here."

Ruanek and Spock exchanged blank looks.

"Spiders!" Kerit repeated, impatient with such stupidity. "Tie up the system in webs, trace you right down the strands. Get you good, maybe, if you're cyberlinked, even brain burn or something synapse-scrambling."

"Narviat," Ruanek said helplessly. "Can you just locate him? And then get out?"

"Sure as the Pit hope so. Just in case, get ready to run when I give the yell."

"Understood. All of you," Spock said over his shoulder, "pack up anything that might be considered incriminating. And be ready to *move*."

Kerit, muttering to herself once more, was flashing through floor plans, screen after screen. "Lot of rooms . . . secret ones. See? No clear way in, out. Cells, bet you. Cells Dralath doesn't want anyone to know are there."

"Go on," Spock urged, studying the screen as the charts scrolled by, "on." The concentration needed for an accurate scan of quickly moving data helped focus mind and will. And Kerit, he was learning, could process data almost as swiftly as he: most satisfying. They scanned together, swiftly hunting . . . hunting . . . "There! Stop. Close in, Kerit . . . yes. Stop. A bit closer . . ."

"Can't get any closer. Lots of spiders around there. Lots and lots of them, all sorts of stuff, all around just that one little room."

"That one little cell," Spock corrected. "That can only be the location of Narviat's prison. No other isolated room would be so thoroughly guarded."

Ruanek stared at the screen. "I know where that is!" he exclaimed. "Really know, I mean, specifically. My patro—my former patron had a file of . . . well . . . routes that are not exactly public knowledge in and out of the whole complex. He never let me know the entire file, of course; didn't trust me—ha, didn't trust any of his security that much, but I do know that one."

"Could you get in?"

"Well, yes, but—"

"Uh-oh," Kerit cut in. "On to us. Bailing out, *now!* No, dammit, can't, they've locked on to us, can't get out—"

"We can." Spock calmly ripped the console from its connections in a flurry of sparks, and every screen in the room went dead. "Did they have time to get the coordinates?" he asked the sharp-eyed Kerit.

Staring, she shook her head.

"Excellent." Putting down the dead console, he added, "Someone may be here shortly to investigate the sudden surge, then drop, of power, so I would advise moving from here to the main room."

That sounded, Spock thought, *quite logical. At least I trust that it did.* Coherent thought was coming and going in maddening, ever-widening waves. *Let me but see this mission through.*

As they hurried back into Room 235, blocking up the telltale hole in the wall with the heavy cabinet, Spock warned Ruanek, "We cannot wait. Complete evidence or not, we must attack before the remnants of Volskiar's fleet return. Dralath must not have the propaganda value of a military victory, even if—"

They all froze at the sudden sound of a wary knock. Ruanek, stalking noiselessly forward, dropped his hand to a disruptor he wasn't wearing, and swore softly, closing his hand about the hilt of his Honor Blade instead. At a nod from Spock, Jarrin opened the door. A tall figure entered, shrouded in a scholar's dark, hooded cloak.

Ruanek shot forward to block the figure's path, Honor Blade glinting in his hand. "No civilian carries himself like that!"

"Stand aside!" a crisp male voice ordered.

"Not a chance in all the hells!"

Spock hastily moved between the two Romulans. "Sheathe that blade," he snapped at Ruanek.

"But—"

"Sheathe it!"

The hooded stranger, brought face-to-face with Spock, drew in his breath in a sharp hiss. *"You!"*

For one brief, illogical moment, Spock wanted to react to that instant hatred with an attack of his own. *I will not blindly strike at someone I do not even know!* Rigidly controlling himself, he began, "I am—"

"I know who you are. And what you did to me and my commander." The stranger pushed back his hood, revealing a lean, strong, cold Romulan face—and eyes that burned with utter hatred as he stared straight at Spock. "Do you not recognize me?"

Spock, clinging to precarious self-control, said, "I fear not."

"I am Commander Tal, Fleet Second. I was Subcommander Tal back then. When you betrayed my commander, Noble Born Charvanek, to the Federation."

Memory flashed to life: a much younger Tal, staring at Charvanek—she whom Spock had betrayed—with astonished, angry eyes as though unable to accept that his commander might, after all, prove fallible.

"That was as it was," Spock said coldly. "Times and people change. Right now it is your commander we seek to help—as well as all the Romulan people!"

"True," Ruanek added, moving to stand shoulder to shoulder with Spock and glaring at the newcomer. "And you may be a commander, you may be the secret Master of the Empire for all I know—but right now, all you are is a nuisance!"

Tal ignored him utterly. "I swore an oath to Commander Charvanek," he said to Spock. "When she was taken prisoner after Narendra III for being the only warrior there to protest turning honorable war into a massacre, I swore an oath as though she were still my own commanding officer. I returned to Romulus to meet with Admiral Narviat—only to be told that he'd been arrested on charges of high treason. I went from there to his Imperial kinsman—only to be told that Emperor Shiarkiek had suffered a relapse and been taken into protective custody by the praetor.

"I thought my trail had gone cold. But even as I was hurried out, a servant whispered to me that yet another kinsman existed, the Academician Symakhos, and told me where he might be found. And what I find now is you, and even more treachery!"

Ruanek snarled an oath at that, and Tal turned sharply to him. "And you, are you to be another warrior who loses his honor, his home, his life because he has listened to this man's lies?"

"We do not have the time to discuss morality," Spock interrupted before Ruanek could reply. "What happened those years ago was a ruse of war—and do not think it did not cost me my own honor. But I was then under orders from my own commander. Now, if you will not believe me, here are all these others who will state that we work for the good of Romulus against a praetor who would destroy all honor. And if you will not believe them," Spock added, "then we must see that you tell no one of this meeting."

That startled Tal into the slightest of steps back. He fell into an instinctive crouch, ready to fight, and once again, Spock felt an answering surge of anger—

"We haven't got time for this!" Ruanek cut in. "Hear me, Commander. I'll put my life in your hands if that will speed this along and get you out of here: I was Subcommander Ruanek of House Minor Strevon, in service to my patron, Senator Avrak. You could take that knowledge, and the knowledge that I am here, with these folks, report it to the right people, and I'd be condemned to death for treason. Along with Admiral Narviat. And Commander Charvanek, to whom you boast of having such loyalty."

Tal's glance flicked from Spock to Ruanek to Spock again. "What are you," Tal murmured, "to command such loyalty in those who should be your foes?"

"My foe," Spock said, "is Dralath. Commander Tal, this place is no longer safe—and your presence has added to our danger. If you have proof of what actually occurred at Narendra III, let us see it. If not, let us all leave before Dralath finds us!"

A great shudder racked Tal's lean frame. "I have spent too many years hating you to forgive the careers you destroyed. Hers. Mine. But . . . for Commander Charvanek's sake . . ." He pulled a small golden amulet from the folds of his cloak. "The commander gave this to me. In it is a complete record of what truly happened at Narendra III. Use it honorably, or I swear I will see your lifeblood drip from my Honor Blade."

He looked very much as though he wanted to say more. But without another word, the commander pulled the hood back up to hide his face, and strode away.

Ruanek let out his breath in a great sigh of relief. "Wasn't sure how it was going to go. And with this arm, I didn't know if I could take him. I . . . didn't really want to fight him, not over his loyalty to Commander Charvanek."

"Neither did I," Spock admitted softly. Ignoring the other Romulans, who were whispering together, he glanced at the wide-eyed Kerit. "How efficient are you at hacking into information broadcast systems?"

She grinned, eyes sparkling with the challenge. "I'm good. I'm really good." She glanced at the others. "Remember that spot, in the middle of the news, other day or so? The bit about—"

"That was you?" Ruanek exclaimed. "That, ah, really explicit—"

"Explicit is not what we need," Spock cut in. "But stand ready, Kerit." He closed his hand about the little amulet. "First, we must make a precise copy of what this contains. Then, if all succeeds, we will need a sudden and quite satisfyingly illicit broadcast at any time."

"Can do. Got friends to help."

Ruanek grinned at her. "Do it, and I bet you get a good spot in the new administration."

"Honest? Could you put in a word for me?"

Spock cut in dryly, "I doubt Narviat would dare risk not having you on his side."

He handed the amulet to Kerit. "I can also take out some of

those security devices," she added, almost shyly, "the ones around the admiral's cell, I mean."

"Without leaving any evidence that the systems have gone off-line?"

After a second's hesitation, she nodded.

"You must be certain of that," Spock warned. "Our lives may depend on your skill."

She nodded again, wide-eyed. Turning to Ruanek, Spock said, "The same holds true for you. Assuming that your knowledge is accurate and you can find Narviat's cell, you and I are about to commit what the Terrans call a 'jail break.' "

TWENTY-SEVEN

KI BARATAN, ROMULUS, DAY 9, SECOND WEEK OF TASMEEN, YEAR 2344

Their jail break, Spock thought, almost stopped before it began. They heard an officer's barked command to the clerk in the atrium to stand aside, followed by the heavy footsteps of armed guards.

Ruanek had time only for a quick "Damn!"

"We are scholars, going about our business," Spock murmured. "This does not concern us."

In the next instant, guards came rushing down the gray-walled corridor, hands on disruptor butts and heading straight at Spock and Ruanek. For a wild instant, the Fires blazed up in Spock: *Enemy males, a challenge—*

"Out of the way," an officer snarled as he raced by. "Praetor's business."

Spock and Ruanek obediently flattened themselves against a wall, the hoods of their drab scholars' cloaks hiding their faces as the rest of the troop clattered past them. As the guards disappeared down the corridor, Ruanek muttered, "Guess where *they're* going in such a hurry."

"Guessing is illogical." The guards were, without a doubt, headed toward Corridor B, Room 235. "They will be disappointed."

"We hope. Yes, yes, I know, hope is illogical, too."

But if the praetor's guards seized Kerit, Jarrin, Ridda, any of the others, they had lost before they even started.

"Not completely. Go on now. The way is clear."

He had to bite the words off to keep his voice steady. Spock's heart was still racing with alarm, the Fires blazing in his mind. *Logic,* he thought with all his will. *Logic is sanity . . . logic is control . . . logic.*

And gradually, his sudden fury died to embers. Spock frowned, suddenly aware of Ruanek's uneasy sideways glance. Not surprising that the Romulan should have noticed behavioral changes.

"Ruanek, hear me. What is happening to me is nothing contagious, nothing to endanger you. More," he added truthfully, "than you are already endangered." The Fires burned, whispering, *No more. Tell no more.* "Do not ask anything further." It came out as a harsh croak.

"But—"

"No further!"

But Ruanek, who was after all, a warrior unafraid of threats, continued, "I have heard rumors about Vulcans, and . . . ah . . . certain matters. Is that—" He stopped, tried again, "Can that be what—" Ruanek broke off with an exasperated, *"Akhh!* I'm not sure what I am trying to ask. Romulans do not—"

"Romulans," Spock snapped, "do not know when to stop prying!"

That startled two clerks and, more alarmingly, a guard. Dropping his voice, struggling to fall back into Symakhos' controlled cadences, Spock asked, "Where is this shorter route that you promised me?"

"This way," Ruanek said curtly. Spock could not tell from his deliberately impassive face what he was thinking. So long as the Romulan was loyal, Spock decided he did not wish to know.

Narviat stirred, shivering. Even through eyelids squeezed shut against the oppressive light in his cell, he thought it had diminished. Worth a try. He moved his arm away from his face, and peered about his cell. The noise and those damnable subsonics had actually stopped for the moment. He cautioned himself not to get used to it: All the crueler, to give a prisoner a taste of hope before it all began again. *Definitely something Dralath would do.*

Damnably chilly in here. Nothing to see: No window, of course, not even in the door, although air filtered in from tiny vents in the ceiling. The only furnishings were the bare shelf-bed on which he sat, and the less-than-civilized waste-disposal unit. Floor, walls, and ceiling were of the seamless composite used to coat warbird hulls: nothing short of a disruptor blast would make a mark on them. The shelf-bed was another seamless slab, with nothing he could break off or unscrew; the waste disposal was equally seamless. Daring, noisome escapes were hardly in his style, but if the waste disposal had not been too narrow, he really thought he would have had to at least try to break free, like a trapped *h'vart* that gnaws off its own paw and limps to freedom.

Melodrama is not in your style either, he scolded himself, and returned to scrutinizing his cell. How many times did this make?

Do you truly expect, in your current condition, to see something you missed before? he asked himself, and knew it was just another question for which he had no answer.

The door was the one weak point, since it must open and close, but whoever had designed this cell had been shrewd enough to put the hinges on the outside, where an ambitious prisoner couldn't get at them.

At least it *was* a door, and not a transparent forcefield such as one found in a warbird's brig; at least he had the illusion of privacy.

Illusion, indeed. Narviat glanced up. Must be a surveillance camera up there—*he* certainly would have included one—but he couldn't find any sign of the lens. He fought down the urge to make an obscene gesture at whoever was watching. He also fought down any movement that might have been taken for despair.

The blazing lights and the subsonics, Fires take them and Dralath too, came back on in a nauseating surge. Far worse to give a man an instant's relief, then torment him again, and Dralath knew it. Narviat swallowed hard, squeezed his eyes shut, and gritted his teeth, fighting the urge to curl up, rejecting the world.

If he didn't have an Empire to fight for, he could easily think of despairing under these conditions. Far too easily.

This is not a trap, Spock told himself firmly. *It is merely a . . . maintenance tunnel. Farther underground than one might prefer. But merely a tunnel.*

It was a long, dank corridor smelling faintly of mold, dingy gray paint peeling from the walls. No Romulan, Spock thought, was going to waste time or money in upgrading anything so far from public sight. Widely spaced ceiling fixtures of archaic design gave off a miserly amount of ghastly blue-white light. Some even more archaic instinct whispered to Spock of *the caves, the World of Ever-Dark*—

No! *It is a* tunnel, *nothing worse.*

Ironic: Had Dralath put Narviat into a high-security prison, they would have had little hope of a rescue. But such a move could never have been kept secret, and Dralath could hardly afford any negative publicity.

There will still be guards down here, though, and security devices . . . although if Kerit has done her job, few of those devices will be functioning.

He had loaded an appalling amount of responsibility on the shoulders of a child, even one whom his companion trusted. If she failed—

Worrying about what cannot be altered is the height of illogic.

"We are now," Ruanek whispered, "directly underneath the bureaucratic complex. Told you: semi-secret maintenance tunnel. And," he added with a fierce grin, "it connects with each and every one of the buildings—including, if one but knows the proper way in, the one containing Admiral Narviat's prison cell!"

"And Praetor Dralath's office?" Spock murmured. "How very illogical of the designers!"

"Well, maybe not all that illogical. Depends on who designed this thing. Wait . . . yes, this way. You have to squeeze through this doorway, and watch the low-hanging pipes . . . right. You couldn't actually get up to the praetor's office," Ruanek continued softly as they continued down the dingy gray corridor, "try your hand at assassination or anything like that. But as for the rest of this . . ." He shrugged. "Makes it easier for workers to get back and forth without interrupting government affairs. Bureaucrats think of convenience first and foremost, not of defense or—"

Spock silenced him with a sharp glance: two cold-eyed guards stood directly ahead, blocking the corridor.

"Halt," one snapped.

Arms out to show his lack of weapons, Spock began, "We were merely attempting a shortcut—"

"No one allowed down here right now. Question of security."

"Of course."

Spock and Ruanek exchanged a quick glance. They lunged, Ruanek to the right, Spock to the left. Spock caught his guard in a quick nerve pinch, then whirled to see Ruanek straightening, face gone gray. "Forgot about my arm," he muttered. "Should have just stabbed him. Hells, never mind; I've suffered worse. Let's get going before these two wake up."

Spock fiercely suppressed a surge of distaste: Ruanek was, after all, a Romulan warrior used to casual violence. That he should, despite that background, be so honorable—

Spock stopped short. Fire suddenly blazed along his nerves, stabbing through his head. A sane corner of his mind recognized, *Subsonics, to wear down Narviat. We've entered the range.*

But sanity had no bearing here. Four guards patrolled ahead, faces hidden by protective, sonic-muffling helms, and Spock—

—could not remember what prisoner they were guarding. Saavik—

Why he should think that—but it was Saavik, Saavik because the subsonics were tearing at him and the Fires were rousing—

Saavik! It was Saavik they held captive, it was Saavik they would dishonor, it was Saavik—

The Fires blinded him, deafened him. There was nothing but *Saavik* and flame all around him, flame—

Flame—

Flame . . .

Someone was touching him. Someone was daring to catch his arm, risking calling him by name: "Spock! Stop it! Spock!"

He savagely backhanded that someone, heard a startled cry of pain, whirled and saw:

"Ruanek!"

Ruanek was huddled against a wall, clutching his injured arm once more, this time with green blood staining his fingers. His breath hissed between clenched teeth.

I did that. I hurled him aside so roughly his wounds reopened. An ally . . . a friend, and I . . .

"Ruanek," Spock repeated more softly in entreaty.

The Romulan straightened slowly, warily releasing the pressure on his arm, his glance unreadable. "I'll be all right."

"I did not mean—it was my—my condition, not me."

"I know." A pause. Ruanek met Spock's eyes. "I do know."

The guards, Spock realized, sprawled limply on the floor. Blood pooled beneath the helm of one; the other's leg jutted at a physiologically impossible angle. "Did I . . . ?"

"Kill them? No. Not," Ruanek added shortly, "for want of trying. I don't *think* any of them had time to get off a warning before you attacked. And you—you tore the gadgetry right out of the walls—no more noise or damned subsonics, hear?" He shook his head in amazement. "Never saw anything like that outside of the vidshows. One against four, and *they* were the ones outnumbered."

"Ruanek, my mind may be clear again, but the clarity will not last long. And we have certainly triggered alarms somewhere."

One of the guards bore a tiny keypad—and had lazily left a code accessible. For the cell door? Or an alarm straight to Dralath's office? There was no logical alternative but to try. Spock keyed in the code, his fingers reassuringly steady, for once, and pressed the correct button. . . .

Yes! The cell door slid soundlessly open. Within was a blaze of light, and a figure—

Narviat's worn, weary face was a study in quick contrasts: first, a flash of anger and cold pride, then astonishment, then sheer disbelief and the dawning of hope.

But he had not risen to the rank of admiral by wasting time. Springing to his feet, staggering only slightly, he said, "I have to speak to the people . . . tell them . . ."

Spock all but shoved him toward Ruanek. "Get him to Kerit. Safely. She'll have the commander's testimony. The sooner you can break in on the broadcasts . ." He faced Narviat, trying to see him as "ally," not "male" and "rival." "There is something you must know."

Narviat's quick glance was wary. "What?"

"Charvanek," Spock said brusquely. "She has been taken. You will give her rescue the diversion it needs. Now, go!"

TWENTY-EIGHT

Workers lounged in the courtyard outside the office complex, drinking *khavas* and trying hard not to look as if they were waiting for someone. They almost succeeded, Spock thought, as he emerged.

Recognizing him by his by-now-dusty and disheveled scholarly robes, they came alert, then damped it down. After all, there was nothing unusual about a scholar's stopping to ask for directions from workers.

"Well?" Jarrin demanded, more sharply than a worker would ask such a man.

"He has been freed." They hardly needed to know who "he" might be. They might not be warriors, but Romulans had discipline, and they were all too well schooled in the ways of rebellion to shout. But their eyes blazed with relief that Spock found . . . gratifying.

"Now," Spock continued, "we must be able to say the same for Commander Charvanek. Have any of you been able to confirm her status?"

"In transit," a woman said tersely. "One of our people just reported a small convoy of vehicles, including a closed groundcar bearing the insignia of General Volskiar, leaving his estate, heading directly to Ki Baratan."

Obvious, Spock thought. Logically, too obvious. "How many vehicles in the convoy?"

"Three. A military vehicle leading the way, then the closed groundcar, and then a second military vehicle."

"Were either of the other two vehicles also closed?"

The woman blinked, confused. "Yes, the last one, no windows at all. The driver would have to operate strictly on instruments. But you wouldn't transport a state prisoner in a wreck like . . . oh. Right." She grinned, showing teeth but no humor at all.

"Exactly," Spock said.

A sudden blare of noise brought their heads up, their hands reaching for weapons no one would expect workers to be carrying. Announcements resonated from speakers set all about the courtyard, stating—warning—that Dralath, Praetor of the Romulans, would shortly be making a proclamation, "One to stir the blood and cheer the heart of every true Romulan. All shall make ready to hear!"

"All shall make ready to clog traffic," Jarrin muttered.

Spock wasn't really listening. Someone was following them. He subtly waved the others to one side and drew back into the mouth of an alley, waiting—

"It's me," a wary voice said.

Ruanek! Yes, and dressed in a remarkably ill-fitting uniform. Spock moved back out of shadow. "I thought you were to accompany Narviat."

A shrug. "I did, up to a point. We ran into Kerit and some of the others, so I handed him over to her, saw them safely off to their broadcast facilities—such as they are—and decided I'd be more useful here, instead. Caught a soldier off-guard, even if he wasn't quite my size. At least, now, I'm in uniform. They can't say I'm a spy."

"You do not trust me?"

"Hells, no," Ruanek said bluntly, "not the way you are right now!" But a quick flash of a grin took the sting from the words.

"There is no time for discussion." Drawing the others into the alley with himself and Ruanek, Spock said, "We need a vehicle. . . ."

As a sleek black groundcar came their way, Spock stepped out in front of it, facing it, coldly rigid as a figure out of myth. He had time for a surge of not-quite-suppressed alarm that the driver, being Romulan and evidently in the service of someone of importance, might speed right over him—

But Spock's luck—illogical though such a concept might be—held. The startled driver did stop, so suddenly the vehicle nearly slewed sideways. The rebels swarmed over the driver before he could draw a weapon, tearing him from the groundcar. Spock hurried to the passenger side—

And found himself looking into the mouth of a disruptor. "Not you," said Commander Tal. "Not again."

A wave of Spock's hand held back the others. "We cannot waste time. I say only this: We go to free the Noble Born Charvanek from a shameful death. To do it, we need this groundcar. Leave, or be ejected."

"Tell me your plan," Tal countered, just as tersely, "or die right now."

Quickly and concisely, Spock told him, then watched the emotions storm across that narrow, hungry face: Commander Charvanek . . . her betrayal and all the long years of shame . . . Commander Charvanek . . . her life against his . . .

Suddenly the cold eyes blazed. "I must be as mad as you! I'm letting you destroy my life a second time—but damn you, *damn you,* I—I cannot see my commander die a traitor's death."

He hurled himself into the driver's compartment and seized the controls. Spock and Ruanek barely had time to scramble into the back before Tal sent the groundcar hurtling forward. They sped through the city by the back ways, careening left, right, dodging other vehicles, scraping their sides in showers of sparks. Tal, his lips drawn back in a savage, humorless grin, never once braked. Jim Kirk had driven this recklessly. But recklessness had been part of Jim's nature. Tal was letting out years of frustration with this madness!

Pedestrians scattered for their lives, shouting curses that penetrated the car's soundproofing. Ruanek, slammed against Spock and trying to shield his injured arm, did a fair amount of cursing as well. But as they blazed out of Ki Baratan, Spock saw that Ruanek's lips were peeled back in the same desperate grin as Tal.

They are Romulans, he reminded himself. *"Our lives may be ruined, but at least we die in a blaze of glory!"*

But not just yet!

Charvanek sat alone in the darkness of the closed ground transport's back compartment. She refused to continue looking for some means of escape. She already knew there weren't any. There hadn't been any when Volskiar's ship had returned to Romulus. There hadn't been any when she'd been hustled from the ship to what she'd guessed from her one brief glimpse of land and sunlight was his estate. And there certainly weren't any now that she was headed off . . . wherever.

At least, Charvanek thought dourly as they left the estate behind, the transport jouncing a little over potholes, she hadn't been molested. Charvanek had quite coolly steeled herself for the indignities likely to be inflicted on a woman prisoner, but aside from some malicious whispers the guards had meant for her to overhear, there had been nothing. She was as untouchable as she was invisible.

Of course I am. Dralath doesn't want his prize damaged in any way.

Logically, it had to be Dralath who now had control over her: It would hardly be politic of him to allow Volskiar a victory procession. Dralath, then, or that cold-blooded head of security, Zerliak, would be sure to interrogate her.

Let them come! This would be her one and only chance to say what she *really* thought of the praetor and his reign. A small satisfaction before what would, she knew, be an exceedingly unpleasant death. But, Charvanek thought grimly, one took whatever satisfaction one could.

Narviat, do you know what's become of me? Is your information network that good? A little shiver raced through her. *I know how you feel about me, my kinsman. But don't try anything foolish. Romulus needs you alive.*

Do only this, Narviat, my . . . friend: Say the Rites. Remember me.

If she had no escape, at least she had one consolation.

My crew, my eaglets . . . at least you will not face a traitor's death. You were, they will say, only following orders. You will, at the very worst, be granted swift execution. While I . . .

Akhh, she had another. Her execution would be finite. No matter how agonizing, no matter how drawn out and humiliating, it would, at last, be over.

She would, one way or another, die free.

The road toward Volskiar's estate ran through a narrow cut between low ridges of rock stripped of ground cover. Where, Spock wondered, was the air support? Were he the one bringing a valuable captive to Ki Baratan, he would have at least one surveillance ship overhead. But Volskiar was impulsive, even for a Romulan. His arrogance, his certainty that no one would dare attack him, was about to recoil on him, Spock thought with a satisfaction too fierce to be strictly logical.

"There," Spock said suddenly. "Directly ahead: Volskiar's convoy."

"I see it," Tal snapped. "Hells, I approved the route. Get down, both of you."

The groundcar roared forward at top speed. Whether or not the guards recognized it for Tal's, they knew themselves to be under attack. Disruptor fire raged about it, scorching it, nearly overturning it, but Tal, eyes like cold flame, kept the vehicle steady.

Outmatched by his determination, the convoy broke apart as, the drivers of all three vehicles fought to avoid a collision with this maniac who was going far, far too fast to be attacked—

The third transport skidded as they raced past it. It struck the rocks edging the road and overturned in a shriek of metal crashing against stone. Finally, it skidded to a stop on one battered side. Tal braked so fiercely that the groundcar nearly flipped over as well, slewing around in a circle, sparks flying.

"Charvanek! Commander!"

The impact had broken the lock and twisted the hinges of the wrecked groundcar's passenger compartment. They heard a kick from inside, and the door parted. A hand, undeniably feminine, pushed it open the rest of the way. Disheveled but unhurt, Charvanek began to scramble out, already searching for cover. Tal started the groundcar toward her. She stared, recognized her rescuers, laughed, and leaped. Spock caught one arm, Ruanek the other, and they pulled her safely into the car. Charvanek sprawled ignominiously across Ruanek for an instant. As he flushed dark green and Spock fought down a surge of fire at her touch, she managed to squirm into a more dignified position, crowded in next to him on the one seat.

"Get us to Ki Baratan!" Spock snapped.

Tal accelerated with a roar of the groundcar's overworked engines.

And, in a wild storm of dust and small stones, they were away.

"You three," Charvanek said, panting, "have talents that I never suspected. No, I am not mocking you! Believe me, I never thought to see freedom again. But . . . what now? Where is Narviat?"

"If all goes as it should," Spock said, "he is doing what humans call 'making broadcast history.' "

The way Ruanek and the commander raised their eyebrows was, he thought, almost Vulcan.

TWENTY-NINE

KI BARATAN

Narviat, following little Kerit, looked covertly around the featureless corridor in this shabby building in this . . . less refined sector. His mind and body ached with weariness, but damned if he was going to show it. Damned, too, if he was going to show that he knew his mission, no, no, his life lay in the hands of one scrawny, unsocialized little girl-child.

Ruanek, on whom he'd expected to be able to depend, had deposited him unceremoniously into her keeping, then vanished. Narviat did not think Kerit would deliberately betray him. She had too little respect for he'd heard her call "the Authorities" for that. And as far as she was concerned, he, Noble Born admiral or not, was the ultimate rebel.

But what if she just grew bored, or was overwhelmed by the sheer joy of rebellion? What if she—

"We're here," Kerit said, and rapped lightly on the rusty door at the corridor's end.

"Where is 'here'?"

"Told you. This corridor's Tech Crew's, so they can get equip-

279

ment to and from the studio, you know, without tripping up everyone. No one but the crew knows about this, crew and me, of course."

"Of course."

The door opened a crack. A male face, just as skinny and young as Kerit's own, peeked out.

"Amarik," she said, " 's us. Let us in."

The boy's eyes widened. "Eyah, fancy! Double-shine! You made it!"

Wonderful. My life is in the hands of slang-talking children.

As Narviat stepped warily into a singularly crowded and downright shabby room—a broadcast studio, by all the Powers— a swarm of curious young people engulfed him. Most of them had lanky hair just this side of Imperial long and wore mismatched clothing that looked old and baggy enough to have belonged to their grandparents. Odd bits of jewelry glinted here and there: an earring made from a disruptor safety clip, a necklace of old computer parts.

My constituents.

Ah well, the young of every generation had to find some way to prove their nonconformity! At least, Narviat thought, the children did seem genuinely delighted to see him. The boy who had opened the door, Amarik, was staring at him in open awe.

"You are Admiral Narviat? I mean, really?"

"Course he is," Kerit muttered. "Don't be stupid, Amarik."

Amarik ran a hand nervously through stringy black hair that badly needed washing. "You gotta understand, uh, sir, this is just too—like—you know, *double-shine!* You—I mean, I've been tracking you, what you've done, been doing—"

"And that is . . . ?" Narviat asked, very carefully.

"Surviving." The boy flushed, but continued, "Can't be easy for you, being who and what you are, you know? A real balancing act. Especially with You Know Who in charge. And yet you not only stay alive, you, you know, speak up for us, the nobodies. Not easy, sir. And we—well, uh, we appreciate it. Honor to you, and—and all that."

So-o! Narviat thought, seeing the sharp intelligence in the young eyes. *Serves me right for judging by exteriors alone. This child is no fool.* He dipped his head in courtesy. "One does what one can."

"Right, and—and—well, look, we've got a broadcast setup here, just a small one, licensed program, though: 'Romulus Roars,' that's us. You've . . . heard of us?"

"I rarely have the time to watch broadcasts of any sort," Narviat told him solemnly.

"Right. Stupid of me. Well, anyway, the Powers That Be let us live, we're too small to bother them. We, uh, kind of tiptoe 'round subversive with our stuff, try to plant the seeds, you know?"

"Stuff," Narviat repeated.

Amarik's grin was quick and sharp. "Take a look. They toss out new gear all the time. Top of the line we've got here, even if it's put together from other stuff."

Narviat admitted to himself that he was hardly a technician. But from what little he did know, the hybrid network of equipment there amid the clutter did look amazingly advanced and, unlike anything else in the room, meticulously maintained. "Has Kerit told you what I need?" he asked. "What *we* need?"

"Needs a break-in," Kerit said with a grin. "Into the middle of You Know Who's broadcast."

Amarik blinked, staring. "Eeee. You don't think small. No, damn, course you wouldn't."

Narviat eyed him skeptically. "Can you do it?"

"I don't . . ."

"Or," Narviat prodded, "are you capable only of pornographic stunts?"

Amarik flushed, looking accusingly at Kerit. "He knows it was us?"

She shrugged. The boy licked his lips nervously, glanced at Narviat, glanced at the studio equipment, glanced at Narviat again. And all at once the nervousness was gone. All at once Amarik was as deadly serious as a man twice his age.

"This is it, then? This is when it begins."

"This is when it begins," Narviat agreed. "And, I hope, where. *Can* you do this? You will be going up against the most sophisticated equipment at the praetor's command."

Amarik ran a hand absently through his hair again. "Eeee. I—"

"Think of it as a challenge," Narviat goaded.

"Yes!" Kerit cut in impatiently. "We can. Trick of it is, you don't go face-to-face with the big stuff, you just slide under or around it! I know how, honest."

"She does," Amarik agreed. "Kerit here's the best."

Narviat sat down suddenly, all at once drained and hopeless as he hadn't been while in prison. "With what?" he asked wearily. "What evidence do we have?"

Amarik stared. "Didn't anyone tell you? Admiral, we have *the* tape, the whole blood-burn tape, the truth, you know? About Narendra III—what really happened! I, uh, I think Commander Charvanek taped the whole thing herself during the battle."

Charvanek . . . Liviana . . . hold on.

"Uh . . . Admiral?"

Maybe his weariness wasn't that well hidden after all. With a nod of thanks to Amarik, he accepted a grimy cup of what looked like *khavas,* despite the iridescent sludge floating on its surface. It went down like acid, but at least it was hot.

"Got this, too," Kerit said shyly. "Saw this get dropped. You know, when you were arrested. Thought you might need it."

She slipped a little package into his hands. Inside . . . Narviat's breath caught in his throat. Therakith's marriage bracelet, and with it . . . "Oh Powers . . ." With it were the delicate strands of hair from the scholar's murdered babies.

"Admiral . . . ?"

"We will do it," he said. "We will bring Dralath down."

"All right, then!" Amarik yelped. "Come on, we gotta get started before You Know Who does! Come on, all you dreebs, stop staring at me. 'Romulus Roars' is about to do a very special broadcast!"

* * *

Dralath had planned his personal appearance very carefully. His hair was elegantly groomed but not too precisely styled, his uniform tailored to be flattering without being totally severe. All in all, he thought, glancing into the mirror held by his fearful dresser, perfect: a living being, not a godlike icon—a paternal figure who would see that all would go very well for his children.

"Yes," he said, shooing away the dresser with a wave of his hand and taking his place before the cameras there in the main conference hall. "I am ready."

Dralath took a steadying breath, waiting for the technician's signal: Now!

Keeping his voice smooth and friendly, Dralath began, "My comrades, my fellow Romulans," knowing the words were going out over the entire world, over all the planetary data links and viewscreens, "today I come before you with joyous news. A potential threat to the security of our homeworlds has been eradicated. Thanks in part to the heroic deeds of—"

Frantic activity was going on behind the scenes. Dralath swept his hand brusquely across his chest, signaling a stop and snapped, "What is it?"

The technicians glanced at him in utter terror. "An override, m-my praetor," one of them stammered out. "Someone's sending an illegal broadcast out over our signal."

"Then cut him off, idiot! Locate him, cut him off, and I shall have the traitor eliminated!"

Dralath sat there, fuming, while the technicians worked feverishly, swearing at each other under their breaths as they tried frequency after frequency. Suddenly, the interloper's voice thundered through the room, calm, reasonable, and persuasive. Dralath sprang to his feet.

Narviat!

The children had found Narviat a prop tunic that looked almost like the real thing once it was pinned in place. They had cleared a wall, plain and unornamented, for his backdrop. *Good enough,*

Narviat thought. *No theatrical setting needed. What I have to say is dramatic enough.*

He endured while Amarik, behind the camera, and Kerit, at the keyboard, counted down the seconds till: Now!

"Romulans," Narviat began gently, "for those of you who may not recognize me, I am Admiral Narviat, retired from the Imperial fleet and now a member-at-liberty of His Imperial Majesty's government."

He glanced at Amarik and the skinny boy who was the sound tech, and got enthusiastic nods from them both: The broadcast was sending perfectly, sliding on top of Dralath's signal.

"I trust that some of you do know me," Narviat continued smoothly, "and know too that I honor our people and our home-worlds."

Amarik, with beautiful timing, tightened the focus so that there could be no mistake to anyone watching. Never mind the lack of insignia, the shadows under the eyes: This was no trick; this actually was Narviat.

"I was reluctant to come before you. Reluctant, since it is always difficult to be the messenger of tragic news. But speak I must." Surprising himself at the genuine horror that was slipping into his voice, Narviat said into the camera, "For—is not treason always tragic? Particularly when it is treason against the Romulan people—against all of you! It is our praetor who has betrayed us. I do not say this lightly. I would not lie about so serious an issue. But I cannot conceal this truth!

"Praetor Dralath has acted in a cowardly, dangerous manner. He has attacked, and attacked without provocation not warriors, not those able to defend themselves. He has attacked Narendra III, a Klingon outpost, yes—but a civilian base! I swear to this on my honor as a member of His Imperial Majesty's House: Our noble praetor has murdered unarmed *women,* he has murdered *children,* he has made war on weak, helpless, dishonorable targets!

"Hear me, my people. It is your gold that went toward this

murder, the gold that should have fed and housed Romulan citizens! It is your honor that has been bought and sold!

"But there is yet another horror to tell. In the process of murdering the helpless, Praetor Dralath has lost no fewer than four warbirds! Four warbirds and all their crews—How many of your children, how many of your husbands or wives will never return from that shameful action?

"Ask yourself this, my people: How many brave Romulan warriors have died for no reason—no reason, that is, save for the cause of Praetor Dralath's vanity?" Kerit was signaling to him, *We have it!* "And, lest you doubt my word," Narviat continued smoothly, "here is the proof, taken at the very heart of the massacre—taken by one who the praetor dared call traitor, but who you will see is the truest of Romulans! I call her name: Commander Charvanek!"

So blazing with anger he could not stand still, Dralath paced the conference room. *I will kill you, I swear it, Narviat, I will tear you apart myself!*

"Find him!" he shouted. "Find that thrice-damned Narviat and whatever scum of a broadcast pirate is helping him. Find him and *silence him!*"

"But . . . my praetor . . ."

Dralath almost casually backhanded the technician who had dared say even that much across the face. "Be glad that my hand held no knife," the praetor snarled at him as he cringed. "No excuses! Is that understood, all of you? There can be no excuses!

"Find me that traitor! Silence him—or by all the twisted fates, I will have you put to death, one by one!

"Silence Narviat *now!*"

Narviat was dimly aware of Kerit, giggling to herself like a manic creature of legend, as she jumped their signal from frequency to frequency, always keeping one step ahead of their pursuers. His head was pounding fiercely by now. But he dared not stop. As long as Amarik was waving to him, *Open air, go on,* he could not waste this precious chance to get his message across.

"Do you believe me?" he asked his unseen audience. "Do you believe me now that you have seen the evidence shown to you? Or do you, can you possibly, think the whole tape but a sham? Come now, let me show you more so there can be no doubt at all! Let me pile horror on horror, not out there in the darkness of space, but here at home, here in the very heart of our homeworld! Let me tell you of a scholar, an honest, innocent scholar and his family, tell you how Praetor Dralath decided to degrade this family. He took the wife and children hostage, did Praetor Dralath, with a promise to the scholar: 'Spy for me, and I shall free your family.' What could he do, that scholar, but obey? But then, but then . . . then the praetor lied. Then the praetor showed himself of no honor, none! For he murdered those innocents, wife, children.

"Do you wish proof?" Gently, Narviat took out the strands of fine baby hair he had removed from the belt of the guard who'd done the murders. "Do you see this? See how delicate it is, how silky? Do you see this baby hair, torn from the scalp of . . . of . . ."

It hit him then, that murdered baby, robbed of life almost before it had begun, that loving family destroyed, Therakith and his final, anguished courage . . . To his utter horror, Narviat realized that he was on the verge of weeping, as he had not been during all the years of combat, as he had not been during his time in Dralath's cell, as he had not been . . . since the day so many years ago . . . when his own wife and heir had died in what had been called an accident, a stupid, senseless transport accident . . .

Discipline, Narviat told himself. He must continue. Exhaustion and old grief were not excuses for failure.

"Dralath m-murdered the family." He must *not* break; Powers, he must not weep on screen! "The—the scholar, the scholar slew himself . . . h-he died in my arms . . ."

No. He could not go on. A hand over his eyes, Narviat waved desperately to Amarik with the other, *End it!*

"And . . . clear," he heard the boy say. But for a time Narviat could not move, head bent, both hands, fisted, over his eyes, fiercely willing the tears away.

You idiot! You weak, timorous idiot! What type of image did you just project to the whole planet?

At last he dared straighten, thinking, *Ah well, it was a good run while it lasted.*

The youngsters were all staring at him. Not surprising, since they could never have dreamed of seeing a military man, a retired admiral no less, break down like this. But Narviat realized with a jolt that they were all wide-eyed not in shock or dismay, but with genuine awe. He heard one of them murmur something about, "Such courage . . ."

Courage!

Little Kerit was suddenly at his side, looking up at him, her eyes burning. "That was the bravest thing I have ever seen," she told him earnestly. "I mean, nothing fake there, nothing lying—you let them all see you, how you really felt—you even let them see you weep! Now, that's really brave: You're so strong you can even afford to let them see you weep!" Kerit snorted. "Can't see the stupid praetor ever being half that brave."

Ah. Well.

At least I still have these allies, Narviat thought with heavy irony. *An army. Of children.*

As they reentered Ki Baratan, Tal slackened the groundcar's mad speed to a saner one. Swearing under his breath, he made some quick adjustments to the controls, then pounded the control panel angrily and slowed yet again. "We aren't going to get much further in this vehicle."

"Overheating?" Ruanek asked.

"To the point of burnout . . . damn. We walk from here."

Spock sprang from the groundcar. "We must make haste. Dralath must already have begun his proclamation."

Haste, yes. The rescue, all that violent action, might indeed be holding back the Fires, but one could, Spock thought wryly, only fight off Nature so long: The respite this time was going to be far shorter, he could feel that very plainly, and the backlash would be so much the stronger.

At least I have accomplished this much. At least Charvanek will not die a traitor.

She held up a hand, demanding, "What about my crew?"

"We don't know where they're being held," Ruanek began.

Spock waved him to silence. "If we succeed, they will be freed. You must be content with your own freedom for now."

Had that been too curt? Charvanek eyed him strangely as they wove their way through the maze of streets, heading towards the Central Court.

"What?" Spock asked.

"I thought, I hoped you had left. Yes, I know, that is a hopelessly illogical thought, but . . ." Charvanek studied him again, bit her lip, then leaned toward him. "Know this." It was a murmur too soft for Ruanek and Tal to hear. "If it—when it—when you can no longer endure, I—I will give you the last mercy a friend can grant."

"Final Honor."

"You—" She swallowed dryly. "You shall not suffer madness, exposure, or humiliation."

"Charvanek . . ." And then, more softly, "Liviana . . ." But he dared not look at her, and there was nothing else to say but, "Thank you. I do not need that mercy yet."

Ruanek frowned, looking around, his hand resting nervously on the hilt of his knife. "Streets are too empty for this time of day. Where is everyone?"

Spock shrugged. "An illicit broadcast cannot be common. Doubtless, everyone is watching Narviat."

"He *can* be persuasive," Charvanek murmured. "But where is he?"

Ruanek glanced at her. " 'Romulus Roars.' "

Spock raised an eyebrow. "An interesting metaphor, but—"

"It's a program, one of those, uh, 'angry young people letting off steam' types of shows. Borderline legal."

"And you listen to it?" Charvanek murmured with the barest touch of weary humor.

"I," Ruanek said with immense dignity, "like the music."

"I think we've found our crowds," Tal cut in. "Listen."

Ahead was a muted roar that could only be a disturbed crowd on the verge of turning into a mob. Spock hurried forward, Charvanek at his side and Ruanek and Tal behind—and found out in one startled moment why no one had been on the streets.

"What," Charvanek gasped, "has Narviat done?"

THIRTY

KI BARATAN, ROMULUS, DAY 9, SECOND WEEK OF TASMEEN, YEAR 2344

What Narviat had done, Spock thought, was obvious: he had created utter chaos.

Spock, Charvanek, Ruanek, and Tal fought their way out across the city square through a frenzied crowd and a descending storm of the praetor's guards. The four of them dodged frantic fists and the guards' truncheons, working across to the relative safety of an alley. There, panting, Spock glanced up at a viewscreen in time to see a replay of Narviat's broadcast: Narviat, face anguished, stammering out broken words about Therakith's murdered babies, the murdered family.

He weeps. *That is not feigned emotion. This once, Narviat is revealing his true, honest inner self. Will he ever forgive himself, I wonder, for exposing it?*

It had been enough, the final spark to ignite the smoldering unrest in the city, possibly over all of Romulus, into mob hysteria. All around him, people were shouting, screaming, crying out in pain or anger. Spock struggled to block the surging waves of

emotion from his mind, struggled not to respond, struggled not to
join the chaos—

*No! I am not yet mindless! We must tame this wildness, control
and shape it. Otherwise, Dralath will deploy his heavy arma-
ments, and there will be a massacre—we cannot allow that!
There is no Surak here to keep the Empire from tearing itself and
its people apart.*

"There!" Spock snapped at Ruanek. "Is that shopkeeper not
one of the Underground? We need him, and as many of the others
as we can reach."

Ruanek glanced at him, angry at the autocratic tone, then
quickly registered the truth: Spock did not mean to command
him, but dared not, for the sake of what sanity remained to him,
plunge into that chaos himself. "Right," Ruanek said without
argument. "Good idea."

He charged off through the crowds, quickly snagged his target
by the arm, and nearly dragged the man back with him. This was,
Spock remembered, Arket, a merchant with the wiry build of an
athlete—and right now, a startled, angry one. "Subcommander!
Let go of me, dammit, Ruanek! What in the name of all the fates
do you—Symakhos? What is going on?"

"We cannot allow a bloodbath," Spock told him tersely. "For
the crowd's sake, for ours, we must direct the mob's mind."

"How—"

"Do not argue! Can you locate any of the other members of the
Underground?"

Arket nodded. "We were starting to gather to meet with
Admiral Narviat when"—he gestured—"all that exploded. Even
so," he added hastily, watching Spock's face, "I can still collect
us all in one place quickly enough."

"Excellent. Here, then, is what you must do. . . ."

Narviat glanced impatiently about at his young admirers. "We
have to know what's happening out there! Amarik, can't you get
us an outside view?"

The boy pounced on a keyboard. "Sure can. We have . . . well, let's just say we can preempt a few cameras. Tricky, but . . ."

"Tricky's us," Kerit said, and pushed Amarik aside, taking over the keyboard. "Here, I'm quicker at this. Wait . . . getting something . . ."

"Eeee!" Amarik yelped. "Would you look at that! You've started a dark-blood *riot* out there, Admiral! Here," he added as Narviat rushed to his side. "Look at this screen. View's focused right on the main square."

It took Narviat a few moments to make any sense out of the swirling mass: commoners, merchants, even some of the lesser nobility, and through it all, Dralath's guards, helmed, their truncheons rising and falling with grim efficiency. But the crowds were growing, and Narviat thought in horror that it was just a matter of time before the guards drew disruptors and the square became a battleground.

Powers help us all, I didn't want this! "He'll kill them all! I've got to—"

But then Narviat froze, staring. "Amarik! Kerit! One of you, get me a close-up!" He stabbed at the screen. "There! Hurry!"

No mistaking that face: The Vulcan! But he no longer looked even remotely like the solemn academician. For an instant, Narviat stood in speechless astonishment. Such elegant ferocity, such fierce, terrible dignity—

I could almost believe I watched a noble from the homeworld's ancient past! What madness is this . . . ?

But then Narviat recovered and snapped, "Sound, give me—"

The sudden blare from the speakers made everyone jump. Amarik made some hasty adjustments, and they heard the Vulcan's voice ring out over the roar of the crowd, cold and clear as the edge of a blade, the voice of one trained to be heard.

"It is Narviat who shows courage, true courage!"

He was never in one place for more than a few moments, never long enough for Dralath's guards to reach him. And each time he paused, the Vulcan shouted anew:

"It is Narviat who should be praetor! Narviat!"

Stopping here, there, even leaping up onto a low column for a daring moment, the Vulcan all but forced the crowd through sheer willpower into a chant of:

"Down with Dralath! Narviat for praetor! Narviat! Narviat!"

Yes, yes, and there were some of the Underground in that crowd: Arket and Ruanek and—oh, Fates guide her, that was surely Charvanek, free, but in the heart of all that new peril! Yes, and there were who knew how many of the others, helping the Vulcan, leading the shouts:

"Narviat! Narviat! Narviat!"

Narviat's first thought was *Damn him, he's going to get himself killed.* His second was *Damn him indeed: He's stealing my moment!* "I must get out there! Don't argue! What have you got for a disguise? A cloak, a blanket—curse it, there must be something—yes!"

The cloak was old and reeked of developing fluids, but Narviat didn't care. Flanked by his youthful army, he plunged out into the mob.

Dralath caught an attendant by the throat, dragged the man to him. "Get this damned studio makeup off me! Hurry, curse you! And you—yes, curse it, you! Get my advisors in here if you have to drag them in, yes, and Zerliak, too—Watch it, you idiot," he snarled at the trembling attendant trying to remove the makeup, "that's my eye! I don't want to look like that weepy traitor."

He shoved the man away as the advisors scurried in. "There you are, you miserable excuses for aides: What do you make of *that,* eh? Eh? That's a mob out there, if you hadn't noticed, and it's chanting Narviat's name! What now, idiots?"

"You, uh, you must make a public announcement, my Praetor," one of them began.

"An *announcement?* Do you think I'm going to make that traitor's words and that cursed tape go away with a pretty little *announcement?* Assuming, of course, that whoever's sending that illegal broadcast actually lets my signal through—dammit, why hasn't someone tracked down that broadcast source yet?"

"It, uh, keeps changing, my Praetor. It . . . even was, uh, routed through your own offices at one point."

"The fires burn you all!" As Dralath stalked about the room, advisors stumbled over each other to get out of his way. "Have I not one competent aide on the entire planet? That's enough," he added to the attendant who was frantically trailing him, dabbing at his face with a makeup sponge. "I said, *enough!* Zerliak!"

The head of Security saluted with crisp *I, at least, am a professional* perfection. "My Praetor."

"Get the emperor here, *now!"*

"Ah, my Praetor, the doctor has just, uh, given him his medication. He may not be in any condition to—"

"I don't care if he has to be carried here and propped up against a stake! I need him! I am going to make an announcement, all right, but it is going to be a public appearance, out there on the Praetor's Balcony."

"But is that safe?"

Dralath whirled on the advisor who'd dared ask that, staring at him with such cold, calculating rage that the advisor sagged, knowing he'd just destroyed himself.

"Safe?" Dralath spat. "Those are my people out there, rioting with another man's name on their lips, and you're worried about *safe?* I am going to make that public appearance to show the populous that *yes,* I am alive, and *yes,* I am well, and *yes,* damn them all, I am still very much the head of this government! And Emperor Shiarkiek will be at my side to prove it!"

Sanity was but one thin, shimmering ribbon of light almost lost amid the flames, but Spock held fast to that ribbon, telling the Underground clustering around him in the mob, "Dralath *must* make an appearance. It is only logical. But where?"

"There," Ruanek cut in. "That's the Praetor's Balcony, overlooking the Square of Heroes, where he makes all his personal appearances."

Spock studied it as best he could while the crowds swirled about him, their emotions a hot blaze engulfing him, tempting him with mindless, illogical, satisfying violence—

No, I will not surrender! No, I will not strike out every time they jostle me! I will hold on, just this short, short while longer. And then . . . then if need be, Liviana can find me and give me the Final Honor, and I will be at peace. . . .

Just a little longer.

"Can you get us through?" he asked Ruanek.

"Not easily, but yes."

But where is Narviat? I felt certain this would draw him. But if he is not here, all this is for nothing!

"What in the name of all the fates are you doing?" a voice said in his ear, and after the first startled instant, he recognized the voice: Narviat, after all.

"Ah, you *are* here. Perfect."

But Narviat's attention was all on the slender figure at Spock's side. "Charvanek . . ." he breathed. "I did see you. They did get you out. You're safe."

Her raised eyebrow paid tribute to his worn and stained disguise. "Safe as possible under the circumstances," she said after a long moment.

"Which," Spock cut in, "are not likely to improve—"

"Unless I act," Narviat finished, pulling the hood of his disreputable cloak further forward to hide his face. "Agreed. The Praetor's Balcony, I take it?"

Ruanek nodded. "We need a diversion."

Arket grinned. "Leave that to us. You'll have one!"

The route Ruanek followed took Spock, Narviat, Charvanek, with Tal in wary attendance, as well as several members of the Underground, through a convoluted new maze of bureaucratic corridors.

Necessarily convoluted, Spock told himself sternly. *The fewer guards we encounter, the better.*

His head was pounding painfully, and he could not seem to find the control to will the pain away. The wild blood surged in his ears, distorting his hearing, and the Fires blazed within him, confusing his vision.

Keep going, Spock thought, *simply keep going. There is an end to everything.*

There was a time of no thought at all, only vague snatches of having fought this guard or that, and he was—

—clear-minded again, with a shocking suddenness, knowing only that he had not lost awareness for very long. But what had happened in that time? Where were they?

And . . . what have I done? Spock consoled himself, *It could not have been anything so terrible, or the others would surely still be reacting. I—we—disabled some guards, then, no more.*

I did not kill.

I trust I did not.

The others . . . he could not be sure. A knife glinted in Narviat's hand, others in Ruanek's and Tal's. None of them were under the restraints of Vulcan morality. Ruanek's face was pale; his wounded arm must be paining him. But his eyes were grimly determined.

If he can hold out, Spock thought with the weariest flash of irony, *so can I.*

Ah. They were in a wider corridor, and Spock could see the bright glare of daylight at its far end. "Up ahead," Ruanek mouthed. "Dralath."

Sure enough, there he was, trailed by an entourage of guards and attendants, two of whom were virtually carrying a tall, lean figure who sagged in their arms.

"The emperor!" Charvanek breathed.

"He looks drugged," Ruanek added in horror.

"He is," Narviat snapped. "And I will see their blood for it!"

Dralath was stepping out onto the wide balcony.

We need that distraction!

And they got it. As Dralath appeared, he was greeted by the rest of the Underground, infiltrating the crowd, and by what sounded like the entire crew of "Romulus Roars," their shrill young voices rising above the others.

"Down with Dralath!"

"Dralath Child-Killer!"

"Narviat for Praetor!"

"Narviat! Narviat! Narviat!"

"Now," Spock snapped, and charged.

The guards, Dralath in their midst, were all watching the commotion below—a fatal mistake as the Underground rushed them from behind. Knives flashed, men and women fell, and Spock smelled the coppery tang of blood, saw the deaths, ached to killkillkill—

"No!" he gasped, and hurled a guard aside hard enough to stun but not, he hoped, break bones. "I . . . will . . . not . . . *kill!*"

A second guard rushed him, and Spock hit him sharply on the side of the head with the flat of his hand, felling the man. A third guard—but Ruanek cut this one down, hissing to Spock, "Stay back! I know you are ill—shouldn't fight—stay back!"

How could he stay out of this battle? The guards—

But the guards were already overcome, and Dralath bowed his head in seeming surrender . . .

Only to straighten, smiling fiercely, a disruptor pistol aimed at point-blank range directly at Narviat.

Everyone on the balcony froze. Down in the square, the wild turmoil continued, but it seemed a light-year removed; here, there was only intense silence. Narviat very carefully raised his hands, smiling as if to say, *Ah well, at least I tried.* Dralath's finger began to tighten. . . .

A sudden sharp giggle rang out: the emperor. Dralath's startled glance shifted—and Spock lunged, shouting at Narviat, "Down!" As Spock grappled with Dralath, trying to tear the disruptor from him without lashing out in a lethal move from *tal-shaya*, the praetor fired. Spock forced his arm up, and the blast raked the far wall, sending hot stone splinters flying. Narviat, who'd dropped to hands and knees, lunged up from the floor, crushing Dralath back against the near wall, beating his hand against the stone till Dralath, cursing, lost his grip on the weapon.

"Someone hold on to this filth," Narviat said shortly, and stepped back as the Underground rushed in to engulf Dralath. "Thank you," he added to Spock, who dipped his head. Dropping the disreputable cloak and straightening his clothes and hair with hasty hands, Narviat told everyone, "Now, excuse me. I have work to do."

Face carefully composed, he stepped to the front of the balcony, and a roar went up from the crowd below, from the guards—who were not averse to suddenly changing sides—as well as the civilians.

Now it is his moment, Spock thought, *and I can finally—*

But Dralath was watching him intently. "Who are you?" Dralath asked, and again, more urgently, *"Who are you?"*

Who, indeed? "The Eater of Souls," Spock said, and withdrew into the shadows. A Vulcan must not be seen by the people, for here on Romulus, except to a very few, he could not exist except as an enemy. Tal noted—but Tal, face impassive, turned away: His loyalty now lay utterly with Charvanek again, and he would do nothing that might harm her in any way.

Meanwhile, Narviat had slipped easily back into the politician's role, his voice, Spock thought, smooth as rich cream, his face that of a loving father.

"You all know me by now."

"Narviat!" they obligingly shouted back. Some of them added, "Praetor Narviat!"

"That is as may be. But you know only part of why I am here. I have already told you of Dralath's crimes, of his most terrible treason. There is nothing I could add to that; his crimes of murder, of corruption, of greed and utter disregard for all things a Romulan holds honorable speak for themselves.

"But I do not wish you to think I am alone in making these charges. Commander Charvanek, if you would?"

She moved to his side, as dignified in her prison garb as though she still wore her uniform. "I was there," Charvanek said. "At the cowardly attack on Narendra III. Listen, and I shall tell you of a Klingon elder—yes, a Klingon, a grandfather, who proved far more honorable than any Romulan that day. Listen, too, and I shall tell you of the Federation's gallant *Enterprise*, of hundreds who died that day in the effort to stave off that massacre.

"Listen, and I shall tell you of Romulans who laughed at the very mention of honor!"

As Charvanek continued to tell her side of the Narendra III story, Spock silently congratulated her. How delicately she avoided the fact that *she* had attacked Romulan ships!

"Do you hear the words of this brave woman?" Narviat demanded. "Do you hear them?"

He waited just long enough for the predictable shouts of "Yes!" and "Glory to Commander Charvanek!"

"And do you know how treacherous Dralath rewarded her for her bravery?" Narviat continued. "With *prison!*"

"No!" the crowd roared.

"With accusations of treason!"

"No!

"Does that seem terrible enough? But there is more, my friends. Dralath, treacherous Dralath, rewarded this brave commander with a *sentence of death!*"

"No!" It was a collective scream this time.

"Dralath is the traitor!"

"Kill Dralath!"

"She *is* a traitor!" Dralath shouted, struggling in his captors' grips. "Listen to me, you idiots! This woman you revere fired on our own warbirds!"

But no one save those on the balcony heard him.

"And as further proof, were proof needed, of Dralath's crimes,"

Narviat continued in a voice that shook ever so slightly, "see what he has done to our beloved emperor!"

With the help of Charvanek and two assistants, the old man was gently brought forward, head lolling, clearly unable to speak.

"Drugged . . ." The murmur swept the crowd. "Dralath drugged him . . . Dralath tried to kill the emperor! Dralath tried to kill the emperor!"

Narviat threw up both arms in a deliberately theatrical gesture, glorying in his control over the crowd. "No!" he commanded, and the crowd, startled, fell silence. "We are not beasts, my friends, we are not madmen. We are Romulans, people of honor. We do not descend to mob frenzy."

That was clearly the signal the "Romulus Roars" crew had been awaiting. "Praetor Narviat!" they began. "Praetor Narviat!"

Others in the crowd took it up. "Praetor Narviat!"

Now they were all shouting it. "Praetor Narviat! Praetor Narviat! Praetor—"

They fell silent as he threw up his arms again. "If such is truly the will of the people."

"It is!"

"Praetor Narviat!"

"Yes!"

Narviat slowly lowered his arms. "Then—I accept."

He waited for the cheers to die down, then added, "I hereby decree a new regime not of terror and shame but of honor! And as my first act as your praetor, my friends, I place under arrest that traitor known as Dralath!"

This time the cheers had a bloodthirsty edge to them. Narviat let them continue just long enough, then said, "I declare today a day of holiday! Go, my friends, enjoy yourself. But forgive me for not joining you just yet. There is much to be done in this our bright new order!"

Well done, Spock thought, *oh, most well done. But how much of that do you actually believe?*

Clearly more than Dralath did. Narviat paused before the former praetor, studying him.

"So," Dralath spat. "Am I to be sent a sword? Or will I take my place in your cell? I warn you, I will be avenged. Your life will never be safe."

Narviat shrugged. "At least I will not have you to bother me. Commander Jarok." He turned to a stocky officer with a bruise on one jowl. "Will you kindly lend me a disruptor?"

But Ruanek moved to block Narviat's path. Voice soft but urgent, he said, "Sir, no. Forgive me, but you cannot start your reign with murder. That—that is Dralath's way."

"Damn you." Narviat's growl was almost too soft even for Vulcan ears. "Damn you, you're right." Raising his voice, instantly all politic smoothness, Narviat proclaimed, "I shall not stain my administration with cold-blooded murder. There shall be an honorable trial of criminal Dralath in accordance with our sacred customs."

There was a suddenly flurry of alarm, cries of, "Watch out! He's got a disruptor!"

Dralath! He'd taken advantage of the few moments of inattention to kick and bite his way free, then grab a weapon. He fired, fired again, filling the air with shards of stone and the reek of vaporized flesh. Amid the screams and smoke, Dralath shouted, "Code Four Five One—*now!*"

He was suddenly surrounded by the shimmering of a transporter effect—and in the next moment, was gone.

Narviat spat an oath. "We should have expected this. He was devious enough to have made contingency plans. Much harm may they do him!"

With a savage sigh, he turned to Charvanek. "Take charge of our kinsman the emperor until we can get a surgeon we trust for him, will you, my cousin?"

She cast a glance at the wavering old man, another at Spock, and set two fingers on Narviat's wrist. He covered them gently with his hand, but shook his head.

"Must I ask you twice?"

Whatever else Narviat might be to her, he was now her commanding officer. Charvanek turned obediently to support the emperor, Tal in attendance.

Spock tried to rouse at that, tried to summon the strength to manage his own escape. But he had done too much, fought too hard. Now Narviat could rid himself of the Vulcan who should never have been there at all.

At least I have helped in Dralath's defeat, Spock thought. *Even though no one will ever know the entire role I played, the Federation and the Empire both are free from his plots.*

At least I have that much satisfaction.

Then *Plak-tow,* the blood fever, engulfed him, and Spock felt himself sag against the nearest wall.

And then he thought and felt nothing more.

THIRTY-ONE

ROMULUS, THE NEUTRAL ZONE AND FEDERATION SPACE, STAR DATE 21163.4

Ruanek followed Narviat's glance to where Spock stood . . .

No. Not stood. What he saw turned Ruanek's spine to ice. In the shuddering figure who leaned against a wall, his fingers steepled, no one would ever have recognized the Vulcan ambassador, the Romulan academician, the Starfleet veteran whose life was still forfeit to the Empire on charges of espionage—or the brave man who helped the Empire regain its honor. Some of its honor.

He can't stay here! Ruanek thought with a surge of near panic.

Narviat was a man of honor—but honor could be stretched too far. It would be dangerous for a new praetor to admit he'd been aided by a Vulcan, and downright fatal to admit that said Vulcan had helped him to his office. What easier way to be rid of the danger than to claim that Spock carried some deadly, highly communicable disease?

But the way Spock is now . . . how can he ever hope to escape?

Ruanek's mind answered him, unbidden, *Would you trust him with a ship?*

No, of course not. Spock was very clearly not fit.

So, Ruanek's mind continued with relentless logic, *someone has to go with him. No, you must go with him. Get him home to Vulcan where they can help . . . where he has his only chance for life—*

Leave the Empire? Defect? Ruanek thought in shock, *No Romulan has ever defected!*

But it wouldn't be a defection . . . would it?

"Sir," Ruanek said softly to Narviat before he could talk himself out of it, "please hear me." Ignoring the praetor's impatient glare, he hurried on, "We both know that, ah, Symakhos cannot remain here. But he—I—" Desperately, Ruanek continued, "I will not stain my honor with his death, nor will I allow you to stain your own."

For an instant, staring into Narviat's suddenly chill eyes, he was sure he'd gone too far. Stupid, unbelievably stupid, to lecture the new praetor not once but twice, and the Empire punished stupidity almost as ruthlessly as treachery.

But to his surprise, it was Narviat's gaze that dropped. "Do you know what you say?"

Ruanek's wounds ached just enough to be nagging. In fact his whole body and even his mind ached. Just then he would have liked nothing more than to hide in some safe corner where he could collapse. Where he could avoid agonizing decisions.

Instead, Ruanek forced his reluctant body to military attention. "Yes, sir, I do. I mean to get him home."

"But you—Ruanek, the law is as it is, and I—I cannot make an exception: If you leave the Empire, if you land on some Federation world, you can never return."

Oh Fates. He'd forgotten about that law. To give it up, everything . . .

Such as what? A chance for promotion, weighted against the betrayal of a friend? "Who better to go?" Ruanek countered. "I have no immediate family, sir. I am of a very minor house and have no personal ties. Not now." *How can you sound so calm about this?* his mind screamed at him. *You are destroying all your life!* Frantically trying to convince himself as well as Narviat, Ruanek burst out, "Would you not give your life for your people?"

"Yes, of course, but—"

"Well then, so would I give my life for a friend!"

For a long moment Narviat was silent. But other voices were calling for their new praetor, military and politicians alike in urgent need of direction, and he spat out an oath and turned away. "I don't have time for this now! Charvanek, would you kindly see that our gallant commander fully understands what he's volunteered for?"

Ruanek almost corrected the praetor yet again, almost reminded him, *That's "subcommander," sir.* But Narviat had known exactly what he'd said: Commander. Instant promotion. Instant shift of patronage, too.

Narviat knew how to turn the knife in the wound.

Oh no, don't do this to me. Don't make the choice even more painful. I always swore, my life for the Empire, but this is hardly what I had in mind.

And Commander Charvanek—*akhh*, so recently freed from sentence of death herself, she hardly needed to be burdened with his troubles!

But Charvanek, after a quick, startled glance at Narviat, gently detached His Imperial Majesty's hand from her arm, murmuring soothingly to him, and entrusted him, still weaving from the drugs Dralath had fed him, to the medical officer now standing at her shoulder. She saluted the emperor as if he possessed all his faculties and all his power. Then she moved to Ruanek's side and laid a hand on his shoulder.

It was a warrior's grip. "You come with me," she hissed.

Come or be dragged. Experience told him the commander was running on combat reserves, wit, and the sheer audacity that had always been her best weapon. *If I had had a patron like her . . .*

You'd probably be dead already.

"You," she snapped at Ruanek, "will you stop and think, truly think, for once in your impulsive life?"

"This once, I have! Do you want him dead?" he demanded. "Do you want to give him Final Honor yourself? No? Neither do I."

"The law states—"

"I know! Once made, the choice can't be recalled."

"That law was passed because of *me*, Ruanek!" It was a cry of anguish. "Do you understand me? Because I made one too-quick decision that landed me in Federation hands, you must suffer."

"Because of that decision, he came here! Commander, lady—"

"I was repatriated—but you won't be, you *can't* be! If he starts his administration by breaking the law, he violates everything he's always stood for. Ruanek, listen to me," she said, tightening her grasp. "Spock might not even survive. And then what? His life gone; your life wasted when you could have had . . . Are you ready to live in exile?"

"No, Commander," Ruanek said with bitter honesty, "I am not. But I'm not ready to live with his death on my conscience, either."

"So be it!" she exploded. "A scoutcraft is already fueled and ready. It was," Charvanek added ironically, seeing his surprise, "the first thing I had done after returning here, just in case. I'll have the ship cleared for takeoff. But I must warn you: It was the only ship I could find, and it is barely worthy of the name 'Romulan.' "

"Understood."

But all at once Charvanek's fierce gaze softened. "I know you are not a defector," she murmured. "No one who knows you could think you a traitor. And . . . your loss need not be fatal. It was not so for me."

Ruanek, blinking fiercely, saluted her.

Acting with wonderfully feigned casualness, Charvanek moved to Spock's side, spoke to him quietly and with even greater gentleness than she had used with the emperor. They did not touch, and Ruanek managed not to flinch at the storm of emotions he sensed. When Charvanek returned to Ruanek, the Vulcan followed her, his breathing ragged, his face pale.

"Centurion Tomalak will take you to the port, Commander," she said.

Commander. She gives me what honor she can.

Ruanek saluted again, then gestured for Spock to come with him. For an instant, the Vulcan's eyes focused on him, and he managed not to flinch from the madness in the dark eyes. Charvanek nodded, then shrugged and went to stand beside Narviat. He smiled as though he had noticed nothing of what had just occurred, and held out his hand to her. Charvanek smiled as well, and clasped it. And turned her back on the past.

Spock's eyes rolled up in his head until he really did look like the Eater of Souls.

"Come on, sir!" Ruanek urged.

No motion. Ruanek summoned all his courage and touched Spock's arm. The Vulcan slapped his hand away, but followed.

If the Fates were kind, perhaps Spock could restrain himself from battle madness long enough for them to get offworld.

Safer for both of us if I keep him locked in the scout's cabin till we reach Vulcan. Assuming that we have even a chance of getting there.

Centurion Tomalak had commandeered a groundcar to take them to the port. "You're really going to go through with this?" he asked Ruanek.

"Yes."

"Better you than me . . ." The word he did not say but let Ruanek sense was "renegade."

I need him, dammit. I have to let him live.

Besides, Ruanek added with weary honesty, *right now, I'm not sure I could take him.*

Tomalak laughed silently. At the port, he watched with curiosity and a good deal of cynicism as Ruanek leapt out of the car, then tried to extricate Spock. He did not offer to assist.

"We have to go, sir," Ruanek told Spock as if he were sane enough to understand. "Let me help you."

As the Vulcan emerged from the groundcar, his knees buckled. In what was either the bravest act of his life or the stupidest—there was plenty of recent competition for that, Ruanek thought—he wedged his shoulder under Spock's and half-carried him to the landing slip and the waiting scoutship.

"Must not . . . kill," Spock rasped as if wandering in nightmare.

"Not if you want to get home, sir," Ruanek agreed. "You don't like to kill. We both know that. You didn't even kill that traitor back on Obsidian. So you won't kill me."

There might be some who'd say *he* was a traitor—no, he wouldn't think about that.

"You do not understand!" Spock's words came out in a rush, savagely edged.

"Just a few more steps, sir," Ruanek kept his voice cheerful, if low. "I understand that you're sick and that they can help you on Vulcan. So I'm going to need your cooperation to get you there. I can't pilot if you break my neck."

To his astonishment, the madman actually chuckled. "Logical," he said and gave no further opposition.

Fates. Ruanek stared at the scout in utter disbelief. Commander Charvanek hadn't been exaggerating: The damned ugly, antiquated thing should have been cut into scrap years ago. But if she thought it was still spaceworthy . . .

Cuts and muscles aching, Ruanek heaved Spock into the decrepit ship, secured him in the copilot's chair—which creaked alarmingly—and demanded final clearance from the port. Tomalak's sardonic voice—how had the aggravating bastard gotten to ground control so fast?—gave it.

Speed, Charvanek had urged, and Ruanek had promised to obey. The engines whined in protest, but they did start, and assuming that the cracked instrument panel could be trusted, power was building properly.

Now! High-G restraints engaged as the full thrust of takeoff pushed them back into their seats. All around them, the ship groaned and wheezed, but the cursed thing flew.

"Safe voyage!" Centurion Tomalak wished in a voice that made Ruanek want to turn the ship around and teach him manners.

He accelerated, not even putting on screen a visual of the setting sun, the moons' rise, or the homeworld he was abandoning. He would have faced down executioners, but a final sight of the homeworld would have broken him.

Once out of atmosphere, Ruanek, very carefully not thinking about what he was doing, engaged the standard preset course out of the homeworlds' system, then turned to Spock.

The Vulcan had bitten his lip. Green blood trickled down his face.

"Let's settle you more comfortably, sir," Ruanek said, and bent to release the Vulcan's safety gear.

Spock struck at him. Damn good thing, Ruanek thought, that the Vulcan had been weakened by whatever his condition was, or the move might have ripped out his throat. "You don't want to do that, sir," he told Spock. "I'm a friend, remember?"

"No . . ." Spock muttered. *"I will not kill!"*

Better lock him up right now, Ruanek decided.

He had pulled Spock out of the copilot's seat, one arm over his shoulder, and was half-walking, half-dragging him toward the cabin when a savage impact hurled Ruanek and Spock to the deck. The ship yawed wildly for a heartrending few moments before autopilot regained control.

To Erebus with the robots, Ruanek thought, struggling up; nothing matched a living pilot for skill. Damn whoever was shooting at them, he wasn't going down without a fight!

Damn this junkpile of a ship, he corrected after a few tense moments. There hadn't been an attack. A scout this size had only rudimentary shields—but they should have been enough to ward off whatever debris they'd just hit. Or rather, they should have stayed up, not faded without so much as a warning! Ruanek brought them up and accessed damage control simultaneously.

Damn, again. A bad hit. The hull hadn't been breached, but the sensors showed, as much as they showed anything, that a plate was badly damaged. If the angle of impact had been only slightly different, he and Spock would already be subatomic particles.

The viewscreen's image flickered and faded. Ruanek fought with the instruments for a time. Then, with a snarl, he hit the screen with the flat of his hand and got a clear visual long enough for him to grunt in irony.

What they'd hit had been a fragment from one of Volskiar's wounded warbirds.

Where there was one fragment, he suddenly realized, there might well be another!

And Fires take it, there was! Ruanek, cursing instruments that weren't giving him accurate readings, banked the ship sharply away from new danger, only to be shocked by another impact. At least the shields stayed up this time, deflecting the worst of it. Still, Ruanek felt the whole ship shudder until he wondered if was going to shake itself apart. The lights dimmed, and for one horrifying moment, so did life-support.

But then the lights brightened and the antiquated air pumps started up again. Ruanek let out a breath he hadn't even known he was holding. Something somewhere in the engines groaned like a living being, then the ship resumed course.

Ruanek checked navigational readings. He groaned, too. More bad news: already out of the homeworld system, he would be entering the Neutral Zone in one point twenty-five *veraks*. At that point, his problems would promptly increase: he would be facing both a ship that wanted to die and Federation enemies who'd want to see *him* die.

The ship's responses were sluggish, but after three tries,

Ruanek managed to activate the arms computer. Not much fire-power, but you could do damage with even a child's blade.

Whose ship *was* this? Klingon manufacture, presumably; no one else's handiwork would be so shoddy. He refused to be para-noid enough to think it part of a convoluted plot on the part of the praetor—the former praetor. Or—and the thought made his blood run cold—had Narviat used his kinswoman and consort to set up one rival and one inconvenience for an easy kill? After all, Ruanek had contradicted him not once but twice, and been right both times—did Narviat see *him* as a potential rival, too?

Dammit, that really was paranoid.

But, live or die, Ruanek realized, he would never know the truth.

"Emissions . . ."

To Ruanek's astonishment, Spock was dragging himself over to the copilot's seat. "Faulty instruments . . . you cannot trust the readings. Check for emissions . . . sign of hairline cracks . . ." His eyes rolled back in his head, then focused again on Ruanek. There was no sanity in them, nothing but blood madness. But it was not aimed at Ruanek.

"Give me weapons control!" Spock rasped out.

Fates! "Sir, no sir, there's no enemy out there. Just this damned ship. I'm a warrior, not a technician. Can you, uh, help me with it? What can be fixed, I mean?"

"Yes . . . I . . . yes."

That sounded reassuringly normal. If Spock was sane and capable, their chances of survival had just risen—*akhh,* he was no Vulcan to reduce his life to probability statistics.

He started when warning lights suddenly flashed from the life-support monitors and alarm buzzers sounded. Ruanek swore. Now what?

Spock toppled back into the copilot's seat, his hands shaking so badly he could not manage the restraints. In the greenish lights of the instrument panels, he looked like something risen from the dead.

"Can you manage that?" Ruanek let the doubt echo in his voice, hoping to provoke the Vulcan into at least a hint of fighting strength.

"There is no . . . logical alternative. You are, as you say . . . no technician."

Dead if he did and dead if he didn't, as the saying went. Ruanek released instrument control to the madman beside him.

"Emissions . . . yes! Ruanek, there is a hairline breach—seal off sector fifty-five by five, now!"

Ruanek stabbed at the appropriate buttons. Some didn't light, and he wondered—

The ship lurched! "Shields down," Spock read as calmly as though announcing the time.

Damn this ship to Erebus! Buzzers sounded on the life-support systems as the cabin slowly filled with acrid smoke.

I'm not ready to go to Erebus with it, Ruanek thought, and kept the ship as steady as he could.

"Got . . . it," Spock muttered. "Hold steady. Hold it . . . hold it . . ."

The long fingers did not tremble in the slightest as they danced over the control panel. Maybe concentration would help him, Ruanek thought wildly, burn whatever fever rode him out of his system. Or perhaps he would go irretrievably mad this time.

Suddenly the weakened hull plate exploded out. Spock's hand shot out, slamming down on the controls. Ruanek had time for a quick thought: *Either he sealed off the breach or we're both dead.*

Then the scout erupted into a storm of warning lights, smoke, and debris, and Ruanek shouted with shock and pain as his wounded arm was slammed against the control panel. He heard real agony in Spock's voice as the Vulcan was hurled from his chair.

No time to look. Ruanek, clenching his teeth against the pain, bent to engines and life-support. No cloak for this ship: that was certain. Cloaking devices consumed power, and right now he needed all the power he could get.

Ha, yes. The engines were stable as they were going to get, and clearly the breach had been successfully sealed off. Life-support: nothing he could do about that.

Ruanek turned toward Spock, terrified of what he was going to find. The Vulcan lay facedown upon the bridge. Green blood pooled beneath his head and shoulders, and Ruanek unfastened himself from his chair and knelt at Spock's side. Most of the blood, to his immense relief, seemed to be coming not from some mortal wound but from a slash across the Vulcan's forehead: those always bled spectacularly. But what internal damage there might be—no way of knowing that. And when you factored in whatever was already wrong with Spock . . .

It wouldn't matter. There would be nothing left for either of them, Ruanek knew, unless he could coax his ship and his Vulcan charge into a safe haven.

No time for more than a cursory exam. Back to the pilot's seat. Start running diagnostics, see what was left. A vision of *that* day-dream—the peaceful desert at dawn—flashed into Ruanek's consciousness, then flickered out, as unattainable as everything else he had ever wanted.

No, you idiot, no time for self-pity!

He began diverting power around trashed systems, thanking the Fates that he knew how to do it. Unfortunately, main life-support was one of those now-useless systems. Even the backup was flickering.

All right, no place for panic. Just find a way to conserve energy, nurse the thing along.

Ruanek reduced ship's gravity, ship's temperature, to save on power. He ran diagnostics on the warp engines, heart racing . . . then nodded at the results, almost reassured. There was a chance. Maybe. If some Federation ship did not see a Romulan, one wing down, as it were, emerging from the Neutral Zone and decide to score an easy kill. Fates knew he would have done so in what seemed like another life and exulted in the kill.

He got to his feet, thinking that at least the lighter gravity was keeping his knees from buckling. Crouching beside Spock, he turned him over. In addition to the cut across his forehead, the Vulcan was bleeding from the mouth and nose; but that could have been from the fall he took. Peeling up the Vulcan's eyelids, Ruanek began to check him for injuries. The head wound was the least serious, merely messy. The worst Spock had suffered seemed to be were deeper cuts on his neck and left shoulder. Any deeper, and he would have bled out by now.

Don't think of Therakith with his slashed throat. The ambassador needs your help, not your fears. You went into exile to get him home, so, by all the forgotten powers, you will damned well do it.

Ruanek snatched up the medkit and bandaged the wounds deftly, as he had been trained. Spock was beginning to shake, so Ruanek wrapped him in the one thermal blanket that seemed to be the ship's total emergency supply.

Not enough. He pulled the bedding off the cabin's bunk, then added his own uniform tunic, already much the worse for wear. Most of his own cuts had opened up again, and his undertunic was sticking to his body. It would have to be soaked off, assuming he lived that long.

"Home . . ." Spock's eyes met his. To Ruanek's astonishment, they were almost sane, as if his wounds had drained the madness.

"Ship's got painkillers," Ruanek told Spock. Vulcans were close enough in physical type that drugs that helped Romulans would probably help him. Wouldn't they? Damn all doctrine; he hadn't been trained for this! Damn again, what he needed now was that Evaste. Saavik. Whatever. She would know what to do.

The incongruity of that idea struck him an instant later, and he laughed.

Spock raised a somewhat battered eyebrow. The familiarity of that gesture tore at Ruanek.

"No painkillers," Spock muttered. "Need . . . the pain. Need to . . . focus." He flung up a hand, as if seeking anchorage.

Ruanek provided it in a strong handclasp that Spock tried to return.

"Punch in . . ." Spock gasped.

"What's that?" Ruanek asked. He might respect the Vulcan more than anyone except perhaps the emperor and his dead father, but this was *his* ship! His first independent command— even if it was also his last.

"Distress codes. Recognition symbols," Spock whispered. His voice was going weak, and the shivering had started again.

"Can I get you something hot to drink?" Ruanek asked.

"You can obey!"

That had the authentic bridge commander's snap. Ruanek didn't even try to argue, simply entered the codes and coordinates Spock dictated.

"There will be Federation ships on patrol," Spock said. "By now, I may have been missed. Or Saavik." His voice softened on the woman's name. "Do not let . . . them know," Spock whispered.

That you and she both were on Romulus illegally? "Let them know what?" Ruanek asked and forced a grin.

You are a Romulan, he told himself. *Invent a satisfying lie. The day you can't fool a bunch of Vulcans . . .*

But Vulcans abhorred lies and liars. He would not willingly earn Spock's distaste.

"I'll tell them I'm from the Romulan Underground. That I have information about the recent overthrow of the praetor. And that I claim political asylum on Vulcan in return for my information."

All of that, strictly speaking, was quite true.

"What about you?" Ruanek mused. "I can say you are my brother. It . . . *is* a lie, of course."

"Not . . . not substantially . . ."

"Oh." Spock had probably meant only that the two races were related, but it still felt amazingly comforting. "Then that's what I'll do. I'll get you home, Ambassador," Ruanek promised too frantically for his age and rank. His . . . new rank. "Or die trying."

"That is indeed the logical alternative. This . . ." He coughed. Ruanek dabbed gently at the blood on Spock's face. At least he wasn't bleeding from the mouth like a dying man.

"If you are hailed by a Federation ship, repeat this. . . ." Spock recited words and code groups that meant nothing to Ruanek. He managed to get his tongue and teeth around the strange terms on which their lives might depend, but, with the best will in the worlds, they came out accented.

Spock sighed. "Practice. But now . . . must try . . ." His breathing rasped, fought to steady itself, then grew more and more rhythmic. It grew deeper, steadier, and then softened until Ruanek set fingers to the pulse in Spock's throat and bent over his face with a piece of shiny metal.

"Do not fear," Spock rasped, the barest whisper, his eyes shut. "It is a Vulcan discipline. Another of the gifts the Empire has been denied."

If Ruanek lived, he realized, he might have a chance to observe such disciplines, perhaps even study them himself. If he lived . . .

Instruments showed that the scout had entered the Neutral Zone. Alone and uncloaked. Broadcasting Federation distress signals. *Might as well open the ship to hard vacuum while I'm at it,* Ruanek thought.

Instead, he jury-rigged a fan to keep the air reasonably breathable and nursed his ship along; he practiced the codes Spock had taught him before lapsing into the trance that was keeping him alive; and he thought, begging Fate in a way unworthy of a child, let alone a warrior.

They were almost out of the Neutral Zone when the warp engines gave out. Impulse power now; not enough power left, though, to actually get anywhere. Except, maybe, toward the ships that Spock claimed were out there.

Maybe. For the first time in his life, he knew total helplessness. Warriors knew better than to invoke "fair," but Ruanek remembered what he knew of Spock's life: how he had fought Sered, the cool nerve with which he had dared the Empire's

316

heart, the countless lessons he had given, from loyalty to sheer viciousness in the face of overwhelming odds. And he knew it would be neither fair nor right for Spock to die thus.

Should I try waking him? How? Besides, what would I wake him to? Pain and death?

Instead, Ruanek reached for communications and, real time, frantically called for help on any hailing frequency he could access.

And—yes! A ship was forming on the flickering viewscreen—

A ship coming after him. Out of the Neutral Zone. Ruanek recognized the predatory curves and deadly green of a warbird and sank back in his chair with a bitter laugh.

Now I know what happened to him. And now we die. At least we'll go up in a burst of glory.

THIRTY-TWO

U.S.S. STARGAZER, STARDATE 21191.0

Jean-Luc Picard, captain of the *Stargazer,* glanced about the bridge. It all looked perfectly, utterly normal. As though, he thought, they had never received the news of Narendra III. As though the *Enterprise* had never died, and all those Klingon civilians had never been massacred . . . But he knew that even at maximum warp, the *Stargazer,* posted on the far edge of the Neutral Zone, would never have made it to Narendra III in time to make a difference.

So what else can I do but continue as is? I have my orders. Maddening though they might be.

At least Melville Colony was still safe; there was that much. And if the politicians did their work, there would be no war, either.

At her communications station, fresh-faced young Tricia Cadwallader was pretending to be very busy with minute adjustments. Beside her, Science Officer Lisuni's narrow, gray-skinned face showed no emotion at all—but then, Ochati faces weren't suited to human expressions.

Beyond him, Gerda Asmund, Helm, and her twin sister, Idun, Navigation, exchanged quick, unreadable glances. Deceptively calm, those two; but Picard remembered their grief and rage when they'd heard the of the loss of Narendra III and *Enterprise*.

I could almost howl with you. We should have been there at Narendra III. Instead . . . we endlessly, uselessly, patrol the Neutral Zone. And . . . we . . . wait.

Walker, Picard thought yet again, *you should have called me in.*

Surely he could have gotten in-system in time to at least divert *one* warbird. It might have sufficed to turn the tide. And he might have done more.

Cadwallader suddenly straightened at her station. "Message coming in, sir. Encrypted, but not eyes only."

"I'll take it here. On screen," Picard ordered. He exchanged a quick, wry glance with his first officer, tall, dark Gilaad ben Zoma. Even an admiral's face would be a welcome sight by now.

"Message decrypted, sir," Cadwallader said. "On screen now."

It was Walker Keel's image, barely degraded by the light-years the signal had traveled. His eyes were deeply shadowed, his face that of someone who's gone without sleep for far too long. "We've received word from Vulcan," he said without any words of greeting. "Your objective has been retrieved."

Picard sat forward in his chair, just barely biting back an oath. "By whom?"

"By *Enterprise,* ironically, and then transferred away from *Enterprise* by a shuttle crew. Four out of seven hundred." Keel added wearily. "They missed the battle. So as far as you're concerned, Jean-Luc, this mission's over. New orders are attached to this signal packet, but in brief, the *Stargazer* is to go on to Narendra III. Help them assay the damage. Keel out."

"Confirm receipt," Picard ordered Cadwallader.

"Confirmed, sir."

All that waiting. For nothing.

Indeed . . . ?

"Lay in a course for Narendra III, sir?" Helm asked. Picard could feel the emotional temperature on the bridge drop about thirty degrees.

Of course. Neither Gerda Idun nor Asmund would want to leave without vengeance.

Picard held up a hand. "Make it . . ."

"Captain," Cadwallader interrupted suddenly, "I'm getting a distress signal from a . . ." She turned sharply about to face him, her freckled face gone pale. "Captain, it's a Romulan scoutcraft."

"Red alert!" Picard ordered. Sirens howled and red lights pulsed over the bridge. Where there was one Romulan visible, there were likely to be cloaked warbirds, just waiting for some unwary Federation officer, God help him, to snap at the bait. "On screen. Magnify."

Yes, you could see it now, a small, badly battered vessel struggling into range.

"It doesn't look like even impulse power's fully on-line," Picard thought aloud. A . . . Romulan horse? Dead in space was a game both sides had played before.

"Shields up," Idun Asmund reported tersely. "Phasers on-line."

Red alert first; questions second. And phasers a distant third, if you didn't want to start a war. Another war.

At least they might see action now. Such as it was.

Helm and Weapons exchanged swift, savage smiles. They would be happy to take out even a small Romulan ship.

"Steady," Picard cautioned them.

"Captain," Cadwallader cut in, "I'm getting something. . . . It's a distress signal, sir!"

Underestimating Romulans was a damn good way to start a war. Or lose one.

"Commander Lisuni!" Picard snapped. "Real or feigned distress?"

The science officer studied his instruments intently, narrow gray Ochati face furrowed with concentration, then glanced up in alarm. "It's real, all right. That scout's been badly damaged. It's rapidly losing life-support. Rapidly losing structural integrity, for that matter."

"Life signs?"

"Two. One's very, very shaky."

"Lieutenant Cadwallader," Picard ordered, "open a hailing frequency and patch me through."

"Hailing frequency open. Go ahead, Captain."

"This is Jean-Luc Picard, captain of the Federation star cruiser *Stargazer*, to the master of the Romulan scout. Are you aware you are in Federation space?"

A burst of static answered. And then came a response that made Cadwallader gasp. "That's a Federation recognition code! Patching it through to your station, sir."

Good work, Picard thought. It was Federation, all right, and high-level enough that you didn't want it blurted all over even a starship's bridge.

In fact, he quickly realized, it was the highest-level security known to Federation civilians—one that the Romulans should *not* have known.

Probably Romulan. The voice repeating it had such a heavy accent that Picard could barely understand him. And the static breaking up the transmission didn't help it at all.

"It's the correct recognition code," Cadwallader confirmed, "but that's definitely a native Romulan speaker."

Ben Zoma moved to Picard's side, murmuring, "And where do you suppose he got that code?"

Meaning, of course, just how bad is the Federation's security leak? "Suggestions, Number One?" Picard asked.

"I'd say blast that ship out of space, but that's just a gut reaction. Captain, the Romulans could have set up a crippled scout with an injured crew as a decoy."

"Let's hear what this one has to say. Lieutenant Cadwallader, raise the scout again."

"I'm trying, sir. . . ."

With a sudden crackle of static, the channel came alive. ". . . need of immediate assistance," the heavily accented voice said. "We were damaged as we left the homeworld."

"We? Who's we?"

Idun Asmund said, "Photon torpedoes on-line, sir," and glanced Picard's way hopefully. Picard got her thought easily enough: *Just one good shot.*

"Belay that," he told her.

The Romulan continued wearily, "I am . . . was . . . Subcommander Ruanek . . . House Minor Strevon . . . We are— my brother and I—are, you would say, dissidents. Refugees." He broke off, coughing rackingly, then continued, voice hoarse, "My brother's unconscious. We . . . we claim political asylum. On Vulcan."

"Vulcan!"

"Captain," Lisuni cut in, "I'm picking up gravity fluctuations from the scout."

Had gravity gone on *Enterprise-C* along with light and life-support before the ship blew? Had its people had time to fear? Had they feared, yet fought for life just as this Romulan did?

Dammit, no, you don't condemn even a Romulan without a fair trial.

"It doesn't matter for me," the Romulan continued. "But my brother . . . He is older than I and wiser. He knows . . . he understands. They can heal him on Vulcan."

The Vulcans would hardly be likely to take in this scout crew—or . . . would they?

"Cadwallader," Picard ordered quickly, "raise Starbase 9. Report to Admiral Lynn on our status. Commander Lisuni, start a scan for any other ships out there." Romulan warbirds would run cloaked, but Lisuni knew enough to check for emissions signatures as well.

"Aye, aye, sir."

Meanwhile, *Stargazer* was left holding the bag. Or the crippled Romulan scout.

Ben Zoma glanced at his captain. "The way our luck's been running lately, the minute we beam those two aboard, three warbirds decloak. Romulans wouldn't hesitate to blow up a spy."

Subcommander Ruanek caught that. In a heavily accented, most frustrated tone, he exploded, "If I were a spy, would I be this—this damned incompetent?"

Picard took a deep breath, tried not to laugh, then failed. "We're not Romulans, Gilaad. And if we let these two die, we're no better than they. Besides, no Romulan is that good at making himself ridiculous on purpose!

"All right, Subcommander. Prepare to beam over, you and your brother. Unarmed."

"Understood," the Romulan rasped.

"Gilaad," Picard ordered in an undertone, "get down to the Transporter Room. Now."

As the turbolift doors whooshed shut behind ben Zoma, Gerda Asmund implored Picard with her eyes, *Me, too!* He shook his head. The last thing he wanted was a human with a grudge down there.

"Transporter Chief, make no move until Commander ben Zoma and Security Chief Joseph arrive. Security to Transporter Room. Attention. Now hear this: Security to transporter room. I will give you the order to beam over the Romulans. As soon as you have them, signal, and I will raise shields."

"Ben Zoma in the transporter room," came the report over in-ship communications.

"Excellent," said Picard. "Ready to gamble?"

"Biggest bluff of my life. I'll raise you two Romulans, and I'll call."

"No, Cadwallader will do that. Lieutenant, tell the scout crew to prepare to beam over."

"No reply, sir. Their communications are off-line."

"Life-support off-line as well," Lisuni cut in.

"Transporter room," Picard snapped. "Energize."

"Aye, Captain."

Picard winced as violent light erupted from what had been the Romulan scout. Had he waited a few moments too long? "Transporter Room!"

"Got them, Captain."

"Shields up!" Picard ordered. "Helm, take us out of here. Maximum warp." That should catch any pursuing warbirds off guard—he hoped.

Over the audio, he could hear the Security chief snapping an order, then another.

"Captain." Ben Zoma's voice was as controlled as if he were in ship-to-ship action. "We have a situation. Can you get down here?"

Just what Picard needed: another damn crisis.

"On my way," said Jean-Luc Picard.

THIRTY-THREE

U.S.S. STARGAZER, STARDATE 21203.6

As Picard entered the Transporter Room, ben Zoma warned him in an undertone, "Careful. He's got a knife."

I thought I said "unarmed." Is he that foolish? Or that contemptuous of us?

But then a flash of data memorized from who knew what briefing reminded Picard that all Romulans of rank carried a knife known as an Honor Blade. This Romulan probably hadn't even considered his as anything as common as a weapon. It was part of him.

But it was a weapon now. The Romulan—Ruanek, he'd named himself—had one arm about the sagging body of his unconscious brother. Both were battered and stained with soot and green blood—but the knife gleamed, unmarked, never wavering in that clenched fist. The Romulan's face was cold and hard, but his eyes . . .

Picard had seen that look in the eyes of humans, too: those who had been pushed far too hard under unbearable conditions for far too long. Those who had reached the edge of total collapse.

One wrong word, and he either attacks in sheer despair or uses that blade on himself.

Neither option is acceptable.

He quickly considered and discarded command voice: Subcommander Ruanek was in no condition to hear anything military from anyone he would consider an enemy.

All right, then. Gamble. Picard muttered to the Security crew, "Put your phasers down."

"But sir—"

"That's an order!"

He waited a second for their compliance, then took a wary step forward, hands half raised to show their emptiness.

"You brought your brother to us for help." The translator should handle that easily enough, and his soothing tone should register even if the words didn't. "That means you trust us with his life. The way you talked, it means more to you than your own. But we can't help him if you won't let us near him. Surely you know that."

Something flickered in the Romulan's eyes. Not relief, exactly, but a desperate surrender that said, *I trust him; I have no other option.* "Captain?" It was said in his heavy accent but the urgency in his voice was unmistakable.

"Yes. Jean-Luc Picard, captain of—"

"Go!" Ruanek was clearly fighting with his exhausted mind for the right words in this unfamiliar language. "Warp drive—get this ship away!"

Damnation. He was *followed.* Picard gestured subtly to ben Zoma, who just as subtly shrugged: No news from Lisuni. "Who—"

"No questions, no . . . no time. Here, I show you honor, you show me the same."

He sheathed the knife and offered it and its scabbard to Picard. A spark of inspiration moved Picard to say quietly, "I know that is an Honor Blade. And I give you *my* word of honor that no shame shall befall it." As he tucked knife and sheath respectfully into his belt, thinking, *An unlikely ornament for a Federation captain,* he saw the relief on the Romulan's face. "Now, let us get your brother to sickbay. Yes, and you, I think, as well. For treatment," Picard added wryly, seeing how Ruanek tensed, "not torture. I don't know what you've heard of the Federation, but one thing we are not is torturers."

"Captain." Cadwallader's voice over the comm was sharp. "We've picked up another ship on our sensors. It just decloaked. And—Captain, it's coming straight at us out of the Neutral Zone."

I knew it! Our refugees did *have friends.* "Belay that," Picard snapped at Ruanek. "Only your brother goes to sickbay. You've got work to do. On my way," he added to Cadwallader. As Picard rushed out, he snapped over his shoulder to Security, "Get him to the bridge on the double!"

Even before he'd left the turbolift, Picard was ordering, "Go to visual. Maximum magnification."

"Aye, aye, Captain."

He settled into the command chair, staring. Nothing at first. Then ben Zoma, standing at Picard's shoulder, straightened. "My God, will you look at that."

With alarming majesty, a warbird bigger than any Picard had ever seen formed against the backdrop of space. The curve of its immense double hulls was graceful and terrible in one, like the shape of some vast, dull-green, merciless predator, and its disruptor array glowed the poisonous green that had terrified intelligent beings from Q'onoS to Earth . . . to Narendra III.

"Red alert!" Picard commanded. "Shields! And get that damned refugee up here."

"Do we fight?" That was a hopeful cry from Idun Asmund.

Are you insane, woman? Whatever that is, some new type of warbird, it's at least three times our size and probably mounting a hell of a lot greater firepower. Now I know what took out Enterprise.

"Not yet," Picard said flatly. "First, let's see who's out there.

We've had pretty good luck with that lately. Ensign Cadwallader, open hailing frequencies."

A few tense moments, then: "Hailing frequencies open, sir."

"This is Captain Jean-Luc Picard of the *U.S.S. Stargazer,* hailing Romulan Star Empire warship. You are in Federation space, Commander. Repeat, you are in Federation space. Do you require navigational assistance?"

That might give them an honorable way to retreat, Picard thought. As the seconds slipped away, he was aware of the faint whirr of his ship's life-support, aware of the pulsing lights of red alert, aware that his hands were beginning to sweat.

No response.

Picard tried again. "Romulan vessel: You are in direct violation of treaty! Identify yourself and withdraw!"

No visual formed. But a harsh voice snarled out swiftly translated words, "I am your nemesis. You cannot withstand me. I am," here the translation failed, *"ketrakath!"*

"Analysis!" Picard snapped.

The doors to the bridge slid open. Subcommander Ruanek, still dazed and unsteady, stood there, flanked by Security guards. Out of the corner of his eye, Picard saw the Romulan tense at the sight of the warbird on the screen, and heard his angry hiss. The subcommander moved blindly forward, nearly falling, catching himself only by an equally blind grab at a rail. Ignoring that, ignoring the guards close behind him, he focused utterly on the Romulan ship, eyes fierce.

"Replay," snapped Picard. Once again, the warbird's threat rang out over *Stargazer*'s bridge. "What is *that*?" Picard snapped at him. "And what is *ketrakath?*"

"That, Captain," Ruanek snapped back, the translator catching his words, too, "is the ship of our beloved ex-praetor, Dralath."

"What's he doing in Federation space? Trying to get himself a trophy to take home?"

"A trophy? Oh no, Captain. That," Ruanek said, loathing in his voice, "is a foulness a decent soldier prays never to see:

Ketrakath means a suicide run, attack without restraint or hope."
He balled his hand into a fist and brought it down on a guardrail.
"Fires burn him to Erebus! Having no honor, he does not choose
Final Honor. Instead, he steals the lives of his crew!"

"Meaning?"

Ruanek shot Picard a savage glance. "The warriors on board
that ship have no choice. Dralath has drugged his crew so that
none will turn on him or rebel against the course he has set. *It is
a thing utterly without honor!*"

Honor be damned, it's their firepower *we need to know! We'll
have the sociology lessons later!* "Commander Lisuni: Any
data?"

Lisuni promptly rattled off figures: approximate mass, approximate type of weaponry.

Right. Three times our mass and definitely *more firepower.*
"Helm, move us back. Keep us out of disruptor range."

The Romulan had pressed forward until he leaned against the
rail less than a meter from Gerda Asmund. Absorbed in minute
course corrections, she did not even growl a warning. For an
eerie moment, the disgust on both their faces, half masked by the
rhythmic flash of red alert, made them seem close kin.

"They're moving with us, Captain," she warned. "Still closing."

"They still show no signs of hostility," Lisuni noted.

"Overt, anyhow." That from Idun Asmund.

"As you were, Lieutenant," Picard snapped. "Helm, warp
eight. Lisuni, what's this thing's top speed?"

"Unknown. The fastest recorded speed we have for the older
ships is a little over warp nine point three, but it—"

"Does not apply," the Romulan interrupted sharply. "This is a
suicide run. Start by assuming he's diverted all available power to
engines and weapons systems, and know Dralath will push his
ship's engines to destruction to take us."

The Romulan swallowed hard, licking his lips as if he
thirsted . . . for what? Revenge? Atonement? Or was he merely
battling his own exhaustion?

Damned if I understand you. A shame it's the Vulcans who'll get to debrief you—at least I assume it will be the Vulcans, also assuming we survive this.

"Ship's unshielded," Gerda Asmund reported sharply.

"Doctrine, Captain," Lisuni added. "A ship whose captain chooses not to shield displays peaceful intentions."

The Romulan barked out a laugh that made Picard want to flinch. "Federation doctrine, maybe! The only time Dralath ever told a truth was when the truth was deadlier than a lie."

"Warbird's closing," Gerda Asmund snarled. "Captain, it's accelerating. Warp eight point five . . . six . . . warp nine. Nine point one!"

"It's powering up disruptors," Idun Asmund reported.

"It's firing!" Lisuni cut in.

"Helm!" Picard shouted. "Evasive!"

A blaze of poisonous pale green energy engulfed *Stargazer.* The ship lurched and trembled. Lights dimmed for a heartrending second—then brightened again.

"Damage control," Picard snapped. "Lieutenant Asmund, return fire!"

"Photon torpedoes away—Direct hit!" she added in a shriek of triumph as light blossomed out.

But it was followed almost immediately by Lisuni's discouraging, "Minimal damage. Even with lowered shields, that is one powerfully built ship."

Damage reports were flooding in from all over the *Stargazer.* No structural damage, only minor injuries—

We won't be that lucky next time. If we can't damage that ship head-on, there has to be some way . . .

Ha, yes, here we have our very own Romulan military advisor!

"All right, Subcommander Ruanek," Picard told him sharply, "you've made your point. That ship is out for blood. I'll put all my cards on the table, and frankly I don't care whether you think this is honorable or not: We have clearance to land you and your brother on Vulcan—but we're not going to get there unless you know some weakness in that warbird!"

"*Akhh!*" It was a cry of pure frustration at his own weakness. "As well starve a child and expect it to fight." The pulsing red-alert signals flashed across the Romulan's drawn face, glinting off a desperate, humorless grin and glazing eyes. "The Klingons who died with honor at . . . Narendra III were right: It is a good day to die." He pulled vaguely at his battered tunic, trying to straighten it. "I had thought before . . . of taking Final Honor. I do not fear . . . the Last Review."

"Well, I'm not ready for it, if it's all the same to you," Picard said. "Helm—"

"Wait . . . wait . . ." Ruanek blinked, shook his head, clearly struggling to clear his mind. "No shields, no shields . . ."

"Disruptors gathering power," Lisuni warned.

"Not . . . a frontal attack . . . too strong there, even without . . . without shields. But . . . you are human, Captain . . . devious. You will think of something . . . ."

Ruanek's sudden grin was sharp. Picard felt a predator's grin twist his own face: the first time in the history of the races, he thought irreverently, that Federation and Romulan officers had conferred on tactics. "They can outshoot us and outrun us. But outmaneuver us?"

He slapped in-ship communications open. "Engineering!"

"Aye, Captain?"

"Phigus, I want you to reinforce *Stargazer*'s structural integrity field for all it's worth."

"Aye, Captain."

Picard dropped his voice, as if the madman on that Romulan ship could hear him. "Cadwallader, open speakers. Order all hands to strap in. You, too, Subcommander! Don't want to lose you now. Helm, on my mark!"

"Everyone," Picard announced, adrenaline riding him hard, "we are about to perform the Federation's first Immelmann turn in space."

That got the response he'd expected: blank looks from the

Romulan and most of the bridge crew, a few gasps from those who knew their Earth military and aviation history, and a silent whistle of admiration from ben Zoma.

"Asmund, Weapons." Picard specified name and position deliberately: he could *not* risk confusing the twins just now. "Be ready to fire the *instant* I give the order."

"Aye, sir."

"Asmund, Helm: prepare to warp us out the instant she fires."

"Aye, sir."

"Engineering!"

"Ah, sir." Simenon's usually subdued hiss seemed to spray from the speaker across the bridge. "No disrespect meant, but you're going to do *what*?"

"An Immelmann turn, Phigus."

"Well yes, but—"

"I gave you an order, Engineer. Ready? Then: On my mark— *engage!*"

Engines roaring into full power, *Stargazer* leaped forward, whipping into an impossibly tight loop. Happening fast, so fast, no time to think, no time to worry at the whine of the inertial damping system, the shuddering of the ship as its structural integrity field threatened to collapse. Support struts trembling, groaning—any more strain, and *Stargazer* would destruct and at least take that damnable warbird with it—

So fast—so quickly through the loop and braking, ship shaking all over again with the sudden deceleration, threatening to tear itself apart. The warbird had fired again, but they'd been too quick for it. The disruptor blasts missed them completely, and—

Stargazer was right behind the warbird, looking at that unshielded flank—

"Fire!" Picard shouted.

With twin shrieks that tore at his eardrums, Idun Asmund fired both torpedo banks, and her sister brought them into a sharp bank and full speed away from the warbird.

Did we . . . ? Did we . . . ?

"Got him!" someone yelled. "Right up the—"

The warbird exploded in a savage blaze of white-orange-red flame, debris gouting in all directions. The shock wave buffeted them—almost negligible after their wild ride. And then: space was empty again, silent . . .

"Hei-ya-hai!"

That shout of triumph erupted from the Romulan refugee, who stood shivering, still clinging to the rail with his good arm. Picard spared him a quick glance. Subcommander Ruanek had clearly reached the end of his endurance and would need to get to sickbay pretty soon.

But first, Picard faced a more important task. "Damage report," he ordered, heart racing.

Reports came flooding in, and with each in turn, he felt as though a vise were loosening around his mind and heart.

He'd done it. He had taken the gamble of a lifetime and destroyed a ship with three times *Stargazer*'s fighting strength. And there was no major damage, either to his ship or his people.

O God, thy arm was here! The King's line from *Henry V* after Agincourt rang in his head.

Picard drew a deep breath, playing for the few seconds he needed before he could be sure his voice would not shake.

"Helm, Weapons, well done. And you, too, Engineering." Commendations for all three, no doubt about it. And maybe, just as a reward, even though the subcommander had wanted to save his own neck and his brother's, a favorable mention of him, too.

"Now," Picard ordered, "put us back on course for Vulcan. Warp factor nine, Phigus, if you think the engines can take it."

"Captain, after this, nothing will surprise me." The chief engineer's voice sounded a little hollow.

"Cadwallader, encrypt and transmit a message to Admiral Lynn."

"Contents, sir?"

"Ah . . ." Picard smiled faintly. "Encountered warbird. Sank same." Admiral Lynn would appreciate the joke. "Advise him that a more detailed report will follow shortly.

"Now, Subcommander, you're going to sickbay. Guards, give him a hand."

Security laid surprisingly gentle hands on Ruanek's good arm. The Romulan shrugged them off.

Proud *and* stubborn, Picard thought. But it was all catching up to Ruanek now. He looked like hell, greenish-pale with exhaustion, shaking, soaked in perspiration, eyes wild with pain and the realization that he'd just helped kill a Romulan praetor.

Ex-praetor.

Still, Ruanek had enough will left to give Picard a sharp, ironic grin.

"Congratulations, Captain. You are now a Hero of the Romulan Empire. Very impressive decoration, by the way."

Despite his usual self-control, despite the Federation injunctions to good order and discipline, which no doubt did not include captains joking with Romulan refugees on a ship's bridge, Picard had to laugh.

"I won't go to collect my award, if that's all the same with you. Now, off with you. I don't need a refugee fainting on my bridge."

But Ruanek got in the last shot. In the instant before the turbolift's doors whisked shut, the subcommander drew himself up and, face carefully bland, gave Picard a full Romulan military salute.

THIRTY-FOUR

VULCAN, DAY 6, SECOND WEEK OF HARAVEEN, YEAR 2344

The destruction of Narendra III had shattered the peace of
Sarek's town house in ShiKahr. Day and night alike, the high-
ceilinged rooms teemed with aides, attachés, scholars, and senior
diplomats. It left him little time for meditation or even private
thought.

Sarek compelled himself to admit that this was almost a
relief.

As Federation diplomats focused on the Klingon Empire's
desire for permanent alliance, Sarek's negotiations with the
Legarans, at another critical point after 60.54 Earth years, were
temporarily suspended.

The Klingon Alliance should have been my son's task, Sarek
thought.

It would have been the crowning achievement of Spock's
diplomatic career, just as Coridan and perhaps the Legarans
would be Sarek's. But Spock remained missing, this time without
even a hope that his *katra* could be recovered.

If Spock were dead, surely Saavik would not survive, Sarek told himself. *Saavik has always been so strong, so determined. . . .*

Illogical or not, he could not endure to think of that. Of course he should not go anywhere near his son's betrothed at such a moment, but, with Spock still missing, he was the closest thing Saavik had to a "next of kin." It was therefore his duty to arrange for her care.

This could be the last contact I will ever have with my child. With my children.

A tactful cough made him turn. Aram Korel, Sarek's stocky young human chief of staff, had just emerged from his private office.

"Ambassador, Starfleet Sector Admiral Lynn is on a secured line and wishes to speak with you."

This level of security in Sarek's own home was unwelcome, but logical under the circumstances and therefore to be endured. Stifling an admittedly emotional but very heartfelt sigh, Sarek went to take the admiral's call.

Admiral Lynn sat in the position Spock had identified for Sarek long ago as "at attention," an indication of great respect. Respect notwithstanding, the admiral attacked without waiting for the civilities of formal greeting.

"How is Commander Saavik, Ambassador?"

"Very ill," Sarek said, and left it at that.

"Do you think she'd be up to answering a few questions vital to our investigation?"

Did the human understand why that question was such a breach of good taste—no, of course he did not. "Commander Saavik cannot answer questions now, Admiral."

"I see. Ambassador, would you like to know the progress of Starfleet's investigation of Commander Saavik's unauthorized foray into Romulan space?"

"Only if you are able to tell me," Sarek countered. Humans could not understand the clarity of Vulcan logic: If Saavik was innocent, she would be cleared. If she was guilty, the truth must be known. Whether she . . . lived or died.

Lynn smiled ever so slightly. "The news media are screaming that the *Enterprise* reached Narendra in time—in time, they call it!—because 'one gallant officer penetrated the Romulan Neutral Zone, learned of the assault, and escaped, carrying a warning at the risk of her life.' What do you think of that story?"

"I find it," Sarek said, "overly dramatic."

"It's spectacular public relations," Lynn said, as though disappointed at Sarek's calmness. "Thought you might want in on it." He paused, smile fading. "Ambassador, are you all right?"

No, human, I am not. My son is missing, my daughter lies near death— "I ask forgiveness," Sarek murmured. "So many different tasks . . ."

"I'm afraid I'm going to have to ask you to take on another one. One of my most reliable captains has pulled two Romulans out of a wrecked scout. They—the one of them who's conscious—call themselves part of their underground."

"The one who is conscious?"

"The elder Romulan is comatose, apparently injured in a shipboard accident. The younger wants asylum on Vulcan for himself and his brother."

Sarek raised an eyebrow.

"I see a certain logic to this." Admiral Lynn drove his point home with a certain relish. "Who can tell better than a Vulcan if a Romulan is lying? Or provide tighter security?"

"I assume that your questions are rhetorical, Admiral."

"Also, Vulcan is probably the safest place in the Federation if we are to protect these Romulans against reprisals. The port admiral concurs."

"Logical," Sarek conceded.

But underneath the logic, the smallest flame of hope would not be denied.

Oh my son, my son, may it be you!

Without breaking eye contact with Admiral Lynn, Sarek coded messages for security to meet him at the Medical Center. "I will assume responsibility for these Romulan refugees."

337

Admiral Lynn all but beamed his relief. "That's fine, Ambassador. The ship will approach Vulcan, beam them down, and then leave. You won't even have to know its name."

No. Of course I do not need to know that it is the U.S.S. *Stargazer.*

"Ambassador? Have we got a deal?"

"Your terms are satisfactory," Sarek said, and broke contact.

T'Selis, the Healer Sarek had brought to attend Saavik, intercepted him on his way to the transporter room.

"Thy daughter has had another seizure," she stated. A tiny woman in Healer's brown, highly talented despite her undeniable youth, she was as much priestess as physician. "They grow in intensity. If we are to preserve her mind undamaged, I should undertake the *katra* ritual now. I calculate that, at this point, it has a three in five chance of success. Those odds drop to one in one hundred and fifty if she suffers another seizure, and fall further with each one."

Lacking her katra, *will Saavik have the will to fight?* Sarek thought. *Her grasp on life is already so fragile.* "You will not perform the ritual," he ordered.

T'Selis raised an imperious eyebrow. "Ambassador, you risk losing all that she is."

And you point out the obvious. "I am convinced," Sarek said, consciously exercising discipline to keep his voice calm before a woman who looked as if she had never lost a night's sleep, let alone anyone she valued, "that, were my daughter capable of choice, she would choose to continue fighting."

Security Chief Osmanski, a tall, sturdy human from Vulcan's Starfleet base, glanced at Sarek. "Vulcan Space Central reports UFP ship within transporter range. Passengers are ready for transport. Shall I . . . ?"

"If you would," said Sarek.

"Energizing."

As the familiar transporter shimmer began, the Starfleet security guards tensed, drawing their phasers.

Sarek raised an eyebrow. "I trust that those weapons are set only to 'stun'?"

Some quick, nervous alterations assured him that *now* they were.

Two figures materialized on the small platform. A tall Romulan in a very battered, stained military tunic braced a lean figure against his shoulder, one arm flung about him protectively to keep him upright.

The Romulan stood motionless, staring at the guards.

Taking in his first sight of Vulcan, Sarek thought. *It is regrettable that it need be so militant a view. Welcome, Ruanek. That is who you, logically, must be. And is that . . . is that . . . my son you hold with a true friend's care?*

Except for the disrepair of his uniform, the Romulan carried himself well. His features, somewhat closer to the Vulcan than to the hawklike Romulan norm, had hardened into the tense, arrogant mask Romulan officers assumed among enemies or outsiders. Lines much like those etched into Sarek's face were starting to show around his eyes and mouth. *This man is too young,* Sarek thought, *to have spent that much time under that much stress.*

"Subcommander Ruanek?" Sarek began in Romulan before any of the starbase personnel could intervene. "I am—"

But Ruanek, judging by that quickly suppressed gasp of relief, had already identified him. "My Lord Ambassador."

It was said in shaky but credible Vulcan. The subcommander forced himself to attention. He attempted to bring up his free hand in a Romulan salute, but his arm was clearly paining him, and his hand shook. He clenched his fist, as if angered at how his body betrayed him, and a guard tensed. "Sir," Ruanek continued in his careful Vulcan, "I have brought your son home."

Can it be, can it be . . . ? The odds against it . . .

As the guards moved in, the refugee staggered down from the

transporter platform, bearing his unconscious companion with him. Gently, he lowered him to the padded floor, kneeling beside him, hand still clasped on the figure's shoulder.

Deliberately so, Sarek thought. *Even in healing trance, one preserves some knowledge of the waking world—but how has Ruanek deduced this?*

The Romulan was looking up at him not like a hardened warrior but almost like a child willing Sarek to make things right. Rigidly self-controlled as he had not needed to be since his wife's death, Sarek gazed down at his son.

Spock's face was even more drawn than Ruanek's, and greenish scars raked his throat.

But he is alive. My son is alive.

"We've had a rough flight, sir," Ruanek said, as though trying to spare Sarek's feelings. "A defective ship nearly took us with it, but your son saved us. But . . . he is very ill." He met Sarek's eyes fully for an instant, then quickly glanced away.

So he knows. Or suspects.

But Ruanek, clearly suddenly dizzy, swayed, eyes half-closing. Sarek hastily knelt beside him, catching his arm with what to the Starbase guards must look like no more than a steadying hand— and felt, as he'd expected, the rush of the Romulan's emotions. This was not a mind-meld, of course; Sarek was not about to risk that, or the immense breach of propriety.

But, forgive me, Ruanek, I must know about you, and swiftly.

And there was in one quick flash . . . utter weariness . . . shock to the point of trauma . . . a mind on the edge of collapse from too much change come too swiftly . . . but there was also, first and foremost, a sense of honor like a blaze of light, honor and honesty both . . . and sharp, clear worry, friend for friend, yes, and of course for himself, lost and utterly alone . . .

So, now, Sarek thought in that flash of time, *this one is worth the saving.*

In the next instant, Ruanek had recovered, and Sarek lowered his hand.

"Your pardon, sir," the Romulan said. "I, uh . . . as I said, it's been a . . . rough trip."

"Indeed."

"But you should have seen him fight to keep us alive. Even after he could barely talk—" Ruanek shook his head. "After Captain—I mean, Ambassador Spock was injured, he entered what he called . . ." His Vulcan abruptly abandoned him.

"A healing trance," Sarek supplied. "Yes. You may release him."

The reluctance with which the younger man did so spoke well for him.

With a gentleness he had never shown Spock awake, Sarek put out his hands to touch his son's temples. He knew he would sense the elevated temperature and deranged metabolism characteristic of the last stages of *Plak-tow*.

Spock suddenly tensed, then struggled against his hands, and Sarek slapped him. Slapped him again, all his love, his fear, his exasperation in the blows. They were not hard enough.

"Sir, what are you doing?" Ruanek cried in alarm, reaching out to stop him.

Instantly, suspicious guards surrounded them. Sarek waved them away.

I will be the judge of Ruanek's trustworthiness, not Starfleet Security!

"Pain helped him enter the trance," Sarek explained. "It will help him focus now that he struggles to wake."

Sarek gestured at a guard to signal Healer T'Selis to attend him now.

My son has a chance. I would calculate the odds at . . . But Sarek's mathematics, like his logic, were uncertain where his son was concerned.

If he can be waked and brought to Saavik . . . it is improper to think of such things . . . but . . . my son has a chance to live!

Ruanek glanced from Spock to Sarek almost fearfully.
"If he feels himself under attack, he will strike out. And he—"

"Sir?" The security guard nearest to Ruanek gestured with his sidearm. The Romulan turned to Sarek, sudden despair in his eyes.

"There is no need for alarm," Sarek told both the guard and the Romulan. "I will debrief our guest myself. Later. After he is rested and refreshed. *I name thee guestfriend,*" he told Ruanek in Romulan.

Ruanek drew in a sharp breath of relief. He began to sag—*How long since he has truly been able to rest?*—then forced himself back to desperate attention.

"Ambassador Spock," Ruanek said. "I should stay . . . I promised . . ."

"You will only be in the way here," Sarek told him. "And you require medical assistance yourself." Impatience was illogical—but where was that Healer?

"I am sure you have someplace secure where the subcommander can rest," Sarek added to the guards. No guestfriend of Sarek's House would be thrown into a Starfleet brig. "Perhaps," he added after the most delicate of pauses, quickly considering the problems of a Romulan amid all those officials in the town house, "away from ShiKahr with all its security constraints. Perhaps . . . yes, within my own estate."

Sarek's statement provoked the storm of human outrage he had expected. Inwardly begrudging the time, he waited till the humans paused to draw breath, then asked, "Do you believe I am not capable of dealing with the situation?"

"But Ambassador!" Osmanski protested. "The man *is* a Romulan!"

"Indeed?" Sarek raised his eyebrow disdainfully. "One injured man. Alone and weary. Ah, perhaps you think me unable to keep one weary Romulan secure! Or perhaps you credit the Sundered with supernatural powers?"

"But—you can't—"

" 'Can't'?" Sarek asked very mildly. "I was under the impression that Vulcan was a sovereign world. Am I, then, mistaken?"

Osmanski opened his mouth, closed it again, grudging appreciation in his eyes, his slight nod saying without words, *I yield to a master.* Sarek returned the nod, serenely opened the personal communicator he generally carried—an ambassador never knowing when or where a message might need to be sent or received—pressed the proper code, and said into the sudden waiting silence:

"Aram Korel."

The human, competent as ever, had been expecting the summons. "Sir?"

"Return to my estate, if you would. You will be receiving company there shortly. One . . . distant cousin. Provide my guest, please, with fresh clothing. Give him water, as if it came from me. Offer him the services of my physician."

The human must have been bursting with curiosity, but all he said was "Understood, sir."

Sarek closed the communicator and glanced at Ruanek, who was staring at him as though expecting him to sprout wings. "Subcommander, I will speak with you soon."

"I'll have to post guards, sir," Osmanski said desperately. "And report this."

"By all means," Sarek agreed. "For my guest's protection." He snapped open the communicator again, added smoothly to Aram Korel, "One thing more. My guest will be accompanied by Starfleet guards. See that they are treated with proper courtesy, too—and that they do not intrude upon my guest's privacy unless it becomes necessary."

Was that the faintest hiss of indrawn breath? But the unflappable human replied with only a second "Understood, sir."

Sarek closed the communicator, glancing mildly about at the others.

"Worry not," Ruanek said in his shaky Vulcan. "I pledge you my word to remain."

He started to bring up his fist in salute, then remembered where he was, and bowed instead. Managing a nod at the guards, he allowed them to lead him away.

T'Selis' light footsteps in the corridor caused another eruption of security guards. In the confusion, no one was looking at Sarek. He took this second of privacy to shut his eyes and let out his breath in a silent sigh of unbearable relief.

My son, my daughter are both here now. Let them live. They must live. It is illogical that after having come so far, my children would not have a chance at life!

THIRTY-FIVE

KI BARATAN, DAY 13, THIRD WEEK OF TASMEEN, YEAR 2344

Charvanek linked her hands behind her back, stretching at her desk in her makeshift office there in the bureaucratic complex, trying to work a stiff spot out of her muscles.

It was . . . what . . . five days since Narviat had become praetor, and here she was, still busy overseeing the sorting out of political prisoners—and her crew, her freed eaglets—from genuine criminals. Most of the latter had either been scheduled for more accurate retrial or efficiently eliminated.

Charvanek let out her breath in a silent hiss, glancing over the piles of printouts, court accounts, and various holographic documents. She had also spent far longer than she wished going over former Security Chief Zerliak's records, witnessing his interrogation under drugs, or questioning him herself.

She had a terrible premonition that she might have to take over his job.

If I become a tenth as twisted as Zerliak, I will merit assassination.

Someone was at the door. Charvanek's hand shot, almost of its own accord, for the weapon that—

Wasn't needed, she reminded herself. But just in case, she let that hand stay within easy reach of the sidearm. "Who?"

"Serik, my lady. I, uh, have a message from Praetor Narviat. He, uh, asks to see you." She raised an eyebrow at that "asks," and Serik rushed on, "As soon as is convenient."

Which, of course, meant *now.*

Not that I won't welcome an excuse to get away from this aftermath of "the Glorious Revolution," or whatever the reporters are calling it today. "Tell him I'll be there shortly."

With a quick bow, Serik scurried out. Now, there was a survivor, Charvanek thought: Dralath's personal aide, who'd also been an utterly loyal spy for the emperor. He would, of course, be sent back to the emperor very shortly, since Praetor Narviat was hardly going to allow even an Imperial spy near him.

The Fates only know who has placed what on my *staff. When affairs become a bit less chaotic, I shall do some careful private research.*

Odd thought. For the first time since Charvanek could remember, she would go to an audience with the praetor without fear or disgust.

Charvanek found Narviat in what had been Dralath's private study, sitting at that massive desk and going over his own mountains of printouts. He glanced up at her, eyes brightening.

"Ah, Charvanek."

He looks so weary! Illogical thought: Of *course* he was weary! Hunting for something neutral to say, Charvanek glanced about the room. "You've gotten rid of all the mirrors."

He snorted. "I had to get rid of them. It was like living in a room full of clones. Charvanek . . . Liviana . . ."

Oh.

". . . please be seated."

Taken aback by the use of her private name, she . . . sat.

Without a word, Narviat pushed a broken bracelet across the desk to her. Charvanek gasped.

"*Akhh,* Narviat . . . this is the wedding bracelet of that poor, murdered woman. Therakith's wife."

"Katara. Yes. I thought you . . . as a woman . . ."

"Of course. I will gladly honor the slain family's memory with the women's rites."

Silence. Narviat glanced down at his printouts, riffling through them as though impatient.

Is this all you wanted of me? And am I relieved or disappointed?

But then Narviat pushed a second bracelet at her, and her heart gave a great start. The bracelet . . . had his and her personal insignias entwined, hastily carved into what had been a plain silver band, but all the more touching, somehow, for the haste.

Narviat was staring at her, clearly taking her silence for reluctance. He burst out in frustration, "Dralath left affairs in an unbelievable mess! It is going to take years just to get everything straightened out to the point where I know what needs to be corrected. I desperately need someone I can trust at my side."

Not very romantic, Charvanek thought dryly. *But then, he can't allow himself the liability of romance. For that matter, can I?*

It didn't really matter: She knew exactly what he was feeling but didn't dare express. She'd known for years.

Without a word, Charvanek took the bracelet and slid it onto her wrist; it would be properly adjusted at the ceremony.

"It's . . . not exactly elegant," Narviat said. "I incised the symbols myself; didn't have time for a silversmith. You don't have to—"

"Oh yes, I do . . . Devoras."

It was the first time she'd called him by his private name. Glancing up, she saw, just for an unguarded moment, honest love shining in Narviat's eyes. He hesitated, then, in one of the few spontaneous actions in his whole carefully planned, meticulously scripted life, leaped up from his chair. As it crashed back against the wall, he reached across the desk to catch her in an awkwardly angled but passionate kiss.

Just like a man. He could *have taken the moment more to go* around *the desk.*

Then she stopped thinking for a time.

But the edges of that desk were just too damned sharp for either of them to hold the pose for long, and they were hardly a pair of love-starved youngsters to collapse onto its surface, scattering the cursed printouts. As they let go of each other, not quite meeting each other's eyes, Charvanek thought ironically, *Ah well, there are worse fates than this!*

She always had felt a warmth toward Narviat. That well might yet turn to something stronger. And they needed each other.

Farewell, Spock. May you live long and prosper with your Saavik.

"My friends," Narviat began his latest proclamation from the Praetor's Balcony. "My fellow Romulans. Today I come before you with news of our continued efforts to root out corruption . . ."

". . . to root out corrup . . ."

"Dark-blood stupid rez!" Amarik exploded, staring at the screen. The image danced, broke up, and went to black. "Get that backup running, now, dreebs, we're broadcasting, got it?"

His crew of two swore, fiddling with connections until: "Got it! We're broadcasting again!"

"Double-shine!" Amarik grabbed the microphone. "All right, all you wildings out there, here we go: Coverage direct from the Praetor's Balcony, live, wildings, as only 'Romulus Roars' can bring it to you!"

Kerit giggled.

"What?" Amarik asked.

"Our break! I mean, this is it! We were in on the start of it, and here we are—This is our real, double-shine, *break!*"

". . . rebuilding as a people willing and able to defend

ourselves, yet wise enough to know which are honorable targets . . ."

It has all happened so fast, Commander Tal thought, watching Charvanek watching Narviat, *so many changes to my life in so short a time—I could almost believe in the Fates. After all those bitter years, I have a career again.*

More than that: I have my honor back as well.

He glanced sideways at Charvanek's aide, young M'ret . . . boy no longer. Though there were no visible scars, combat and imprisonment had hardened him; there was a new tightness to the set of his mouth, and a hint of shadow in his eyes.

But his spirit has not been crushed. Nor his honor.

And now he and the rest of the younger generation will have a chance to grow up clean.

". . . furthermore, repairs to our vital spaceports and customs buildings are already under way . . ."

Hasmonak, One-Eye, saluted the image of the new praetor. He didn't need two good eyes to see how the repairs to this Customs Hall were progressing. The inlay on the walls had already been replaced, and the stonework shone. More, a new ventilation system dispelled the smells of damp, of fear, of misery.

Next, he told himself, looking at the still-fearful crowds, *we work on the people.*

Eh, what was this? Someone passing through had left a small box behind—

A box with his name on it, and . . . Commander Charvanek's insignia. Hasmonak warily opened it, and heard himself gasp.

An Honor Blade lay gleaming within, a finer one than the likes of him could ever hope to buy. A piece of paper fluttered from the case, and he caught it up.

A keepsake, it read. Unsigned, but with a signature glyph he had seen on proclamations.

Hasmonak straightened proudly. By all the Hells, there still was honor within the Empire after all!

He put the blade away and braced himself, smiling slightly, for the next onslaught of travelers.

". . . and freed the political prisoners who had been arrested for no reason other than standing up to what they knew was wrong . . ."

Senator Pardek, one of those liberated, sat at his ease in the study he'd never thought to see again, a glass of pale golden *vetiris* wine in one hand, and ironically saluted Narviat's image on the viewscreen. The man really was too tall, too handsome, and too fearless to go on living.

Never mind all the glittering words. We both know what life is all about, don't we, Narviat? Power. Winning against the odds.

Surviving.

". . . and now, all loyal citizens of the Empire, I bring you splendid news: Our beloved Emperor Shiarkiek has made a full recovery . . ."

"So I have," Shiarkiek said to the monitor set over the tank of gleaming red and silver *tarak*. As he sprinkled feed into the tank and watched the *tarak* gobble it up, the emperor added slyly to Narviat's image, "And I am *still* not naming an heir."

"And in conclusion," Narviat told the citizens of the Romulan Star Empire, "the corrupt and cruel former Security Department has been, this very day, eliminated! In its place will be a shining new force for justice, incorruptible and forever honest.

"I hereby make this proclamation, my friends. In honor of Emperor Shiarkiek, let this new force for justice bring naught but glory to his name."

THIRTY-SIX

Despite what he had heard Ambassador Sarek command, Ruanek had half-expected to be cast into a prison cell, or at best to be ushered into a minimum-comfort, high-security "guest room." His expectations had sunk even lower when his guards hustled him into a closed vehicle as though they held him personally responsible for Narendra III. The ambassador must have been overruled, then: It would be a prison cell, definitely. Or rather, indefinitely.

But to his utter surprise, he and his "escorts" had traveled swiftly through the rapidly fading Vulcan day to end up here, instead, at the ambassador's secluded estate somewhere out of the city. On the border of the desert he'd dreamed about all his life. The guards hadn't given him a chance for even the quickest of glances about, hustling him inside almost before he could catch his breath and footing.

After that—*akhh,* after that, things had happened too quickly for a mind dazed by hope and exhaustion; he couldn't quite keep events in order. Ruanek vaguely remembered meeting Ambassador Sarek's chief of staff, and being so worn out by surprises by this point he'd barely raised an eyebrow over the fact that Aram Korel turned out to be a human.

And a sensible one: The man had taken one look at him, plainly registering both "Romulan" and "exhausted," and had wasted no time in conversation. Instead, he had ushered Ruanek, along with that unshakable entourage of guards, on to Sarek's own physician.

Another sensible person, that, competent and not ungentle, far better than that coldhearted doctor aboard the Federation ship, who had scanned him quickly and thoroughly, assured him that the knife wounds were well on the way to mending, that the main cause of his weakened arm was nothing worse than badly strained muscles—much to his relief, since Ruanek had already been thinking *permanent damage*—and that all injuries would be healed once he finally got sufficient rest. He'd also assured Ruanek, his words carefully guarded, that yes, Spock, back in ShiKahr, would survive.

Somewhere along the way, too, there'd been a blessedly efficient sonic shower that had finally let him rid himself of all the grime and stains of the various battles. Someone had taken his filthy, battered uniform, asking dubiously if he wanted it cleaned.

Did I really tell him, "Burn it!"?

At any rate, he'd been genuinely grateful for clean clothing— and genuinely surprised that he'd been permitted to keep his Honor Blade. He had a hazy memory of having eaten and drunk something somewhere about then—no memory at all of what it had been—so foggy-brained by that point, he hadn't even considered that the food or drink (whatever it had been) might be drugged. Which it hadn't been.

The human guards had not intruded in any of that. He was fairly certain of that . . . yes. In fact, Aram Korel, invoking the ambassador's name more than once, had finally managed to usher them out of his immediate vicinity. He was finally, blessedly, alone.

Ruanek rubbed a brisk hand over his eyes, trying to get them to stop burning. Now that his body had some nourishment on which to work, if not yet the rest it craved, he could at least begin to think again.

I do not understand these people. I do not. Unless . . . is this all a snare? Set me off my guard with kindness, and then, when I am properly weakened—

No. He could not bear that thought.

This room—this suite, rather—that he'd been allotted was downright luxurious, in a tranquil, sparsely furnished way. For all Ruanek knew, there still *could* be security systems monitoring his every move, although so far he hadn't been able to locate any sign of surveillance.

And where are the guards? Lurking outside? Or in nearby quarters of their own? I cannot believe that they've gone altogether.

No matter, for now. The illusion of privacy was . . . quite agreeable.

After some experimenting, he found the controls for the lighting and adjusted it so that the walls glowed a soft, soothing tan and the bare, blue-patterned tile floors gleamed. The only furniture in the main room was a low table, a desk with a computer console, and chairs, all of some sleek, golden-brown substance that looked like wood but, given that this was a desert world, was probably a synthetic.

He explored further, finding a sleeping alcove hung with tan and brown draperies and holding a wide, comfortable-looking bed. Ruanek warily tried it out even though, for all his weariness, he'd never felt further from sleep. Comfortable, yes, more so than any he could remember since childhood.

Too comfortable for a warrior, he decided, and forced himself back to his feet with a great effort, ignoring a body that clamored for him to just stay flat. *If I am still a warrior.*

No, don't think of that. Not yet.

Off the alcove, a door led to, amazingly, a separate room for the sanitary fixtures. Ruanek explored the various devices, and found them easy to operate and most agreeably modern; far better than the dingy, rusty things he'd known in the barracks in Ki Baratan.

Restlessly prowling, too tired, paradoxically, by this point to rest, he returned to the main room, examining the small, intricately wrought bronze firepot on a stand in the corner: cautious sniffing revealed no hidden drugs, only a pleasant incense. Some ritual item? Probably.

And here, in this corner: Ha, a small cooling device. Ruanek even managed to get himself a fruity drink that, after some wary study, he figured out how to dial (to his secret delight, feeling almost like a child) to just the right chill.

Almost decadent, all this, he thought, sipping the drink as he looked about, especially when he compared it to the one cramped room that for so many years had been his quarters back in Ki Baratan. That, at least, he was *not* going to miss!

Akhh, but . . .

No. Don't even try to think. Not of past. Not of future. Not yet. Concentrate only on here *and* now.

Easy to say, when he didn't even know who or what he was anymore. Ruanek glanced down at the clothes he'd been given: a flowing tunic cinched in by a woven belt, fitted trousers that seemed almost made for him, both in some soft fabric that was— he had to admit it—a great deal more comfortable, as well as more becoming, than a uniform. Nice, flattering shades of blue-green, too, as though someone, that human chief of staff or maybe even Ambassador Sarek, had actually *cared* how he looked. The thought sent a little stab of appreciation through him.

After all, you didn't care how a prisoner looked.

But . . . agreeable though the outfit might be, it made him a stranger to himself. The Honor Blade that Picard had returned to him no longer seemed a natural extension of what he was, but something exotic, strange—

All right, all right. Get away from this dangerous track of thought, now!

Ruanek put down the drinking glass and hurled open the room's shutters, sure he was going to find bars or armed guards ready to shoot—

Instead . . . oh Fates, it was the desert, the open, peaceful sweep of space of his daydreams. Ruanek stood frozen, drinking it in, trying to pull the quiet of it into his spirit. He didn't doubt that there were security devices and guards out there. After all, Ambassador Sarek was not a fool. But it was so easy to pretend that there was only that wide, tranquil expanse, and the equally vast sweep of slowly darkening sky.

The sky that, as the night came on, became far too dark . . . But, Ruanek reminded himself hastily, there were nights on Romulus just as dark, times when none of the moons were visible, and he—he wouldn't think of that.

The breeze was shifting, blowing in off the cooling desert, and Ruanek took a deep breath of dry, fragrant air. Why had he never guessed, with all his daydreaming, that the desert might smell *sweet?*

But without any warning, the scene suddenly changed in his mind, and it was all at once alien, all at once far too alien. Ruanek quickly closed the shutters, hands not quite steady, and went to sit at the desk, trembling, staring at the console on it, the one even remotely familiar item in all his surroundings, in all this entire foreign world.

No. There was one other. One very familiar item. His . . . Honor Blade.

With a sharply indrawn breath very much like a sob, Ruanek drew the weapon from its sheath, studying its unmarred beauty.

Fates. Maybe this was the answer after all. Surely, Ruanek thought bitterly, his vow to rescue Spock was fulfilled. He had seen Spock safely home and, Fates willing, reunited with his mate. There was, when one came right down to the hard facts of it, absolutely no more point to his life, nothing else to hold him here. . . .

At least I got to see the desert.

But—Ambassador Sarek had given him hospitality. It would be the height of dishonorable behavior to stain that hospitality with even an honorable suicide.

For what seemed an eternity, Ruanek sat shivering, unable to grasp the knife in the proper position, unable to leave it alone. In a burst of panicky strength, he put it down on the desk and, desperate to stop himself from doing anything else, switched on the computer console. The screen, mercifully, came instantly to life. Studying the cryptic Vulcan menus revealed, Ruanek frowned slightly, feeling the faintest stirring of curiosity shiver through the weight of despair.

What programs had been left for him to access? Some easy-to-understand story, probably, full of simple action. Something to amuse the stupid warrior.

No . . . this was . . . a text of some sort. Yes . . . in Vulcan, but he could more or less manage the written as well as the spoken language. This was, he saw, a text in Vulcan *about* Vulcan. Land, climate, history . . . all here, though probably at a child's level—

No, again. Whoever had left this program ready for him to access was definitely not patronizing him! Difficult going, but Ruanek scrolled down, intrigued in spite of himself, struggling to understand the flood of new concepts, new ideas. There was probably a voice control, but he wasn't sure enough of his Vulcan accent to attempt that.

Akhh, he'd come to a whole page of choices! Too many. *Pick one,* he told himself, and stabbed at "Linguistics" at random. New images formed almost instantly, new lists of words, ideas, modern Vulcan and Old High Vulcan, and—look at this! He knew this phrase, but knew it as Romulan! Close, so close—yes, and here was a whole proverb, Old High Vulcan maybe, but Romulan, too. Ha, more links, tying in to more subjects, related studies of culture and custom, and even though Ruanek knew he really should stick to one thing at a time, the flood of information, so rare, so new, was just too fascinating, far too fascinating for that!

And no one to arrest me, no one to name me traitor for
learning.

The Honor Blade lay, forgotten, on the edge of the desk as
Ruanek lost himself in the raw joy of knowledge.

Sarek's palmprint soundlessly opened the door to the guest
suite. There, as Aram Korel had assured him, was the Romulan,
awake and unhurt, staring intently at the computer screen,
scrolling down through the files with almost Vulcan speed. Sarek
coughed discreetly, prepared for a warrior's whirl and crouch.

To his bemusement, though, his guest's first reaction was an
over-the-shoulder attempt to wave this intruder away and an
impatient, "Not now!"

In the next instant, Ruanek realized who had entered, and nearly lost his balance jumping to his feet and trying to give a military salute and a civilian bow at the same time. "My Lord
Ambassador! Forgive me, I, ah—"

"The hunger for knowledge," Sarek assured him, "is no reason
for embarrassment."

"But—Spock? Sir, how is—"

"It is likely my son will survive," Sarek said, "but my daughter
may not."

"Saavik? But . . ." Ruanek began, but Sarek stopped him.

"Let us speak of other matters," the ambassador said. "Might I
see what you study?"

Ruanek quickly stepped aside, only just barely keeping from
snapping to military attention. Sarek glanced at the screen.
Vulcan desert ecology . . . , he noted, *interspecies symbioses . . .*
"I mean no insult by the question, but do you understand this?"

The Romulan's eyes were blazing with the near-hysterical
excitement that came from utter exhaustion mixed, Sarek
thought, with what Terrans quite accurately termed "information
overload." "Some of it, sir. I—I lack a good deal of the vocabu-
lary, but, well, I can more or less bridge the gaps with, uh, logic."

But then the cold, hard mask slipped back over his face. *As though,* Sarek thought, *he is afraid of revealing anything more about himself.* The ambassador said with carefully controlled irony, "I am hardly about to betray you to the praetor. This is not meant as censure, Ruanek, but how is it that you speak and read Vulcan?"

"Federation Standard, too." It was a muttered admission. "More or less. Less, to be perfectly honest."

"Indeed! Explain, if you would."

"It's nothing very dramatic, sir. There was a long, boring winter one year, and you can only do so many military exercises. I . . . well, you can get a few not-quite-legal items in a city the size of Ki Baratan, if you know how."

"Items, I assume, such as language tapes."

"Exactly. I could only find a Federation Standard book, though, no tape, so my accent is terrible. Nearly got your son and me blown up."

"Then you have an interest in languages? Obviously, you learn them swiftly."

"Yes, sir, I do."

It was said as though Ruanek were confessing to a crime. Sarek, eyebrow raised, prodded delicately, "But I should think that such a skill would be an asset."

"An asset! Knowing Vulcan and Federation Standard could have gotten me executed as a spy!"

"Do you speak any . . . less perilous languages?"

"A smattering of Barolian," the Romulan muttered, "and some Zerik: That's a pretty straightforward tongue, no genders for nouns or—

"Sir," he added so suddenly that Sarek blinked, "are you trying to bribe me?"

"I . . . beg your pardon?"

"With knowledge. It's—I—sir, you don't understand. I am . . . I was the son of a House Minor. Not very high on the status ladder, but too high to let someone like me legally do anything but go into the military, try to find a good patron, and hopefully rise through the ranks. I have a decent general education, of course; I *am* of the nobility. But I was not, legally, permitted to study anything above that level in any depth 'lest I become distracted from my proper service to my patron.' "

What a supremely illogical policy! "There are no such restrictions on Vulcan, I assure you." Sarek paused. "But if Romulan law was so strict, why did you risk your life to learn?"

Ruanek glanced down. "I . . . I don't know how to say this, sir, and frankly I'm too weary for pretty words. Maybe it was one of the reasons I never made it past subcommander." He stopped with a jolt and added almost as though he didn't believe it himself, "Commander. Commander for a few hours, anyhow. Sir, I couldn't endure *not* learning, even if it meant running risks."

"And perhaps a tiny piece of it was the enjoyment of that risk? The knowledge that you ran the danger of getting caught both with contraband and illegal knowledge?"

The quick, startled flash of a smile told him he'd struck home. "You're good, sir. Yes, there was a bit of that, too; things got pretty dull at times, always in Avrak's shadow, watching for danger that almost never came. But it was, truly, that I, I *needed* to learn."

Not all would be as strong-willed as Ruanek. *How many of their brightest minds have our cousins destroyed?*

That was a matter for later consideration. "Ruanek, I must speak of Federation and Vulcan law."

The light left the Romulan's eyes. "Of course. I did expect this."

"Perhaps not. This will not be a standard interrogation, nor will you be harmed in any way."

"Sir?"

"I wish to attempt a mind-meld. Do you know what that is?"

"Yes, sir. I saw it done once."

Not by the slightest twitch did Sarek reveal his surprise. "Indeed?" *By whom? No Romulan, surely. My son? Did Spock . . . ?* "Then you know I do not say this lightly. Nor do I demand it. But if you grant me permission, I may then pass on a report of your innocence to the proper Federation officials. They will then leave you at least in relative peace."

When Ruanek hesitated, clearly uneasy behind that mask of warrior arrogance, Sarek added, "I will not invade your private thoughts, nor alter any, my word upon that. I already know that you have great personal honor."

He saw the faintest hint of a pleased smile quiver on Ruanek's lips at that. "You honor me, sir."

I will not tell you how I learned even that much, Sarek thought. "But," he continued, "there is a darker matter that must be resolved: Are you a weapon? Has your mind been altered without your knowledge?"

The mask shattered. Genuine horror flashed in Ruanek's eyes. "They've already done that." It was little more than a whisper. "My patron—former patron—Avrak, curse him to the Outer Darkness, he—he would sometimes have secret codes implanted in my mind." White-faced, Ruanek continued, "I had no choice, I never did. They always swore to me no harm had been done, no change had been made, b-but how would I know?"

He straightened with desperate pride. "I will not be used as a weapon against you or your son. I grant you permission, sir, to do what you must. And if . . . if I am, indeed, a weapon, I ask of you only this: Tell me that I may choose the Final Honor with my mind still intact."

"I trust that it will not come to that," Sarek said gently, and sank to a chair. "Come, sit opposite me, within my reach . . . yes."

He leaned toward Ruanek, fingers outspread, feeling the Romulan first flinch at his touch, shivering, then hold resolutely still.

"My mind to your mind," Sarek began with the ease of many years' experience . . .

. . . and as swiftly as thought, he was there, one with Ruanek's mind, allowed in by the Romulan without more than a moment's uneasy resistance . . .

... traveling through bright flashes of hope, shadows of memory, blaze of green—violence, recent memory—*fightknifedeath,* an enemy falling, Kharik, cousin-foe, savage stab of joy at being free mixed with a weary horror at needing to kill yet again ... then brighter memories of *Spockfriendolderbrotherhonor* ... a confused montage of *rebelsundergroundperil* ... of Narviat ... strangely seen, bright with hope, dark with *uneasinessuncertainty,* of a woman, a commander, Charvanek, seen only in *purestwhitehonor* and the emperor, a blaze of cleanest gold ... hunting, all the while hunting with utmost delicacy through the web of thoughts for wrongness, tampering ... yes, and yes ... here were old sites of tampering, but no traces of lasting damage ... no sign of harsh black signaling altered synapses, altered neurons ... no sign of hidden peril and now ...

Out.

He sat with the patience of experience, waiting for his mind to accept that he was not Romulan, not an exiled rebel, that he was ...

I am Sarek ...

Yes. He was himself again, in his own mind and consciousness.

"Sir ... ?"

It was a very nervous sound. Opening his eyes, Sarek told the anxious Ruanek, "All is well. And yes, your mind is your own. There is no trace of intrusion."

"Hei-ya-hai!"

That, Sarek suspected from Ruanek's instantly embarrassed expression, was a Romulan warrior's cry of triumph.

"Do not claim victory just yet, Ruanek. We are not quite finished. I said that I would not invade your private thoughts, and I have not. However, I could hardly have avoided your memories of the revolution, or your ambivalent feelings—quite understandable under the circumstances—toward the new praetor."

"I don't believe he will be an aggressive foe to the Federation, sir, if that's what you want to know—probably, given the state of confusion Dralath left behind, not a foe at all. I . . . assume you know the rest."

"Save for this one thing: How were my son and his mate involved?"

"They did nothing treasonous! I swear to that on my honor. Sir, your son is a hero, he and his lady, too. They risked everything, down to their lives, for peace. And . . . it may sound melodramatic, because . . . because . . ." Ruanek rubbed a hand over his eyes. "Because I'm so weary by now I'm not sure what I'm saying . . . But, well, your son helped both the Empire and the Federation and . . . and I will not betray him, sir, not even to you."

"Quite acceptable." Sarek had already gained enough data from the mind-meld to be able to put together logical excuses for his children's . . . adventures. *Not that I will not be questioning them myself, when they . . . if it becomes possible.* "Then that is all."

"Your pardon, sir, but it's not. What happens to me now?"

"You are my guest, Ruanek; you need not fear that I will simply throw you out into the desert." He paused, watching Ruanek's face. "I will, assuming that you wish it, provide tutors and whatever educational tapes we both think logical. Since you show an affinity for languages, perhaps linguistics should be the main subject of your study, though I would advise a wider curriculum including the other sciences as well."

Most gratifying: Ruanek could not suppress a gasp of sheer wonder.

"One thing more, Ruanek," Sarek continued smoothly. "I shall also provide a Healer for you."

That brought back the cold-faced warrior, snapping, "I don't need . . ."

But his voice trailed into silence when Sarek pointed to the unsheathed Honor Blade still lying on the desk. "In the days ahead," the ambassador said gently, "you may find the burden of your life's total change too heavy to bear alone. This is not a weakness or a reason for shame, but merely a logical fact. The

Healer's name is T'Selis, and I believe that you will find her both discreet and quite competent."

"B-but why are you doing this? Why should you care what happens to me?"

"You saved my son's life even knowing what it would cost you. More, you are Spock's friend, and I have learned over the years to trust his judgment." *In that, at least.* "I also do not believe in wasting an intelligent and honorable life."

Judging from Ruanek's eyes, exhaustion was finally overwhelming consciousness. But he fought back, saying, "I'm not a Vulcan; I can't control my emotions as you do . . . and, and, to be truthful, sir, I don't know if I want that."

"No," Sarek agreed, "you may never totally learn such control, not at this stage of your life. However, that is not necessarily a handicap. My chief of staff is human, and I find him, for all his occasional emotional outbursts, quite competent. And you surely know that my late wife, Spock's mother, was human."

"Yes, but . . ."

"You may or may not also know that, among my other duties, I am Vulcan's Ambassador to Earth. As such, I am always in need of aides who have both a gift for languages and a firsthand understanding of emotions. To say nothing of the usefulness," Sarek added, and only another Vulcan could have read the hint of wry humor in his eyes, "of an aide who may become a bodyguard should an emergency arise."

"Sir . . . are you offering me your . . . patronage?"

"I am offering you the chance to make your own choice."

Ruanek all but radiated sudden sharp joy at that thought—presumably the first time he had ever *had* such a choice—but he protested, "I am a Romulan!"

"Truly? Seeing you dressed as you are, an outsider would find it difficult to name you Romulan or Vulcan. You are, after all, in a very real genetic sense, my distant cousin."

"But everything I do, everything I say—what *of* my emotions?"

"Of course you are emotional. Were you not raised on Romulus?"

That was almost too subtle for someone who by this point was struggling just to keep his eyes open. But then Sarek saw the sense of it strike home as Ruanek straightened: Down through the centuries of the two races' spacefaring, there had occasionally been Vulcan prisoners taken, Vulcan or half-Vulcan children raised as Romulans.

"I . . . sir, I . . . should be . . . saying something more . . . arguing or . . . or . . . something . . . but I—I can't think . . . thank you, that's all. Can't find words for—for anything else . . ."

"You should be saying nothing. Come, Ruanek, *stand!*"

It was snapped out sharply as a military command, and it brought his guest staggering to his feet. Eyes glazing, the Romulan followed Sarek's lead to the sleeping alcove. Without another word, Ruanek collapsed down across the bed, finally surrendering to the sudden, dense sleep of the utterly exhausted.

Excellent. Now he may begin to heal.

Since there was no one to see, Sarek permitted himself the slightest of satisfied smiles. Turning down the light, he left.

THIRTY-SEVEN

Even before the transporter effect faded, sunlight hit Dr. Leonard McCoy—Federation Starfleet admiral, retired, thank you very much—as if he, not Vulcan's Forge, were Eridani A's anvil. In this heat, the collar of his dress uniform, which had always fretted him, chafed even worse than usual. He tried not to tug at it like an ensign with his first dress uniform.

Damn! I'd forgotten just how uncomfortable the things were! At least it still fits, more or less.

He strode forward boldly, refusing to trudge as if his knees were hurting (which they were, even though this was, and blast the first person who said it, a *dry* heat), toward the somber figure, hooded and faceless in the noon sun, who stood waiting for him. Behind the figure rose the austere white walls of the Vulcan Science Academy's Medical Center.

The hood was pushed slightly back to reveal a strong, absolutely unreadable face. "Live long and prosper," Sarek of Vulcan said, hand raised.

"I come to serve," McCoy responded. "Peace and long life." At least, for once, his stubborn fingers didn't tangle on the split-fingered formal greeting. "I'm thankful I was already en route to Vulcan when I got your message."

Sarek dipped his head slightly in courtesy. "It is good for Spock to have his friends with him at such a time."

They started toward the Medical Center together. It was just as well, McCoy conceded to himself, that they'd drafted all the old Klingon hands. God knows, he was one of the oldest.

I could use some of that ice on Rura Penthe right now. Oh well. Mad dogs and Starfleet officers . . .

The bronze gates stood open beneath the plaque stating simply in flowing Vulcan calligraphy, *There is Healing within for any who have need.* Vulcan men and women in Healers' brown robes stood aside, gaze politely averted, granting the visitors privacy. Sarek and his human guest crossed a small courtyard ornamented with a carefully raked sand garden set with three rocks of intricate black basalt—*Great for meditating,* McCoy thought, *if you don't get sunstroke first*—and entered a shadowy corridor.

McCoy gave an involuntary gasp of relief. It was blessedly cool in here. For Vulcan, anyway.

Without any words of explanation, Sarek pointed him toward a blank white door and stepped back. "Your pardon, Doctor. I have some final arrangements to make."

McCoy tentatively pressed the door chime.

No answer. He glanced back at Sarek, who had his back to him, murmuring into a communicator.

All right, try again.

McCoy held the button down for a little longer this time. Still no answer.

He nearly jumped when the door slid noiselessly open a fraction, revealing Spock in robes of a red so dark it was almost black, the fabric glinting coldly with the sigils of his house and rank. He was so drawn and weary that McCoy said "Are you all right?" instead of "Hello."

Spock, voice a harsh whisper, said, "McCoy." He stepped back enough to allow McCoy a glimpse inside.

My God, McCoy thought.

He knew all about Vulcan strength, of course. Even so . . . what he saw represented Vulcan strength crossed with a total loss of emotional control. A massive bed, looking heavy enough to have given a Klingon pause, lay on its side, bedding and cushions shredded and strewn about the room, and an equally massive chest had been smashed to kindling. Everything that could be overturned or smashed had been, save perhaps for the still-glowing firepot.

So much for incense fumes being calming.

But he knew how, well, savage Vulcans could be on the rare occasions that they let their feelings come out. And under the circumstance, he certainly understood that Spock would be acting without restraint.

He was suddenly strongly aware of being watched. McCoy turned warily and saw Saavik, seated at a mirror of some presumably shatterproof material, looking at him without blinking.

McCoy's breath caught in his throat. God, she looked . . . he couldn't find the right word. Exhausted, yes, but . . . radiant. Magnificent.

Alien.

Yes. Exactly. After all these years of friendship, of knowing them both so well, he looked at Spock, at Saavik, and for the first time, saw *alien.*

Helluva time for a revelation.

Or maybe not all so alien at that. What was that old saying: "You have your marriage for yourself, you have your wedding for the relatives." Never mind *Pon farr,* these two were newly made husband and wife. No wonder Sarek wouldn't come in. This was no sight for a father.

Amazing woman. Amazing species! He had hung on until he could reach her, and she had fought back against all the odds until they could be together. Her cure, and his, had in the end been simple: throw them together and stand back!

No wonder there hasn't been any ceremony till now, McCoy thought, *the wedding had had to wait until their* Pon farr *fires were slaked, at least somewhat.*

McCoy saw Spock and Saavik glance at each other, new fire sparking in their eyes, together with an intensity of love they never would have permitted him to see under normal circumstances. And he thought, *Got to say something, now, or the ceremony will have to wait another few days!*

"I guess we can forget about the bride and groom not seeing each other before the wedding," he managed to say.

To McCoy's relief, he saw the faintest hint of humor glint in Saavik's eyes. Spock relaxed minutely.

Daring, McCoy continued, "Come on, Spock. Maybe I should be afraid you'll knock me to kingdom come, but I'm not."

"Perhaps you should be." It was that harsh, barely controlled voice.

"Spock, I guess I'll just have to take that chance. Now, let's see about getting you both to the church on time!" Dammit, was he going to make bad jokes all the way to the ceremony? Hell, yes, out of sheer relief that his friends were really going to get a chance to live long and prosper!

He was giddy and he knew it, but he couldn't resist one parting shot as he ushered his old comrade out:

"Spock, my friend, don't even *think* of trying to get your room deposit back!"

THIRTY-EIGHT

VULCAN, DAY 8, SECOND WEEK OF HARAVEEN, YEAR 2344

Once again, McCoy stood on a plateau in the middle of nowhere, a semicircle of dark, weathered lava rock open to a wide sweep of Vulcan's stark red desert and mountains. He easily picked out Mount Seleya, a jagged silhouette in the light of Vulcan's afternoon. The only entrance—other than up that steep cliff where the plateau dropped away—was the way he'd just arrived, through an archway of smooth reddish stone. In the center of the plateau was a second semicircle created by more rocks of dark lava, roughly worked to form bridged, upright columns that reminded him vaguely of Earth's Stonehenge, and within that circle was a single firepit and a single curving column. A hot desert wind blew in from the desert, carrying scents that were sweet and acrid in one, like nothing at all of Earth.

McCoy nodded. Spock's family's ancient place of *Koon-ut-kal-if-fee*. Nothing much had changed.

No, wait: the green Vulcan jadeite gong hanging from that central pillar was new. The hot wind drove particles of sand against it, making it hum softly.

Of course they'd have replaced the broken one. Wouldn't want any reminders of the last time they tried to marry Spock off.

He steadied the not-exactly regulation sunhat on his head; the tri-ox might be keeping him breathing normally and helping him bear the heat, but it wouldn't ward off the sun. McCoy had no intention of risking sunstroke.

The first time he'd been up here, during that near-disaster with T'Pring, he and Jim had been beamed almost directly to the site. The last time, he'd managed the long, long walk. This time, McCoy had been unashamedly glad to ride up the rough, rocky way, even if ritual demanded that the last stretch be not in a groundcar but in that ridiculously old-fashioned litter.

Dr. Leonard McCoy: Potentate. Felt like I should be waving to the crowds and tossing largesse. At least I didn't have to worry about the litter-bearers dropping me. One human couldn't have been much of a burden for four strapping young Vulcan men.

Youngsters who had handed him out as courteously as though he'd been the late, still-lamented T'Pau.

At least Spock can climb up here on his own.

It had made McCoy more uncomfortable than he ever would have admitted to think about his friend reduced to . . . well . . . savagery. But satiated *Pon farr* apparently ran its course reasonably quickly, Nature not wanting to kill off the species.

Odd, McCoy mused, to be here after so many years—wonderful to be here knowing (or praying) that this time there would be no more surprises.

He looked about at the other wedding guests. Fewer than he would have liked: there'd been no time to do more than fire off messages to other old friends like Sulu, and yes, David Rabin, Spock's boyhood pal, off there on Obsidian with his wife and kids, and a grandchild on the way.

Couldn't be helped.

Ah, but look who *was* here: Uhura, having her own sources of information. God, even after all these years, she was still beautiful. With the indifference to protocol you could get away with if you essentially ran Starfleet Intelligence, she was wearing not dress uniform, but a flowing robe of kente cloth, intricately patterned in red and black and gold and green. A headdress of the same fabric nestled like some tropical bird in the glowing silver corona of her hair. Around her neck, a pendant wrought of hammered gold caught Eridani 40 A's bloody light and reflected it back like a tiny sun.

Looks a damn sight more at home here than I do, in all these medals.

What she did not look was at all surprised to see him.

McCoy edged past three silent Vulcans to her side. "Madam," he said with a broad grin and a broader bow, "you look even more beautiful than I remember."

"Leonard, you flatterer!" Uhura's smile outshone the light glinting on her necklace and earrings. "I promised to dance at Saavik's wedding, and I certainly can't dance in a dress uniform."

"At least you can dance," McCoy retorted. "I should have got my knees upgraded five years ago."

But he would try, even if Uhura insisted on leading. There was something else he wanted to try. "So we have our happy ending after all," he said.

Uhura's smile brightened. "We do indeed, Leonard."

He mimed a salaam—McCoy as Potentate again—and won a grin from her.

Now, if only nothing got screwed up at the last minute.

Hoping for distraction from that thought, he turned.

Directly in front of him loomed a tall figure in a hooded cloak. "Someone else who doesn't want to risk sunstroke, I see," McCoy remarked. Vulcans might not make small talk, but this human was going to try.

The figure turned, agreeing in not-quite-certain Vulcan, "The sun is brighter than I would have—" He broke off, staring. "Makhoi . . . ?"

No Vulcan ever called him that; they could pronounce his name accurately enough. But there had been someone else, years ago . . . McCoy frowned, studying that teasingly familiar face . . . Now, if it were a bit younger, a bit less hard . . .

"Ruanek!" he burst out. "Centurion Ruanek—or whatever rank you hold now!"

"Ruanek, yes. No longer a centurion, or the commander I was just before . . ."

He stopped awkwardly, and McCoy shook his head in wonder. "You're that Romulan refugee, aren't you? The one I heard brought Spock home and—Here now, stop looking at me like that! I know I've aged and you haven't, not all that much, but that's the way we humans are. I still have all my wits, son, wrinkles notwithstanding."

"And your sharp tongue. And kind heart."

Clearly embarrassed at what he'd just said, Ruanek looked away, staring out over the wide vista of desert and mountain.

"Look familiar?" McCoy asked.

"In a strange way. The gravity and atmosphere are so similar, the—the faint sense of active seismic life, too, but the light is so much brighter than that of Romulus. The air is so much hotter, dry enough to pull the moisture from one's skin. Yet . . . it is all so very beautiful . . . and it somehow feels . . . *akhh*, I don't know: right."

"But?"

"But . . ." Ruanek shook his head in confusion. "There are friendships here, Makhoi, and no one needs to watch one's back. Ambassador Sarek—he goes about unaccompanied, unguarded!"

"That's a bad thing?"

"No! It's merely . . ."

"Too foreign?"

"I will cope," flatly.

Brittle as glass, McCoy thought, and put a comforting hand on the younger man's shoulder—just as his mind screamed, *Oh, bright move, touching a Romulan warrior!*

But with what was clearly a great effort, Ruanek kept from striking out at him. "Steady there, son," McCoy said gently, and backed off a step. Sensing Ruanek's uncertainty, he cut through it with a wry, "How's the horse business?"

The Ruanek of old had had an ironic sense of humor. So, it seemed, did the current one. "I am not in the horse business. I am in the political refugee business."

"Kill the wrong man, did you, son?" McCoy asked. "That cousin of yours for a bet. Yes, and got yourself into more political hot water than that sulfur pool over there."

Overstepped the bounds again. A curt nod was his only answer.

"Tell you what," McCoy said after an awkward moment. "When all the ceremonies are over, you and I, we'll get together over a drink or two and compare notes."

Ruanek turned to him, face controlled but eyes betraying a very fervent gratitude. "I would very much like that, Makh—ah, Doktor McKoi."

"Better, son. Much better."

The distant chiming of bells, clear in the desert silence, made them both straighten. "It's beginning," McCoy said.

In other words: Here comes the groom. Let's hope he's sane.

Spock entered through the archway alone, straight-backed and noble in his flowing, dark-red ambassadorial robes. His face was composed as that of a statue, utterly unreadable. Without so much as a glance at the assembled guests, he strode straight for the central column and struck the ritual gong a powerful blow. The sound rang out across the desert, so deep and pure that it shivered along McCoy's spine.

A new whisper of bells sounded in the distance, carried on a hot breath of desert wind.

"The bridal party," McCoy whispered to Ruanek. He added as the Romulan looked at him inquiringly, "Yep. Been through this before. This time, let's hope it's done right!"

A second litter was carried into the circle. A shrouded figure was helped out, assisted to the cushioned stone chair. This must be . . . who?

The figure threw off the dark cloak, revealing blazing red robes, a fine-boned, fierce, ancient face—

"T'Lar!" McCoy breathed. God, the High Priestess must be close to three hundred by now, but—*Damn, I wish I felt as good as she looks.*

As though she'd heard him whisper her name, T'Lar turned. The ancient eyes studied first Ruanek, then he, himself, recognizing him. McCoy bowed to her with full Southern gallantry. She gave him the barest dip of her head in return, then turned away.

Beside him, Ruanek shuddered, then forced himself almost to military attention. "She knew what I am at a glance," he whispered. "She knew, and didn't reject me."

"I wouldn't be at all surprised. Shh. Here they come."

First, came attendants shaking those blasted *systra,* the banners made of rows of tiny shrill bells. The stiff tunics of their ritual, archaic garb glinted molten in the sunlight.

Then . . . ah, there was Ambassador Sarek, every bit as aristocratic as his son, his robes of state darkest blue glowing with metallic embroidery, his hair blazing silver.

Ahh, here came the bride, or rather, here came her attendants. That must be the Healer, T'Selis, the one Sarek credited with saving his daughter-in-law's life. She'd put off Healer's brown in favor of the white and red robes of a priestess from Seleya. Beside her, somewhat to McCoy's surprise, was a fair-haired human woman who looked just as out-of-place in the close-fitting Starfleet dress uniform as he did. Frances Stewart, he realized. The *Enterprise*-C's junior medical officer.

But here was Saavik, eyes properly downcast, her flowing silver robes gleaming like a river in a wasteland. Seeing how her gaze met Spock's and rested there, McCoy sighed.

The attendants shook their *systra* one last, maddening shake, then fell blessedly still. Far overhead, a hunting *shavokh* gave its shrill call, cutting into the sudden silence. McCoy fought not to glare up at it. *I hope that's not a bad omen,* he thought, then told himself as sternly as Sarek that omens were illogical.

He braced himself, abruptly terrified that history was going to suddenly repeat itself and that the next thing he was going to hear would be the dreaded *"kah-li-fee,"* the challenge that meant a fight to the death and a doomed marriage.

But of course there was no challenge. In fact, McCoy suddenly realized that they'd already gotten through that part of the ceremony, the "acceptance or fight" or whatever they called it in Vulcan. T'Lar, her ancient voice strong and sure as Vulcan's very soul, was already beginning the chant, "As it was in the beginning . . ."

Across from him, McCoy saw Frances Stewart sniffling quietly, trying very hard not to let her human emotions bother anyone. But McCoy couldn't fault her. *Note to self,* he thought: She and the three other crew members who'd flown Saavik to Vulcan could use a chance to talk with him. After all, he knew what it felt like to lose an *Enterprise.* He—was he going to get all misty-eyed, too, at his age? *You bet I am. Damn, but I wish Jim could be here. And the Lady Amanda.*

Hell, I'm human, I don't need to be logical: Maybe they are!

Had he ever doubted, though, that Vulcans, too, had emotions? There was not the slightest sign of anything but composure on either Spock or Saavik's face, but McCoy could have sworn he felt the force of their love radiating between them—a love that had pulled them both back from the brink of death.

He lost track of time for a while . . . Too many ritual words, archaic forms that he couldn't follow, and enough heat to really be getting to him. God, what he'd do for a mint julep right now . . . or just a big glass of iced lemonade . . . they had something like lemonade on Vulcan . . . no lemons, though . . .

McCoy dragged his wandering mind back with an effort.

Spock and Saavik, not quite touching, knelt before T'Lar. Very gently, with never a quiver in her thin hands, she touched their temples. They raised their hands to touch each other's temples as well.

And, with spectacularly right timing, lightning flashed over Mount Seleya.

Now there's an omen for you! Even Sarek started at that one!

Only T'Lar was unmoved. Almost, McCoy thought uneasily, as though she'd been expecting it. She gestured, calmly imperious, and T'Selis, face carefully composed, came forward with a plain, earthenware cup. T'Lar signaled, *wait,* and said directly to Spock, "We always had a plan for thee. Thee shall fulfill it." And to Saavik, "Thee shall be guardian."

Great, now we've got a prophecy. Or is that sort of thing routine at the end of Vulcan wedding ceremonies, like wishing them good luck?

Dammit, this place is getting to me.

T'lar took the cup, then gave it to Spock. He offered it to Saavik first. She sipped, then returned the cup to him, her gaze never leaving her mate. To McCoy's utter and delighted fascination, before Spock drank, he turned the cup so his lips rested where hers had.

Where'd he get that? Been reading Earth novels on the sly, have we?

T'Lar merely raised an eyebrow. "Thee will need that deep a bond," she said without the slightest trace of expression. "Now recite thy vows."

McCoy heard them murmur:

"Parted and never parted."

"Never and always touching and touched."

T'Lar gestured to the couple: Rise. "Thee are wed, Spock, son of Sarek, son of Skon, son of Solkar, and Saavik, Vulcan's Daughter."

Tactful way of putting it, McCoy thought.

And that, he realized, was that. No "You may now kiss the bride," no cheering, no rushing forward to embrace the bride. Nothing— except for the Vulcan version of the reception line. Which in this case meant meeting T'Lar. One by one, the guests were formally presented to her; one by one, she blessed them and said a few words.

When it was McCoy's turn, he found himself nearly shivering from the impact of the strength in the wise, ancient eyes.

"Ma'am." He dipped his head as he would before royalty.

"McCoy. Thee does not regret choosing the danger?"

"No, ma'am. Not when a friend's life is at stake."

He bowed, and felt her hand, warm and dry, rest very briefly on his head as she murmured what he trusted was a blessing in Old High Vulcan.

Ruanek was next, falling to one knee in what McCoy guessed was Overawed Romulan fashion. She knew what he was, all right: McCoy heard her say, almost warmly for her, "Welcome home."

Hearing Ruanek's breath catch, McCoy moved on. Ruanek quickly caught up with him, face troubled, and the doctor asked, "How are you doing, son?"

"Overwhelmed. In addition to everything else, Ambassador Sarek says that at Spock's request, he wishes me to speak at the Vulcan Science Academy."

McCoy suppressed a grin, remembering some Vulcan-style knock-down-drag-outs between Spock and his father on the subject of Unification. But he supposed this new development was only logical: Sarek, being Sarek, would never let politics get in the way of learning. Pity more politicians weren't like that.

McCoy gave the refugee his best patented "tell me more" look. "And how do you feel about all this?"

"Happy, yes. Sad, yes. Romulus was my birthworld. . . . This . . . I don't know. Can it ever really be my home?"

McCoy grinned. "Someone seems to think so. Look."

T'Selis was watching Ruanek with the candid, logical, interested gaze only a young, lovely Vulcan woman could show. One of the Vulcan guests, noticing Ruanek's stare, murmured with a touch of indulgent understanding, "She is a Healer, and not bonded."

"But who is she . . . ?" Ruanek breathed.

"Her name," McCoy began, "is T'Selis—"

"*That* is T'Selis? Are you certain? Yes? Fates . . ." Ruanek shook his head, grinning. "Suddenly, Doktor McKoi, Vulcan really does begin to seem like home."

* * *

Spock drew a cautious breath. Sanity had returned so suddenly, he was not certain yet if it would stay. But he must be sane, because he knew he had just survived the ceremony. Saavik was his wife. *My wife,* he thought, awestruck.

Saavik, standing beside him, was sane, too. Watching the interesting exchange of glances occurring between T'Selis and . . . was that not Ruanek? She glanced at Spock, unconsciously echoing Charvanek's words: "What a fascinating complication!"

Spock looked into her eyes. "Jealousy is illogical, my wife."

She whispered back at him, "On Romulus, I could not take my eyes off you."

And, as suddenly as that, they were close to losing control again. Sarek, watching, gestured, *this way.* Spock touched his wife's fingers with his own and led her away. Sarek stopped them only long enough to say, "I am . . . pleased that your wedding has gone so well."

Spock knew that this was as close to an apology as he was ever going to get from his father on the subject of T'Pring. Wisely, he merely bowed. In any event, he was not certain he could have spoken coherently. Saavik's hand, touching his, trembled. Not much longer now.

Sarek stepped aside and let his children pass.

They went down from the plateau together, out into the desert. The day was already fading, and long blue shadows lay across the sands. Side by side, touching each other's minds, they recited their vows together, alone:

"Parted and never parted."

"Never and always touching and touched."

Then, since they were alone, they held hands like any other lovers and together watched the sun set. There was work for them in the galaxy, but they would get to it soon enough.

For now, this time was their own.

OUR FIRST SERIAL NOVEL!

Presenting, one chapter
per month . . .

The very beginning of the
Starfleet Adventure . . .

**STAR TREK®
STARFLEET: YEAR ONE**

A novel in Twelve Parts®

by
Michael Jan Friedman

Chapter Ten

Hiro Matsura had retrieved his pod and was about to break orbit when his navigator notified him that the *Maverick* was in the vicinity.

Matsura hadn't expected any company at Oreias Seven. "On screen," he said, settling back into his center seat.

A moment later, Connor Dane's face filled the forward viewscreen. He didn't seem pleased.

"Tell me you had better luck than we did," said Dane.

Matsura shook his head. "My team didn't find anything of significance."

Dane scowled. "Maybe we'll figure something out when we compare notes with Shumar and Cobaryn."

Matsura couldn't keep from smiling a little. "You really think so?"

Dane looked at him. "Don't you?"

"With all due respect," Matsura told him, "I think we can sit and compare notes until the last days of the universe, and we'll still just be groping in the dark."

Dane's eyes narrowed. "And you've got a better way to dope out what happened?"

"I think Captain Stiles had the right idea," said Matsura. "The only way we're going to find the aliens is by going out and looking for them."

"It's not that big a system," Dane responded. "We don't *all* have to be looking for them."

"It would speed things up," Matsura noted.

"Or slow them down," said Dane, "by putting all our eggs in the wrong basket. Depends on how you look at it."

Matsura was surprised at the man's attitude. "I didn't know you had such deep respect for research scientists."

Dane's mouth twisted at the other man's tone. "You mean butterfly catchers, don't you?"

Matsura found himself turning red. "I don't use that terminology."

"But your buddies do," the other man observed. "And don't insult my intelligence by claiming otherwise."

"All right," said Matsura, "I won't."

That seemed to pacify Dane a bit. "At least you're honest," he conceded.

"Thanks. Now, I'm sorry you took the trouble to fly all the way over here, but I'm leaving to try to hook up with Stiles and Hagedorn. You're welcome to join me if you'd like."

Dane snorted. "I'll put my money on Shumar and Cobaryn."

"Suit yourself," said Matsura. "I'll—"

Suddenly, his navigator interrupted him. "Sir," said Williams, her face drawn with concern as she consulted her monitor, "we're picking up a number of unidentified vessels."

The captain saw Dane turn away from the viewscreen and spit a command at one of his officers. He didn't look happy.

For that matter, Matsura wasn't very happy either. "Give me visual," he told Williams.

A moment later, Dane's image vanished from the viewscreen, to be replaced by that of three small, triangular vessels. They were gleaming in the glare of Oreias as they approached.

The aggressors, Matsura thought. It had to be.

"Raise shields," he announced. "Power to all batteries."

"Raising shields," Williams confirmed.

"Power to lasers and launchers," said his weapons officer.

"You still there?" asked Matsura over their comm link.

"Yeah, I'm here," came Dane's response. "But I've got to tell you, I'm not much of a team player."

No big surprise there, Matsura told himself. "I'll try to work with you anyway. Leave your comm link open. If I see an alien on your tail, I can give you a holler."

"Acknowledged," said Dane.

Then the enemy was on top of them. Or rather, the triangular vessels were plunging past them—so intent on the colony, it seemed, that they were ignoring the *Christophers* above it.

Matsura took the slight personally. "Lock lasers on the nearest ship," he told his weapons officer.

"Targeting," said Wickersham, a fair-haired man with a narrow face and deep-set eyes.

"Fire!" the captain commanded.

Their electric-blue beams reached out and skewered the enemy vessel—failing to disable it, but getting its attention. It came about like an angry bee and returned fire, sending out a string of scarlet fireballs.

"Evade!" Matsura called out.

But they weren't fast enough. The energy clusters plowed into the *Yellowjacket,* sending a bone-rattling jolt through the deckplates.

The aliens packed a punch, the captain realized. He had made the mistake of judging their firepower by their size.

"Another one on our port beam!" said Williams.

"Split the difference!" Matsura ordered.

At the helm console, McCallum worked feverishly. What's more, his efforts paid off. The *Yellowjacket* sliced between the two triangular ships, preventing them from firing for the moment.

Suddenly, the third vessel loomed on Matsura's viewscreen, its underbelly exposed, filling the entire frame with its unexpected proximity. He had never had such an easy target and he might never have one again.

"Target lasers and fire!" he commanded.

At close range, their beams seemed to do a good deal more damage. The enemy staggered under the impact.

"Their shields are at twenty-eight percent," Williams reported.

A barrage of atomics might take the alien out of the fight, the captain noted. But before he could launch one, the enemy was bludgeoned with blasts of white fury.

Dane, Matsura thought.

"Their tactical systems are offline," his navigator told him.

The captain could have finished off the alien then and there. However, the vessel wasn't in a position to hurt the colony any-more, and he still had two other marauders to worry about.

"Where are the others?" he asked Williams.

She worked at her console. "Right here, sir."

A moment later, he saw the two still-capable triangles on his viewscreen. They were going after the *Maverick* with their energy weapons blazing, trying to catch her in a deadly crossfire.

Unlike Matsura, Dane didn't make an attempt to dart between his adversaries. He headed straight for one of them, exposing his starboard flank to the other.

It was a maneuver that depended on the enemy's being caught by surprise and veering off. But if that didn't happen, it was suicide.

Had Matsura been fighting both the aliens on his own, he might have made an effort to do something similar. As it was, he found the move reckless to the point of insanity.

You idiot, he thought—and not just because Dane had endangered his own ship. By placing himself in jeopardy, he had made it necessary for the *Yellowjacket* to expose herself as well.

Matsura frowned. "Pursue the vessel to port, Mr. Weeks! Target lasers and fire!"

Weeks managed to nail the enemy from behind with both blue beams. He hit the triangle hard enough to keep it from striking the *Maverick* with an energy volley, but—unfortunately—not hard enough to cripple it.

As they dogged the alien ship, trying to lock on for another shot, the captain saw the other triangle peel off to avoid the *Maverick*—just as Dane had gambled it would.

But as surely as the *Maverick* had climbed out of the fire, the *Yellowjacket* was falling into it. As Weeks released another laser barrage, the enemy to port looped around with amazing dexterity. Then it came for Matsura and his crew, its weapons belching bundle after bundle of crimson brilliance.

"Hard to starboard!" the captain called out, hoping to pull his ship out of harm's way.

But it was no use. The alien's energy clusters dazzled his screen and rammed the *Yellowjacket* with explosive force—once, twice, and again, finally wrenching Matsura out of his captain's chair and pitching him sideways across the deck.

Behind him, a control console erupted in a shower of sparks. Black smoke collected above it like a bad omen. There were cries of pain and dismay, punctuated by frantic status reports.

"Shields are down!"

"Hull breaches on decks five and six!"

"Lasers and atomics are inoperable!"

Dazed, Matsura watched someone grab a fire extinguisher from the rack on the wall. Ignoring a stinging wetness over his right eye, he dragged himself to his feet and made his way back to his center seat.

On the static-riddled viewscreen, the battle had advanced while Matsura was pulling himself together. Somehow, Dane had incapacitated another of the enemy's vessels because only the *Maverick* and one of the aliens were still exchanging fire.

Abruptly, the commander of the triangle decided to change tactics. The ship broke off the engagement and went hurtling out into the void. And just as abruptly, its sister ships departed in its wake.

Matsura's first instinct was to follow them. Then he remembered that the *Yellowjacket* was in no shape to pursue *anyone*.

Without shields and weapons, she was all but helpless. The captain looked around at his bridge officers. They looked relieved that the battle was over, especially the ones who had sustained injuries.

"Casualties?" Matsura asked, not looking forward to the response he might get.

Williams, who looked shaken but not hurt, consulted her monitor. "Sickbay has three reports, sir, but more are expected. No fatalities as far as the doctor can tell."

The captain frowned. "Dispatch a couple of engineering teams to see to those hull breaches."

Williams nodded. "Aye, sir."

Matsura turned to Weeks, who was holding a damaged left arm and grimacing. "Tacticals are a mess, sir," he got out. "I'll see to bringing them back online, but it's going to take a while."

"First," the captain said, "you'll get yourself to sickbay."

"But, sir," Weeks protested, looking even more pained than before, "we're in need of—"

"Repairs? Yes, we are," Matsura told him. "But they can be carried out without you."

The weapons officer looked like he was going to put up a fight. Then he said, "Aye, sir," and made his way to the lift.

Matsura was about to check on his propulsion system when Williams spoke up. "Sir, Captain Dane is asking to speak with you."

His jaw clenching, the captain nodded. "Link him in."

A moment later, Dane appeared on the viewscreen. "You look like you took a beating," he observed. "What's your situation?"

"The situation," said the captain, doing his best to keep his voice free of anger, "is I've lost my lasers, my atomics, and my shield generators. And that's just a superficial assessment."

Dane grunted. "Tough luck. We suffered a little damage ourselves." He began tapping a command into his armrest. "I'll contact the others and let them know what happened here."

Matsura's mouth fell open. That was it? he wondered. No thanks? No recognition that he had put his ship and crew on the line to bail out a reckless fool of a comrade?

If this had been an Earth Command mission, Matsura's wing-mates would have been quick to acknowledge what he had done. But this wasn't Earth Command, he reminded himself bitterly. It was something completely different.

And Connor Dane was still a Cochrane jockey at heart, taking low-percentage chances as if his life were the only one at stake.

Matsura was tempted to lash out at the man, to tell him how he felt; but he wouldn't do that with two complements of bridge officers privy to the conversation. He would arrange a better time.

"You do that," Matsura said. "And when you're done, I'd like to speak with you. In private."

For the first time, it seemed to dawn on the other man that his colleague might not be entirely happy with him. "No problem," Dane answered casually. "I'll tell my transporter operator to expect you."

"*Yellowjacket* out," said Matsura—and terminated the link.

A moment later, Dane's face vanished from the screen, replaced with a view of his *Christopher*. Matsura studied it for a moment, his resentment building inside him.

Then he got up from his center seat. "You've got the conn," he told Lieutenant Williams and headed for the *Yellowjacket*'s transporter room.

As far as he knew, *that* system was still working.

"I'd ask you to pardon the mess," Dane said, "but I might as well tell you, it's like this all the time."

Matsura didn't say anything in response. He just frowned disapprovingly, looked around Dane's cluttered anteroom and found an empty seat.

Obviously, Matsura wasn't pleased with him. And just as obviously, Dane was about to hear why. Removing yesterday's uniform from his workstation chair, Dane tossed it into a pile in the corner of the room and sat down.

"All right," he told his fellow captain. "There's something you want to get off your chest, right? So go ahead."

Matsura glared at him. "Fine. If you want me to be blunt, I'll be blunt. What you did out there a minute ago was foolish and irresponsible. Leaving your flank exposed, forcing me to go in and protect it . . . you're lucky you didn't get us all killed."

Dane looked at him. "Is that so?"

"You're damned right," Matsura shot back. "No Earth Command captain would ever have taken a chance like that."

Dane shrugged. "Then maybe they should consider it."

"Are you out of your mind?" asked Matsura, turning dark with anger. "You're going to defend that gambit—after it crippled my ship and injured seventeen of my crewmen?"

Dane smiled a thin smile. "Given a million chances, I'd do it a million times . . . hands down, no contest."

Matsura was speechless.

"Of course," Dane went on, "I'm not one of the noble black and gold, so none of my skill or experience means a flipping thing. But I'll tell you what . . . I've met a few Romulans in my day too. In fact, I was blasting them out of space long before you ever warmed your butt in a center seat."

Matsura's eyes narrowed. "There's a difference between experience and luck," he pointed out.

"Men make their own luck," Dane told him. "I make mine by pushing the envelope—by doing what they least expect. Come to think of it, you might want to think about pushing the envelope a little yourself."

"Me . . . ?" Matsura asked.

"That's right. Dare to be different. Or do you want to spend the rest of your life living in your flyboy buddies' shadow?"

Matsura's jaw clenched. "I don't live in anyone's shadow—not Hagedorn's or Stiles's or anyone else's. What I do is carry out my mission within the parameters of good sense."

Dane grunted. "Right."

"You think otherwise?"

Dane shrugged. "I think good sense is what people hide behind when they can't do any better."

"Says the man who hasn't got any."

"Says the man who accomplished his mission," Dane noted.

Matsura flushed and got to his feet. "Obviously, I'm wasting my time talking to you. You know everything."

"Funny," said Dane, keeping his voice nice and even. "I was just about to tell you the same thing."

Matsura's mouth twisted.

"And just for the record," said Dane, "I didn't expect you to protect my flank. As I said, I'm not much of a team player."

The other man didn't respond to that one. He just turned his back on Dane, tapped the door control and left.

The captain shook his head. Matsura had potential—anyone with an eye in his head could see that. But the way things were going, it didn't look like he was going to realize it.

Not that that's any of *my* headache, Dane told himself, leaning back in his chair and closing his eyes.

Matsura was still boiling over Dane's remarks as he left the *Yellowjacket*'s transporter room . . . and on an impulse, headed for a part of his vessel he hadn't had occasion to visit lately.

Men make their own luck, Dane had told him.

But Matsura had done that, hadn't he? During the war, he had been as effective a weapon as Earth Command could have asked for. He had risen to every challenge thrown his way.

But Dane wasn't talking about efficiency or determination. He was talking about thinking outside the box. He was talking about a willingness to try something different.

You might want to think about pushing the envelope . . .

And, damn it, Matsura would do just that. He would show Dane that he could take the direction least expected of him—and do more with it than the butterfly catchers themselves.

Neither Shumar, Cobaryn, nor Dane had discovered anything of value with all their meticulous site scanning. But with the help of his research team, Matsura would turn up something. He would find a way to beat the aliens that his colleagues had overlooked.

Or do you want to spend the rest of your life living in your flyboy buddies' shadow?

Matsura swore beneath his breath. Dane was wrong about him—dead wrong—and he was going to make the arrogant sonuvagun see that.

The captain had barely completed the thought when he realized that his destination was looming just ahead of him. Arriving at the appropriate set of doors, he tapped the control pad on the bulkhead and watched the titanium panels slide aside.

Once, this relatively large compartment on Deck Eight had been a supply bay. It had been converted by Starfleet into a research laboratory, equipped with three state-of-the-art computer workstations and a stationary scanner that was three times as sensitive as the portable version.

It was all Clarisse Dumont's doing. If the fleet was going to conduct research in space, she had argued, it might as well enjoy the finest instruments available.

Matsura hadn't been especially inclined to make use of them before; he had left that to those members of his crew with a more scientific bent. But he would certainly make use of them now.

"Mr. Siefried," he said, addressing one of the three crewmen who had beamed down to the colony to collect data.

Siefried, a lanky mineralogist with sharp features and close-cropped hair, evinced surprise as he swiveled in his seat. After all, it wasn't every day that Matsura made an appearance there.

"Sir?" said Siefried.

"What have we got?" asked the captain, trying his best to keep his anger at Dane under wraps.

The mineralogist shrugged his bony shoulders. "Not much more than we had before, I'm afraid. At least, nothing that would explain why the aliens attacked the colony."

Matsura turned to Arquette, a compact man with startling blue eyes. "Anything to add to that?" he asked.

Arquette, an exobiologist, shook his head. "Nothing, sir. Just the same materials we saw before. But I'm still working on it."

"Perhaps if we had a context," said Smithson, a buxom physicist who specialized in energy emissions, "some kind of backdrop against which we could interpret the data."

"That would be helpful, all right," Matsura agreed. "Then again, if we knew something about these aliens, we probably wouldn't have needed to do site research in the first place."

The scan team looked disheartened by his remark. Realizing what he had done, the captain held his hand up in a plea for understanding. "Sorry. I didn't mean that the way it came out."

"It's all right, sir," said Smithson, in an almost motherly tone of voice. "It's been a frustrating time for all of us."

Matsura nodded. "To say the least."

But he wasn't going to accept defeat so easily. Not when Dane's smugness was still so vivid in his memory.

"Do you mind if I take a look?" he asked Smithson.

"Not at all," said the physicist, getting up from her seat to give the captain access to her monitor.

Depositing himself behind the workstation, Matsura took a

look at the screen, on which the Oreias Seven colony was mapped out in bright blue lines on a black field. He hadn't actually seen the site in person, so he took a moment to study it.

Immediately, a question came to mind.

"Why does the perimeter of the colony follow these curves?" he asked, pointing to a couple of scalloped areas near the top of the plan.

"There are hills there," said Siefried, who had come over to stand behind him. "Not steep ones, mind you, but steep enough to keep the colonists from erecting their domes."

Makes sense, the captain thought. Why build on a slope when you can build on a flat?

Then again, why build near hills at all? Matsura presented the question to his mineralogist.

"Actually," Siefried noted, "it would have been difficult to do otherwise. All the regions suitable for farming have hilly features. The area the colonists picked is the flattest on the planet."

"I see," said the captain.

He studied the layout of the colony some more, looking for any other detail that might trigger an insight. Nothing seemed to do that, however. Without anything else to attract Matsura's eye, it was eventually drawn back to the two scalloped areas.

"What is it, sir?" asked Arquette, who had come to stand behind the captain as well.

Matsura shook his head, trying to figure out what it was about those two half-circles that intrigued him. "Nothing, really. Or maybe . . ." He heaved a sigh. "I don't know."

But it seemed that a visit to the colony was in order. And this time, he was going to go down there *personally.*

As Bryce Shumar materialized on the *Horatio*'s transporter pad, he saw Cobaryn standing alongside the ship's transporter technician. Obviously, the Rigelian had decided to wait there for him.

That came as no surprise to Shumar. What surprised him was that Connor Dane was waiting there too.

"Welcome to the *Horatio,* sir," said the transporter operator.

Shumar nodded to the man. "Thanks, Lieutenant."

"About time you got here," the Cochrane jockey added. "Hagedorn and Stiles have probably finished all the hors d'oeuvres."

The remark was unexpected—even more so than Dane's presence there in the first place. Shumar couldn't help smiling a little. "I didn't know you were a comedian," he said.

"Who's joking?" Dane returned.

"I hate to interrupt," Cobaryn told them, "but now that Captain Shumar is here, we should get up to Captain Hagedorn's quarters as quickly as possible. I wish to be present when the decisions are made."

Shumar agreed. Together, the three of them exited the transporter room and made their way to the nearest turbolift, which carried them to the appropriate deck. From there, it was a short walk to the captain's door.

They knew that because the ships they commanded were exact replicas of the *Horatio*, designed to be identical down to the last airflow vent and intercom panel. Anyway, that had been the intent.

As the doors to Hagedorn's quarters whispered open, Shumar saw that there were at least a few details there that diverged from the standard. More to the point, Hagedorn's anteroom wasn't anything like Shumar's.

It had been furnished economically but impeccably, the walls decorated with a series of small, ancient-looking iron artifacts, the clunky, standard-issue Earth Command table and chairs replaced with a simpler and earthier-looking version in a tawny, unfinished wood.

Interestingly, there weren't any of the *customary* personal effects to be seen. Not a medal—though Hagedorn must have won lots of them. Not an exotic liquor bottle, a musical instrument, an alien statuette, or an unusual mineral specimen. Not a hat, a globe, or a 3-D chessboard.

Not even a picture of a loved one.

Shumar found the place a little off-putting in its spartan outlook, in its minimalism. However, it looked considerably bigger than Shumar's own anteroom. So much so, in fact, that he didn't feel cramped sharing the space with his five colleagues.

Then it occurred to Shumar that only *four* of his colleagues were present. Matsura was conspicuous by his absence.

"Come on in," said Hagedorn, his manner cordial if a bit too crisp for Shumar's taste. "Can I get you anything?"

Shumar noticed that neither Hagedorn nor Stiles had a drink in his hand. "Nothing, thanks. Where's Captain Matsura?"

Stiles frowned. "He'll be a few minutes late. He wanted to check out the Oreias Seven colony himself."

"Didn't he do that already?" asked Shumar.

"Apparently not," Hagedorn replied, obviously unperturbed by his colleague's oversight.

"You forget," said Stiles, "some of us aren't scientists."

Shumar hadn't forgotten. He just couldn't believe his fellow captains hadn't seen a value in examining the colonies firsthand.

"Why don't we get down to business?" asked Dane. "We can bring Matsura up to speed when he gets here."

Shumar had never heard Dane take such a purposeful tack before. Was this the same man who had lingered over his tequila while everyone around him was scrambling to fight the Romulans?

It seemed Connor Dane was *full* of surprises today.

Stiles glanced at Hagedorn. "I agree. It's not as if we don't know where Matsura will come down in this matter."

Hagedorn must have been reasonably sure of Matsura as well because he went ahead with the meeting. "All right, then," he said. "We're all aware of the facts. We've scanned all four colonies in this system, including the two the aliens have already attacked, and we haven't discovered anything to explain their aggressive behavior."

"Fortunately, we've shown we can track them down," said Stiles, picking up where his comrade left off. "But we can't match their firepower or their maneuverability unless we come at them with everything we've got."

"Even with the *Yellowjacket* damaged," Hagedorn noted, "we've still got five battleworthy ships left. I propose we deploy them as a group in order to find the aliens and defuse the threat."

"It's the only viable course of action open to us," Stiles maintained. "Anything less and we'll be lucky to fight them to a draw again."

Silence reigned in the room as they considered the man's advice. Then Hagedorn said, "What do the rest of you think?"

In other words, thought Shumar, you three butterfly catchers.

Cobaryn was the first to speak up. "I agree with Captain Stiles's assessment," he responded.

Shumar was surprised at how easily his friend had been swayed. It must have shown on his face because the Rigelian turned to him with a hint of an apology in his eyes.

"Believe me," said Cobaryn, "I wish we could have come up with another solution to the problem. However, I do not see one presing itself, and the colonists are depending on us to protect them."

It was hard to argue with such logic. Even Shumar had to admit that.

Dane was frowning deeply, looking uncharacteristically thoughtful.

"You seem hesitant," Stiles observed, an undercurrent of mockery in his voice. "I hope you're not thinking of hanging back while the rest of us go into battle."

Obviously, thought Shumar, some bone of contention existed between Stiles and Dane. In fact, now that Shumar had occasion to think about it, he was reminded of an exchange of remarks between the two at the captains' first briefing back on Earth.

In response to Stiles's taunt, the Cochrane jockey smiled jauntily. "What?" he asked, his voice as sharp-edged as the other man's. "And let you have all the fun?"

Ever the cool head, Hagedorn interceded. "This is a serious situation, gentlemen. There's no place at this meeting for personalities."

"You're right," said Stiles. "I was out of line." But neither his expression nor his tone suggested repentance.

Hagedorn turned to Shumar. His demeanor was that of one reasonable man speaking to another.

"And you, Captain?" he asked.

As his colleagues looked on, Shumar mulled over the proposition before him. Part of him was tempted to do what Cobaryn was doing, if only for the sake of the colonists' continued well-being.

Then there was the other part of him.

Shumar shook his head. "Unfortunately, I'm going to have to break with the party line. I'll be beaming down to Oreias Seven in order to continue my investigation."

"Are you sure you want to do that?" asked Hagedorn.

Shumar nodded. "Quite sure."

"What about your ship?" Stiles inquired.

Shumar understood the question. Stiles wanted the *Peregrine* to go with the rest of the fleet to increase their chances of a victory. What's more, Shumar didn't blame him.

"My ship will go with you," he assured Stiles.

"Under whose command?" Stiles pressed.

"That of my first officer, Stephen Mullen. From what I've seen of him, he's more than qualified to command the *Peregrine*. In fact, considering all the military experience he's got under his belt, you'll probably feel more comfortable with *him* than you do with *me*."

But that didn't seem to be good enough for Stiles, who shot a glance at Hagedorn. "As it happens," he argued, "we've got an experienced commanding officer without a viable vessel. Why not put Captain Matsura in the center seat of the *Peregrine?*"

Shumar didn't like the idea. After all, Mullen had demonstrated an ability to work smoothly with the *Peregrine*'s crew. Besides, he wasn't going to let Stiles or anyone else decide whom to put in charge of his vessel.

But before he could say anything, the doors to Hagedorn's anteroom slid aside again and Matsura joined them, his forehead slick with perspiration. "Sorry I'm late," he said.

"It's all right," Stiles assured him. In a matter of moments, he brought his Earth Command comrade up to date. "So, since Captain Shumar has decided to stay here, we're talking about putting you in command of his ship."

"Which isn't going to happen," Shumar interjected matter-of-factly. "Captain Stiles may have missed it, but I've already decided who's going to command the *Peregrine*."

Stiles's look turned disparaging. "With all due respect, Captain—"

Matsura held up his hand, stopping Stiles in mid-objection. "There's no need to argue about it," he said. "As it happens, I'd prefer to stay here with Captain Shumar."

Stiles looked at Matsura as if he were crazy. "What the devil for?"

Shumar wanted to know the answer to that question himself.